"Why are we stopping?" Bahr asked.

Grey Beard sneered. "We can't make it. The enemy is too close. Prepare yourselves. We must fight."

"Shit," Nothol muttered under his breath and drew his sword.

They formed a tight semicircle and waited. Clashing steel rang out from the darkness, followed by a deep groan and then shouting. The same was repeated from another part of the forest. Bahr flexed his grip on his sword. His muscles trembled from over exertion. Heart pounding, he prepared for battle. The wait wasn't long. Short, squat shapes of more than one hundred Dwarves emerged from the dark. Rekka and Ironfoot raced ahead, narrowly avoiding being swarmed by the enemy.

Nothol dropped his sword and set an arrow to string. Finding no point in taking time to aim properly, he fired into the massed enemy soldiers and was rewarded by seeing one pitch backwards. Enraged, the others broke into an all-out charge.

"Get down!" a deep voice roared from behind Bahr, prompting him to obey unquestioningly.

Crossbow bolts sliced through the space where Bahr and the others had just stood. The front rank of advancing Dwarves was decimated by the unexpected assault.

A WHISPER AFTER MIDNIGHT

Book Three of the Northern Crusade

CHRISTIAN WARREN FREED

Copyright © 2020 by Christian Warren Freed

Excerpt from *Empire of Bones* 2021 Christian Warren Freed
Cover design by Melissa Andres
Cover copyright 2021 by Warfighter Books
Author Photograph by Anicie Freed

Warfighter Books
Holly Springs, North Carolina 27540
https://www.christianwfreed.com

Second Edition: August 2021

Library of Congress Cataloging-in-Publication Data
Name: Freed, Christian Warren, 1973- author.
Title: A Whisper After Midnight/ Christian Warren Freed
Description: Second Edition | Holly Springs, NC: Warfighter Books, 2021. Identifiers: LCCN 2021912388 | ISBN 9781736804438 (trade paperback) Subjects: Epic fantasy | Military fantasy | Paranormal

Printed in the United States of America

10 9 8 7 6 5 4 3 2 1

Law of the Heretic
Immortality Shattered Book I

'If you're looking for a fun and exciting fantasy adventure, spend a few hours in the Free Lands with the Law of the Heretic.'

Where Have All the Elves Gone?

'Sometimes funny and other times a little dark, Where Have The Elves Gone? brings something fresh and new to fantasy mysteries. Whether you want to curl up with a mystery or read more about elves this book has something for everyone. Spend a few hours solving a mystery with a human and a couple of dwarves - you'll be glad you did.'

For my beloved wife, Anicie. I am all things with
you by my side.

Cold winter winds kissed the broken mountaintops. This part of northern Malweir was a wicked and cruel place, filled with nightmarish despair, the perfect place for the Hags to roost. The three harpies were sisters, wretched and cunning. They claimed the broken peaks and forced away smaller animals and other predatory birds. Men seldom came this far north without truly understanding the perils in the mountains. Only a tribe of Giants occupied the valley at the top of the mountains: Venheim, the fabled forge lost to time and legend. It was here the Hags chose to maintain their watch. And wait.

Freina flexed her clawed feet, tilting her head back to enjoy the breeze. Her dark eyes watched the mountain pass far below and focused on the small band of travelers with their wagon. She was surprised they had made it this far with all the odds thrown against them. Amar Kit'han and the Dae'shan seemed intent on killing them all but one, yet nothing they had done worked. Freina attributed that to the wizard, Anienam Keiss. The last of his kind, his magics came from deep in the earth and were stronger than anything she remembered encountering before. The wizard made her and her sisters cautious, perhaps overly so. The Hags bristled at their defeats.

Brom crooned, a strange combination of pain and impatience. "We should not have agreed to help the devils."

Freina spread her wings, dark feathers tipped with frost. "These choices are not ours to make. Our kind swore an oath and we are honor bound to adhere. Do not question my decisions, Sister."

"She speaks what we all feel, Freina," Garelda snipped. Smaller than Freina, Garelda's heart bled with hatred. "This is not our war."

"Men are weak," Freina countered swiftly. "The Dae'shan herald the coming age of the dark gods. It is wise to serve them now so that we are remembered when the proper time arrives."

"At what cost?"

Freina cocked her head. "Explain your question."

"Our kind has exhausted itself to near extinction following the corrupt orders of the Dae'shan. So few of us remain it is impossible to rebuild. We are dying, Sister, and your blind obedience will see us put in the ground as well. It is time to break away from the dark gods and find our own path."

Brom jerked back, shocked by her sister's boldness. Freina clenched her fists, claws digging into the calloused flesh of her palms. "We serve as our ancestors did. There is no greater cause than that given to us by our birth. To do less would be blasphemy."

"Against what? We do not worship the dark gods, Freina. Is it not time to reclaim our lives and rebuild the great aeries?"

Freina seemed to consider the wisdom behind Garelda's comment. The thought of building a nest, a place to raise hatchlings and become queen of her race enticed her, but not to the point of abandoning her oaths. Honor spoke otherwise. They were Harpies, as ancient and venerable as the great Dwarven kings of old.

"Our kind has never worshipped the gods. We are sisters of sky and mountain, yet we have sworn commitments. The Dae'shan command us now."

"The Dae'shan will see us all brought to ruin before this ends," Garelda countered.

"What say you, Brom?"

The larger Hag puffed out her chest, dark feathers glimmering in the moonlight. "The winds have changed. We are not the owners of our lives. Difficult decisions must be made, but all for the better of our kind."

Freina waved her claws dismissively. "Everything I do is for our kind. There is no personal motive, Sister."

"I have doubts," said Brom before falling silent.

Too much had happened since Amar Kit'han first ordered them to follow the Delrananian princess. They'd been given free rein to kill as many of her protectors as necessary but had yet to come close enough to make this a reality. The desire to sink her claws into human flesh was becoming overpowering. She needed to feel the thrill of a kill, the taste of flesh and warm blood filling her belly. The Hags hadn't killed in so very long, giving her pause to believe this lay at the center of their discord.

Turning to her sisters, Freina said, "We have much to do if our charge is to be fulfilled, but we obey on empty stomachs. Too long has passed since our claws enjoyed ripping flesh. There is a small Man village at the base of the mountains. Let us go and fill our bellies and relieve this tension."

The prospect of hunting again stole away seditious thoughts, for the moment at least. Brom nodded and took flight first. Garelda, ever distrusting of her sister's true intentions, followed suit, leaving the frigid elder sister along on the small outcropping with dark thoughts coursing through her mind. The past remained unchangeable, but the future was locked in doubt. She very much wanted to see her sisters free again but lacked the foresight to discover how. With a heavy sigh she launched into the midnight sky and hurried after her sisters.

Far below, the wagon rambled on, unaware of the forces gathering against them. Only the Hags watched their passing.

ONE

Ambushed

Pale moonlight cast the world in a haunting glow, broken only by heavy storm clouds and overshadowing mountains. Light snow drifted down, adding to already deepening drifts pouring down from the mountain peaks. Cold winds howled like wolves on the hunt, shredding through the pines in unabated wrath. Winter had come to the Murdes Mountains, the vast range separating Delranan and Rogscroft.

Only a fool would dare cross the long-forgotten passes high in the clouds. Only a fool or a man so desperate it was all he could do. Mahn and Raste were desperate. Their kingdom had fallen to the combined might of the Wolfsreik and an army of Goblins from the east. Their king lay dead, murdered at the hands of King Badron himself. Deposed, what remained of the army broke into bands and retreated to the relative safety of the mountains.

Older, Mahn watched the trees with casual interest as the pair of scouts nestled into the snow. Younger and more energetic, Raste looked bored and impatient. There was so much more to be done than hiding in the snows. Many of his friends died during the sack of Rogscroft, leaving him with a growing darkness in his heart. Revenge called.

"Stop moving. You'll give us away," Mahn scolded quietly.

Raste rolled his eyes again. "Away to whom? We haven't seen so much as a deer or rabbit since sundown."

The older scout shook his head. Raste had been a hothead since they'd first met but the war only pushed him farther. Excessive exposure to violence and death threatened to undo the man Raste was capable of becoming. Mahn didn't know what to do. The loss of King Stelskor and the burning of their city inspired hatred in much of the youth and, while

Mahn could never bring himself to forgive the act, he understood it on a base level. Wars were won by will, and the Wolfsreik showed more of it.

"Prince Aurec sent us to watch the mountain passes for a reason," Mahn replied. "We have to know enemy troop movements so we can retake our kingdom."

"Prince Aurec hides in Grunmarrow while we waste our time counting snowflakes." Fires burned in his eyes. They'd spent two weeks hunting Goblin war parties before this assignment and Raste chafed at being suddenly left out.

I am losing him. This war is stealing our very souls. Nothing will remain but the burnt husks of what we were. And for what? That monster Badron only wants power and is willing to plunge Malweir under the blade to get it. Still, Raste has a point. Aurec has become a hollow reflection.

Mahn's last glimpse of Aurec was of the youth hunched over a small fire at their refuge in Grunmarrow. The look of despair wallowed deep in his spirit. His father's death robbed him of what might have been. Aurec was a fine man, but not the experienced warfighter his people needed to lead them through the dark times. A prince at dawn, king at dusk. Mahn grinned ruefully. Aurec was a king without a kingdom.

"Leave Aurec to his sorrows for the moment. No man should come to the throne by such means," Mahn said.

"The prince has…"

A sudden snap, crisp and echoing across the deepening night, stopped him in midsentence. Another followed. And another. Heavy boot steps turned into a loud roar. Armor jostling and weapons clanging joined in. Mahn's eyes narrowed as he tracked the sounds. Both scouts forced themselves deeper into the snow as the front ranks of a company of Goblins marched into view. Their squat, grey bodies came in ragged ranks deep into the narrow pass. Mahn smiled coldly.

The scouts had been chasing rumors of Goblin troop movements since the initial displacement from Rogscroft in late autumn. Winter slowed most military action considerably, giving the beleaguered defenders the opportunity to gather their strength and refocus their efforts. Badron decided to keep his ten-thousand-man Wolfsreik in the lowlands to secure the kingdom and sent the Goblins into the mountains to root out the rebels and the Pell Darga tribes. The war quickly devolved into a brutal series of ambushes and hit-and-run engagements.

Mahn started counting as the Goblins went past. This marked the first time in two weeks he and Raste had seen the enemy. Fifty had already gone by, causing Mahn to swear under his breath. At least a full company was in front of them. For so many to be in one place meant something big was about to happen. The armored column continued. Every few Goblins carried torches. Each flicker threatened to reveal the scouts. Neither would last long if they were forced to flee. Goblins might be slow witted and better suited to fight in caves, but they were exceptional trackers and notoriously vicious.

A small Goblin with a torch stopped abruptly and turned his head up to the air, sniffing deeply.

A second barreled through the ranks. "What is it? What do you smell?"

"Man stink."

Howls and grunts spread through the column. Short swords, the traditional weapon preferred by Goblin infantry, were drawn in anticipation of battle. They were an animalistic race, bred for warfare. Carnage and slaughter were like an elixir from the gods to them. Heads swiveled, peering into every shadow and snow drift. They strained. Chests heaved. The Goblins ached to be set loose.

Mahn slowly reached over to tap Raste's shoulder. The younger scout immediately understood and, using the Goblins' own noise for cover, started worming his way back down the slope. They might have a chance of escape if they could make it to the pine stand where their horses were tethered. The distance was only one hundred meters, but the going was narrow and treacherous due to the weather conditions. Ice coated the rocks and drooped from pine needles. Loose snow went down nearly a foot at its deepest. Mahn knew there wasn't that much luck in the world. Any hope of escape he harbored vanished the next instant.

"Find the humans! Bring me their heads and it's an extra ration of grog!" the Goblin commander roared.

The column broke apart like a hammer stroke in a chorus of howls and cheers. Deprived remnants of the first Dwarves, Goblins lusted for the taste of flesh. They drew sword and axe. Their breath came in ragged plumes of steam. Anger filled their eyes; hatred filled their hearts. They split into squads and began to hunt, the promise of dining on Man an unquenchable lust. Mahn cursed again. The Goblins were better organized and moving much faster than he anticipated. They torched nearby trees and brush with enough foliage to burn. Soon thick clouds of choking black smoke wafted up. Snow began to melt at their feet.

"We need to run," Raste hissed. The fear of death held no sway over him, but he knew folly when he saw it.

Raste had lived through the first campaign of the war; an act of guerrilla attacks on the Wolfsreik before the army managed to bring its full might to bear on the plains. He'd survived the siege of Rogscroft with barely a scratch despite watching too many friends die. Weeks of skulking in shadows and striking from the blind side took their toll but he was still fully mission capable. But this, waiting in the snow to be discovered by over a hundred Goblins, was plain madness. Every instinct screamed for him to run. The scouts were cut off, leagues of hostile terrain separating them from the rest of the army. Death stalked the pass, its icy fingers crept towards his throat. It was all he could do not to scream. His heart thumped, threatening to burst. His mouth went dry. Raste knew it was the end at last.

Mahn didn't argue, but the horses were still too far away to offer any real hope. Desperation filled his heart. He knew he had failed king and kingdom. Deep down he knew they weren't going to make it. A high-pitched voice snapped out from a stand of nearby trees, breaking his dismal thought process.

"Run!"

Raste didn't wait for further encouragement. Beside him Mahn lurched to his feet and ran as fast as his old legs could go. Goblins spotted them almost immediately and roared in alarm. Others stopped looking and rushed towards the fleeing scouts. The hunt had begun. The frozen earth trembled beneath the thunder of so many boots as the Goblin company converged. Raste darted past Mahn. His eyes fixed on the horses and freedom. Mahn lagged. Weeks of huddling in snowbanks and living off of frozen foods drained his strength. He felt the Goblins drawing close, ready to reach out and grab him by the nape. Fear propelled him, blinding him to all else. Entirely focused on escape, he failed to notice the crisp whistling sound flash past his left ear.

A spray of hot blood whipped across his back as the first Goblin fell dead. Several more followed quickly. Mahn refused to look back. If this was death, he'd rather not see the poisoned blade arching for his back.

"Form ranks!"

Arrows continued to spit into the Goblins' light armor. A wave of bodies soon littered the mountain pass. Less than a minute and the Goblins had been reduced by a fifth. Their advance faltered, stopping altogether as the survivors huddled around, unsure of their enemy. Heads twisted to find their attackers. Their commander, his flat face peering out from under a leather faceplate, snapped his elongated jaws open and shut rapidly. Every instinct demanded he order them to charge. Cowardice held no place among the deep cavern dwellers.

A cry erupted from the back ranks, cut off abruptly with a gurgle of blood. The captain spun and bellowed an animalistic fury unlike any Mahn or Raste had ever heard.

"Ambush! Behind us!"

Brute force a favored weapon, the Goblin captain bellowed an attack. He watched helplessly as the first rank of

Goblins was skewered on a wall short spears popping up from deep snowbanks. Confused, he hesitated. That hesitation proved his undoing. Spears joined the arrows and Goblins fell by droves. Screams and cries of pain sang amongst the thin pines. Mahn froze and watched in muted shock as what had seemed a certain death situation turned into something else. He'd never seen the like.

What remained of the Goblin ranks crashed into the spear wall with a thunderous sound. Lines of Pell Darga warriors emerged from the trees in measured step. Garbed in various pelts, the short mountain warriors hacked and slew the Goblins. Their dark brown skin in contrast with the grey Goblins, the Pell were equally cunning and murderous. They killed with prejudice, slaughtering the invaders without thought. The battle quickly turned into a rout. Not a single Goblin survived.

Mahn finally found the strength to rise. Mouth agape, he stared at the dark blood strewn recklessly across the fresh snows. Once, such a scene would have appalled him. Six months of desperate combat left him largely immune to such scenes. Each new battle stole another piece of his soul and made him less human. He looked down on the bodies with as much detachment as the gods provided. For that he was glad.

Splattered in blood, the Pell warrior shouldered his spear and stopped before the scout. "I am Gol Mad. We have followed these," he gestured with a sneer to the corpses, "for three days. More come."

"How did you find us?" Mahn asked. His heart beat a little slower now that the immediate threat had passed.

Gol Mad grinned savagely. "Cuul Ol sent us to guard pass. We watched you for many hours."

"You could have showed yourselves sooner," Raste said angrily. "They nearly killed us."

"Death very active here," Gol agreed, ignoring the youth's venom.

Mahn scolded Raste with a sharp glare. "Thank you, Gol Mad. We must return to Grunmarrow. The prince will be expecting our report. The enemy is finally moving and we aren't prepared to stop them all."

The Pell paused to consider the words, his face thoughtful and dark. Until King Badron of Delranan invaded Rogscroft, the Pell had been a peaceful people, content to live in their mountain homes with little to do with the rest of Malweir. War changed that. Youthful inexperience drove the warriors into battle, each eager to prove himself against the most feared army in all the northern kingdoms: the Wolfsreik. Instead, Gol and many like him were relegated to fighting the grey skins in less-than-honorable combat.

"This war not ours," Gol finally said. "Many Pell died. We hunt, we kill. That is the way of the world. Life does not care about our concerns."

"This war will claim your way of life. You must understand that," Mahn insisted. "The Pell are no longer safe in these mountains. King Badron will hunt you down and destroy you one hunting party at a time until nothing remains but bone and dust."

"We will do as we must. It is the Pell way."

Raste puffed an angered breath. "Look, we need you to win the war. The Wolfsreik and their Goblin allies are too powerful for us to fight alone. Why can't you see that?"

"You are young, despite your experience. Time may change this. Go back to your prince. Cuul Ol has spoken."

Mahn stopped Raste from coming forward, and making a fatal error, with a swift backhand to the chest. "Cuul Ol also gave his word that the Pell would come to our aid when we required it. That time is now. Thousands of Goblins roam the mountains and lowlands. You can't possibly think to hide from them all, can you?"

"We do as we must," Gol repeated. His stance shifted, becoming more defiant.

Mahn cursed silently. He wasn't a politician or a diplomat. Dealing with a relatively primitive tribe as the Pell Darga brought him more frustration than anything else he'd ever done. It only reinforced his feelings of exhaustion and mental fatigue. So much had happened so quickly he struggled to comprehend most of it. There wasn't much choice, however. In the end, he simply followed orders and did the best he could in a terrible situation.

Mahn decided to push a little further. "Does the honor of the Pell extend to following Cuul Ol completely?"

Gol's fingers whitened on his spear shaft. Fresh anger flared just behind his eyes. "You seek to challenge me?"

The older scout raised his empty hands. "No. I seek to awaken the truth your leaders once inspired in you."

"Our leaders know the value of honor! We fight when Cuul Ol commands. Not before."

Gol Mad fell silent, forcing himself to calm down. He knew what Cuul and the other chiefs had decreed. The Pell Darga weren't strong enough to fight the combined armies ravaging their lands. Not even the remnants of Rogscroft could contend with such might. So many men had gone to the dirt before their time. So many families shattered by needless violence unsought and undeserved. Three of his brothers died fighting the wolf soldiers during the initial stages of the war; it was enough to fuel his need for vengeance as well as inspiring his caution. He learned that he was not the warrior he once imagined. There was much needed to be learned before he could return the fight sufficiently.

Sensing the internal conflicts, Mahn backed off. "Very well. Raste and I shall return to the prince and let him know of your decisions. We thank you for rescuing us. The Goblins would have torn us apart and eaten us alive if you hadn't showed up. Thank you, Gol Mad."

Jerking his head towards their horses, he and Raste started to leave. Enough had been done for now. Mahn once bent a knee to offer fealty to King Stelskor. That bond passed to Stelskor's son upon the sack of Rogscroft. Many men died to ensure Aurec escaped alive to fight for what remained of their kingdom. He and Raste were two of the most valuable assets the new army had available. They made it barely a handful of strides before Gol called out.

"Wait. We come. The honor of the Pell shall never be questioned. Cuul Ol will understand," he explained. He turned and barked orders in their crude language. The Pell warriors immediately collected what useable spears and arrows lay scattered across the scene and melted back into the small pine and scrub brush.

"What about them?" Mahn gestured at the dead.

Gol gave a final look at the corpses and shrugged. "Food for wolves."

TWO

Grunmarrow

The night passed swifter than Mahn had hoped. His fingers and toes ached, tingling from the extreme cold weather at such elevations. Winds continued to strengthen the lower they went. He glanced back at Raste, watching the younger scout shiver uncontrollably. Not even the bearskin cloak offered much protection from prolonged exposure. They needed a fire and something warm to eat and were still many leagues from being able to make that happen.

A wolf bayed off in the distant valleys, followed quickly by another. Their song echoed a haunting melody that sent fresh chills down Mahn's spine. Once, long ago, wolf song soothed him. Now it only served to remind him of the Wolfsreik and their wave of carnage sweeping across the north. Shadows came alive. Each tree and bush hid an enemy soldier waiting to kill. He knew it was mere childish superstitions. He knew they were creatures doing only what nature created them for. That didn't stop his apprehensions from growing.

There was nothing natural about the Wolfsreik. They were the ultimate fighting force in the northern kingdoms, perhaps rivaling those of the king of Averon far to the south. Their name inspired deep fears. Made the mightiest tremble at the knee. Mahn once thought they had a chance to stop the Wolfsreik, but then Badron unleashed an entire army of Goblins. The initial invasion campaign ended quickly, but not without massive casualties. He and Raste and what remained of the scouting corps infiltrated the ruined carcass of the city to discover how badly Badron's armies spent their strength breaking down the walls. What he saw surprised him.

Hundreds, perhaps thousands, of Goblins lay where they fell. In fact, most of the bodies littering Rogscroft were the squat, grey warriors. Very few men lay among the dead, leading Mahn to believe that all was not well with the alliance between Delranan and the Goblins. That fact could be exploited if only it could be confirmed. Scouts were sent repeatedly out to the lowlands with specific instructions to find any truth in Mahn's suspicions. Most failed to return, forcing the young prince to withdraw his forces and wait out the winter.

"The nights get too cold up here," Mahn said, trying to spark conversation from the sullen Raste.

The younger scout frowned and nodded. "Winter has been very harsh this year. Do you think the Pell will fight?"

"Hard to say. I know they want to, despite the reluctance Gol stated. They are a proud people unused to being cowed in their own lands. This band will join us."

He left the thought hanging. Too many variables obscured his normally good hunches. New snow started to fall. The flakes were cold as they melted on his near frozen face. Mahn had suffered through many winters colder than this but he'd always had the comforts of a warm home and spiced wine after. The Murdes Mountains were no place for sane men to travel under the best conditions, much less the dead of winter. A thought crept in, strange and alien. He suddenly felt regret for having wasted his life in servitude. Any chance of having a wife, family, and any normalcy in his life were gone, slashed away like so much detritus. His shoulders slumped just a touch.

"We're going to need more than this bunch," Raste said. "Badron has to have at least twenty thousand troops committed to this war. Even with the Pell we wouldn't be able to half that."

"Haven't you learned anything, Raste? Look at what Aurec managed on the plains before the Wolfsreik brought their full force to bear."

"And for what?" Raste countered darkly. "Rogscroft still fell. The only way to win is by using their own tactics against them. We need to make Delranan fear us."

Mahn looked at Raste sadly. *How do I tell him that has never been our way? We were largely a peaceful society until the war began. He's letting his anger drive his emotions. It will be the death of him.* "Prince Aurec will figure it out. We can win this war if we stay true to our principles, Raste. Don't let the enemy change who you are."

"They already have."

The scouts rode on in silence, disturbed only by the sounds of the iced-over snow breaking beneath each footstep.

Grunmarrow was everything a military camp should be. Secluded in the foothills of the Murdes Mountains and accessible by a single road, the stone buildings were well protected from attack and concealed just enough to keep others guessing its whereabouts. In the six weeks since Delranan had invaded, not a single patrol, Goblin or man, came close to discovering the hidden base. Massive stone formations ringed the camp. A small stream flowed down from the mountains, providing drinking, cooking, and washing water. Ancient pine trees filled the small draw.

Foresight and careful planning filled the storehouses long before winter set in. Stelskor was a very prudent man and had taken every precaution to properly equip the defenders at Grunmarrow for a long winter. Sacks of grains and flour, dried meats, canned fruits and vegetables, as well as grain for the herd animals, filled dozens of specially built storerooms deep into the mountainside. Candles, cloth, blankets, weapons, and armor filled even more. The two smiths echoed metalworking constantly long into the night. Fletchers cut arrows from ash limbs. Fishermen and farmers provided for the ample civilian population. Grunmarrow was everything a military camp should be. It only lacked morale.

Prince Aurec sat upon his favorite tree stump, lamenting the loss of his beloved Maleela. He failed to accept that it was his kidnapping of her that instigated the war. Badron had had his eyes on Rogscroft since both he and Stelskor were boys. He used Maleela's disappearance as an excuse. The resulting wave of destruction proved almost incomprehensible. None of the survivors ever thought to see death and wanton destruction on such massive levels. Six weeks later and Aurec was still in shock.

His eyes focused on the flames dancing up before him from the small fire at his feet. Gold, red, and orange flickered around the tiniest hint of blue, buried deep in the flames. Aurec didn't want to look away. Didn't want to accept responsibility for the thousands of men, women and children, his people, living in Grunmarrow while two enemy armies ravaged their kingdom. Didn't want to be more than a lover to Maleela and perhaps one day a father. He'd never asked to become king, but his inner council decided it was past time he accepted the crown and bore the title of king of Rogscroft. He'd argued. Oh how he'd argued. Rogscroft was no more, reduced to an occupied territory. What use did the displaced have for a throneless king? His words fell on deaf ears. The people needed leadership and it was his inherent responsibility.

The ceremony was set for the end of the week, giving Aurec plenty of time to daydream about running away. Again, he'd protested against one. Venten and several others put him back in his place by reminding the young prince that the ceremony was for the people's benefit, not his. He could wallow away his nights in solitude as long as the citizens of

Rogscroft took some measure of comfort in seeing a new king crowned. So much had happened that the coronation might be the only thing keeping many a good man or woman from ending it all in the cold winter. Too many had already died, leaving the rest a precious commodity.

Sergeant Thorsson saluted crisply and considered waiting for Aurec to reply before giving his report, briefly. "Sire, Mahn and the other scouts have returned. They…ah brought guests as well."

Aurec scarcely looked up. "Guests? We have no allies, Sergeant. Who will have come?"

"The Pell Darga."

His immediate reply shook away some of the disease clinging to Aurec. The Pell had openly declared war against the Wolfsreik and Goblins but had yet to do much about it. The war continued at an agonizingly slow pace with very few engagements since the capital city fell. Having their representatives in Grunmarrow might be the catalyst they needed to turn the war and begin a new campaign. A spark flared. The old Aurec started to awaken.

"Is it Cuul Ol? How many have come? Are they ready to fight?" he asked too fast.

Thorsson enjoyed seeing the prince regain some of his old self but the questions were too much to handle. He held up his hands in mock surrender. "I don't have the answers you seek, sire. Perhaps Mahn can address them."

Aurec shot up. "Take me to him, Sergeant."

Thorsson grinned and led the way through the small huts and homes, emerging into the camp's outer defensive perimeter. There awaited Mahn and the compliment of Pell hunters. Any hope Aurec had of using the Pell to overpower the Wolfsreik died upon seeing too few arrayed in the open field. The Pell hadn't come after all.

"So few," he whispered.

Mahn and Gol Mad noticed the prince first and quickly made their way to his audience. The older scout immediately noticed the growing despair in Aurec's eyes but was warned not to question by a stiff shake of Thorsson's head. Instead, he saluted and began his report. "Sire, this is Gol Mad, from Cuul Ol's clan. He's brought fifty warriors."

Eyes flicked back and forth as Aurec silently processed the news, or rather what hadn't been said. Mahn carefully avoided mentioning any sort of formal commitment by Cuul or whether these Pell had agreed to fight in the lowlands. Stifling his sigh, Aurec reached forward to greet the Pell.

"Welcome, Gol Mad. You are most welcome to Grunmarrow. I would offer to throw you and your warriors a feast, but we are slightly underprepared for such festivities."

Many of the words were lost on him, but Gol still managed to sound courteous. "It does the Pell good to see a new king in Rogscroft. We come to fight. To kill wolf soldiers and their foul-skinned friends."

So much for small talk. Mahn added, "There is still no official word from the larger clans, leading me to believe Cuul Ol and the others already have their hands filled. The Goblin column Gol saved us from was at least one hundred strong. Never before have their numbers been so high in the mountains. Sire, I believe a new phase of the war is beginning."

"In the middle of winter? Badron has to be mad if he expects to tackle the Pell and nature in these blasted peaks," Aurec responded.

"Agreed but the two most likely courses of action are the Wolfsreik scouting for an open passage back into Delranan for reinforcements and supplies or they are preparing to find and destroy as many of the clans as possible before spring. No one in their right mind would expect a full assault this deep into the winter," Mahn said.

"I need to know numbers, Mahn, before I can commit what little forces I have to the fight. We've done well enough raiding supply columns and striking scouting parties, but if what you say is correct we won't stand a chance against so many." Aurec turned back to the Pell. "Does Cuul know the Goblins are moving in force against the clans?"

"Many Pell have given their lives against the grey skins. We fight. Cuul Ol and other leaders swear to kill all that come."

Thorsson nodded approvingly. His opinion of the Pell improved, slightly, making him wish more of his own men were ready and willing to commit themselves so wholeheartedly to the cause. Perhaps then they might have a chance to win the war properly. He glanced back over his shoulder at the sound of approaching footsteps and saw the freshly reinstated General Venten wearily make his way to Aurec's side.

"Damned illness is keeping me from doing my job," he coughed and spat. Bright red blood laced the phlegm. "I guess our friends decided to come down from the mountains and join the fun."

"General, you are hero in some circles," Gol acknowledged with a bow. "Many warriors sing your glory."

"I didn't know I was a hero, but I'll take it," Venten replied with as much of a smile as he could manage before another fit of coughs wracked him.

Mahn's eyes crossed ever so slightly at the mention of heroes. Leaning close, he whispered, "Have you got a story to tell?"

Venten shrugged.

"Gol Mad, please make yourself at home among us. We are honored to host the Pell at our fires," Aurec continued.

"My apologies, prince. We cannot stay. I am here to hear your words for Cuul Ol."

"I don't understand."

Gol adjusted the grip on his short spear. A good foot shorter than Aurec, he was also in contrast to the more well-fed lowlanders. His body was a mass of muscle and terrible strength, folded and shaped by years of harsh living conditions and the fires of combat. The lines on his face came from constant beatings by the weather and his eyes were hard as flint. Shoulder length black hair framed his wide shoulders, giving him a wild, unkempt appearance. Gol Mad and his Pell warriors were natural killers from old times. All they needed was a little push in the right direction.

"The council of elders agreed to war, but we are not strong enough to fight in big battles like you want. We strike at our enemies in the mountains and trees. That is where we are best. At home. Your kind call us Shadow People, and we are. I come to see your camp, your army, and return to Cuul Ol and tell him what I saw."

Aurec paused, taken aback. He'd been expecting an army of Pell coming down from their mountain haunts to take the fight back to the Wolfsreik. Instead, he found a meager war band that might have the drive to fight but were restrained by complicated orders. He felt like hitting something. "Of course, Gol Mad. Please, take food and drink by our fires. Rest the night before returning to the mountains."

Satisfied, Gol said, "We will eat and rest for a time. Thank you, prince."

They waited until he returned to his people before speaking. Aurec began. "You could have done a better job convincing them to join us. Cuul Ol's proclamation happened months ago and we still haven't seen much support."

"Sire, I don't think they have much support to give," Mahn countered. "My impression is that they are beleaguered under Goblin attacks. This band saved Raste and I from a serious problem. We owe them a lot."

"I could use about a hundred of them to help train the new recruits, even some of the old ones. I'm not cut out to be an instructor. My talents are wasted in camp," Thorsson said. His desire to be out in the field almost overpowered his sense of duty to the new king.

Venten coughed again, understanding exactly how the sergeant felt. He'd been with Aurec since birth and had earned his place during the opening campaign of the war.

Unfortunately, his health continued to decline since the fall Rogscroft. He couldn't take to the field any more than the wounded Thorsson. "We all have new jobs, Thorsson. I was just a bodyguard until Grunmarrow. Now I'm the chief of state."

"Don't forget hero," Mahn added.

He frowned.

"There must be something we can do to convince the Pell we need them. It's not a matter of just getting them to fight. Any fool can do that, but we will lose this war without their full support. Mahn, how were the Goblins equipped?"

"Heavy infantry. They were hunting," he answered. "Though for us or the Pell I don't know. We didn't have much time to analyze the battlefield afterwards."

Aurec shook his head and placed both hands on his hips. "Keep working on them, all you. We have to find a way to get them to fight. Otherwise…"

Venten laid a gentle hand on Aurec's shoulder, much the way a father would his son. "Go and take some rest, sire. We'll figure out how to break them."

"I hope so, for all our sakes," Aurec said and returned to his hut. His thoughts had already turned back to Maleela and the broken love they shared.

THREE

Doubts

Far away, at the southern end of the Murdes Mountains, rambled the much abused wagon carrying Maleela and her companions. They'd set out from Venheim a week ago and were still trapped in the dark limestone and granite mountains, all despite Groge's assurance that he knew the correct paths down out of the mountains. Of course, he'd never been out of Venheim before, a fact none of the others bothered to consider before setting out.

Maleela wasn't herself. She doubted any of them were these days; especially after all they'd been through. Kidnapped by the love of her life from her very bedchambers, she'd been hunted ever since. Bahr, her uncle, unwittingly aided her father in stealing her back, thus paving the way for his invasion of Rogscroft. She felt helpless; like it was all her fault. Worse, she discovered a dark hatred festered deep in her soul, but for what she didn't know.

"You seem troubled," Anienam Keiss, the odd wizard, commented from his driver's seat on the wagon.

"We should all be troubled, Anienam," she answered. "How does any of this make sense to you? We're chasing ghosts."

The wizard snickered softly. "What do you mean?"

She shot him a withering glare. "Seriously? Look at us. A boy. Two sell swords that I still haven't decided if they are mentally capable or not. A foreign woman who's killed more men than any of the rest of us except perhaps Boen." She gestured towards the massive Gaimosian Knight riding at the front of the group. "I'm convinced you're borderline insane and I don't know what I'm doing. That brings us to our Giant wonder boy who's never left home. And what are we doing? Travelling halfway across Malweir in search of an ancient weapon that may or may not exist to defeat powers that have existed since the dawn of life. Have I left anything out?"

"Our friend Ionascu," Anienam added. "He's perhaps the most broken of us all. I truly don't trust him."

"Precisely my point! None of us belong together and you expect us to save the world from something that seemingly can't be defeated. What's the point?" she asked.

A few of the others paused to look her way but were wise enough to stay silent. They each faced demons of a personal nature.

"The dark gods will enslave the entire world, Maleela. Nothing will be left sacred to their depredations. Right now, at this singular moment in time, we are all that stands between total annihilation and at least the opportunity for peace. Daunting, I know. Destiny rarely calls upon us at moments of our convenience. This is one of those times."

She listened to his explanation but remained angry. "Why us? What makes any of us so special the fate of all Malweir should fall into our hands?"

"I like to think I'm fairly special. Leastwise my father and his kind were. But that's not my point. Perhaps none of us are truly special, which is what makes us all special if you follow my meaning," he said.

"You're talking in circles again," she growled.

He snuck a cautious glance before acting indignant. "What? Circles? How dare you, young princess! I am the last of my kind and have been granted a certain amount of flair in my manner of speech. It's not my fault that you can't follow!"

He finished with a stern harrumph. Maleela watched him with vicious eyes, suddenly tired of the mirage being played. She'd been through more than any other woman her age and still had so much more to go before the end. Emotionally she wasn't sure she had the strength to last. Traumas heaped upon her like waves breaking against the rocky shore. Hope started to fade, leaving her in a position of mass confusion.

"You can't carry the deeds of others on your shoulders," Anienam said after noticing the internal battle wage deep in her eyes.

"What choice do I have?"

He smiled softly. "Doing so will only bring you low, dragging you down into an impossible hole you can never climb from. I know, for I've done it too many times. This world is not a kind one, no matter how many times we try to make it so. Oftentimes our good deeds get reduced to tragedy, or worse. I'd like to tell you that it will all work out in the end, that each of us will go on with our lives unchanged. I can't."

"That doesn't give me much hope for the future," she countered.

He shrugged. "Hope is what you make of it. Have I ever told you the tale of how I managed to talk a group of Trolls out of waging a civil war? Silly creatures really. They'd come upon a claim in the Bairn Hills that the Dwarves had missed. Gold is a powerful thing, especially to smaller minds. Why, I recall how they…"

Maleela rolled her eyes and tried to focus on the strong back of her uncle Bahr, riding alongside the Gaimosian.

"She should not have come," Boen grumbled to Bahr after listening to their banter.

Bahr nodded crisply. "I agree, but where else should she be? The One Eye will kill her if she stays in Delranan. We can't take her back to Rogscroft. The list of safe havens seems rather small."

Born without a home, Boen spent his life roaming the kingdoms of Malweir, paying for a crime he wasn't alive to commit. The fall ancient Gaimos was the most storied legend in all the lands, a tragedy unrivaled. The idea that any Gaimosians survived this long provided testament to the strength of their convictions. He, and those few hundreds like him, were a scourge on the world.

"At what point does your charity turn to liability?" he asked. The thought of continuing to babysit the princess and a few others almost insulted him.

Bahr felt his cheeks flush. "She is my niece, Boen. No matter what else happens I can't ignore family."

She's the only true family I have. My brother has finally become a tyrant and I am as much of an exile as you are. He knew something about being displaced as well. The black sheep of the family, Bahr left home at an early age, leaving the kingdom to Badron. The open sea called and he gleefully threw himself into her bosom. Decades of pirating the northern coastline earned him the nickname Sea Wolf but, despite having an impressive estate on the outskirts of Chadra, he never truly felt at home in Delranan.

The decision to return hadn't been of his choosing. Harnin One Eye, first among Badron's lieutenants, bore special hatred for the forgotten son and used deception to enlist Bahr in rescuing Maleela from Rogscroft. It had all been a ruse. She'd never been kidnapped. The kingdom never in jeopardy. Harnin and Badron used him to start a war. Now neither Maleela nor Bahr could go home. Images of Bahr's estate burning to the ground haunted him continually: a visual reminder of what might have been.

"You are letting your emotions compromise the mission."

"We're trying to save the world, Boen," Bahr replied. "I think a task like that will need all the help it can get."

Boen scowled. "You know what I mean. This is no game, Bahr. What we've seen and done is nothing if what the wizard says is true. This is going to get messy before the end."

"Is there a choice? Neither of us was looking for a war, but one has been thrust upon us. My home is gone. My kingdom taken over and turned into a dictatorship and my brother has gone to war with a perceived enemy for the sake of his own vanity. I feel like Maleela and that bothers me deeply."

Boen almost suggested the old man get back into the sea where he was more comfortable but the *Dragon's Bane* had been burned to the waterline for Harnin's amusement. Nothing had gone right since. "Bahr, you aren't used to this life. I've spent my life going from one bad time to the next without any hope of finding a home. I know the risks. I accept them. You should take her and find a place to settle down while you still can. This quest will claim us all."

"You're sounding like that cracked wizard," Bahr said. "My brother won't stop with Rogscroft. And if the rumors are true, he's got an army of Goblins working for him." He shook his head. "None of this makes sense to me. There's no way he should have been able to gain so much power without anyone knowing."

"A spy?" Boen suggested.

The implication lurking behind the comment disturbed Bahr. He'd known Ionascu was one of Harnin's lackeys and had taken appropriate measures to keep him neutralized. At least he had until Harnin turned on his spy and left him a broken shell of a man. Ionascu remained haunted, something sinister lurking just under the surface. No one else seemed capable of turning against Bahr. They'd been chosen for their friendship, loyalty, and knowledge of combat. Only Rekka Jel and young Skuld remained mysteries. The boy was easy enough to figure. He'd overheard a conversation between Dorl Theed and Nothol Coll and decided to try and get rich on their coattails. Rekka Jel, however, was an enigma from the moment she arrived on the docks. Bahr didn't like surprises. Between the strange woman from the southern jungles and the wizard she looked up to, Bahr didn't know where he stood. What began as a quest to rescue his niece quickly spiraled out of control and left him mired in an unending string of misery.

"After all we've been through I can't see how anyone is working against us. Even young Skuld was tortured by

Harnin's men," the Sea Wolf answered. "I don't know, Boen. Explain to me how the enemy always seems to know what we're doing before we do."

For once the Gaimosian had no answer. His well-honed combat instincts whispered of being watched, forcing him to look back over his shoulder far too many times. No matter what he did he couldn't shake the feeling and that perplexed him terribly. He was a man that needed to fight, more comfortable in battle than civilization. The thought that some darkness haunted him and stayed hidden was beyond infuriating.

"I would like to get my hands around the neck of whoever it is," he finally said. "I feel like we are running away. That doesn't sit well with me, Bahr."

"Running don't sit well with any of us but this isn't like anything we've seen before. The whole damned war is unnatural."

Boen shifted in his saddle, his lower back sore. "I need a stand-up fight. Never been any good with sneaking around."

"Agreed." Bahr decided to shift topics. "What about the wizard? How much credence can we put in his theories?"

"I think the old man has had too many mugs of bad ale. He's half cracked and taking the rest of us with him. Still, I get the feeling that he might know what he's doing. Found Venheim, with the help of that book of course."

Bahr nodded slightly. "He's mad, that I agree. I still can't figure out why he showed up on my doorstep that night, but he's guided us true the whole time. I suppose it's better to have a wizard with us than against us if this war is going to continue."

"War, that would be nice. Instead we're going halfway across Malweir in search of a weapon that might not even exist," Boen grumbled. "All those Giants and they send us a mere apprentice. I don't know about you but they'd have given us a more experienced person if they believed their own tales."

The Giants had been reluctant to accept their small band and more than eager to get rid of them. Venheim was one of the last true hidden places in Malweir, and for good reason. Giants were largely extinct throughout most of the world. Poor breeding contributed to increasingly low population numbers. Whatever they might have been, the Giants of Venheim were now a secluded, superstitious clan cut off from the rest of civilization and mired in their own demons, self-created or otherwise.

"Groge seems a good enough lad," Bahr said. "What better way to get experience is there than by going out into the world? His size and strength will definitely come in handy if and when we get into a real scrape."

"Size doesn't make a good fighter. That boy hasn't swung a sword in his life."

Bahr carefully peered back over his right shoulder to the Giant walking casually alongside the wagon. "He doesn't need to. Very few have ever seen a Giant and I'm guessing they'll wind up pissing themselves when they do. We have a small advantage at least."

"He's also big enough that we can't hide if needs be. Groge is twice as tall as I am. He'll be a liability."

"One I'm willing to accept. Legends say their hides are so thick no mortal weapon can pierce them. He doesn't need to fight well if there's any truth in it. Damnation, he can step on a man and kill him!"

They shared a laugh, the thought of Groge squashing a grown man to pulp oddly amusing. Nothing had gone right since accepting Harnin's mission to rescue Maleela from Rogscroft and now, even with their recent additions and knowledge, the tunnel continued to lengthen. Bahr would have very much liked a platoon of Giants at his service but instead he only got a young apprentice smith. Something being better than nothing, he recognized their need to include Groge. If what Anienam said was correct, only the Giant could handle the legendary Blud Hamr.

They needed to find it first.

"What's our next move?" he asked Boen, hoping the Gaimosian had a better sense of things than he did.

"Those snowstorms kept us pent up in the mountains for too long, not to mention getting lost in the damned foothills. We've lost a lot of time. The quickest way is down the short road to the Kergland Spine and then the Fern River. Rekka says we can move faster by boat and I agree. The current will be with us on the voyage down. Getting back will be more difficult."

Bahr considered the route. "The Kergland Spine takes us into Dwarf territory."

"It's the fastest route."

They both knew the reputations surrounding Dwarves. Bitter and reclusive, the mountain dwellers were feared almost as much as they were respected for their craftsmanship. Bahr and the others would do well to avoid any run-ins.

"We're most likely not going to make it in time, if the wizard's calculations are correct," Bahr said.

"A handful of months are far too short to make it all the way down to the southern jungles and back again. There is no time. We'll be fortunate if we make it half that far."

A cold wind shuffled through the rocky corridor, blasting them with unabated fury. Bahr, no stranger to fierce weather, ducked down into his bearskin cloak in a futile attempt to keep the wind out. His curses were lost on the low growl of the wind.

"You're getting old," Boen laughed. His deep voice boomed with each syllable. "There was a time when the mighty Sea Wolf would have spit in the face of such a breeze."

"There was a time when he also had a boat, but look where he is now," Bahr countered. "I think I'm going to go have a talk with Anienam. See if I can get him to reread that part in the book that basically tells us if we're screwed or not."

The Gaimosian nodded. "I will keep point. The way out of the foothills is clear now. We shouldn't have any trouble."

Bahr failed to remind Boen he'd said the same thing a week ago.

FOUR

Doldrums

Every rock looked the same. Every snow-covered mound, lichen-covered rock, and moss-striped tree looked the same. The ground offered nothing new. The same sky continued to look down mockingly. The northern reaches of the Murdes Mountains might be filled with many foul and dangerous things, but the southern end drove men to despair. Not a single aspect of the mountains had changed since leaving Venheim. Nothing except it got much colder without the heat of the massive forges.

Dorl Theed took a long pull from his canteen, swirled it around in his mouth and then spit. The makeshift goggles cut out of pine bark helped reduced the glare from the snow to the point he found it almost manageable. Weeks of wandering aimlessly down from the peaks threatened to break his spirit though, a thing he never thought possible. Not even Harnin's torturers managed to do much more than break a few bones.

He began to regret the decision to sign on with Bahr. Nothing good had come from it. The old man wasn't the adventurer he once was. Nor did he seem to care too much about the fate of Delranan. Any other man would have snapped already. Home, boat, any chance at a normal life all wiped out on a madman's whim. Dorl found himself growing angry over the indignity of it, and nothing had happened to him!

"Your mind is clouded," Rekka Jel said softly from his side.

He smiled. He couldn't help it. She was the one thing going right for him since leaving Delranan all those weeks ago though he still wasn't sure what she saw in him. Rekka came from an entirely different culture far to the south, a tribe locked deep in the jungle and given the purpose of defending something more ancient than the gods themselves. She'd come so far on sheer faith, bearing a warning for Bahr. The selflessness of it impressed him greatly. Though he couldn't help but wonder why she'd chosen him.

He answered, "Because I can't seem to make it up. None of this is right, Rekka."

She appeared confused. "What is wrong? We have the wizard, a Giant to wield the hammer and we know where it is located. I don't believe we're missing anything."

You've got to be kidding me. Not missing anything? How about common sense? How about knowing what in the world we are doing in the first place? Dorl wanted to tip his head back and shout at the top of his lungs in the hope of bringing the mountain down on his head to relieve the frustration. Too many questions and doubts kept him down and he had no one to ask that fatal question to: why?

"Rekka, what made you come to Delranan in the first place? There has to be more than your elders decided it must be you."

She stiffened slightly, caught off guard. "One does not question the gods. Our elders commune with the spirits of the gods and of the earth. Knowledge comes from them alone. We must all obey or the cause is lost."

"Cause?" he asked, deciding to press further.

"Good and evil must coexist in order for the world to spin with symmetry. One cannot vanquish the other or all we know will be plunged into total chaos. Yet there cannot be too much of one. Balance must be maintained. We are the keepers of the balance. My people have long defended the temple masters but we are very few. We serve righteousness and justice. The Dae'shan and their masters threaten to undo us. Therefore our cause is in great peril. You were all chosen for reasons that go beyond my comprehension."

Rekka fell silent, having said more than enough. She'd been given specific instructions not to get involved with the brutal and barbaric northerners. Not to tell more of her life than necessary to accomplish her mission. She had questions of her own. How would she know the right ones to approach? Would they be pure enough? The elders brushed off her concerns and sent her on her way with the knowledge that she was setting out to help save Malweir from eternal darkness. Fortunately, many of those questions were answered easily when she stumbled across Anienam Keiss. Now that they'd been together for a few months, Rekka came to doubt finding him was an accident.

The wizard guided her through those dark patches she couldn't navigate, helped her understand the much larger picture her elders had either forgotten or never knew. He always knew precisely what to say and when. Every time she felt the tug of doubt he was there to wipe her concerns away. No, finding him was no accident. Anienam Keiss had been searching for her from the beginning. He too must have guessed the time of confluence was fast approaching. A time when the dark gods would make their next attempt at returning to claim their vacant thrones.

And he should. The ancient order of Mages once held those dark forces at bay. Born from the trials of a handful of Gaimosians, the order slowly became the dominant body on all Malweir. They were sought for their great wisdom and abilities to heal and more. Everyone celebrated their society at Ipn Shal until they made the crystal of Tol Shere. The dark gods infiltrated the Mages and used the crystal to wreak unspeakable horrors on the world. In the end, only a handful of Mages lived. One of them was Anienam's father.

Centuries of hit-and-run battles and weak attempts at regaining power filled the space between the fall Ipn Shal and now. Centuries of unprecedented grief and despair. Anienam's father gave his life to the cause, stopping his arch nemesis, Sidian the Silver Mage, in what he thought had been the final battle. History proved him wrong. The dark gods lingered on, ever hungering for their return. Dakeb eventually passed. Now only Anienam remained: the last of his kind. Magic was dying and there was little room left in Malweir for it. People didn't want to be reminded of what magic did to them. How badly it had altered their style of life.

When Dorl spoke again it was slow and thoughtful. "I don't believe I will ever understand you, Rekka Jel, but you have my devotion. Never doubt my intent to remain at your side, no matter how dark the night becomes."

She reached out and squeezed his offered hand before riding to the front of the column.

"I don't believe I just heard that come from your mouth."

Dorl narrowed his eyes on his oldest and best friend, Nothol Coll. "Just had to open your mouth and spoil the moment, didn't you?"

"I had to open my mouth to vomit," he replied with laughter. "If I didn't know better I'd say she had your balls in a little pouch around her neck."

Dorl, angered, pointed an accusing finger. "Just you listen up, I can take a fair amount of abuse from you, *friend*, but I draw the line when it comes to her."

"So she can't abuse your ears?" Nothol asked.

"You know damned well what I mean!"

Laughing harder, Nothol held up his hands. "Relax, Doral. I'm only playing and you know it. What are friends for, right?"

"They're not for this. I can tell you that much."

"Nonsense." Nothol stopped laughing. "We're heading deep into it here, my friend, and I need to know you've got my back just like before. We can't trust too many of the others, in case you haven't figured it out. That means we need to stick together no matter what. I don't mind helping out on an important cause and all but I'm not ready to give up my life for it just yet."

"When have you ever been willing to die for something not your choice?" Dorl asked, still upset with how easily Nothol had crossed the boundary.

"I never have and I doubt I ever will, but if what the wizard says is even half true then we might have a real shot at immortality."

"Now you want to live forever? I don't get you. You're starting to talk like that crack pot old man," Dorl said, shaking his head.

Nothol reached out and smacked him on the back of his head. "No, stupid. Ain't nobody can live forever. I'm talking about my name. How many future generations will look back on our deeds and say, 'There was a true hero! A selfless man.' Think about it, Dorl. We have the chance to become heroes."

Dorl couldn't believe what he was hearing. Nothol Coll was normally a reserved and prudent man, now he talked like Skuld at the beginning of the quest. Dreams of treasure and greatness had filled the young boy's head, at least until they ran into trouble and he saw how wrong he'd been. Now Skuld only hoped to make it home alive. And Nothol suffered from delusions of grandeur.

"Heroes die young," he finally said. "I'd like to live awhile longer if it's all the same."

Nothol shrugged. "Now, later. What difference does it make? In the end we all go back to the dirt and fade away."

"Have you been drinking?"

"Not yet. I didn't know we had anything left," Nothol replied.

Frustrated, Dorl spurred his horse forward to confront Anienam on filling his best friend's head with nonsense. Nothol watched him go, pausing only to glance up at the wagon. He found Skuld looking back at him. The blank look on his face told Nothol everything. Suddenly disturbed, he looked skyward. Not sure what he'd find, he searched the grey clouds for answers, truths, for any sign that he was making the right decisions going forward. His eyes focused. *Is that? Perhaps I'm too tired. Long nights in the saddle have robbed me of my senses. But I know what I saw. Three dark specks drifting into the clouds. We're being watched!*

"Are you certain?" Boen pressed.

The gentle cackle of their fire filled the background of the small vale they'd camped for the night in. Everyone gathered after a brief meal of old bread, dried meat, and what was left of a wheel of white cheese. Now they listened to Nothol explain what he believed he'd witnessed a few hours earlier.

He nodded. "Absolutely. They were much too large to be birds, even the great condors of the higher peaks."

Bahr poked at the fire with a blackened stick. "What do you make of this, wizard?"

"It could be something, might not be," Anienam replied. "There aren't many birds in this part of the world. Nor dragons or any such nonsense. I honestly don't know what they are."

"Not exactly confidence inspiring, is he?" Maleela whispered to her uncle.

Bahr suppressed a grin. "Hush girl. We've known we're being followed for a while now. This might be the break we need."

"We know Badron is allied with dark powers, could they be some construct of the Dae'shan?" Rekka asked.

"Possibly, but unless you can manage to shoot one down I can't know for certain." Anienam shook his head, frustrated at the continuing depth of the puzzle. Much of his plans were centered on speculation, preventing him from learning the truth in too many areas. Blinded, he had no choice but to carry on with his original plans. And pray they worked.

Nothol shook his head. "No. They were much too high to shoot down."

Ionascu suddenly broke out in bitter laughter. His crippled hand thumped down on his thigh. "Fools. Run and hide. Stand and die. What difference does it make? The One Eye will find us and kill us all!"

Boen's fist clenched instinctively. He looked to Bahr. "Say the word and I'll cave his skull in."

Bahr gently shook his head.

"Violence is not the solution to every situation, Gaimosian," Anienam scolded. "This man is damaged, broken in mind and body, but he may yet be of use to us."

"The big man goes down!" Ionascu cackled before ambling off to his bedroll.

"I really don't like him," Boen grumbled.

Ignoring him, Bahr asked, "What do we do about our spies? They'll give us away the moment they figure out where we're going."

The wizard shrugged. "What can we do? I have no spell that can bring them down. Deception will merely delay us to the point of failure."

"About that," Bahr asked. "Are you certain you read that book correctly? Because according to your timeline we're already late."

Anienam paused. He'd never considered being wrong; so few times in the past had he ever been. But Bahr brought a valid point. Perhaps he had misread the book. "I can certainly go back and reread it, but that's not the issue at hand. I have concerns about those creatures Nothol claims to have seen."

"Saw," Nothol corrected sharply.

Anienam waved him off. "Irrelevant. There is a village not far from here. I think we should make for it and regroup. Perhaps that will throw our trackers off."

"Fine, but what do we do about him?" Bahr asked, pointing at Groge.

The Giant lingered just outside of the range of the fire. Towering over everyone, he still didn't feel comfortable being around them. Groge had never seen another species before and found he was fascinated by them. They bickered and argued like old friends. Bore grudges contrary to their actions. They made no sense. He found it all oddly refreshing. Life in the forges held so little variation.

"I will remain in the forests," Groge finally said. "Your kind will not take kindly to seeing me, if what our elders say is true."

"True enough. Giants are extremely rare these days," Bahr said. "I think your best move is to remain hidden for as long as possible. We don't need any more unwarranted attention."

Groge nodded, that feeling of seclusion steadily growing stronger. He wanted to be part of their group, part of something that mattered for a change, but his size and race set him out as the oddity. The idea was absurd. They needed him to wield the fabled Blud Hamr when the time came. They needed him. He found the idea comforting but remained apprehensive. Humans were vastly different from his people. Certainly not what he imagined.

"Rest up," Bahr told the group. "We need to move quickly. I don't want our spies to grow comfortable while we dither on what to do. I'll take first watch. We leave in four hours."

FIVE

Fedro

Mired in the shadow of the mountains, Fedro was a largely forgotten village. Originally intended as a way station for travelers seeking to go over the mountains, the town quickly sprouted up and grew too far beyond its original intent. Bandits and thieves lined the streets hoping to fleece unsuspecting men and women. Worse, they often set ambushes in the foothills. The Murdes Mountains were lawless, a fact Bahr was counting on. The less law enforcement in the area the better. He knew Harnin would already have bounty hunters and worse scouring the neighboring kingdoms.

Smoke rose from a hundred chimneys, choking the air with subtle pollution. The roads were wet and muddy, sprinkled with light snow. Trees and bushes lined them, giving Fedro a small touch of class. Most of the houses were made from pine, though a few brick homes were interspersed. Bahr suggested they were most likely the homes of merchants and factors. Most people weren't rich enough to afford brick.

Bahr guided them down the two-lane road past the shanty guard houses and into the heart of Fedro. They'd left Groge about a kilometer back in a heavy stand of oaks with enough food and water to last the next two days. He hadn't put up an argument but stood with sad eyes as the others continued.

The size of the group drew stares and gawkers, more than Bahr or Anienam felt comfortable with. They'd been counting on secrecy but only succeeded in drawing attention to themselves. Bahr cursed, knowing he should have left the wagon with Groge and broken the group down into twos and threes. So many newcomers at once were bound to draw the wrong kinds of attention. Too late for that, he pushed them on to the nearest inn.

They'd been on the road for weeks without a rest and a good night's sleep with a roof over their heads was just what they needed to recharge. Leaving Nothol and Dorl to secure stable space for the horses and a berth for the wagon, he, Maleela, Anienam, and Skuld went in to get rooms and pay for their meals. Boen and Rekka went out through Fedro to scout the streets and identify potential escape routes should the need arise. Only broken Ionascu declined to accompany anyone and remained in the wagon bed, curled up under a pile of blankets.

Dawn broke by the time they gathered together for breakfast in the common room. The smell of bacon cooking assaulted their senses, making stomachs growl. Heaps of apples and fresh cheese were brought out along with pitchers of ice cold mountain water and freshly made dark bread with jam. Bahr paid a little extra to have eggs as well, knowing they needed the protein. The group's mood instantly improved and soon the room was alive with genuine laughter. Every care seemed forgotten, for the moment.

The door opened suddenly, allowing a small child in, accompanied by a strong gust of wind. He walked right up to their table as if he'd known they were going to be there. "You are the Sea Wolf," he stated to Bahr. "I have been sent with a message. The Old Mother wishes to see you. She has necessary knowledge to aid you in your quest."

"Go away, boy. We've no need for cheap parlor tricks this morn," Boen frowned.

Anienam waved a cautious hand at the Gaimosian. "Careful, Boen. This boy is more than he appears. You're a *taken*, aren't you?"

The child cocked his head, studying the wizard. Recognition flashed in his dull, brown eyes. "We have met before, old one. Long ago, in a distant land. Does this new body throw you off? Perhaps you'd recall my previous form? An elderly man with no right eye in Alloenis."

"What devilry is this?" Bahr snarled, reaching for his sword.

"Patience, Bahr. This is a very rare creature. They are known as *taken*, ancient souls that travel from body to body."

"Demons!"

The *taken* laughed, a terrible hissing sound escaping grit teeth. "Your knowledge of the world is limited, Sea Wolf. My kind has walked these lands since the first dawn. We are neither angel nor demon. We simply…are. But that is unimportant. The Old Mother commands your audience and you would do well to follow."

Deflated, Bahr dropped his hand back on the table and leaned back in his chair. "Very well, *taken*, where can I find this Old Mother?"

"Come with me, but only two may go. She is not one for large groups and the message will be diluted if there are more than two." The *taken* edged back towards the door.

"I do not like this," Boen rumbled.

Rekka added, "I agree. He smells of foulness."

"The *taken* are many things but deceptive is not one of them. I shall accompany you," Anienam said. "If what he says is true we have had dealings before."

"This smells bad, like Rekka said," Dorl said. "Could be a trap."

"No, I have heard of this Old Mother. Some say she has visions. What she says might prove useful in the coming days," the wizard said.

Bahr finished the last of his eggs, the golden yolks running down the stubble on his chin. "Very well. Let us get this over with. I am anxious to be out of this town. And someone make sure Groge gets enough food. Wouldn't do to let him starve out there."

The *taken* smiled and opened the door.

Tucked away in a forgotten part of old Fedro, the Old Mother's home was small and unassuming. Moss covered the walls to the roof. Vines and angry bushes lining the house set back most curious passersby. Candlelight glowed through the gloomy windows. Smoke gusted from the low chimney, dark and fetid. The *taken* ignored their cautious looks, leading the pair up to the front door.

"I can go no further. The Old Mother awaits within," it said.

Bahr and Anienam exchanged wary glances but said nothing. Any ill that might happen was bound to whether they wanted it or not. By the time Bahr looked back to the *taken* it was gone. A dark cloud settled over his head. He started to speak but was cut off when the cottage door opened suddenly.

"It seems we go in," Anienam mused.

On edge, Bahr grunted and pushed inside. His nose itched from the overpowering stench of so many herbs and spices. Gloom clung to walls and ceiling, impenetrable and oppressive. He immediately felt confined. He felt trapped in a cave. *How can anyone choose to live like this? A lesser life might be had in better places.*

An ancient voice crept through the gloom. "You disparage my home, Bahr, son of Brogon."

"How do you know my name?" he asked defensively.

"Bah, I know many things the light never finds. Come closer so that I may see you."

He waited for Anienam's encouragement before delving further into the cottage. Odd, exotic plants hung from the rafters. Flowers he'd never seen sprouted from rows of pots along the walls. Very little furniture filled the interior. A broken down chair by the fireplace. A small table under the largest window. Dirt covered the floor, leading Bahr to believe no one had bothered cleaning this place in a very long time, if ever.

Something dark brown scurried away to the far corner. Bahr ignored it and moved towards the sound of the voice. He didn't know why but his heart beat a little faster.

There was a strange power at work here. He felt the power rippling across his flesh. Electrifying his bones. Different from the wizard, this power came from the air. He felt the currents pass through his nostrils, into his lungs. Nausea quickly spread. His head began to ache, a dull throbbing echoing deep in his mind. Anienam placed a hand on his shoulder and he immediately felt warmth flow through him.

"Thank you," he said without understanding. The magical effects began wearing off.

Anienam nodded and kept walking. They found the Old Mother in her bed, too old and fragile to get up. Wiry white hair hung down well past her shoulders. Wrinkles distorted her face. Bahr could just make out the thick hairs on her chin and upper lip. Her teeth were broken, crooked, and stained dark brown. Everything about her screamed she should have already passed to the next world. Everything but her eyes. Her eyes were strong, vivid. They watched Bahr and Anienam approach. The Old Mother calculated every minute fact, every nuance in their stride and stance.

"Ah, you bring the last scion of ruined Ipn Shal," she mused. "I did not think you still drew breath, Anienam."

The wizard stiffened. "Baethesida. You're supposed to be dead."

"You know this woman?" Bahr asked.

"Of course he does. Tell him, wizard. Tell him how your order abandoned my kind. Threw us out to the wolves to fend for ourselves. How dozens of us were captured or slaughtered for our unique abilities. Your self-destruction was the best thing to happen to Malweir."

"You summoned us," Anienam said, ignoring her barb.

She waved him off. "I summoned him. You came because you cannot help but interfere with the affairs of others. How like the rest of your dead kin."

"Some would name you abomination, witch-seer," he snapped. "Ever you and your sisters sought to control the wills of others. Haven't you learned from meddling that life does not follow your desires?"

"Desires are all the flesh is comprised of. Who are you to condemn me for my gifts?"

Bahr stepped between them. "Time is short, Old Mother. You summoned me?"

Her eyes flicked to him. "Indeed. You embark upon an epic quest, thinking the answers are all known to you. You are wrong. Everything you think you know is a lie."

"Speak plainly, woman. I told you we don't have time."

Anienam frowned. "Careful, Bahr. She is old but extremely powerful. It wouldn't be wise to upset her more than necessary."

"I don't understand. She doesn't look like much," he replied.

"Your eyes deceive you, Sea Wolf," Baethesida crooned. "Open your heart and the truth will be revealed."

Bahr felt more frustrated. "I don't do riddles, Old Mother. What is it you want?"

"Want? Nothing. What can an old woman such as I need from the likes of you?" she replied chastely. "I wish to give you information you will have need of before you reach Trennaron."

"How do you know this, witch-seer?" Anienam demanded.

"I know many forbidden facts, *wizard*. You should not have come. My words are for Bahr alone."

"Perhaps she is right. We're getting nowhere like this. Wait outside, Anienam," Bahr said.

The wizard bristled at the indignity but held his tongue. Enough damage had been done to their little band and they couldn't afford more angst. Reluctantly he nodded. "Do not trust what she says. The witch-seers are famous for the poison in their words."

Bahr clasped Anienam's forearm and waited for him to leave before turning back to the Old Mother.

"He will become a problem before the end," she remarked casually.

Bahr frowned. "Why am I here?"

"This war is beyond your ability to win. Your brother is enslaved by the Dae'shan, a willing servant of the dark gods. Soon his power will rival the mightiest kingdom. His spies hound your movements, reporting every turn to their masters. You march across the world in search of a weapon unseen for thousands of years. What is it you hope to accomplish?"

For the first time he realized he had no answer. No personal objective other than mere survival. He'd been drawn into this affair without the opportunity to see any personal gain other than saving Maleela. By all means his task was complete and he should take his few possessions and find a quiet corner of the world to settle down in. Reality and desire seldom crossed paths though. He'd never be safe as long as Badron continued to rule. Others would hunt him to the ends of Malweir just to please their lord and collect the ample bounty.

So what did he hope to accomplish? His only true chance at freedom lay in turning around and stopping Badron, even if that meant killing him. Truthfully, he had no desire to murder his only brother. Nor did he wish to ascend to the throne of Delranan. Leading their group south to find the Blud Hamr wasn't his first choice. Meant for the open sea, Bahr needed the feel of sea spray on his face, the salt in the air. He felt stymied this deep in the countryside.

"Freedom," he finally said.

The Old Mother nodded ever so slightly. "Ever elusive, what you seek. Many never come to know what it means to be free. The choice before you is plain. Continue on the path you have undertaken and it shall claim your life. The dark gods have powers no mortal can understand. Fight them if you must, but you will die. It is as inevitable as the rising sun."

He'd never run from a fight in his long life. The very thought galled him. There was no honor to be found in cowardice, no glory or fame. His nature told him to stand up and confront threats as they come, not run and hide in the nearest hole. Even when confronted by impossible forces his base instinct was to fight. A man like Bahr thrived off intense situations and needed the adrenaline rush to feel alive. His estates in Delranan were expansive, built with the best money could buy, but he'd never felt at home.

"Death never held sway over me. Go frighten lesser men with your warnings and portents."

Baethesida's eyes widened. Decades had passed since one so foolish rebuked her. "You misunderstand me, Sea Wolf. If you continue your quest to find the Blud Hamr, you will know darkness the likes of which your pet wizard hasn't dreamed. Pain and suffering will claim you."

Frustrated, he turned to leave. "We're done here. Good day, Old Mother."

"Wait, Bahr. This has more to do than with your vanity. Maleela will suffer the longer your quest goes on. In the end she will fall to darkness."

Bahr stiffened but said nothing and stormed off. The witch-seer watched him go, quietly debating whether to tell him the truth. Darkness rode the horizon, storming towards him, and he remained blinded. She smirked, knowing the path he had chosen would only lead to horror.

SIX

Seeds of Rebellion

Far to the north, in what had once been the kingdom and city of Rogscroft, King Badron of Delranan sat upon the burned throne of his vanquished foe. Stelskor's corpse hung from the ceiling, minus the head. Badron personally impaled the severed head upon a spear and set it at the gates to the city for all to witness. Armed guards patrolled the area constantly lest one of the former citizens attempt to be noble and rescue their dead king's dignity.

The throne room reeked of rotting flesh. Flies buzzed in thick clouds. Many of Badron's advisors refused to enter, secretly citing the unnaturalness of it all. Their king had lost his mind, surrounded by corpses and puddles of dried blood. Half-chewed bones scattered the corners. Badron sat in amusement as the dogs devoured his dead enemies. Only the senior ranking Goblins felt comfortable in his presence. The dank, musky air and overpowering feeling of death made them feel at home. Badron cared less. His mind walked down paths very few had ever trodden. He looked forward to the whispered promises of the Dae'shan. Amar Kit'han spoke of the coming time when Badron would be crowned lord of the entire north. Master of the world from the west to the east. All he needed to do was kill his daughter and find true freedom.

Lost in one of his now frequent dark moods, Badron failed to notice Grugnak enter the throne room. The Goblin commander marched up to the broken throne, head held high. His black armor was dented and filthy. Hair plastered wildly about his face and neck. His normally dull grey skin seemed pale, gangrenous. The anger in his eyes reflected the hungry flames from the twin braziers flanking the throne.

"Two hundred more dead," he growled in broken speech.

Badron didn't bother looking up. His head rested on a fist, staring off into the distance at visions no one else could see.

Grugnak stepped closer, hand dangerously close to his sword. "Did you not hear? More dead. We must attack!"

"What difference does two hundred make?" Badron asked suddenly. "I have a combined force of close to twenty thousand combat soldiers. Two hundred is nothing."

"Two hundred Goblins! When do men begin dying?" Grugnak demanded.

"Why, since our creation. Do not think to lay claim to unprecedented violence. Man is more terrible than the foulest Goblin."

Badron fell silent again, leaving the Goblin commander to stew. He had better things to occupy his time than a disgruntled puppet. For in the end that was all the Goblin force amounted to: puppets. He planned on sacrificing every single one of them before the end. After all, why waste good, able-bodied men when you had another army willing to fight and die at no cost?

The crisp sound of steel being drawn from the scabbard echoed throughout the room. "Maybe I take my army back to the Dead Lands."

"Maybe you should," Badron countered. "Rogscroft has fallen. I don't need you anymore."

"Maybe we go to Delranan instead."

More swords were drawn as Badron's guards ringed the Goblin. Their gaze went from Grugnak to Badron, eager for the command to slay the foul creature. Badron did nothing. Grugnak snarled and spit.

"Coward."

"Beware your words, Goblin. I had no qualm with sacrificing your troops to take this city and I'll have none in spitting your head beside Stelskor's." Badron rose. His bulk more than a match for the shorter Goblin, he towered over Grugnak with unmistakable menace. "I have no patience for ignorance. Speak out of turn again and I'll have every last one of your people put to death. Am I clear?"

Grugnak swallowed, fingers dancing over his sword hilt. Killing Badron wouldn't prove difficult. Whatever he might be now was but a shadow of his former self. The king of Delranan might have fought many wars but they were long ago. He hadn't swung a sword in combat in decades, giving Grugnak the advantage if he could only get close enough. Reluctantly he sheathed his sword. The time would come soon enough.

Badron nodded, as if the outcome had never been in doubt. "I knew you'd see reason, my friend. Now as to those two hundred of yours. Where were they lost?"

"In the mountain passes."

So the Pell have finally thrown in. It took them long enough. "The Pell are ruthless, far more so than your kind. Digging them out will prove difficult. We must double our efforts. The snows continue to deepen. I want the Pell brought to heel quickly. We march on Delranan in the spring."

"I need more soldiers," Grugnak said, ignoring most of what he'd been told. Badron's dreams of conquest meant nothing to him. He had been sent by Amar Kit'han to assist in the conduct of Badron's war and to help prepare the way for the return of the dark gods. Faithless, Grugnak cared little for gods and conquest. He merely wanted to fight, to feel the ripping sensation of his sword driving into flesh. Nothing else mattered.

Badron rubbed his tired eyes. "I shall inform General Rolnir to detach two battalions. That should provide sufficient strength to accomplish your task, Commander. Now, leave me."

Visibly insulted, Grugnak turned and left without a word. Thoughts of murdering Badron entertained him as he made his way back to his army.

"New orders just came down," Rolnir announced to his gathered commanders. "None of you are going to like them."

Piper Joach cut a slice from his green apple and popped it in his mouth. "I think I can speak for all us when I say we haven't liked a damned thing since entering Rogscroft."

"Keep that noise to yourself, Piper. The king has ears everywhere," Rolnir scolded, disappointed his commander didn't know better. *Or perhaps he just doesn't care anymore. This war is taking a toll on us all. I only pray we have what it takes to make it out alive.*

Rebuked, Piper dipped his head. "Yes sir. What are our orders?"

Taking a deep breath, the red-haired general almost couldn't bring himself to speak. "The king has ordered two full battalions to assist the Goblins in driving the Pell Darga out of the mountains. They are to report to Grugnak at dawn."

"He does hate us, doesn't he," Ulaf, master of engineers, said.

Rolnir couldn't help but grin. "It appears that way, doesn't it? Regardless of his likes or dislikes, he is our king and we are honor bound to obey. Herger, I need two of your best."

The dour-faced Herger grimaced with displeasure. His thick beard hung just below the rim of his chest armor, as black as midnight. "Why my best, General? Chances are the damned Goblins will turn on them the moment they see the advantage."

"Of course they will. Which is exactly why I need the best. Grugnak is about as trustworthy as a prostitute. I'm counting on the Goblins turning."

Piper finished chewing and added, "Gives us an excuse to finally do what's right and get rid of a fair chunk of their combat force at the same time."

While he couldn't disagree, Rolnir realized they were getting off the topic. "Make no mistake, gentlemen, our troops are going up into the Murdes Mountains in the middle of winter to fight the Pell Darga on their own ground. I wouldn't care to take them on under the best of conditions, but the choice isn't mine."

Herger finally nodded, more excited at the prospect of killing Goblins than anything, and said, "Very well. I will go inform the commanders. How long do we expect them to be deployed?"

"Weeks at a minimum. Prepare for a month. We'll resupply as necessary. I want swords sharpened and shields strong. This isn't going to be easy."

"They know their jobs," he said and left the command building.

Piper ruefully rubbed his chin. "You're asking a lot from his infantry."

Rolnir fixed him with a baleful glare. "I'm not the one asking."

They waited until the rest of the commanders left. A hollow silence filled the space between them. Best friends since joining the Wolfsreik, Rolnir and Piper struggled to find the right words, any words, to say. They felt stretched, spread too thin across an enemy kingdom and cut off from the much needed support from home. Every citizen they encountered was hostile, despite the false smiles and occasional waves. Over a hundred men had been lulled to their deaths by the *conquered* people.

Morale began to plunge the moment the Goblin army arrived and continued to drop the longer into the campaign they got. Soldiers fought for varied reasons: friends, the absence of friends, kingdom, or plunder. Not a one wanted to be away from home longer than necessary. They floundered in the occupation. Mistakes continued to rise. Men flooded the surgeons' tents with careless injuries. Drunkenness became a large problem as the winter lengthened. The brig was constantly filled as discipline broke down. Rolnir felt the famed Wolfsreik discipline slipping away and couldn't find a way out. They'd never experienced a prolonged occupation and it was taking a heavy toll.

"What's on your mind?" Piper asked. "I haven't seen you this stoic since you relieved my vanguard a few months ago."

Rolnir got up to pour a glass of water. "Want one?"

"No thank you."

Finishing half of it in a single gulp, Rolnir sat back down and looked his friend dead in the eye. "I'm questioning the authority in all this. It doesn't feel right."

"Yeah, there's a lot of that going around."

"I'm serious, Piper. The invasion was all well and fine, but nothing we've done since has served any purpose I can see. We are an army wasting itself away at the whims of a madman." His voice trailed off to a low whisper.

Piper stared at him hard for a moment, unsure if he was being tested or not. More than one man had been arrested on charges of sedition against the crown. It wasn't a stretch to think Rolnir had been ordered to ensure the loyalties of his command team.

"You… speak dangerous words," he finally said.

"Do you deny them? How many soldiers have we lost to carelessness? How many to drunken altercations with the wrong people? How many have been killed or wounded because they wanted to mingle with the locals? I'm tired, Piper. This occupation should have ended the moment Badron cut Stelskor's head off. We have no right to remain here."

Piper decided to take the opposite stance, still unsure what was happening. "Or you could look at it as we have every right to be here. We conquered Rogscroft. They are defeated, broken and scattered to all four corners of their kingdom. This is what conquerors do, Rolnir. They occupy and pacify newly won territories in the name of throne and kingdom."

"If I didn't know better I'd say you were a spy," the general mused.

Piper forced a grin. "I'm too ticklish. Never be able to hold sensitive information that way. What's really digging into you? You're making me worried now."

Rolnir exhaled a long, slow breath. "I'm hearing reports, rumors mostly, that Harnin One Eye has overthrown the loyalist government and assumed control of Delranan. Badron knows this and is consumed with taking back his kingdom, even if it costs all our lives trying to break through the passes. All indicators point to us on the verge of civil war."

"You know how rumors are. You can't trust them. Too many times a slip of information turns into an avalanche of doom and gloom."

"I wish it were that simple, Piper. I really do, but this information comes from scouts returning to the camp. I took a trip up to Dredl to speak with some of the resupply boat captains."

This is news to me. Explains where you disappeared to a while back though. "And? What did they say?" Piper asked.

"Chaos has taken Chadra. The people live in constant fear. Bodies are found in the streets daily. Harnin has grown more corrupt than Badron." He fell silent, staring off into nowhere.

"That is...distressful. Should we take the army back and restore order?" Piper asked, not knowing what else to say. He'd never dreamed of such a scenario. Briefly his thoughts turned to his friends and family, what few he still had, and the horrors they must be going through. He wanted to go home, help where he could, but one Man wasn't enough to change the world.

Rolnir reluctantly shook his head. "No, we'd never be able to get back in time with enough strength and Badron won't let us leave. Whatever dark purpose drives these two must be some sort of disease. I can't figure it out. We're in this deep, Piper."

They both knew of Badron's gradual change. He hadn't been the same since the loss of his only son back in autumn. Darkness crept into his world. His decisions seemed guided, demented and perverse. Rolnir couldn't make sense of how the king changed. Certain inner circle members whispered of a strange figure lurking behind the throne, speaking into the king's ear. It conspired against Delranan, driven by some unseen agenda. Worse, neither man had been able to find a way to be alone with Badron since the sack of Rogscroft.

"How many dead? Chadra isn't a large city."

Rolnir finished his water. "A few dozen every day. There is one bright bit of news, however. Lord Argis has turned against the king and leads the insurrection."

Piper's eyes flew wide. "Insurrection? We need to return immediately! Rogscroft can wait. Delranan needs us."

"Calm yourself, my friend. We can't. Let Argis run his rebellion and hope for the best. I have a feeling we're going to be needed here before too long."

"So what do we do? Our options grow smaller as the days progress," Piper said. "We don't run. We can't leave. This feels hopeless."

Rolnir snorted a laugh. "Because it is! If I were a lesser man I'd have sent scouts out to find Aurec and negotiate a truce."

He stopped abruptly, instantly aware of the severity of what he'd just said. *Treason! I've spent a life dedicated to soldiering only to succumb to thoughts of treason. Perhaps it's time I stepped down. Retire before my mind gets me into too much trouble.* "I'm tired, Piper. Go and check on Herger. He's a good man but prone to rashness. Make sure he sends the right battalions. We can't afford any mistakes at this junction."

"Yes sir."

Piper saluted and left. Rolnir stared after him for a while before finally drooping his head and letting go of the cold breath he'd been holding.

SEVEN

The Plight of Lord Argis

Armed guards patrolled the streets of Chadra around the clock since Harnin One Eye assumed control of the kingdom. His reach went deep but loosened the further away from the capital the kingdom stretched. Yet for all his show of force, Harnin lacked complete control of Chadra. Argis's rebellion was much stronger than he originally believed. The attack on the armory at the docks showed him how wrong he'd been. The rebellion was stronger than he'd anticipated, forcing him to adjust his initial plans. What he'd intended to be brutally quick and efficient denigrated into a series of hit-and-miss attacks ranging throughout the city and down to Stouds on the coast.

Every day the rebellion continued meant another day closer to the mountain passes clearing. Harnin dreaded the Wolfsreik's return, knowing it would mean the end of all his grand schemes. Not that he was helpless. His agents sent word to the rest of the northern kingdoms for the best assassins. Many declined, citing regicide as going a step too far, but enough were eager to make their names. Their combined guile should prove more than enough to deal with Badron. Or so Harnin hoped.

"Another three attacks last night," Jarrik reported, throwing a stack of parchments to the aged oak table.

Harnin didn't bother looking down. His gaze remained fixed on the rising sun. Sparkling rays of golden light ripped through the veil of darkness. Once, such a sight would have inspired him, but now he felt hollow. Darkness proved more comfortable. He came to despise what the daylight represented, the purity of the light becoming offensive.

"How many casualties?" he asked without taking his eyes off the diminishing night.

Jarrik passed a wary glance to his side, to Inion. "Too many by all reports. Six dead and thirteen more injured. We can't keep sustaining such loses."

Harnin wasn't concerned. "How many rebels?"

Young and thickly muscled, Skaning folded his arms over his chest and spat. "Two."

Finally Harnin turned. "Two what?"

"Two dead. That's it. No wounded, no blood trails."

"We are losing this war," Inion added.

Harnin rose much too swiftly, sweeping the clay jar from the table. It crashed into the wall, stale beer splashing. "There is no room for seditious thoughts in my kingdom, Inion. Another word and I'll have your head."

Inion swallowed hard. Another time and he might have accepted the challenge, but a dark power lingered around Harnin, making it near impossible to harm him. Inion had seen it once. The manifestation of evil lurking just over Harnin's shadow. It disappeared quickly, as if letting Inion know it was there to dissuade the thought of striking out.

Skaning slammed a meaty fist into the table. "Damn it, Harnin, he speaks the truth. We are losing men daily without any notion of the rebels' losses. Our militias aren't recruiting the numbers needed to sustain this conflict."

"Conscript more!" Harnin raged.

"Most of the population is sympathetic to the rebellion. They see the bodies hanging from the streets. The way our soldiers patrol Chadra with iron authority."

"I declared martial law for a reason," Harnin replied. "Keep the people in their homes all day if necessary. I will not let this kingdom fall apart now."

"The curfew isn't working. Rebels violate it at will, raiding storerooms or small guard outposts. The Wolfsreik reserves we have aren't fully trained soldiers and because of it our casualty ratio is worse than three to one. Numbers are against us, Harnin."

Thoughts of having Skaning flayed danced in his eyes. Reluctantly, Harnin was forced to admit he still needed the big captain to secure his newly stolen kingdom. Once that was finished he would have the luxury of disposing of the more uncooperative members at will. "You bring me problems but no solutions. What then do you propose to do about *Lord* Argis and his little insurrection?"

The assembled captains of Delranan shuffled anxiously. Argis had been one of their best. Now a rogue, his knowledge of the inner workings of the kingdom was wreaking havoc on the defenders. Even imprisoned, his name lent strength to those disaffected by Harnin's rule. As much as Harnin wanted to execute him, they knew Argis was more useful alive than dead. A fact that continually gnawed at the one eye.

"Argis rots in our dungeons, but his name inspires many who would otherwise not take up arms," Jarrik answered. "We can't kill him or the entire population will turn against us. They'd rout us out of Chadra Keep in a matter of days and we'd be the ones hanging from the gibbets."

"My torturers are ineffective. Argis has not said a word against his rebel friends," Skaning added. "He's one tough, old bastard."

"Break him! I don't care how, but break him," Harnin snapped. His thin frame trembled with rage. Veins popped out of his temples. His remaining eye threatened to tear. "He is becoming a bane to my rule."

"We can't kill him! Not even secretly," Jarrik reiterated. "He has become the rebellion. Posters and crude images plaster every street and alley. We tear them down but they are back the next day. His name is revered as a god among the lower class. Destroy him physically and all you succeed in doing is making him a martyr."

"At this point I'm willing to make that concession," Harnin replied. "What will it take to bring this rebellion to its knees?"

No one answered, telling Harnin everything he needed to know about his captains. It was time for a change. Delranan wallowed under the ineffective guidance of former leaders lacking the vision to push the kingdom to greater heights. Complacency rendered them all but useless. Only he knew the truth. The truth that history was written on deeds of men willing to step outside of their comfort zones, step forward to make their claim against the stars and even the gods. Men fought and died in the name of kings but the future changed only at the behest of visionaries.

The arrival of the Dae'shan Pelthit Re, initially foreboding, turned into greed, corruption. Harnin came to realize and accept the Dae'shan was a blessing to his dreams of power. He'd languished under Badron's rule for decades, growing increasingly frustrated with the direction the kingdom went. He knew he could do better; achieve more and bring Delranan to the front of Malweir's mighty kingdoms. His dreams rivaled the strength and power of Averon in the south. The north deserved to rule, deserved to take its rightful place among the true powers in the world. Harnin intended to make that happen. He only needed to remove the captains standing in his way.

Hours turned to days. Days to nights and then weeks. He sat in a windowless room, locked in total darkness until time lost meaning. Rotten food and stagnant water was delivered at random intervals. He'd tried keeping track in the beginning but soon gave up. A pair of rats occasionally crawled out from the walls to nibble on his toes and fingers when he slept, scurrying away to safety before he could kill them. He lived in his own filth. The five-by-five-foot room stank of human waste and bile.

Argis had once been among the elite; a noble of mighty Delranan. He'd been the first to charge into battle the night Chadra Keep was assaulted. The first to discover the body of Badron's son. He'd stood beside his king without question through good times and bad. But every loyalty reaches the point of question. His came when Badron announced the final plans for the invasion of Rogscroft. Argis couldn't see why. He empathized with the misery the king felt over the loss of his son and kidnapping of his daughter but didn't see the justification for a full-blown invasion. With no one to turn to, Argis began to doubt. His mind strayed what was right and wrong before deciding that Badron was wrong.

He rebelled. Quietly at first. He made his way through the various social circles, feeling out who would follow him and who might lead. A core group of the most diverse people gradually came together, forming the nucleus of the rebellion. All it needed was a spark. Argis provided the spark. It had been he that unlocked the long forgotten exit at the base of the mountain Chadra Keep had been built on. He alone knew of the attempt to steal Maleela away from her father; a father who hated her with every fiber in his body. Badron had never forgiven her for the death of her mother in childbirth.

For a time the rebellion went well. The Wolfsreik reserve forces were caught off guard and put on the defensive. Argis insisted the rebels only kill when necessary while maintaining maximum enemy casualties. A wounded man was worse than a dead one. Supply depots and arms rooms were raided, stealing from Harnin. Each assault produced a drain on enemy combat strength and, hopefully, weakened their resolve to engage their own people. It worked. Many of the Wolfsreik had friends and family in Chadra, neutralizing them from doing what they did best.

Harnin demanded they assault the city with extreme prejudice, but the commanders refused. The rebellion gained ground, winning the people over. Harnin struck back, placing the kingdom under strict martial law and authorizing summary executions in the street for those unfortunates caught performing subversive acts. Panic soon gripped Chadra. A mass exodus began and Harnin let them go. The smaller the population made it easier for him to conduct his war. Argis knew it was only a matter of time before the rebellion faltered.

He lay on his back and stared up towards the dark ceiling. Eyes open or closed, it didn't matter. Argis had come to accept his confinement. What didn't make sense was why he was still alive. Common sense said he should have been executed long ago. But Harnin had grown wicked and cunning since the army left for the war to the east. His imagination visited odd horrors on the land. At first they came every day to brag about their deeds, attempting to break his spirit. When that didn't work they brought in prisoners and threatened to kill them if he didn't talk. His lips never parted and the bodies were dragged away in trails of blood. Eventually torturers abandoned their earlier policies and introduced him to foul instruments designed to deliver maximum pain. Argis screamed and cried but still said nothing.

Frustrated, Harnin soon abandoned that tactic as well. What happened next was much worse. They simply left Argis alone in his cell. A forgotten relic of what might have been. Food and water were shoved into his cell and the door closed quickly. Light entered for only a fraction of a minute before darkness reclaimed the cell. He began hearing voices. They called to him, beckoning him with impossible promises of freedom and reward. He laughed. Madness threatened to settle in. He briefly thought about trying to escape but the opportunity never presented itself. Nor had anyone come to rescue him. Argis felt trapped, damned.

A noise drew his attention. So faint he thought he imagined it. Sitting up, he slowly swept the cell for any sign of something out of the ordinary. His sight may have been taken, but he'd been locked in darkness for so long the cell took on a haunting glow.

"You cannot see me, but know that I watch you," a hideous voice said.

Argis felt his heart clutch and his skin flushed cold. "Who are you?"

"I have had many names, none of them important to one in your position. Just know that it is through my urgings that the One Eye has brought your kingdom to the edge of permanent chaos. Does that satisfy you, Lord Argis?"

"Set me free so that I might put blade to your throat and I'll be satisfied," he replied. Every syllable was a struggle to maintain what little composure he had.

A foreign sound mocked him from the dark. Laughter? "If a mortal blade could kill me we would not be having this conversation."

"What do you want from me?"

There was a pause, as if his confronter was in thought. "Want? There is nothing a man in your position can offer me. Now if you were a free man…."

Argis never believed in demons. Superstitions were for the weak and old. But the creature in his cell gave him pause. There was an inherently evil quality emanating from the creature. So strong it turned Argis' stomach. So strong he was sure demons did exist.

"A free man is capable of a great many things. The power of the human mind can transcend physical strength. Take you to unexplored heights. Strength and power lie at your feet if only you had the courage to reach out and claim them."

Tears broke from the corners of his eyes. "Leave me, demon. I am not the man you seek."

"Demon? Would a demon offer you the opportunity to rise above all your peers and become the man you should be?"

Weeping freely, Argis replied, "Yes."

"You know so little of the true nature of the world. Ancient dogmas mire your race in decrepitude. I offer you the future and you rebuke me out of what? Spite? Fear? I have no need of such emotions."

Darkness strengthened, threatening to cast Argis into unconsciousness. He swooned. The eerie combination of madness and darkness claimed his mind and when he regained control of awareness he discovered he was alone.

EIGHT

The Hags

The screaming began shortly after midnight. A door broke open. Splinters flew through the front room of the small home. The rush of wings blew out the already cooling fire. Smoke and ash filled the air. Claws ripped and slashed. A sword gleamed momentarily in the cold, pale moonlight before falling to the floor, the severed hand still gripping the hilt. Blood, hot and bright red, splashed across the walls and furniture. The attack ended almost as quickly as it began. Three bodies lay in ruined heaps of flesh: the parents and a small daughter. Each body was grasped by one of the Hags and dragged away to the foothills.

Those foolish enough to venture into the streets watched the three monstrous shapes take flight and disappear into the clouds. Whispers spread quickly. Demons had come to Fedro, claiming the damned and condemning the rest. Grown men and women fell to their knees while performing gestures intended to ward off evil spirits. Some cried. Others slammed their doors and bolted them. Still others went for weapons, anything they could use to defend against the monsters. Fedro became subsumed by paranoia. It didn't take long before those with clear heads turned towards the strangers in town. Blame was only a matter of time.

"They are here," Rekka Jel said from her post by the window.

They'd taken rooms in the back of the first floor, close enough to the rear door to make an escape if necessary. Their foul experience in Praeg set everyone on edge, heightening security and apprehensions. Sleep came lightly even after their time spent in the forge of Giants. Bahr remained filled with suspicions. Having a traitor among them kept him on edge.

Fresh screams rippled through the sleeping village, drawing the weary band to action. Ionascu cackled recklessly from the corner while the rest strapped on weapons and prepared for battle. Dorl resisted the urge to backhand him and followed Nothol out into the hallway. The bow in his hands felt good, like it belonged. He only hoped he didn't need to use it.

"Where?" Boen asked. The easygoing attitudes he adopted for travelling were gone, replaced by decades of hardened combat experience.

Rekka gestured east. "The screams came from the far end of the village. They move this way."

Bahr drew his sword. "Dorl, you and Rekka get up on the roof and cover high."

"You think these are our spies?" Nothol asked.

The Sea Wolf glanced over to the oddly complacent Anienam. "Ask him."

"More than likely," the wizard answered slowly. "But anything is possible."

Another scream echoed. This one closer.

"Enough talk. Blood is being shed." Boen shouldered his way past the others and headed towards the door. Blood pumping, the Vengeance Knight was eager to apply his steel in battle.

The rest broke into groups, Anienam following Rekka and Dorl to the rooftop. Bahr stopped and turned suddenly, fixing Skuld with a wary glance. "Not you, lad. I need you to stay and keep an eye on Ionascu. He may be broken but I don't trust him."

"But I want to fight! I can help," Skuld protested furiously.

Bahr shook his head. "Not this time. My word is final."

The door swung shut behind him, leaving the dejected Skuld glowering.

A soft hand rested on his shoulder. "Don't fret, Skuld. You're not the only one who's not necessary in battle."

His demeanor softened, slightly. "You're a princess. They are protecting you."

"Are they?" She glared back at him. "I call it smothering. How many more need to die because of me? Yet here I stand, helpless as a newborn babe. Life is not kind, nor does it care for our desires. We must all find a way to get along with it or be run over and lost to the cold haunts of the past. The others will return soon. Very little can stand up to my uncle and the Gaimosian."

Skuld took little comfort in her words. His eyes never left the scratched and stained wooden door daring him to exit.

Storm clouds blocked the moon, enshrouding the village in tumultuous darkness. The air smelled of snow and bore a damp flavor. Doors and windows being shuttered rang out from dozens of homes. Fires were lit in the vain attempts of keeping whatever evil stalked Fedro away. Bahr wanted to laugh at the ridiculousness of it. Nothing but cold steel was going to save them. He'd never understood the cattle mentality of humanity. Most would rather button up and hide rather than confront their fears. The weak almost always perished because of that. A handful of men and women came forward to combat the darkness and keep the monsters at bay. While he never considered himself a hero, Bahr had no qualms about defending those who were incapable of doing so for themselves.

Nothol snatched a torch from the nearest streetlight and pushed forward. Visibility was so reduced they needed the light to see. Boen made every attempt to stay ahead of the glare, not wanting the flames to affect his night vision. He contemplated telling the sell sword to get rid of it but knew the light might come in handy if they were indeed fighting the winged creatures they'd spotted coming down from the mountains.

A loud crash came from the alley just ahead and the group began to run. Boen reached the gap between homes first. Throwing caution to the wolves, he charged into the alley with sword poised in a high guard. A large, dark shape burst from the shadows and took flight the moment Boen arrived. Something large fell to the ground and rolled to a stop a few feet away. He peered down already knowing it was a freshly killed villager. Whatever plague had descended on Fedro did so to feed.

"They're airborne!" he growled, stepping over the corpse.

Bahr hardly glanced at the body as Nothol's torchlight fell. Warm blood streaked the broken forearm, hand curled up in mock defiance. "We need to find a way to push it towards Dorl."

"We don't have any weapons capable of dropping one of them," Nothol protested. "They can escape without effort."

The first rain drops spattered Boen's upturned face. "No. They aren't going to run. We fight them here, now."

The Giant would be mighty useful right about now. Bahr grimaced and ordered them back into the main avenue. All eyes focused on the skies, desperately seeking their enemy. Desperate and futile. Whatever hunted them remained carefully hidden in the low clouds. Frustration threatened. Bahr needed to find a way to lure their stalkers down close enough to kill.

"Do you see anything?" he asked if for nothing else than to break the oppressive silence.

Boen grumbled under his breath. "The clouds are too thick. We will not see them unless they want to be seen."

"I'm open to ideas," Bahr countered. *What's the point of having a blasted wizard if he can't do any magic? Now I know why Mages are all but extinct. Damned fools worried more about the stars than trying to help anyone.*

Nothol threw the torch down and stamped the flames out.

"What are you doing?" Bahr asked.

"Bait. We need to draw them in. Or this is just a waste of time," the sell sword replied nervously.

"Don't end up like this poor man," Bahr said and gestured towards the body.

Nothol spit. "Keep them off me so I don't need to worry about it."

He darted out into the middle of the street and held his arms open wide. "Here I am! Come and kill me, cowards!"

Nothol Coll ran, back towards the tavern where, hopefully, Dorl and Rekka sat ready. Otherwise… He looped around the village once before coming back to Bahr and Boen. Each clung to the shadows on opposite sides of the road, watching, waiting. Nothol looked to Bahr as they passed, but the Sea Wolf only shook his head. Nothing. Winded, Nothol continued to run. He began shouting obscenities, hoping to lure the enemy in through a sense of vanity. Unused to being in this sort of situation, he was quickly running out of ideas and options. Just when he was about to give up and head back, the night came alive and attacked.

Winds rushed past. Nothol felt something large and incredibly hard slam into his side, knocking him to the ground with a grunt. Claws raked at his exposed face and hands. Feathers shed down upon him as he struggled to get off his back before he got killed. A pungent odor assaulted him, causing him to gag and retch.

"Finish him, Sister!" a foul voice screeched from the rooftops.

A rock whistled through the night before slamming into the Harpy's head. Her screech made Nothol's ears bleed. Boen rushed in a moment later, tackling the Harpy in a flurry of feathers and crunching bones. He punched three quick times to the chest and face before the Harpy managed to dig out from under his massive frame and burst into the sky. Feathers and blood drifted down.

"What in the Hells was that?" Nothol asked as he rolled back to his feet.

Boen brushed a feather from his shoulder. "I don't know. Nothing I've ever seen before. We should be cautious. I wounded it but there are others."

"Nice shot," Bahr said and pulled Boen up. He knelt and dabbed a fingertip in the small drops of blood. "We've got a trail. I heard the bones snap from the other side of the street. I doubt it's going to fly away quickly, if at all."

"What's our next move?" Nothol asked.

"We kill it," Boen said and stalked after the Harpy. The thrill of the kill aroused him. It was time for the Gaimosian to do what he was created for.

Nothol and Bahr hurried to catch up.

***

"Can't you do anything to help?" Dorl asked angrily. He was getting fed up with having a do-nothing wizard along.

Anienam stifled a yawn. "I've already told you my talents don't work like that. Magic isn't a children's game I can turn on and off at will. There are preparations required and we don't have time for any of them. I don't know why I'm trying to explain this to you. Yours is not an educated mind, my friend, and I will only confuse myself trying to enlighten you!"

Dorl flushed crimson with anger. "Mind your tongue, old man, or I might just forget you saved our asses back in Chadra."

"Quiet, both of you," Rekka scolded suddenly. Her focus never left the area where she'd seen Bahr and the others disappear.

Soon after, the sounds of battle drifted to them. Rekka set an arrow to string and gave her bow a few quick test pulls to loosen it. She inhaled small breaths through her nose and exhaled almost imperceptibly through her mouth. Her muscles relaxed. Her mind cleared as she subconsciously ran through old training drills instilled in her since childhood. She became the weapon.

Dorl peered over the edge, struggling to see what Rekka did. He found only darkness. "What is it?"

She waved him off, merely gesturing with a curt nod. Dorl followed her gaze and was rewarded with seeing his best friend struggling with a winged creature. He briefly considered taking a shot but the distance was too great and he feared hitting Nothol. Instead he cursed and punched the rooftop.

"Patience, Dorl. They are bringing the creature to us."

He didn't understand how Rekka could know but he wasn't in an arguing mood. His inability to help Nothol twisted him with guilt. They'd been through countless bad situations and always had each other's backs. Sitting up here on the top of the tavern effectively removed him from being able to help. Nothol was on his own. Only he wasn't. He had Bahr and Boen. Between the two of them he ought to be fine.

"We need to help them," he insisted, more from the thought of being helpless than anything else.

She ignored him. Rekka's eyes never left the engagement. Boen all but crushed the creature to death as he tackled it off of Nothol but it still managed to take flight. Two others leapt from a dark light post and helped their wounded comrade escape the Gaimosian.

Rekka slowly drew her bow and aimed. Her breathing slowed to a bare hint. Her eyes locked on the already wounded creature. She exhaled and counted to three. Rekka fired. Feathers tickled her cheek as she released. The arrow sliced through the air and plunged deep in the creature's chest. It, *she*, screamed in rage and agony and would have fallen to the ground if not for the others. Rekka mechanically reached back for a second bolt and took aim as Dorl fired his first shot.

The three Harpies pulled up and away. Dorl's bolt crashed harmlessly into the cobblestones below. The largest of the three glared down with baleful eyes, marking their faces. A day would come when revenge demanded justice. Slowly the Harpies pulled away and were lost to the clouds.

"Save your bolts. They are already out of range," Rekka cautioned upon noticing Dorl setting another arrow to string. "We have wounded them and that is enough."

Dorl reluctantly did as he was told. "They'll be back. Nothing is ever this easy."

Rekka cocked her head, regarding him with a quizzical look he couldn't read. They were all at the point of exhaustion. Tensions ran high and no one seemed in the mood for the usual banter that accompanied their journey. Only now did Dorl realize his muscles trembled slightly. He wanted nothing more than to collapse on a soft bed and wake days later.

He looked to Anienam and asked, "Don't you have anything to add?"

The wizard sighed. "No. Not at this time. Bahr and the others are coming. We should go back down."

Giving a final look to the cloudy skies, Dorl let out a deep sigh and followed the others inside. He'd had enough excitement for the night.

NINE

Debates

Fedro laid leagues behind them, but the adventurers kept their eyes to the sky, fearful of another attack. Bahr tried to calm their nerves by claiming, rightfully so, that the Harpies had only attacked *after* he and the others infringed upon their hunting raid. A week had passed since that night and they hadn't seen so much as a sign of their hunters.

Anienam finally determined the creatures were Harpies. A taste of their blood and a few feathers mixed with random chemicals told him everything he needed to know. The temptation to throw his use of magic back at Dorl nearly won through but he maintained enough composure to let it pass. Besides, he'd had his share of being wrong already. Their fragile group didn't need any more distractions to their cohesion.

"Harpies?" Skuld asked. The wonder in his voice was almost innocent, refreshing.

Anienam waved generally. "An ancient race but one quickly dying out. Humanity has encroached upon their roosts. Much of the world has changed since their kind filled the skies. We are a blessing and a bane to all that came before us."

Bahr grunted. "Seems to me the bane comes from those flying monsters."

"They kill because they have no choice."

Boen broke out in deep, bellowing laughter. "You don't find deer trying to kill us for taking their lands, old man! Those bastards are killers, no doubt about it. They are hunting us and we still don't know for whom. I can't wait to wrap my fingers around one of their necks."

"Life requires more than acts of mindless violence, Gaimosian," Anienam snapped back. "There comes a time when thinking is more important than skill with a sword."

Boen waved him off. "Say what you will but keep your propaganda for youth like Skuld here. I've seen enough of Malweir to know where true strength lies."

"Pay him no mind, Skuld. His kind has lost much and their plight formed the paths of their lives. There is no changing a man like that," Anienam told the boy. He watched Skuld, constantly evaluating the former street urchin to see if he had the potential to take his place as the last in the line of Mages and wizards. His nightmares revolved around the order finally dying. Anienam wasn't a strong man, nor were his convictions solid enough to change the world, and the thought of Malweir being unguarded against those dangerous powers lurking in the dark propelled him on. Besides, his father would have wanted it.

The wagon rumbled on, ever drawing nearer to the Kergland Spine and the next stage of their journey. He hadn't been through Dwarf lands in decades and proved little help to the planning process. A quick study showed none among them had much experience with the Dwarves. They were a secretive race, mistrusting and unwilling to interact with the other races unless necessary. Once, long ago when the order of Mages first came to power, the Dwarves were an important part of Malweir politics. They held offices across the lands and ran banks and other institutions. The war for the crystal of Tol Shere forced them back in seclusion and concreted their suspicions towards the other races.

"This is all so new to me," Groge commented after sensing Anienam's deep sorrow. "I know only the granite mountaintops and the crisp bite of winter winds. This, this is almost alien to my kind. Wondrous and tempting."

"There is much the lowlands offer that cannot be found lost in the mountains. A shame you didn't come down in the summer when the flowers bloom and the birds roam free," Anienam said and smiled. "The abundance of life refreshes the soul."

The Giant nodded without understanding the concepts Anienam presented. "The very air is changed. I can smell no forge, no folded steel. Much of the oppression in the atmosphere is not here. I can breathe freely."

"Wait until you witness the seduction of the seas for the first time, my friend," Bahr added, riding up alongside. "Once she takes your hand she will steal your heart."

"I have read of the sea," Groge said, smiling. "Is it true the water goes on forever?"

"Damned near. I've sailed much of the northern seas and there were times when I was certain all land had faded away. It can make a man feel very small."

"What about a Giant?"

Bahr laughed. "Even a Giant. The majesty of the sea is without compare. Not even your mighty forges hold sway with the raw power of the water."

"The elders would never allow us to leave Venheim just for the sake of witnessing something they deem trivial," Groge said sadly. "Will we have the opportunity to go there on this journey?"

"I don't know, but there is always a chance," Bahr replied.

"Time and Fate often have little to do with one another," the wizard added. "Anything is possible. I haven't been able to foresee much since we left Delranan."

"What of the war consuming your homelands?" Groge asked after a few moments. "We have had no part in wars for centuries."

Anienam snapped the reins and pushed the horses slightly harder, leaving Bahr to deal with talk of wars and killing. He had no stomach for either. Soon even the sound of their banter drifted to mumblings. So much of his life had been dedicated to helping others; to altering the course of things for the better of all Malweir. He selflessly abandoned any chance at having a family, an heir, any hope of a normal life, for the greater good. There were times he wasn't sure he could continue, but the next dawn always found him putting one foot in front of the other. Anienam was tried and tested but remained constant.

The threat of the dark gods returning hounded his conscience. How many times in Malweir's long history had they tried to return? To reclaim what once belonged to them and bring the world to ruin? He knew of at least five. Much was necessary if the dark gods had a chance of being released into the world. A great confluence of powers needed to happen first. He felt such power in the air. It rode the currents and charged the atmosphere. Anienam could taste the powers of the dark gods as they strained against the immaterial fabric of their prison. They wanted back as much he needed to find a way to keep them out.

What little warmth offered by the sun faded moments after kissing his aged skin. Time was an enemy, he contemplated glumly. No man should have to endure the amount of sorrow and hardships he had. Not the most wicked. He acted in the vain hopes of defending his new friends and what they stood for, but even as he rode among them he knew many would not live to see the end of this adventure. Death forever hounded their footsteps. That only a few were claimed thus far was miraculous.

A handful of crewmen from the *Dragon's Bane* were murdered upon returning from Rogscroft, Anienam hadn't the heart to tell Bahr that part, along with most of the survivors of Ionascu's men. Badron's absence left Delranan a mess, especially when Harnin One Eye made his bid for power. So much wanton destruction for what? The hastening of the end of the world? Anienam wished he could find a way out, a chance to end the threat of being lost under the crushing weight of the dark gods forever, but it was not in his visions.

All enemy powers seemed focused on stopping the small band of would-be heroes. The Dae'shan knew what dangers Bahr truly posed and would stop at nothing to kill him before he got to the Blud Hamr. Too many careful plans stood in the balance for the Sea Wolf to be allowed even the slightest chance of success. The Harpies were testament to that but were most certainly not the only tool at the Dae'shan's disposal. Evil collected more evil. Any manner of nightmares could be awaiting them just around the bend. The old wizard found the thought daunting and he nearly gave thought to turning and abandoning the quest.

The idea threatened to steal his sanity so he gave a final look to the looming mountains and handed Skuld the reins. He then climbed into the wagon bed and retrieved the ancient text they'd nearly died for in the caverns under Chadra. Clues to their great mystery rested within and remained to be discovered. Without it they never would have found the Bergin Pass and the road to the forge of Giants. Venheim had been undiscovered by man for centuries, making them the first explorers to interact with that ancient race in recent history. At any other time it would have been a tremendous achievement worthy of celebration. Too much rode on their shoulders for it to be anything less than life threatening.

A shame really. I should have liked to stay and learn more. They are a remarkable people with much to contribute to the younger races. He sighed. *If only.* Anienam turned the pages daftly and with the care of a new mother. His initial time tables suggested they needed to have the hammer back in Delranan a week ago. The absence of the dark gods told him how wrong he'd been but that only strengthened his worries. Their lives depended on how accurately he could translate the book. *Nothing like a little extra pressure just when I don't need it.*

"Is there anything I can do to help?" Maleela asked upon waking from her nap. Long days and even longer nights left her exhausted. The others tended to forget she'd been on the road the longest, having been "kidnapped" by Aurec and taken to Rogscroft months ago. The horrors of that first night plagued her dreams almost as much as the thought that her life with Aurec appeared unobtainable. To reduce the stress she took to sleep.

Anienam didn't mean to ignore her, but he was already engrossed in the book.

She made a show of clearing her throat and nudged him with a boot. "I am perhaps the only person in Delranan who's read most if not all the books in the royal libraries." *Not that the library was much to boast on.* She doubted it contained more than one hundred books.

"You haven't read this one," Anienam said absently. His lips silently mouthed phrases and paragraphs as he dug deeper.

"You're not giving me a chance, again. I grow tired of being ignored, wizard," Maleela said sternly. As princess, she was unaccustomed to being so casually dismissed.

The wagon rumbled on in awkward silence.

They camped at dusk. Only Boen and the wizard had ever ventured this far east and their recollections of the terrain were vague at best. Boen and Bahr studied the handful of maps purchased in Fedro, hoping to find the quickest route through the mountains and the river beyond. Added pressures of time running out and being hunted burdened both men. Their troubles in the Murdes Mountains weighed heavily, forcing them to debate each decision no matter how minor.

The gentle cracklings of the small campfire broke the monotony of an otherwise silent encampment. Ionascu, crippled and broken, hummed a childhood lullaby from the edge of the small glade they'd confiscated for the night. His wild eyes darted from person to person. Plots formed and dispelled. He hated each for different reasons but reserved his true hatred for the One Eye. They'd once worked together, comrades and hesitant friends, but Harnin's betrayal left Ionascu a hollow fragment of the person he had been. He vowed to kill Harnin before this nightmare ended.

"I don't trust him," Skuld quietly told Maleela. His continued exclusion forced him further from the main group and left him seeking companionship from the fallen princess and the wizard. All his dreams of being a sword-wielding hero gradually faded away.

She poked at the fire with an already charred stick. "Who?"

"Ionascu. He is a bad man."

Maleela paused and glanced over to where the older man rocked gently, knees drawn up and head down. "There are many bad men, Skuld. He's the worst sort, a traitor. My father used dozens of men like him while he consolidated power. Ionascu was once Harnin's most trusted spy. I'm not sure what went wrong."

"They would come to the streets and hire boys to spy for them, do odds jobs after the sun went down. I never thought they were touchable."

She offered a half smile. "Everything has changed in Delranan. Men like Ionascu aren't necessary past their singular uses. Harnin has always been a rat. He showed his true colors the moment my father departed for the war."

"Why do we keep him with us?"

She had no answer. Whatever Bahr's motivations were he failed to inform her, a fact Maleela found increasingly frustrating. She hated being left out, forced away from plans and thoughts. Objectively she knew it made sense. She was the daughter of the king and a liability, regardless of her strained relationship. That didn't prevent her from gnawing on growing anger. She'd been stolen twice, once against her will. She'd endured harsh treatments from her captors and witnessed more fighting in the last few months than in her entire life. Men were dying in her name and it sickened her. She wanted to ball her fists and scream to the heavens. More, she wanted to be left alone. And if that wasn't going to happen, she wanted, needed, to be involved in the planning process, if for no other reason than peace of mind.

When she spoke at last it was with heavy tones. "Because he is just as much of a misfit as the rest of us. He can't go home any more than we can."

"I wish he weren't here. I don't trust him." Skuld went back to finishing the chunk of slightly stale dark bread. Whatever solace he searched for in the fire remained private but that didn't prevent him from brooding while he ate.

Maleela empathized. Her trust diminished the longer the quest took. She gave Ionascu a last look before going back to the fire.

"We should go north and circle around the mountains," Boen's voice dominated the camp suddenly.

Bahr, face red, vehemently shook his head. "That adds too much time. Time we don't have. We need to get south by the quickest route possible. Going around the entire mountain range will add weeks of extra travel."

"The Spine is not as forgiving as the Murdes," Boen said and frowned. "We barely made it down from them. The rock is different too. Sharp and wicked. The bones of many travelers decorate the passes. I would not try it with such a large group in the dead of winter."

"We're running out of options, Boen."

Boen folded his arms across his massive chest and gestured with his chin towards the wizard. "Have you come up with an answer yet?"

"This isn't exactly easy reading," Anienam snapped, tired of being interrupted. "It was written in a dead language that I could hardly recall properly if I had all the resources of Ipn Shal at my use. This takes time, Gaimosian."

He snorted. "Time which, according to you has already come to pass."

Anienam slammed the book shut and rose to confront Boen. "Do you wish to hear I made a mistake? Is that it? You have this overpowering urge to know I was wrong about something? Fine. I was mistaken. I misread some of the key passages."

"Enough of this. We don't have time to see who's got the bigger ego," Bahr said and stepped between them. "Anienam, have you been able to decipher anything?"

"Yes. No, some of it, surely, but my initial calculations were too far off the mark to provide any use here."

"You got some of it correct. We found Venheim when no one else could. I need you to keep trying. We have to know when the dark gods will attempt to reenter Malweir." *Otherwise we're just wasting our time and running from death.*

Leaving his darkest thoughts unsaid, Bahr resumed his argument with Boen. "Just because we don't have a definite answer doesn't give us the luxury of burning time. I say we push through the mountains and reach the river."

"The passes are sure to be filled with snow by now! Attempting a crossing would be tantamount to suicide. And let's not forget the Dwarves. They won't take kindly to us marching across their territory uninvited."

Damnation. I'd almost forgotten about them. "Everything I know of Dwarves says they won't bother us if we don't bother them."

Boen barked a laugh. "Believe that if you wish, but I have known many Dwarves. Fought with them and even made a few friends. Fought against them too. They're mean little bastards when it comes down to it and I'd just as soon avoid them altogether. Besides, Dwarves hold grudges that travel from clan to clan. We'd have every Dwarf in Malweir out looking for us."

"What's another few thousand hunting us?" Nothol asked. He couldn't shake the feeling that whatever dark powers were active in the north were sending every tool at their disposal after the small band.

"He's got a point," Boen said. "But that doesn't change the fact that we don't need a legion of Dwarves after us. You can kiss your precious hammer goodbye that way."

"The Kergland Dwarves won't bother anyone," Anienam said suddenly.

"How can you know this?" Bahr demanded.

The wizard shrugged casually. "I have friends as well. They will know me. We should be quite welcome."

Bahr doubted that. The wizard was a quirky old man, but he was off his rocker. Given his track record, Bahr decided Anienam was just as likely to draw someone's ire as their friendship. He couldn't take that chance. "We need to avoid contact. The fewer know about us the better."

"But the Dwarves…"

Bahr pointed at Groge. "Have no love for him. Do you want to start a war?"

"All right, all right! Have it your way. I'm going back to my book."

He ambled back to his already cold seat and picked the book back up, leaving the other two with bemused looks.

"We should scout the nearest pass. If it's blocked we go around," Dorl suddenly added. "It's the only way to end your arguments and keeps us moving forward."

Bahr hid his smile as Boen unfolded his arms warily. The decision to bring along the sell swords continued to pay off, making Bahr glad of what few friends he had. They'd proven themselves invaluable a dozen times over since first leaving Delranan and he held every expectation they would continue to do so in what was sure to be dark days ahead. Still, the decision to enter the mountains or go around weighed heavily. *I need the wizard to give me an accurate timetable. We're trapped until he does.*

TEN

Dwarves

They travelled east for another two days. Ahead, the jagged fangs of the Kergland Spine continued to rise higher. Shadows cast about their base, locking the closest land in semi darkness. Tensions continued to rise as well. The group was decidedly torn between which approach best suited their needs. Boen adamantly championed marching around the northern edge of the mountains. So unlike his usual self, Bahr had to wonder what the Gaimosian knew and wasn't telling. That worried him more than anything else since leaving Fedro.

Reluctantly, the Sea Wolf agreed to send Dorl and Nothol forward to scout the passes. Deep down he knew enough snow had fallen to block their passage, though he refused to believe it until the report came back. He needed to be right. He needed to know he was still capable of making the right decision. So much had gone wrong since the night Harnin came to him and besieged him to rescue the princess. Bahr looked back at Maleela and found any ill will difficult to maintain against her. She was just a pawn.

Dark had grown his thoughts the further away from Delranan they travelled. He began to see things in his dreams; terrible things beckoning the doom he felt he couldn't prevent. The world burned around him and all he could do was laugh. Bahr felt a foulness clutch the edges of his soul, waiting, watching. The notion was absurd. He'd never been superstitious and held no beliefs in another world lurking in the shadows. It took much to swallow what the Old Mother had foretold and even that didn't sit well with his principles. Magic and fantasy might be well and fine for men like Anienam, but Bahr was grounded in the inescapable reality of the harshness of life.

He tried to push those thoughts away and refocused on the nearing mountains. Much of the day had already passed when he ordered a halt. They'd come to the foothills and he agreed not to proceed further until Dorl and Nothol returned. Guiding the wagon into a small stand of ash and pine, he took first watch as the camp was made. Cold winds blew in fresh snow, light and non-sticking. More than two feet of snow already blanketed the lands. He was confident they wouldn't need to worry about it once they reached the river and started moving south.

"Any sign yet?" Boen asked, moving silently up behind.

Any traces of their argument vanished. He was back to being his usual obstinate self, for which Bahr was grateful.

"Nothing. I told them to be back by sundown. We can't risk having them caught in the mountains tonight," Bahr replied.

"Wise. They are good lads. Bringing them along was the second smartest thing you've done."

"What's the first?"

Boen grinned, savage and terrifying. "Bringing me." He stiffened suddenly and pointed. "Look, movement about a hundred meters out."

Bahr followed the line of Boen's finger and squinted against the dying light. He could barely make out the shapes bobbing towards them. Any elation faded when he noticed more than two. "Get everyone prepared. I don't think it's them."

"I knew it!" Boen grumbled. "Gods damned Dwarves. We're in for it now."

He slunk back down the large boulder Bahr had taken up the watch on and quietly roused the others for battle. The camp came alive. Rekka drew her weapons and headed towards the tree line as Skuld and Maleela, secretly, drew swords and headed to the far right flank. Even Anienam rose and headed to the line, though with far different intent. He was certain he could reason with the Dwarves and avoid any unnecessary conflict. Too much death trailed them already. More would just hang around their necks like a plague. If they survived. Only Ionascu remained docile.

"Fifty meters," Bahr hissed and drew his sword. He could make them out clearly. Dorl and Nothol were afoot, their horses nowhere to be seen. A score of Dwarves surrounded them. Each was girded for war.

Golden face masks presented a fierce image. Long beards of every color hung down their broad chests. Plated leather armor protected their torsos and upper thighs. Hobnailed boots gave them traction as they marched. Massive, round shields were slung over their backs, gilded with different runes and Dwarf patterns. Each bore a two-headed battle axe, thick fingers curled around the hafts.

The Dwarves halted at the edge of the trees, planting their feet shoulder width apart and lowering their axes just enough to appear slightly less threatening. Bahr moved quickly, knowing Boen wouldn't hesitate to strike if he saw the right opportunity. The Giant, on the other hand, remained an unknown. One Bahr couldn't take a chance on. Lowering his sword, he stepped into the open with arms wide.

"We don't bring trouble," he started.

The Dwarf captain stepped forward and cut him off. "You are intruding on the Dwarf kingdom of Drimmen Delf. Turn around now and depart or else."

Bahr shook his head. "We can't turn back. Our mission lies to the east. We must be allowed to pass."

"Turn around and find another way or spend the rest of your lives in a dungeon," the Dwarf insisted.

Bahr glanced back over his shoulder, looking to the others for help. Especially Anienam. He needed the wizard to come out and smooth things over. Otherwise…

Making a show of clearing his throat, Anienam drew all attention. "If you think you can take us all then go ahead and try. Otherwise let us pass so we may be on our way."

Bahr's mouth dropped. Swords raised. Axes readied and the Dwarven front rank dropped into battle stance. They were going to charge. Bahr tossed down his sword and jumped between the two groups. "Wait! He doesn't speak for us."

"Lower your weapons and surrender." He put his fingers to his mouth and whistled loudly. Another score of Dwarves popped up from the opposite side of the grove and leveled their dark wood crossbows.

"Your weapons," the Dwarf demanded.

Boen acted first, flipping his great broadsword around and handing it over to the Dwarf. He bore a told-you-so look reserved only for Bahr. Fighting the Dwarves wasn't an issue. He'd had more than his share of run-ins with the taciturn people, but he was impossibly outnumbered and outgunned.

Seeing the Gaimosian surrender so easily prompted the others to follow. Rekka removed the arrow from her bow and handed both bow and quiver over. Even Groge, who could have easily crushed half of the Dwarves without effort, stood with hands clasped submissively at his waist. Rough hands grabbed them and forced cruel metal cuffs around their wrists. Dorl and Nothol watched helplessly, already prisoners. Luck had run out. One by one the members of the group were taken into custody and hustled off towards the now grim-looking mountains. Dwarves swarmed up from the snow-covered rocks and from behind trees to rein in the horses and wagon. Soon everything was on the road to Drimmen Delf.

They halted deep in the foothills. Dwarves swiftly surrounded the captives and blindfolded them with daft fingers, giving Bahr the impression not all was well within the Dwarven kingdom. Speaking only got them beat, a fact both he and Boen learned the hard way. The Dwarves were taking every precaution to ensure their prisoners were treated well but brokered little tolerance when it came to following instructions. Bahr counted his bruises and contemplated revenge.

The air around them changed suddenly. Harsh winds swirled to a stop and warmth flushed their skin. Acidic smells of sulfur and brimstone choked the air along with the combined taint of different metals. Small fires could be heard to their left and right. *We're inside. No escaping now. I hope that damned wizard knows what he's doing or I'll slit his throat myself.*

"Where did you find these?" a gruff voice demanded.

"Wandering along the western border approach."

Bahr could sense the speaker looking them over. Disdain bled through his words. The message was clear. Humans were not welcome in Drimmen Delf.

"So many. Is it a scouting party?"

Dwarves shuffled nervously. "They are girded for war and dangerous, but we do not know whose side they are on."

"We can't take the risk of them being spies. Take them before the king. He will want to interrogate them personally."

More prodding guided the weary band through the halls of the mighty Dwarven kingdom. So many twists and turns along the way made it impossible to keep track of the exit. Bahr quickly relented and accepted his current position. This wasn't the first dungeon he'd been in since the quest began though he hoped it was the last. Finally, after what felt like hours, they were pulled to a stop and told to stand quiet.

Long moments passed when the imagination took hold and started to run wild. All manner of foul creatures lurked just beyond reach, waiting for the command to shred them to pieces. A dark hole, inescapable and forever, beckoned to them. Despair mocked each in a different way. The very whisper of movement was the sound of Giants casting boulders from the mountaintops. Giants who now stood in the throne room.

"Well, well. It has been a long time since I last laid eyes on a mountain brother," the deep voice of the king rumbled through the throne room. "And here I find one in the company of men. Strange times indeed have befallen us. Who speaks for you?"

Bahr immediately stepped forward and was disappointed to hear the rustle of clothes from someone else doing the same.

"Seems you have a disagreement," the king smirked. "Remove their blindfolds."

Rough hands stripped the fabric from Bahr's eyes, allowing him to see for the first time in hours. He was immediately impressed. An onyx throne dominated the center of the chamber. Massive fires burned against the back wall, casting tendrils of shadows throughout. Carved dragon skulls emerged from the hand rests. The back was a mighty stone shield with a war hammer standing through the middle. Power resonated from the throne, unlike any Bahr had ever felt.

Enormous marble slabs tiled the floor, pristine and alabaster. Six columns stretched a hundred meters up to the vaulted ceiling. Bahr felt the urge to whisper upon seeing the stained glass covering the dome. The throne room of Drimmen Delf put the mightiest castle in human lands to shame. The columns were so wide it would take ten men to successfully circle one. Each was carved with intricate designs and runes, much like the armor of their captors.

Twenty armed guards stood at attention on each side of the throne. Each was dressed in crimson armor that reflected the hostility of the fire. Wings stuck out form their helmets. Long, flowing capes hung to the floor. Each guard stood with a massive spear. The tips glimmered, threatening sharpness unparalleled. Bahr bore no illusions that these Dwarves were only here for show. Each was a lord in his own right.

Bahr's gaze finally fell upon Anienam, who'd brazenly stepped forward as well. The wizard's eyes remained focused on the Dwarf lord, refusing to lock with Bahr. The Sea Wolf very much wanted to lash out and exact some measure of revenge but knew that in doing so he would damn them all.

"I am Thord, Dwarf Lord of Drimmen Delf. Now, quickly, tell me your names."

Bahr sidled half a step ahead of Anienam. "I am Bahr of Delranan, a kingdom far to the west. I have co...."

Thord waved him off. "I don't care. We'll get to that later. Now, who is your other leader?"

The wizard bowed respectfully. "Anienam Keiss, my lord. Last of the ancient order of Mages and son of Dakeb."

Whispers spread through the Dwarves massed behind them. Thord slammed the haft of his staff on the marble and the throne room fell silent. "The name Dakeb is known to our kind. He was a good man. It pains me to learn of his passing."

"All things must move on eventually."

Thord grunted thoughtfully. "True words. The name of Bahr is also known. Oh yes, we have knowledge of the infamous Sea Wolf even under our mountain strongholds. Pirate and would-be usurper, some say. For myself I see only an old man past his prime. Why are you in my kingdom? Who sent you?"

Bahr ignored the insult and thought for a moment. Saying the wrong thing now would keep them in irons indefinitely. "We did not wish to intrude and had we known it was a crime to travel through Dwarven lands we surely would have taken the opportunity to go around, but our mission is dire and time is our enemy."

"Time is the Great Enemy of us all, Sea Wolf," Thord said. "Ever do we try to outrun it, yet it still claims us all. What are you running from?"

"War," Bahr replied.

Thord's eyes darkened. His face tightened. "War seems to have a way of spreading. Are you spies? Or do you claim to have no knowledge of the war at our very doorsteps?"

Bahr passed a questioning look to Anienam and decided to let the wizard answer. The old man continued to hold secrets close to his chest.

"I had heard whispers, rumors of a great Dwarf civil war on the eastern side of the Spine but had no way of knowing it for fact," he said. "Our war comes from the west. A combined army of men and Goblins is burning the northern kingdoms in the name of great evil. We seek to stop them and restore peace to the north."

"Goblins and men fighting together? What could have inspired such madness?" Thord almost laughed. The thought of the two races willingly working together for common purpose amused him, so ridiculous it sounded.

Anienam cleared his parched throat. His voice felt scratchy, irritated. "The dark gods once again seek to return and claim dominance of the world."

Thord seemed to think for a while. When he spoke it was with conviction and…something else. "Evil constantly seeks to test us, to push us to the edge of our endurance and beyond. All good races should stand and combat this evil, but the wars of men are of no concern for us. We are besieged by our kin and hard pressed to defend Drimmen Delf. You should not have come here."

"I agree, my lord, but we must go south. The enemy hunts us and every hour we delay hastens a demise I would avoid," Anienam pleaded. "So desperate is our position we risked a trip to find Venheim and enlist the aid of the Giants."

"Venheim," Thord uttered. "Long have I desired to look up the forges of the mountain folk. They have many secrets we Dwarves have long forgotten. Masters of steel and flame. What use for a Giant have a band of Humans?"

Bahr winced. *Don't tell him.*

"We travel to ancient Trennaron to find the Blud Hamr," Anienam said with authority.

Bahr felt his world collapse.

"Trennaron is a myth, wizard spawn," Thord told them. "You waste your time."

Thord's immediate rebuke sparked caution in Bahr. Dwarves were notorious for their love of weapons and precious metals. The prospect of finding a weapon as powerful as the Blud Hamr would be too much to pass up. Any Dwarf hold would be increased exponentially. Human kingdoms would bend knee and pay homage. Bahr wondered what the Dwarf lord's true intentions were now that Anienam gave away their most guarded secret.

"I have walked this world for hundreds of years, never once relying on the wisdom of grounded men claiming what is myth or not. While no adventurer, I have seen my share of things that 'couldn't possibly exist.' Trennaron is one such place. I have seen the cold, grey walls of the ancient, forgotten castle with my own eyes."

Thord held up a staying hand, desperate to stay the wizard's tirade. Anger clouded his face, unaccustomed to being debated in his own throne room. "Peace, wizard. I meant no offense. We Dwarves are solitary folk. Much of the world remains impractical to our needs so we choose to ignore it but I too know a thing or two. Many stout warriors have gone off seeking Trennaron and the Hamr. None have ever returned. Whether from danger or sheer exhaustion from trying to find the impossible I won't guess. We have a saying in Drimmen Delf: keep your eyes to the end of your nose and no trouble will find you."

"Be that as it may, our quest takes us south, to the southern jungles," Anienam added, hoping his tactic of baiting the Dwarf Lord into letting them go out of his own innate greed worked before too much time was lost.

"You'll never make it. The jungles are hundreds of leagues away and there is a war on," Thord said. "You are not enemies. I see that now, but neither are you Dwarf-friend. You may spend the remainder of the night in Drimmen Delf, under guard, naturally, and be sent on your way in the morning."

Bahr interrupted, sensing all was about to be ruined. "My lord, if you could allow us passage through the mountains to the river we will leave immediately. We have no wish to impose upon your hospitality any more than necessary."

"This is not the open water, Sea Wolf. You hold no command in these halls. If it's the river you seek you will need to either go north or south to reach it. Passage through Drimmen Delf is forbidden to outsiders. My decision is final."

Groge, standing at the back of the group, gently cleared his throat. Subtle as the noise was intended to be, the very ground trembled beneath their feet. "Dwarf king, I am Groge, apprentice to master smith Joden. Though I have no experience with the lower world and am barely good enough with steel to earn my titles, I have long desired to see the fabled Dwarven halls and experience what my mountain cousins have to offer."

Thord considered this. "Ha! The Giant speaks better wisdom than wizard and pirate combined. Groge of the Giants, I shall grant you access to our forges, though many will argue and grow bitter at my decision. Dwarven smiths are notoriously jealous when it comes to their forges but even the best of us cannot compare to the skill and craftsmanship of your kind. It is an honor to have you in our halls."

Groge bowed at the great honor. "My thanks, Dwarf Lord. I have but a single concern. You mentioned a war. What war is happening this far to the east, for it seems we have left one war for another?"

If possible, Thord's face darkened more. "The dark clans from across the river have invaded, seeking to lay claim to Drimmen Delf's wealth and status. You and your merry band have blundered into a full-blown civil war."

ELEVEN

Vision Renewed

Prince Aurec stood at the edge of the tree line, staring off into the eastern skies. The wolf-skin cloak wrapped around his shoulders did little to reduce the ferocity of the wind slicing across the open field. His shivers lasted just enough to remind him of how insignificant he was compared to the grandeur of nature. The stubble covering his lower face ached from the cold but he didn't mind. He and agony had become boon companions of late, a maddening spiral he couldn't find escape from.

A golden sunrise turned the snow-covered fields into a mass of blinding light, leading him to question if the gods existed or not. He'd never been a believer. Faith stemmed from more of the use of cold steel than quiet ruminations. He'd never prayed, never felt the need to. Gods were more of an inconvenience than necessity. After all, what use was a supremely powerful being that refused to get involved? No. Aurec trudged through life with focus and individual intent.

Those dreams lay shattered now. Visions of his father's impaled face atop the battlements of their fallen city tormented him at night. Much against his closest advisors, Aurec had snuck back to Rogscroft not long after the siege. He knew he risked too much and should have stayed in Grunmarrow to put together a strong resistance, but he also knew he had to see for himself. Together with a small band of rangers he slipped through enemy lines and stared up at all that remained of the once mighty King Stelskor. His father had not died well.

Now Aurec stood at the edge of everything his world had been reduced to, king and leader of a crippled nation. Perhaps it was time to start believing in the gods. He knew he needed as much aid as possible if there was any chance of winning the guerrilla war now engulfing the kingdom.

Worse, he couldn't help but think about Maleela and what might have become of her. The invasion kept his mind off of his missing betrothed but now both sides had settled down for a hard fight and one of the fiercest winters he could remember.

Maleela. Thoughts of her soft face rivaled any majestic sunrise or sunset. His heart relaxed with a content sigh. One of few he allowed himself of late. Maleela's life was hard, though not as hard as his. Her father blamed her for the death of his wife, her mother, in childbirth. Some hatreds can't be overcome, not matter how hard one tries. Maleela instantly took the blame for their ill-advised scheme of kidnapping. King Badron used it as a catalyst to launch his war.

Aurec's thoughts came too quickly now. He vaguely wondered how he'd gone from admiration of the sunrise to lament and then to his abducted love and now to war. War. The very word once held such romance and dreams of glory, fame. Now Aurec saw how fatal war was. There was no glory to be had. Glory came from the survivors and the horrible scars, both mental and physical, they bore until their dying days. Foolish notions of storming the ramparts to raise the colors was childish at best. Aurec had seen war and never wished to again. He was tired, worn down to the point of ineffectiveness.

The others had seen it. He knew they spoke about him when they thought he wasn't around. The council worried for the prince, now forced to be king before his time. Doubts swirled around the hem of his cloak much like freshly fallen winter snow in the cool dawn. Was he strong enough? Did his love of the enemy princess prevent him from making the tough decisions? Truthfully, Aurec didn't know. He didn't have answers. Didn't have an exit strategy to miraculously save his people and reclaim the throne.

"Your highness, it's time," Sergeant Thorsson snapped from behind, his voice crisp in the chill air.

Aurec sighed again, realizing he did it far too much. "Sergeant, how long have you served in the army?"

"Sire?" Thorsson asked, confused.

"How long have you worn these colors? How many years have you given up the hope of a normal life?"

Scratching his chin he replied, "Seems like forever, especially now, but I figure around twenty years. It's not a burden. Never that. I gladly gave up the doldrums of having a normal family and performing the same job day in and day out. My kingdom comes first. It's the mark of a great soldier. We sacrifice so others don't have to. We know there's no great wealth to be had, no fame or enduring glory beyond living through the next scrape. We do it for you, Aurec. You and every single man, woman, and child in Rogscroft."

Aurec found himself speechless. He'd never expected such passion and depth from a scarred, old veteran. He also felt deeply shamed. So much of his thoughts revolved around his own private miseries he'd neglected too much of his subjects. The idea of being ruler of the kingdom didn't sit well, perhaps it never would. He didn't feel like he belonged on the throne. His father was king and that was how it was. Only it wasn't. Stelskor was gone, leaving young Aurec the only heir to an empty throne.

Hearing Thorsson's rebuke was a refreshing slap in the face. He felt stunned, embarrassed. The time for lament was over. Maleela was gone. She hadn't been in Rogscroft for months and might already be dead herself. His father was a memory, as was his home. What remained was the strongest of Rogscroft. They were leaderless despite how hard his council tried to keep it all together. They needed Aurec to assume the mantle he proved ever reluctant to. The hour had at last come, thanks to the unfiltered comments of a lone soldier who might have otherwise spent his life unknown.

"Thank you, Sergeant," Aurec said sincerely.

Confused, Thorsson asked, "For what, sire?"

Aurec stepped forward to lay his hand on Thorsson's shoulder. "For putting me back in my place and making me realize my own pains and fears were petty. Now come, let us find my council and make plans for taking the war back to the Wolfsreik."

Thorsson's grin was savage, almost feral. Wounded in the fall Rogscroft, he was fortunate to have survived and now, fully healed, relished the opportunity to take a measure of revenge. He nodded happily and led the prince back to the command tent. Heads snapped up as they entered. Many knew from Aurec's bright expression that things were not the same as before. The prince, the warrior, was back.

"Gentlemen, my apologies for being a self-absorbed, absent monarch, but the good sergeant has helped me see the error in my ways. Now, what is the enemy status? Where are we going to go back to war?"

General Vajna had recently returned from the northern reaches of the Murdes Mountains with grim news. "Sire, elements of the Wolfsreik have combined with the Goblins and are moving into the foothills here." He paused to point out the position on the map covering the wooden table. "My scouts estimate their strength at close to one thousand."

"We've known they were working together but never in such a major offensive," Venten added quickly. "Badron seems almost desperate to cross the mountains."

"Or destroy the Pell utterly," Mahn said.

Aurec assimilated the data quickly, having already made up his mind. "The Pell are a major nuisance to General Rolnir but Badron thinks them beneath concern. However, he knows that the mountain folk bar the way back to his homeland. He can't get his army home without engaging the Pell." He paused. "One thousand? How many are Wolfsreik?"

"Two full battalions," Vajna answered. "Close to three hundred men."

"Not exactly the largest chunk we could take out of his combat strength but still large enough to send a message to Rolnir and his commanders. We need to make Delranan fear us again. I think this is a prime opportunity to remove a significant portion of their fighting power."

"Sire, they have an estimated twenty thousand men and Goblins at their disposal. We can't possibly compete with that," Mahn countered.

"A day ago I would have agreed but matters have changed. We've bled them from the moment the vanguard first came down from the foothills. They are demoralized and now realizing they're involved in a guerrilla-style campaign they aren't trained for. This is our moment, friends. We've taken the war to the enemy in just this manner from day one. Now it's time to unleash all our pent-up fury and aggression and make them pay. General, how many soldiers can you assemble?"

Vajna grinned, folding his arms across his chest. "A little more than they have. Enough to give a good fight."

"Numbers are in our favor. All you need to do is drive them up into the mountains and into the Pell. Between your fighters and the Pell hunters we'll be able to crush them to the man," Aurec's voice rose with previously unfelt passion. "This will send a clear message to Rolnir and Badron. We are a force to be reckoned with. There is fight left in us. Today begins a new age. Rogscroft will rise again. We will rebuild our cities, our homes and our families. Today we become a people again and shout in one loud voice that we cannot be conquered! We are the masters of this kingdom! The hour and glory belongs to you, the men of Rogscroft!"

Cheers and applause spread quickly. Too long had they languished under the oppression of uncertainty and lament. Heavy losses forced them underground where they licked their wounds and hid from the enemy. Aurec's bold proclamation changed all that in a single moment. The campaign to retake Rogscroft was at last underway.

Aurec let them cheer, knowing they needed it after so much hardship. Gradually it faded and he continued, "Prepare your troops and leave at your earliest convenience. It shouldn't take the enemy more than two days to get into the mountains where they will be bogged down by the Pell. I have assurances from Gol Mad that the Pell will fight. Venten and Sergeant Thorsson, I want you to step up training of those who remain. Take everyone willing to fight: men, women, I don't care."

"That won't sit well with many of the traditionalists," Mahn said, his own feelings clouded. The possibility of fighting alongside women never entered his mind until Aurec mentioned it.

"The old traditions are dead, Mahn. The only way we can survive as a people is by embracing the change necessary to continue the fight. Besides, we've all heard rumors of warrior women in southern kingdoms. Why not here as well?"

"Agreed. Are there any age restrictions?"

"So long as they can hold a spear or sword and march alongside their compatriots, no," Aurec answered. "We need soldiers to fill the rank and file and I need an army to reclaim our kingdom. Do not let this dishearten you. Ours is a long, arduous road, but one we must travel if we hope to find peace at the end. Nothing easy is ever worth doing. We will survive this and see our days renewed. Rogscroft will become a symbol of righteousness. A beacon for other kingdoms to follow."

"How far will you take this war?" Venten asked. "Your father wanted only peace with our neighbors. Recall he and Badron were once boyhood friends. He would not wish for you to visit such violence on Delranan."

Aurec paused. When he spoke his voice was measured, calculated. "My father is dead. I will take the war as far as I must. Badron will either stand down or surrender."

Murmurs broke out. No one expected him to announce invading the strength of Delranan. The thought was preposterous. Rogscroft had limited resources and a small army. Certainly not enough to tackle a kingdom so powerful. The Wolfsreik was the source of that power. Aurec's plan hinged on being able to break them down and force negotiations. Without the Wolfsreik in the field Badron would have no choice but to fold.

Aurec met their gawking looks with confidence he hadn't felt in weeks. "There is no other way. Anything less is suicide."

"Attacking Delranan will also prove suicidal," Venten argued. "We have neither the strength nor the will to do so. Not with ten thousand Men could we hope to take their kingdom."

"I don't want Delranan. I want Badron gone and reparations made for what they've done here," Aurec countered. "Rogscroft comes first, before all our needs."

"Precisely why we can't risk an invasion this close to being conquered."

"We haven't been conquered yet, old friend. There is fight left in us. I have seen it just by walking through the camp. Our people want to fight but have followed my foolish lead. Paneolus, you have been one of my father's staunchest supporters. You are also the only surviving member of the former government. I need you to continue your service."

The older diplomat shifted uncomfortably, as if he'd just been asked to kill his firstborn child. He'd lost much of his excess weight in their exile, now the unused skin hung from his neck. "My lord, I have spent many long years in the service of the kingdom and, while I would like nothing more than to retire into a life of obscurity, I will do as you ask."

Aurec nodded. "Thank you. My first task to you is to build support for my intentions. You have the gift of speech. Use it. Garner enough support that the minor issue of sex is forgotten for the needs of the greater good. It is the only way."

"It will be done," Paneolus said more quietly.

Aurec scanned those assembled. "Time is of the essence. General, you may depart on your own accord. Mahn, I need you to go back to the field. Travel with Gol Mad back to Cuul Ol's camp and tell him our plans. We must have their support."

"Raste is going to love you," Mahn grinned. "We'll depart in the morning, sire."

Aurec couldn't help but chuckle. The laughter felt surprisingly good. He'd languished for too long and needed mirth. "Begin your preparations. It's time to take the fight back to our enemies."

TWELVE

Unexpected Allies

Vajna leaned heavily on the nearest spruce. His breath came in ragged gasps. His muscles trembled from exertion and his eyes burned from beads of sweat stinging him. Dark blood, so foul it appeared black, washed the front of his armor. Great notches had been carved into his finely honed sword and still the battle was far from over. He wiped his brow with the back of an arm and surveyed the battlefield.

Small, rolling foothills surrounded him, making it next to impossible for the enemy to have any sort of visual range. Coordination and detailed movements became next to impossible and the battle quickly devolved into singular combat. Without the ability to control the Wolfsreik, commanders lost the advantage. Vajna watched as men battled men. The combat was fierce, but nothing compared to the natural ferocity of the Goblins. Born and bred under the mountains, their squat, powerful bodies were perfect for hand-to-hand fighting and their independent aggressiveness ensured they worked better alone than in a regimented unit.

Goblins hacked and bit their opponents. Body parts littered the snow, though the quickly cooling blood melted much of it into a soupy mess. A Wolfsreik soldier stabbed his blade deep into the belly of one of Vajna's men. The bright red tip punched out the spine with a spray of blood and steam. A Goblin fell dead from an arrow buried in its throat. Dozens already lay dead. Scores. And still the carnage continued unabated. Even with the arrival of the Pell Darga, Vajna found it difficult to envision any type of victory. The Goblins were simply too powerful. Neither he nor Aurec took that into account.

Already pushed to the point of exhaustion, Vajna pushed off the tree and readied to lead a counter charge. Three mounted soldiers appeared suddenly from behind, trapping him against the trees. Cold dread filled his heart. He knew he couldn't run. Death had come at last. He raised his sword to a low guard and waited.

The sudden attack didn't come though. The riders pulled up short and watched him from behind their helmet visors. Steam puffed from the horses. Hooves stamped impatiently. Magnificent animals bred for war, they wanted to be free to trample the enemy. Only the strength of their riders prevented that from happening. After what felt like hours, the lead rider slowly removed his helmet. He stared down on Vajna with mild interest, quietly admiring the spirit of the man.

"Lower your weapon. I am not here to fight you."

Vajna didn't move. "What trickery is this? You are Wolfsreik. My enemy."

"Not so much an enemy as you think. I am Herger and I come with an offer from my general."

"What offer?" Vajna remained wary. The long spears could skewer him effortlessly despite his willingness to talk.

"There will be time for that later. For now I propose that we join forces and destroy these Goblin scum. Their very sight offends me," Herger said with a disarming smile.

Vajna searched Herger's face for signs of treachery but his instincts were unconfirmed. If Herger plotted, he did an impressive job of concealing it. Lowering his sword, Vajna nodded. "Very well. I am Vajna. Let us kill the Goblins and speak as men."

Herger returned the nod. "Good man. Captain, order the charge. No man is to be harmed by any Wolfsreik under penalty of death."

"Yes sir."

They watched the junior officer ride off to begin the counterattack. Vajna relished the idea of his enemies turning on each other, knowing how much easier his task had just become. At least for the moment. Battle cries and cheers rose from the men as they ceased fighting each other and turned on the dumbstruck Goblins. The body count rose drastically.

The battle turned to a rout and then an all-out slaughter. Goblins were killed where they stood. Very few escaped. An hour later the combined commanders ordered their forces to halt. Without an accurate body count there wasn't any viable way to ensure every Goblin was accounted for and Herger was inclined to let it be. Enough killing had been done for one day and word would eventually get back to Badron and Grugnak. The alliance was shattered. From this day forward the Wolfsreik and Goblins would be as the gods intended, bitter enemies.

Herger found Vajna being treated for a wound on his right thigh. Medics finished bandaging their general with scowls and harsh words. A leader wasn't useful dead and the new armies of Rogscroft needed their senior commander. He waved off their concerns with gruff comments and a stern look. Good leaders needed to be in the front to inspire their men, putting their own regard last.

"You fought well," Herger commented sharply. "Not many would be willing to put themselves in harm's way for men they hardly know. It speaks greatly for the wealth of Rogscroft, General."

"We are left with very few choices," Vajna replied. "Farmers become heroes and the old rise above the youth. War makes strangers of us all."

"No truer words have been spoken. By the gods, it felt good slaying the grey skins."

"It felt better not having to worry about your wolf soldiers though I can't help but wonder about your true intent. Why did you stop fighting us?"

Herger took a seat on the field stool beside Vajna and ran a hand through his hair. "General Rolnir believes the time has come to part ways with our unwanted allies. The Goblins are no longer necessary to our war efforts."

"You haven't beaten us that soundly, Colonel," Vajna scowled. "Why does Badron send away such a massive force? He has to know he wastes his greatest combat multiplier."

Herger remained quiet for a few moments longer than Vajna felt comfortable with. "King Badron doesn't know."

Even the medics were forced to stop in shock.

Gol Mad and one hundred Pell Darga warriors came down from the foothills with spears in hand. Blood and gore dripped from body and blade and they sang terrible songs of victory and honor. More than one Pell carried a bloodied scalp at his belt. None showed signs of exhaustion, contrary to their lowland counterparts. Every warrior wanted more.

They halted at the edge of battle and curiously stared at the two groups of men. None of it made sense. The Wolfsreik had come to Rogscroft and the Murdes Mountains to kill and destroy two distinct ways of life. Goblins added problems but weren't overly difficult to deal with. The Pell watched the nervous alliance, quietly wondering what was going to happen next.

"This is not good."

Gol Mad thumbed his dulled spear tip. "No. We must be cautious. These lowlanders do not hold honor as we. Perhaps they have good reason to stop fighting."

The first warrior bristled, insulted by the apparent betrayal. "We should attack now, while they talk."

Gol Mad studied the youth, a lad of barely eighteen years. Once, long ago, he held the same beliefs but the war aged him in more ways than he realized. Gol valued patience now, and prudence. There was a time and place for everything. He'd seen too many friends fall because of their own ignorance. Every man had limitations, but fools failed to recognize them in time. Gol Mad was a survivor. He knew that now. It fell to him to train the young, teach them how wars were meant to be fought.

"We do not know why they talk. Attacking is not good, Daf Hu. Rushing into battle unprepared is good for only death. We wait, watch, and learn."

The youth tensed at the rebuke but was wise enough to keep his tongue. He'd seen others beaten for less. They lived but bore the scars of shame for the rest of their days. Daf vowed to abide until his time for leadership arrived.

Gol Mad looked back at his warriors. "Wait here. I will speak with the wolf soldiers and our allies. Eat, drink. Prepare fires and sharpen your blades."

They grumbled consent and followed orders as Gol marched over the blood-painted ground to the meeting place. He bowed curtly to Vajna and halted just far enough away to have room to maneuver should the meeting prove deadly.

"Ah, Colonel Herger, this is Gol Mad of the Pell Darga," Vajna introduced. His voice was stern, betraying no hint of weakness or fear. Vajna knew the Pell's respect hinged on his ability to project confidence and command under the worst circumstances. Anything less would result in the Pell returning to their mountains as enemies.

"We are not friends with the wolf soldiers," Gol Mad said crisply. He planted his feet shoulder width apart, a move intended to show strength and power. It was an old Pell tactic normally used during mating rituals and rites of passage. The Pell were fierce and proud. Only the proper display of force would garner respect from a warrior.

Herger took in his enemy for the first time. Barely taller than a Goblin, Gol Mad had dark brown skin, aged and weathered by constant exposure to foul weather. Everything about the man suggested a cagey warrior capable of killing a man with barely an effort. Herger was impressed.

"Nor does the Wolfsreik consider you a friend," he replied just as strongly. "Your kind has killed many of my warriors."

Gol flexed his shoulders. "As have yours."

Vajna felt his heart ready to burst. He cursed his own ignorance for allowing the two sides to interact. Pell and Wolfsreik had been mortal enemies for generations. Scores had been killed during the war and neither seemed willing to back down and accept the other. Aurec never dreamed of a scenario where all three worlds collided. None of them did. Yet the impossible was developing before his eyes and he felt powerless from keeping it intact.

Gol broke first, pointed teeth showing in a terse grin. He nodded his approval. The challenge had been successfully met and, while neither would ever be friendly towards the other, they respected the other as warriors. "You have a strong voice, wolf soldier. I like that."

Herger extended his thick slab of a hand. "There shall be no more bloodshed between our two clans this day. You have my word, shadow warrior."

Only now did Vajna exhale his nerves. His worst case scenario didn't come to pass, yet. "What about the surviving Goblins? They can bring reinforcements."

"Their main body is leagues away," Herger said. "We don't have anything to worry about in that regard."

THIRTEEN

A New King

Grunmarrow finally came alive on Mid-Winter Day. Normally a day for massive celebrations among the northern kingdoms, it bore special significance for the resistance of Rogscroft. This day of days Prince Aurec was to be crowned to king. Winter flowers were strung across the buildings and cleared pathways. Men and women worked tirelessly to improve the grim camp to a small measure of regality. Huge fires were stoked overnight, and the smell of cooking pig and cattle hovered over the buildings. Children played, giddy in excitement they couldn't comprehend. Finally, the people of Rogscroft had reason to feel good.

Aurec stood under the vine-crusted archway with bowed head as the high priest waved a freshly cut sage branch over each shoulder and the crown of Aurec's head. The prince fought back the urge to cry, so powerful was the moment. He'd never thought the day would come. Pride, elation, and bitter disappointment clashed in his mind, nearly rendering him down to a mass of quivering flesh. His thoughts were focused on his late father, the king. *Only, I'm the king now. Rogscroft has been given to me, to protect and restore. I pray I am up to the task. Father, guide my hands.*

With a nod, the priest bade Aurec kneel. The recently laid wood paneling was cool to his knee. A slight breeze tickled his face. He closed his eyes, locked in furious debate over whether he possessed the merits necessary to be a proper king. He just didn't know and that frightened him to no ends. So many had perished due to the fatal combination of his lack of leadership and the wicked depredations of the Goblins. Worse, he felt alone. No allies had heeded the call for aid. Cuul Ol and his Pell warriors did their best, but they were never many and lacked the training and discipline of a proper army.

A simple diadem was placed on his head. No jewels or gold. Wrought iron hammered and tempered into a practical thing would be the crown of Rogscroft, at least until the time came when the king could rightfully sit upon his throne again. Aurec insisted. The real crown was lost, more likely destroyed when Badron assumed control. That was well and fine. He didn't feel he deserved such richness in these dark times. A warrior king was needed if the kingdom were to have a future. Aurec must become that king or fall into the obscurity of history.

The priest raised his hands to the skies and tipped back his head. "In the name of the gods of light I now proclaim Aurec, son of Stelskor, king of Rogscroft. May his reign be lengthy and his decisions wise. Rise, my liege."

Aurec was so engrossed in his thoughts he almost failed to hear the command. Sniffing back the tears, he rose and turned to face those assembled. *My people*. His knees trembled despite having grown up in the court. This was different. Nothing he had seen or done could have prepared him for what must come next.

Cheers erupted, spreading through the hundreds and hundreds of spectators. Soldiers slammed their swords on shields or stamped their boots. Men and women chanted his name in reverence. They bore no doubts that Aurec was now their king. Select children ran up to Aurec with bouquets of flowers. Trumpets blared, announcing to the heavens that Rogscroft had a new lord. For the moment, all thoughts and memories of the war were replaced by unfiltered joy.

Aurec let them have their moment, for it was as much for his subjects as for himself. The cheering continued for many minutes before finally quieting down. It was time for the king to speak. He'd rehearsed this speech a thousand times, knew exactly what he wanted to say, the message he needed to convey. Here, now as he looked out into the sea of expectant faces, all those carefully prepared words fled. He cleared his throat and spoke from his heart instead.

"My father helped make this kingdom, our kingdom, strong. He gave us a developed economy, a good army, and the ability to live our lives in freedom and prosperity. He gave each and every one of us the option of being good people." He paused to look into as many eyes as possible as he scanned from left to right. "I have none of that. We are at the edge of breaking, balancing against the dim tide of despair. But we are not broken yet! Our hearts beat strong in defeat. I look into your eyes and see the very same pride that fills my heart. You give me hope. Strength. You give me the will to carry on in the hopes that we can once again build Rogscroft to a place of prominence."

More cheers. He flushed with embarrassment. Never had anyone so cheered his name or his words.

Aurec held up a hand for silence and continued. "Today begins a new era. Already our soldiers are taking the war back to the enemy. They fight not for me but for you. You are the heart of our kingdom. Without you I am nothing but a fool with a crown. I cannot promise you victory, only my sincerest pledge to keep fighting until the last beat of my heart. For you and for Rogscroft!"

Drums pleated a steady rhythm, echoing across Grunmarrow with pride, fury, and excitement. Aurec walked back through the throngs, shaking hands and offering praise while accepting it from more than he'd imagined. He was beyond exhausted by the time he managed to worm his way to the feasting pavilion. Cups of wine, confiscated from Wolfsreik supply convoys, filled every hand. He greedily accepted one and drank deep. The taste was bitter and from a berry he wasn't familiar with but he drank it anyway.

Attendants began establishing the receiving line, for it was the king's duty to welcome all his invited guests before the feast could begin. Normally this was done in the finest attire with a small orchestra playing in the background. Grunmarrow offered no such luxuries. Most came dressed in their field uniforms or with whatever had the least amount of stains. While the final preparations were being made, Aurec took the time to seek out his most important guest. He found the Pell chieftain sitting alone beside an empty fountain.

"I cannot thank you enough for coming down from your mountains," Aurec began.

Cuul Ol smiled. "It is an honor, young king."

Aurec snorted. "King. I doubt I will ever get used to the title. It wasn't that long ago that I was an impetuous boy intent on bringing our two peoples together."

"It wasn't long ago we held no desire to interact with your kind. Such strange times we live in."

"Unfortunate times," Aurec added.

The Pell shrugged. "We do not get to choose the time we live in, Aurec. The old gods will use us as they will. Who are we to argue?"

"You are a wise man, Cuul. I could use more like you at my council. I feel overwhelmed. Like this task is above me," Aurec confided. "I know I can do the job, but not sure if I can do it well. These people are on the edge. All it will take is a small breeze and they are lost. This isn't how I imagined my reign would begin."

Cuul surprised him by laughing. "No good leader is born from softness. Trials and hardships are necessary. You have been bled many times since autumn and you do not break. You bend, like any tree in a strong gale, but your roots are deep. I think you will endure this storm. There will be light again."

"Light or dark I can't see a way out of the war without much more bloodshed," Aurec replied. "My offer stands, Cuul Ol. Will you join my council? I need more warriors to plan an effective strategy against Delranan."

The Pell sighed and sat on a cold stone bench. "You ask much. The Pell Darga would be without a leader in these dark times. How can I abandon my people now?"

"I'm not asking you to. What I need is your advice and knowledge," the king replied quickly to alleviate any misunderstanding. "I can't remain in Grunmarrow. The war is progressing again and I need to be able to control it from the field."

"You seek to be a warrior king? Some would call that reckless."

Aurec held out his hands. "What choice have I? The enemy holds all the advantages. They need to be taught fear."

"Fear is very powerful," Cuul agreed. "The wolf soldiers use fear very well. Perhaps not as well as the foul *grugk*. The grey skins are like a plague upon us."

"Cuul, we can beat them. Turn their fear back on them and drive them from our lands," Aurec insisted. "Imagine a day when the Pell Darga can live in the lowlands without fear of persecution. Our two communities can grow as one; rebuild Rogscroft in the image of our forefathers."

"We Pell have no use for living down here. The mountains are our home. It doesn't feel right this low," he finished with a chuckle. "I will think on your idea, young king. Important decisions should not be made lightly."

"I expect nothing less," Aurec said. "Now I believe the time has come to feast and celebrate my coronation."

They shared a soft laugh and entered the pavilion with rumbling stomachs.

Dark mists swirled, filling the ancient stone chamber and clouding the vision. The mists soothed Amar Kit'han, reminding him of the days of the turning. He hadn't started out evil. The lure of power and an uncontrollable desire to be more than himself led Amar down the paths of corruption. The Dae'shan fell from grace and became servants of the foul powers. In the process they lost their physical forms. Hatred consumed what remained of their souls, twisting them into wretched creatures whose only enjoyment came from the suffering of others.

"What are we to do?" Kodan Bak snarled from the shadows.

Amar titled his head back, allowing the mists into his robes. Their cool embrace helped him relax. "Continue as the dark gods decree. Who are you to defy their will?"

"Their will or yours?"

"Ever you seek to replace me and claim the mantle of leadership. Have you learned nothing from your time among us? I am merely an instrument. Should the dark gods wish me replaced then I will step aside. But not until that time. You have neither the ability nor the intellect to succeed me, Kodan Bak."

A great knot of shadows swirled together tightly. Raw power built across the chamber. Ancient evil threatened to rip free of mortal constraints. Amar welcomed the assault, so sure of his dominance.

"Yessss, use your pathetic magic and strike me down. You have wished for this moment for so very long," he taunted.

Kodan Bak hesitated, suddenly unsure of the game being played. His hands trembled from the massive amount of power aching to be unleashed. They'd been adversaries for centuries, old enemies sworn to serve the same masters. Their forced companionship did little to assuage their contempt. Kodan Bak knew he was made to lead. Why couldn't the gods see it? Why must he languish under the misguided rule of a lesser being? There were no answers in any tongue capable of making sense. Of late, his every thought turned towards assassinating Amar Kit'han and claiming dominance of the Dae'shan.

Reluctantly, he released the power back into the ether. A time was coming. He would abide for now. "No. Too much needs to be done if we are to have the paths open for the gods return."

"Indeed," Amar agreed, silently amused at Kodan's lack of will. "Has there been word from the Hags?"

"None since their ill-advised battle with their prey. It seems Harpies aren't very good for much after all," Kodan replied. "Nor has there been word from Pelthit Re. Delranan has grown dark. I can no longer see within."

"Pelthit Re does what he assumes is best. Rebellion has fomented. The kingdom falls into chaos and ruin. We are succeeding but much is still required. It is almost time for the sacrifice."

Red eyes flashed and went pale. "What of the princess and her party? They are already en route to claim the Blud Hamr. More effort needs to be placed in stopping them."

"Worry not about that, Kodan. I have plans in motion that should see their travels waylaid."

"It would be better to kill them outright. Having them around is dangerous. I do not know why but I sense great complications in letting the princess live."

Amar shifted subtly. He'd felt it too but didn't know how she convoluted things. "She could be made to fall. The One Eye is weak, too easily manipulated. The princess would make a formidable ally."

"Can she be turned? Her love for her uncle and betrothed keeps her strong," Kodan countered. "She needs to die. Anything less is too risky."

"Perhaps. Time will give us clarity."

The Dae'shan fell silent, carefully watching the other for signs of treachery. A day was coming when new Dae'shan would be required. The old would get swept away in a great conflagration, leaving only the strongest survivors. Amar Kit'han began plans to ensure he alone stood at the end of the day.

FOURTEEN

Betrayal

"Is this a joke? I'm in no mood for games, Piper," General Rolnir said without looking up from the missive freshly delivered to his hands.

Piper Joach folded his arms across his chest and shrugged. "That is Herger's handwriting. We both know he's rather dour on the best days. I doubt highly he'd pull a prank like this."

"A truce? An alliance even? What is happening here? If Badron learns of this we'll all lose our heads."

"Agreed but what's done is done. There can be no denying the enemy desires to collaborate, at least enough to drive the Goblins back to their mountain haunts in the east. We need to give it serious consideration."

Rolnir flashed an angered glare. "What of the king? He'll be here with all the dark powers at his disposal in a heartbeat. Who was the messenger?"

"I didn't ask his name but he's sequestered in one of the supply tents tucked safely away from prying eyes. The bigger issue is how do you intend on replying?" Piper asked.

How indeed? I've dreaded making this decision since it was first brought up. "I don't know. There is no easy answer."

"Not to mention the Wolfsreik has never turned against a seated monarch."

Rolnir wanted to spit. "Delranan has never had a mad king before either. Badron is not the same man he was before this nightmare began. I fear we are already losing too much of ourselves in this war, Piper. Things aren't the way they're supposed to be. We stand on the brink of history and all I can think of is my men. Do you know how many we've lost since coming to Rogscroft?"

"Seven hundred thirty-seven dead and nearly two thousand wounded. I was there in the beginning, my friend. I know how bad this is turning out," Piper said quietly. Much of his bravado faded at the memory of losing so many soldiers in the opening engagement of the war. His shame deepened the longer the war stretched despite Rolnir's best efforts at dissuading the notion he had failed.

"So many. We are down to seventy percent combat strength and the winter deepens around us. Supply trains have stopped coming. The passes are blocked. What little supplies come by boat take weeks to get to the battalions. How many soldiers will die of frostbite or starvation before the snows melt? Wars are not meant to be fought thus."

"Your argument is moot, Rolnir. We did not seek this war, but it is ours nonetheless. As commanders it is our responsibility to ensure as many of the lads return to their homes as possible. No one ever said leading an army was an enviable task," Piper said.

Running a hand through his thick red hair, Rolnir looked him square in the eye and asked, "What would you do?"

Piper glanced at the half-crumpled parchment in Rolnir's hand. "Herger presents us with the best option for keeping our men alive and a plausible means for removing the Goblin threat."

"You still believe Badron will turn them on us once we return to Delranan?"

"If rumors of Harnin's betrayal are true, yes. The king can't afford to have such a large fighting force in unsure hands. He'll throw us into the fray knowing we will be reluctant to kill our own people, and rightfully so. I've no desire to shed Delrananian blood. It doesn't take much imagination to see him using the Goblins to wipe us out along with Harnin's rebellion simultaneously. Ours backs are to the wall."

Rolnir shook his head. "But how can we be sure? I need to know the next move I make is the best for everyone,

Badron included. He may be demented but he is still our king."

"Kings come and go, you know this. Perhaps the princess would make a better regent once her father is removed," Piper suggested.

Rolnir paused. He hadn't considered Maleela in the equation. More than a century had passed since the last queen of Delranan. Perhaps it was time for the next to arise. She was young but had a very good head on her shoulders and her love for the Rogscroft prince was no secret. Their union would solidify the two kingdoms in ways Badron's ill-advised war never would.

"Something I said?" Piper asked, seeing the quizzical look in Rolnir's eyes.

Smiling, Rolnir said, "Just a thought. Maleela is very young, but intelligent. She might make a fine queen if we can get her to the throne."

"That's the true problem. No one has seen or heard from her since she was brought back to Chadra by the Sea Wolf. The old pirate could have absconded with her again or Harnin might have her head on a pike for all we know."

"True, but we're getting ahead of ourselves, Piper. I need time to think before making a decision," he said.

"What of the messenger?"

Rolnir dropped the parchment into the small tent fire and watched as flames curled up the edges, disintegrating all traces of written treachery. "Take me to him. I want to hear everything he has to say. Perhaps in doing so I will find clarity. All this troubles my mind and soul too much."

Piper only nodded in agreement.

Lodi snapped to attention when General Rolnir entered the tent. He shook nervously as his commanding officer looked him up and down. Nine years in the army and he'd never been this close to the leadership.

Seeing his obvious discomfort, Rolnir grinned. "At ease, lad. I'm not the devil the men think. What's your name?"

"Lodi, General," he replied quickly.

"Lodi, I need you to explain everything that is happening on the front. Don't leave any details out. What you have to say may mean life or death for us all."

Swallowing his suddenly overpowering nerves, Lodi began his tale, "We linked up with the Goblins just south of Rogscroft. They're a foul-smelling lot with nothing but evil in their eyes. Colonel Herger didn't trust them none. The march into the mountains went well enough. They stayed in their column and we in ours. It was a three day trek. Me and a handful of boys were sent out as flankers to scout the lower approaches. We didn't see anything right up into the shadows at the base of the mountains.

"The Colonel deployed us in wedge formations and we advanced. Snows choked most of the passes but we were able to traverse through the foothills without much trouble. The Goblins just pushed right ahead without worry or smarts. They were bloodthirsty and didn't care about nothing but getting to the Pell Darga. They raised a gods awful noise, some kind of battle hymn as they pushed deeper into the mountains. That's when we got attacked. The first salvo of arrows punched into the back ranks before anyone knew what was happened. Dozens of men and even more Goblins went down, dead or wounded."

Lodi paused, trying to get the events right before retelling them. "Colonel Herger ordered us about to confront the assault but it was already too late. The enemy unleashed three or four more salvos. There were so many arrows they didn't need to aim. It seemed like the entire sky was filled at one point. We tried to mount a counterattack but their archers just melted back into the foothills."

"Sound tactics, but that doesn't explain how you got here," Rolnir interrupted, anxious to get to the point. Every battle had a different theme, different tactics and results. This one was no different.

"Orders came down to form ranks and wait. Shields were raised and pikes lowered but the enemy never came," Lodi shook his head, lost in thought. "I don't know how long we waited but the boys started getting anxious shortly after midday. That's when we heard the first blood-curdling cry coming down from behind us. Waves of Pell Darga charged us the same time the enemy massed a cavalry attack. We were caught good, sir."

Piper passed a glance to Rolnir but held his tongue. He'd known the enemy was working in conjunction with the Pell but never had there been an instance where both parties attacked simultaneously. Such implications could prove disastrous if Rolnir failed to pursue the obvious course of action.

"We fought for a good long time. The shield wall collapsed under the weight of their cavalry and it broke down into groups of two and three. We gave as good as we got but it all came to stop all a sudden. The winds could be heard echoing through the hills during the pause. We were all tired by then. I don't know how I managed to keep going. The enemy had numbers on us and with the Pell warriors we all knew it was just a matter of time before we were wiped out. But then something queer happened. New orders came down. We were to side with Rogscroft and attack the Goblins."

His eyes widened, still shocked and amazed by the event. "None of us knew what to make of it at first but we'd all had enough of those stinking grey skins. We attacked harder than against the enemy. It felt good to kill Goblins for a change. Only a few got away before we all settled down in camps and took care of our dead and wounded. The Pell even brought down stags for us to eat. Hells, we had a feast right there in the midst of all that carnage. That's when Colonel Herger summoned me and gave me the message to deliver to you, sir."

Rolnir strode forward to place his hand on Lodi's shoulder. "Thank you, lad. You've done a great service to the Wolfsreik. Commander Joach will ensure you are fed and rested before we send you back to the detachment. You've given me valuable information. I'll have a reply drafted for you to give Colonel Herger. Rest well tonight, Lodi. You've earned it."

The young soldier beamed with pride, gladly nodding his head with approval. "Yes sir. Thank you, General."

Rolnir returned the crisp salute and exited the tent. His mind raced with infinite possibilities, most of them foul. For a brief moment he wondered how painful being hung would be. The crisp sound of breaking necks often haunted him, traitors and prisoners all. Occasionally men swung from the gallows for committing heinous crimes, but those days were far and few between of late. Badron seemed to encourage bad behavior. Rape and murder were no longer punishable crimes. Darkness settled over the Wolfsreik, leaving Rolnir next to powerless to prevent his army from devolving into an angry mob.

Crisp winter air took his breath away and chilled his flesh. Once, he enjoyed the winter air. It invigorated him, rejuvenated his tired muscles and strained head. The Rogscroft winter stole that. He wanted warmer climates without the prospect of being trapped in a war he couldn't fathom. The more he thought about it the more he came towards the conclusion that much more was happening in Rogscroft than he knew.

"Herger played that well enough," Piper said once he was sure they were alone. "He prevented a massacre and restored the morale of his men."

"He also jeopardized his command by accompanying those battalions," Rolnir countered. "Still, there is merit to his actions. We'll need men like that in the coming days. His loyalty is decided at least."

Piper attempted a smile. "You always need to start with one. Several others will go along without question, bringing most of the army with them."

"Most isn't good enough, Piper. I need the support of every battalion I have if we're to make a successful break from the king. Nothing on the horizon is going to be easy."

"Nothing worth doing ever is," Piper countered. "Once the army defects, Badron will be toothless. His only military strength will be in Grugnak's Goblin corps. They can't compete with us, Rogscroft, and the Pell. We'll be able to mop this up in weeks and return home in time to end Harnin's rebellion. This can work, Rolnir."

The general wasn't so sure. All his thoughts led to utter destruction. Not that he worried over his own fate, but his men deserved better than to die as traitors. As a general he expected losses in battle, whether from enemy action or natural attrition. What he couldn't accept was his entire ten-thousand-man force being executed at the behest of a mad king. He wished there was another way, a way in which only the king needed to suffer. That just wouldn't be hard enough. Hardships followed the Wolfsreik everywhere. What was one more thrown on the pile?

"If we move forward we need to do it quickly. Badron's wrath will be terrible."

"You've made up your mind then?" Piper asked.

He did. "I've only got two real choices, Piper. Either I can brand Herger a renegade and loose the wolves on him or I can take the army right now and remove the single greatest threat to Delranan."

"Put that way there isn't much of a choice to make after all. What are your orders?"

"Summon all senior commanders to my quarters. I'll meet them one at a time. Once I'm sure where their loyalties lie we can mobilize. Our first priority will be to isolate Badron. We surround Rogscroft and begin the campaign to reduce the Goblin threat. With Aurec's two armies we should be able to accomplish this in weeks. Goblins are ferocious warriors but not very smart and lack the ability to think tactically. We use that against them and purge this land for good."

"That is the most encouraging thing I've heard since we got stuck in the middle of this nightmare," Piper replied. "What do you wish me to do?"

Rolnir considered his adjutant carefully. Best friends for years, Piper had been Rolnir's best man at his wedding and the first to offer condolences after his wife was taken by the pox. He and Piper were like brothers and now that bond was threatened by a rogue idea Rolnir still wasn't sure where it came from.

"Pick your best captain and a detachment. Send them north to the coast. We're going to need ships. The mountain passes are too congested for us to get home in the next few months. Commission as many ships as possible. We're going to need to make several trips to get the bulk of the army back and assembled in fighting condition before marching on Chadra. We also need to find a way to get word to the reserves."

"They could already be turned," Piper suggested. "Harnin was always a snake. He lied better than the worst of us. It's not so hard to think Badron's lost his mind over here. They could have the entire kingdom militarized by now."

Rolnir frowned. He and Harnin had once been friends. War did funny things to men. "I know but I need to know for sure. We're talking about marching on our own kingdom and taking it over. How many armies in modern history have done that?"

"Just enough for us to make history I imagine," Piper said.

"There are other ways to do that," Rolnir countered. "Round up the commanders and send them over. We need to start now, before those Goblins Herger let go return to Rogscroft."

FIFTEEN

Prisoners Again

Bahr hated being underground. A lifetime on the open sea gave him freedoms he'd never experienced on land, or under it. His heart ached to taste the salt in the air, smell the fresh water and sea birds. The quest was slowly claiming him. Reducing him in ways he'd never imagined. He felt less of himself and that worried him greatly. The Sea Wolf. A captain without a vessel. With the *Dragon's Bane* burned away, he had no choice but to go on land. Only land wasn't so kind either. His estates, built off the riches of a lifetime of plunder and trade, suffered the same fate as his precious *Bane*, leaving Bahr displaced and aimless.

He leaned back against the smooth stone wall and wondered how his life had taken such drastic turns. Royalty never suited him. Even from a young boy he wanted nothing to do with the court or politics. He spent countless hours avoiding his obligations, allowing Badron the love and imagination of their father. Now that decision had turned on them all. Two kingdoms sunk in the downward spiral of war and the dark powers in the world steadily clawed their way back to relevance. Bahr felt lost. Like he stood at the bottom of a great pit without a way out.

There'd never been much love between brothers. One craved only power and the opportunity to carve out a great and bloody destiny. Bahr needed no such trappings. It didn't matter to him if future generations remembered his name. He was here, now. Let the future and past be damned by their own accord. His role in tomorrow's world diminished with each passing day. One day, perhaps soon, the final sun would rise and he could rest eternally.

"You're troubled."

He smirked. "It's the little things like this that make me glad we've got a wizard among us. What do you want, Anienam?"

"I see your troubles, ones the others know nothing of, lord of Delranan," Anienam whispered despite their being alone. "You cannot escape your past, not anymore."

Bahr snorted. "What would you know of my past? My sacrifices, what I gave up to find a better life. I could have let him die, you know. Oh it was long ago, when we were no more than boys. He'd gone out onto ice much too thin to support his weight. I tried to talk sense into him. It was still too early in the season for the ice to grow thick and strong, but he was ever the strong-headed one. He charged out onto the ice and challenged me. I all but begged him to come back to the shore. The ice cracked and gave way, pulling him down into the river. I rushed out without thinking and dragged him to safety."

Bahr paused to laugh. It was a dark and cruel sound. "He never did thank me. Called me a coward and stormed back to Chadra Keep. It never occurred to me how shallow and selfish he was becoming. The gift of hindsight is more a curse I think, don't you, wizard?"

"The past is how we learn, grow, and develop. We can only become better through analyzing our pasts and making corrections," Anienam countered thoughtfully. "Don't think to corner the idea of regret. My father lived during the time of the great Mage schism. He suffered from regret so great it eventually consumed his life. We all have burdens heaped upon us, but it is through our ability to rationalize and move forward that we overcome our pasts. Few creatures in this life have the option to create a better life."

"I fail to see how any of that matters," Bahr said. "If I had let my brother drown none of this would be happening."

"Of course it would," the wizard scolded. "You and Badron are only players in a centuries-old game being played out across Malweir. The dark gods want back in. It is only unfortunate circumstance that your lives are involved and if not you than it would be someone else. That is the way of the world, Bahr. We don't get to choose what happens to us. Life is neither that kind nor cruel."

"You make it sound as if mere happenstance guides us."

Anienam shrugged. "Perhaps it does."

"I can't accept that," Bahr said. "I have too many lives depending on me."

"Most of them are strong enough to see to themselves."

"I'm not talking about our group. I know their worth and it is great. Every one of us, except perhaps young Skuld, is capable of handling their own business. I mean the people of Delranan. With the king gone mad and the One Eye rampaging through the kingdom I've left my people powerless."

Realization dawned and Anienam nodded swiftly. "Delranan's problems aren't yours, Bahr. It was never yours to rule. You said so yourself."

"Even sheep need protecting," Bahr said. "Who better to take care of my people? Maleela is heir to the throne. I will see her put to power before the end or die in the attempt."

The sudden course change in the discussion left Anienam confused. Stopping the dark gods was their first priority, anything after that must wait. He hadn't considered the problems of the northern kingdom as anything more than internal complications. The princess was at the center of great controversy. He scolded himself for not seeing it clearly earlier. Maleela was such a large part of the entire affair and he'd barely noticed. A great destiny surrounded her, but to what end? He saw two paths, opposite and disparaging.

He gave Bahr's words careful consideration. Two paths. One led to enlightenment and prosperity. The other to unending darkness, wicked and vengeful. Which path would she take? He wished there were some way to guide her hand, force her in the right direction but destiny controlled the future. Maleela alone could make her decisions. Anienam wasn't comfortable at all with that.

"You have that dark tint to your eyes again," Bahr said suddenly.

Disturbed, Anienam looked up and feigned a smile. "Nonsense. I've got a little too much on my mind is all. Time is still our enemy. I haven't been able to figure out exactly when we need to return with the hammer but I can feel it in my bones. We need to find a way out of this kingdom and to the river."

"How do you propose we do that? These Dwarves aren't keen on making new friends and they damned sure don't trust you or me."

"Groge is the answer. He's as close to kin as they have, well, aside from Goblins, but I wouldn't bring that up. The wound is thousands of years old but still burns them." He stopped from dissembling again, barely. "We must get Groge to convince the king it's in his best interests to set us loose."

Bahr clapped his hands. "Great. How do we get those two together without being obvious?"

"I have no idea."

Silver platters heaped with mounds of roasted boar and venison were brought in. Baskets of fresh baked bread and fruits accompanied the meats. A wheel of yellow cheese and a barrel of dark ale finished the meal. Dour-faced Dwarves delivered the food cordially enough but said nothing. One actually bowed before closing the door behind him.

Nothol was the first to eat. There wasn't much point in waiting for the food to cool and he was starving. The others quickly joined in and all thoughts of the journey and their troubles were forgotten for the moment. Even Boen stopped brooding long enough to enjoy the bountiful feast provided by the Dwarves. Ionascu snatched a bite here and there, warily watching each of them for signs of treachery. He continued to fall deeper into madness with each passing day, a fact that left Bahr deeply troubled.

"I could almost enjoy staying here so long as they keep feeding us like this," Dorl announced with a loud burp. He used both hands to rub a full and extended belly. "Bahr, why haven't you ever traded with the Dwarves before? Their ale is the best I've ever had."

"You might not have noticed but we are prisoners in all but name," Bahr replied with the slightest hint of anger.

Groge yawned and stretched. The hall given to the group was large enough to accommodate the Giant's great height and was still secure enough to prevent them from getting into the main city. Four pillars stretched up to the smoothly crafted vaulted ceiling. Great murals of battles long past decorated the walls, illuminated by roaring fires from a pair of hearths on opposite ends of the hall. A dining hall, dozens of wooden tables large enough to fit twenty warriors stretched from end to end, leading up to a raised area holding the king's own table. The floor was dirt, a casual reminder for all Dwarves to never forget where they came from.

Groge felt confined this deep in the earth. "They seem goodly enough folk to me, though I have not the experience the rest of you do."

"Dwarves are normally very taciturn, but their civil war has made them worse. I'm surprised the king bothered with the time to see us," Anienam replied. "You seemed to have made quite an impression on him."

"I don't understand how," Groge said, confused. "How can our two races be kin?"

Boen reluctantly set down his chunk of bread to hear what the wizard had to say. The others also stopped what they were doing, placing unnecessary pressure on Anienam. Clearing his throat, the wizard said, "That story is one that comes down from the dawn of creation itself. The gods existed on planes we cannot comprehend. They grew bored and tiresome of their lives and sought to make a lasting legacy. Vastly powerful and without equal, it was inevitable factions grew among them. Some called for iron rule and the domination of all planes of existence. These fell into darkness and were consumed by their desires to obtain power and greed. We know them as the dark gods.

"The second group sought to empower themselves through enlightenment. They wanted to reach across the stars and build an empire that would last until the end of time. Peace and harmony drove their hands and for a while all was well. The gods, while split, continued to explore their universe, creating and destroying as was their wont." He paused to take a drink of ale, smiling at the smooth taste trickling down his throat.

"Some scholars suggest there was a war between the gods but how would any truly know? It's not as if the gods bestow their knowledge upon us. More popular theories tell us that rather than going to war, which would potentially destroy all life on all planes, they settled upon a contest of sorts. The gods agreed to create a world, crafted and birthed from their minds.

"When the gods of light finished building Malweir out of their dreams and desires they realized they needed people to cultivate what they built. Without proper care the world would wither and die, something the dark gods sought to achieve from the moment light first breathed across the lands. Thus the world was divided. Half remained light and half dark. For many years they warred over us, each side knowing what was right and just. Finally, the gods of light knew they couldn't defeat their dark brothers and offered a truce. They agreed to leave Malweir so long as the dark followed. The dark gods grew angry and created perversions among us. That is how Goblins and other foul creatures came to exist. We, my friends, are the unfortunate reminders of their bitter feud."

Anienam looked to each face, giving time for his words to soak in. "The dark is ever seductive. They lulled the gods of light into a false peace and then unleashed their war on Malweir. The battles were fierce. Hundreds died for no reason. With the aid of good men and women or all races the gods of light were able to banish their brothers. Hiding them away in another dimension. Equals, they could not kill one another. So without the presence of the dark gods to taint Malweir, the gods of light agreed to leave us to our devices. We were given the chance to grow and become what we wanted."

He fell silent, already lost in thoughts and possibilities.

"A fine tale, but one that doesn't help us much," Boen was the first to comment. "The Dwarves and Giants may once have been close kin but that relationship is strained."

"I think we're going about this all wrong," Bahr interrupted. He rose and stood in the center of the hall. "We're thinking small, of only our problems. What if we offered King Thord assistance in his war?"

Dorl spat a mouthful of ale. "What? Assistance? I didn't come here to fight someone else's war, Bahr."

"That's not what I'm suggesting. Thord's just like the rest of us. He's trapped in his way of thinking. We offer an outside view of the situation. Perhaps we can see something that hadn't occurred to him or his generals. I say we offer strategies, tactics, anything that will help give his army the upper hand against the other clans."

Boen grumbled. "A sound plan, but only if it works. You're not taking into account Dwarven pride. They will be cautious. Thord has the same weakness as many lesser men, vanity. He sees this war as an affront to his pride. The Dwarf king will be furious to salvage his reputation."

"You argue that this will work," Dorl added after finishing his ale.

The Gaimosian met his mocking with a mild shrug. "It may or may not. Don't be quick to think anyone wants to hear that their plan isn't working. All I know is that if we get the Dwarf king mad there's a good chance we find ourselves in another dungeon, unless the wizard is actually going to perform magic to get us out of this mess."

Anienam narrowed his eyes threateningly. "You know magic doesn't work like that."

Boen snorted and made for the barrel of ale. He'd heard enough and knew there wasn't anything but the waiting for now. Born in battle and raised by a series of bad experiences, he'd seen his share of foolishness and was content to let Bahr and the others stumble through their current predicament. So long as the ale continued to flow.

"We're getting off track," Bahr jumped in. "Groge, I need you to convince the king to let me have an audience."

The Giant chewed the last bit of bread thoughtfully, looking back and forth. He still didn't see how he could help much. Without the benefit of experience or interaction with anyone besides his own people he recognized that he was as much of a liability as the crippled man skulking in the shadows. The knowledge that he didn't fit in weighed heavily on him, but he had sworn oaths. Besides, he was the only one capable of wielding the Blud Hamr, if and when they managed to find it.

"I will do what I can," he finally said.

It was the best they could hope for.

SIXTEEN

Thord

Dwarves arrived shortly after to escort the Giant to their king. Each wore traditional armor with large, round shields strapped to their backs and a small hand axe at the side. Bahr spied odd-looking weapons strapped to their hips in leather pouches unlike anything he had ever seen. Asking questions being a pointless endeavor, the Sea Wolf sat quiet as Groge was taken away and the door slammed shut quickly after.

"Bastards enjoy their privacy, don't they?" Nothol remarked.

Anienam didn't bother looking up from his book. "They are a proud and secretive people, almost as ancient as the world itself. Wouldn't you do the same with so many strangers in your home?"

"That's where you're at a loss, wizard. Dorl and I don't have a home," the sell sword shook his head. "We take what we need and move on to the next job. There's no point in sticking around when we don't have to."

"You have a very narrow view on life," Anienam replied and went back to his reading. Everyone relied on him to give answers he wasn't sure he could deliver. The book was almost as ancient as himself and in broken languages seldom used.

"Why do you goad him so?" Rekka asked Dorl after everything died down. "He is a good man. One we need if we are to succeed."

Dorl thought for a moment and shrugged. "Oh I don't doubt we need him, but that doesn't mean I have to like him. His kind has always gotten under my skin."

"Kind?"

"The ones who acted better than everyone else. Doing what they want under the auspice of impunity," Dorl said and spat angrily. "Time and again I've seen their thoughts lead to foul deeds and corruption. Delranan suffers because of those like Anienam. Despite what Nothol claims I do think of Chadra as my home. I was born there. Raised there. It may not be perfect, but it is my home and I care for it nearly as much as Bahr."

Rekka blinked and cocked her head. "I've never heard you speak of home. I find it refreshing. Your people are so different from mine."

Dorl stayed silent. They'd spoken at great length on her homeland and her strange customs. He couldn't imagine being raised to fight from birth. The idea of watching brothers and sisters die at young ages, thrown to the predators of a hostile jungle sickened him greatly. He knew she was a much better person than he, but at what cost? Rekka never had the chance to find love or make a family. Her entire life seemed dedicated to the cause. That didn't seem right to him but he didn't know how to begin explaining that to her. She was just as proud as the Dwarves, more so perhaps and with good reason.

"How do you do it?" he finally asked.

"Do what?" Rekka asked.

"Live such a solitary life? You're a fine woman in every regard and I'm a better man for having met you, but I don't think I could live the way you do. I've never had much in the way of family except for Nothol but the thought of being so solitary in this world is frightening." Dorl stopped talking, realizing he was making a fool of himself.

Rekka smiled sweetly and cupped his cheek. "Dorl Theed, I am a product of my upbringing. We all do what we must. I was born for this purpose. It is inescapable. If it matters, I am deeply attracted to you."

"I like the sound of that," Dorl said and smiled back. He leaned forward and kissed her, enjoying the taste of her honey-covered lips.

Skuld absently listened to their conversation before moving to join the wizard on the far side of the hall. Still a youth and largely inexperienced, the street rat was forced to adulthood by means he'd once idolized. Dreams of battle and campaigning had filled his head at the beginning of this nightmare. If not for the deep-rooted desire to gain untold riches, he might never have followed Dorl and Nothol after the prince's funeral.

"You have questions, young Skuld?"

Embarrassed, Skuld quickly answered. "I didn't mean to intrude."

"But you did, else we would not be having this conversation. Tell me, what troubles you?" Anienam asked.

Where do I even begin? I used to think the world was small but never realized how wrong I was until now. How do I tell him I'm scared and want to go home? He exhaled sharply, long and pent up with frustration. "I don't think I belong here."

"Of course you do," the wizard grinned. "I've learned that we often underestimate our personal value. You have doubts, for obvious reasons. I know it feels like you haven't contributed much to our overall mission, but the time is coming soon when all that will change. I see a great destiny in you, Skuld. It is only a matter of time before it is revealed to your clouded eyes."

"You speak with a golden tongue, but it doesn't help the knot growing in my heart," Skuld replied. "Everyone here is a great warrior. I'm just a kid living on the streets."

"Do you truly believe that? Look around. Boen is the only warrior among us. The rest fight because they must. Poor Ionascu is better suited skulking in the shadows with a poisoned blade ready to plunge into an unsuspecting soul's back. He's no warrior but here he is. Dorl and Nothol quarrel far too much to stand in a shield wall in battle. They are glorified thieves, mercenaries at best. The princess hasn't needed to get her hands bloody, nor should she. Royalty needn't involve itself in the base adventures of the working class, I think. Do you think I'm a warrior as well? I can't recall the last time I had to kill a man. Monsters and whatnot don't really count or I might well be a mass murderer in some kingdoms. Ha!"

Skuld laughed despite his misgivings. "I'm not really that good of a thief, Anienam. I barely managed to get by before all this. What a fool I was."

"Fools don't often recognize the fact. Don't be too harsh on yourself, Skuld. Many don't learn their true path in life until much older than you are right now."

"When did you realize what you wanted to be?" Skuld asked.

"Me? Well, that's different. I never had a choice. My father raised me to follow in the line of Mages from the moment I made the mistake of speaking my first words," Anienam broke off his thoughts with a chuckle, sorrowful and empty. "I never got to be a child, or at least I don't remember it if I did. Mages and wizards are a prickly sort that take much getting used to, but once they figure things out they seem to do quite well in life. Not that there are any others running around Malweir, none that I know of at least. Come to think of it a few might have escaped the purges of the Mage Wars all those years ago, but they would have been hunted to ground quickly. Magic lost most of its relevance when the dark gods corrupted the crystal of Tol Shere and Sidian."

"You're the only wizard?" Skuld asked. He vaguely recalled having a similar conversation but that was long ago and so much had happened since, he remembered little.

"Unfortunately," Anienam replied solemnly. "I accepted the mantle from my father, reluctantly, mind you. The last of a dying breed is not the legacy you want to carry on."

Skuld was confused. "Why was magic attacked? Didn't people see that it wasn't the Mages' fault?"

"No. Once the war ended and the bodies were laid to rest people needed an outlet to turn their aggression and grief upon. Mage kind seemed the logical reaction given all that had happened. Bounty hunters and mercenaries scoured the corners of Malweir. The purges ended the formality of the order; the majesty had died. Do not be discouraged by this. Magic still exists, if perhaps in a baser form."

Skuld suddenly felt very small. Dreams of fortune fled, casually replaced by the idea of being swathed in regal robes. He imagined collecting power in his hands, becoming the embodiment of greatness in the name of a higher cause. Lost in the romance of it all, he asked, "Where did magic come from? How did the Mages begin?"

Anienam finally set the book down and leaned back, folding his hands over his stomach. "That is a story set in mystery and wonder. Magic, so far as we know, has always existed. A gift from the gods before they left or so the wisest of us wrote. The Mages, however, came from a very specific place. We've theorized that magic is inherent in many of us but can only be awoken by a subliminal trigger. Elves and Dwarves have had such powers long before man evolved, but it was in forgotten Gaimos that magic first appeared in men."

Skuld's eyes widened, forcing Anienam to chuckle.

"That's right. Home of our very own Boen. Gaimosians were highly receptive to the powers channeling up from the earth. After the fall Gaimos many fled east. They were drawn by something none understood. We know now that it was the pull of magic. They seemed destined to rise above what seemed like a war of annihilation and for a time they did. Magic flourished and the order of Mages grew rapidly. Soon enough Mages spread across Malweir in search of others. The order continued to grow. Ipn Shal was built to conserve our knowledge and provide a school to teach and learn. Mage kind soon occupied the most important positions in many courts."

"It must have been a grand time," Skuld said breathlessly.

"I trust it was, one I wish I would have seen," Anienam said. "Ipn Shal is nothing but haunted ruins now. A memory of what used to be. I fear when I am gone so too will the wealth of ages' worth of knowledge. It is a sad thing, but inevitable."

The doors opened suddenly with the quiet echoing sound of hobnailed boots marching in. Groge stalked behind a quartet of guards. His face struggled to conceal the raw emotions chewing his insides. As much as he wanted to shout out the news from Thord, he had been given specific instructions to not speak in front of the entire group. The king hadn't exactly threatened to go to war against Venheim so much as insinuate it. Regardless, Groge decided prudence was his best course of action.

"Bahr and Anienam Keiss, you are summoned to an audience with the king of Drimmen Delf," the Dwarf captain announced with a deep, thunderous voice. Even Boen appeared impressed with the commanding tone.

"It's about time," Bahr muttered under his breath, failing to consider Dwarves' outstanding hearing.

Scowling, the Dwarf captain patiently waited for the Men to join them. Silver ingots were plaited in his long beard, giving an almost regal appearance. Bahr studied the Dwarf as he got closer. Barely four feet tall, he was nothing but a mass of muscle with a perpetually angry scowl. Bahr almost felt they might have been friends in another life. Silver torcs wrapped around his biceps, the same colors as his eyes.

"Follow me," the Dwarf growled and spun about.

Bahr waited until they were well down the torch-lit corridor before asking, "How long did it take to make all this?"

The Dwarf passed a secretive glare to his companions. "All what?"

"Your city."

Muscles flexing, the Dwarf stopped abruptly and whirled on Bahr. "Drimmen Delf is the jewel of the Dwarven kingdoms, matching your Paedwyn."

"I've never been myself but I hear it's a real nice place," Bahr countered, refusing to be cowed by his keepers.

The Dwarf scowled fiercely. He wanted to attack but feared the repercussions from King Thord. Discipline was held highly in their society and any lapse, intentional or otherwise, would be met sternly. A public shaming would hound him for generations.

"Drimmen Delf was built on the sweat of thousands of Dwarves over one hundred years. Few are those permitted within our halls, especially those not of our kind. King Thord is a proud man and brokers no ill will towards other races; neither does he find time for their inconveniences. You would do well to mind your tongue in his presence."

"I've had enough of kings, Master Dwarf. Comes from my brother being a lousy one," Bahr sneered. "I'll show your king the respect due, don't fret."

"Enough of this pointless banter!" Anienam scolded them both. "You are the brother of the king of Delranan and you are the voice of the king of Drimmen Delf. I expect you to behave as such. We have important matters to discuss and I don't need the two of you acting like children."

Properly scolded, Bahr and the Dwarf nodded to each other and continued on to the throne room. King Thord sat well back on the throne, a leg up and chewing on a meat-covered bone. A handful of advisors milled around the base of the throne all muttering for attention. Stacks of parchments piled high upon the old table brought in for these meetings. Thord had little patience for the politics behind running a kingdom. He was bred to be a warrior and only ascended to the throne because of a foolish clause built in to Dwarven law. Never wanting to be king, he reluctantly settled in and realized he was in over his head. He was content to let the advisors try and figure out how best to run the kingdom while plans of warfare fell in his lap.

He looked up at Bahr and Anienam with relief. "Ah, the pirate and his wizard friend returned with my new Giant friend! Thank the gods. I grow wearisome of my advisors and their petitions. The young Giant tells me you wish to speak of the war. Good. I am more comfortable dealing with battles and troop movements. Be gone, lowly ones. I have important matters to discuss."

Thord brushed his advisors off with grease-stained fingers and they filed away with mocking bows and curses under their breath. "Damned bureaucrats will be the death of me. I need to feel a good axe in my hand and the sting of wind on my bloodstained face again. Wars make us who we are. This," he gestured to the expansive throne room, "This drives us all mad."

"Precisely why I never wanted to fall into the trappings of kingship," Bahr replied.

Thord regarded him for a moment, his eyes crisp and accusing. "A wise man. If only I had been so fortunate. Alas I wasn't and here I sit, trapped in a world not of my making."

"There's a lot of that going on, your majesty," Bahr replied. Most of his earlier animosity was gone, replaced by the idea of getting his people set free and on their way to Trennaron.

The Dwarf king nodded thoughtfully. "My captains tell me you have ideations on our little civil war. Tell me, what know you of Dwarf wars?"

"Absolutely nothing but that doesn't mean I don't know war," Bahr said. "As we speak, my brother wages war on two kingdoms. Three great peoples are being subsumed under the heavy strain of combat and slaughter, all at the behest of the dark gods and their pawns on Malweir."

"You expect me to believe this nonsense? There are no gods left on Malweir. Everyone knows that. We are alone here. The old gods fled, leaving us to our own perversions."

Anienam stepped forward. "That's not entirely true, King Thord. The gods may be gone, but the dark gods are forever seeking to return and lay claim. Their agents walk among us, seeking to turn great men evil and ruin as many lives as they can in the process. They have come to the northern kingdoms with lies and temptations. Bahr's brother has succumbed to their whims, no more than a puppet in a great lie. Their war has already engulfed two kingdoms and threatens to spread across the entire north. How long before it reaches these halls?"

"What proof do you have, wizard-son?" Thord asked, eyes raised. His superstitious side wanted to believe, to accept the gods hadn't abandoned Malweir at all. His practical side, however, demanded more than what he'd just heard. He needed proof if he was expected to give in and aid these Humans on their quest. Thousands of Dwarves depended on his judgments to guide them in the right directions. Going to war against the powers of darkness definitely wasn't in Drimmen Delf's best interests.

"Physical proof? None, but your scouts will be able to confirm we are being tracked by a trio of Harpies. We travel with one of the Giants of Venheim, a race practically none thought existed anymore, to the fabled city of Trennaron to retrieve the Blud Hamr. Check with your scholars. They can confirm the Hamr's only use. Don't be so quick to abandon rationale, Dwarf king. Malweir's history is laced with times when the dark gods tried to return."

"I know all that, but what you speak of is ancient history," Thord protested, weakly. "Present times have no need for gods or their return. How will any of this help me in my war against the Dark Dwarves?"

Bahr cleared his throat with a sudden thought. "Perhaps by admitting that these Dark Dwarves were turned by the very powers we seek to stop and come to pen you under your mountains while the true war rages elsewhere, effectively removing you from the equation entirely."

Thord opened and closed his mouth, teeth snapping shut harshly. "You suggest we are not relevant? Dwarves have lived under these mountains for millennia. Much of your great treasures were built from our sweat, human. Don't think to come into my throne room and threaten me when I give in to whim and grant your audience."

"That's not what he meant," Anienam rushed to stop the damage. "Bahr speaks a measure of truth. You are too close to the situation. Too used to thinking the same way. We merely seek to give you an outside perspective that will help you turn the tide and end your war as quickly as possible."

"While convincing me to let you cross my lands on your foolish quest," Thord finished tartly.

Anienam flashed his most charming smile. "We're not really asking for much compared to what we're willing to deliver."

Thord's laughter rumbled across the room like a thunderstorm breaking the heavens. His face burned crimson and tears trickled from the corners of his eyes. "I've fought in many wars, wizard. I know my business well. The Dark Dwarves will break on our shields and flee the field. We are the Dwarves of Drimmen Delf and no greater force can be fielded in all Malweir."

"Let us help you and you can add to your combat effectiveness. We have a Giant and our very own Gaimosian Knight, not to mention the talents of one of the last remaining wizards."

Bahr cast Anienam a reluctant glare. *Not much of wizard if you ask me. I've had better stable boys.*

Thord's expression turned dark suddenly, serious. "And we have weapons the likes of which have never been seen in any other kingdom."

"This is pointless, Anienam. He's not willing to budge and we're wasting our time. Let's just get the hells out of here," Bahr snapped, unwilling to sit through the charade any longer.

"How dare you!" Thord raged. He leapt up, dropping his meat in the process. "I give the courtesy of hearing your schemes and you insult me to my face. By my beard! I ought to have you all strung up by your necks and cast from the mountainside."

"My lord I assure you there is no need for that," Groge interrupted. "These are good people, with good hearts. I confess I do not understand their ways, but I trust them entirely. We must be allowed to find the Hamr. All our fates hinge on it."

Hearing the Giant's words calmed him slightly, but Thord remained incensed at Bahr's casual disregard. Others lost their heads for less. Pride struggling with prudence, the Dwarf king managed to retake his seat and breathe normally. "Were it not for your Giant friend you'd already be dead, but he is kin and I will heed his words. Captain Ironfoot."

The gruff Dwarf captain edged closer, hand hovering over his axe. "My lord?"

"I am putting our guests in your care for now. See to it they are fed and given the opportunity to clean up. Tomorrow they will march with me to the forward command center at Bode Hill. They want to fight our war, let them."

Bahr and Anienam exchanged unmistakable looks. *What have we gotten ourselves into*?

SEVENTEEN

A Different Kind of War

Cold winds whipped across the plain, making Bahr shiver. He pulled his bearskin cloak tight and scanned the gentle, rolling hills stretching for leagues to the south. A wide plain at the base of the hill that was once peaceful and serene had been transformed into an ugly network of trenches, bunkers, and wire obstacles. A scattering of broken skeletons littered the area. He had seen war before, but nothing like this.

Monstrous engines of a sort were dug in positions behind both lines. Mostly iron, they had large, round barrels and were built on carriages. Each was manned by six Dwarves. Stockpiles of ammunition were stored close by. Bahr couldn't imagine any use for them. Catapults and ballistae required leverage and used stone and arrow. All he saw were round balls of black metal.

Thousands of infantry massed in ranks stretching across the valley. The sounds of smiths and armorers repairing weapons and armor hovered over the encampment. Great fires burned, packs of Dwarves huddled around them for warmth. Unlike in the great halls, they were somber. Days of trench warfare had turned to weeks, and weeks to months. They were haggard, ready for the tide to break so they could wipe their enemy from the field.

Bahr squinted as breaking sunlight struck the hundreds of iron barriers in front of the trenches. Each was massive and shaped like an "x." Beyond that lay strand upon strand of wire. Bahr had never seen the like. Wars were meant to be fluid, not static like this. Most armies didn't rely on defenses or barriers. The Wolfsreik attacked with speed and strength, smashing their enemies under great weight. The Dwarves seemed content with digging in and waiting.

"What are those barriers?" he asked.

Ironfoot grunted his displeasure at being questioned by an outsider. "We call them dragon teeth. They are quite effective at halting an infantry assault."

Bahr nearly asked if there was a cavalry threat before catching the foolishness of it. Dwarves held a natural dislike for horses, much preferring to go on foot. They kept and bred ponies for their wagons and merchants but very few bothered to ride such beasts.

"And those machines behind us?"

Ironfoot laughed. "Something special our engineers have developed. They are much more powerful than catapults. We call them cannons."

"Alchemy?" Anienam asked. His curiosity got the better of him and he needed to know more. No other kingdom, in so far as he knew, held such destructive power. He knew this might change warfare for all Malweir too soon. And if the dark gods got their hands on this technology…he let the thought die.

"That is not my place to say nor am I inclined to tell you more, wizard," Ironfoot replied. "We are at war and you are not privileged to know our secrets. It is only by the grace of King Thord that you stand upon Bode Hill."

He led them down into the trenches under the watchful stares of battle-hardened Dwarves who had already seen too much. They quickly forgot their own worries, as well as Bahr and Anienam, and focused on Groge. Whispers spread through the ranks. The Giants had returned! Some nodded. Others raised their fists and cheered. Renewed hope invigorated them.

"You inspire them, Groge," Bahr said. He hoped this would give them more leeway to help and then be set free. Every second they spent dithering here drew them closer to an unwanted end.

Groge only shook his head, trying his best to return their cheers and smiles. "I don't know how. I am just an apprentice and still very young. What can I give to such a strong people?"

Anienam added, "Hope. What more can any army in the field ask for?"

Ironfoot halted outside of a massive iron door and used his axe handle to rap on it three times. A pair of Dwarves appeared to open it and ushered the others inside. King Thord already awaited them. He'd traveled earlier with a small retinue to the front lines to get a better tactical picture of the siege lines. He watched Bahr enter, grave misgivings lurking behind his eyes. The king of the Dwarves had no need for Men or wizards but had given his oath to let them attempt to convince him they could help. So many had already fallen Thord was willing to take almost any chance. The war had to end before their culture dwindled past the point of reparation.

"I trust Captain Ironfoot wasn't too harsh in bringing you here," Thord rumbled.

"We're used to it by now," Bahr replied and quickly added, "You have an impressive defensive array. How similar is the enemy's?"

"Damned near alike," Thord said. "They attack us and we them. Day in and day out it is much the same. This is a war of attrition, nothing else."

"I don't understand. Offense is your best weapon. Why not unleash all your cannons and send the weight of your army? You could crush their lines and drive them from the field."

"Don't you think we've already tried that? The bastards have the same weaponry and are just as effective. Hundreds died in that first assault," Thord fumed. "But we made them pay in return. They broke on our iron and ran back to their trenches."

Bahr walked over to the large table dominating the room. A detailed terrain map filled it, complete with moveable icons for units. Bahr had seen maps before but this was much more. It couldn't be picked up or taken places. Reminding him of his childhood toys, the map was more of a playground than anything else. He studied it intently, ignoring everything and everyone else. The river laid a few leagues to the east, almost entirely inaccessible from the bunker. Enemy trench lines extended to the banks in a failed effort at cutting off Thord's troops from potential reinforcements from other holds.

A series of four trenches filled the space between lines. Each was interconnected with bunkers and heavy weapon emplacements. Bahr couldn't imagine the destructive firepower either Dwarf army had and for two equally matched forces to be in the same valley was tantamount to the end of the world. He didn't see any way around the battle that wouldn't take them weeks out of the way. Bahr started to think they'd made a mistake coming into Dwarf lands.

Then he spied what he was searching for: a small forest running the length of the mountains south. Certainly not big or thick enough to hide a large attacking force but more than adequate for him to sneak a handful of men behind enemy lines. The Dark Dwarves would have picket lines established well into the trees, perhaps even to the base of the mountains. The way wouldn't be easy but he was almost confident he could manage under the cover of darkness.

Besides, it was the only way he found that even remotely led to them being set free.

Staving off depression, he turned to the bank of windows stretching across the main wall. Observers and map caretakers busily noted troop dispositions and made adjustments to the map table. Senior commanders conferred in hushed tones from various corners. While all eyes were focused on the enemy, no one had any fresh ideas that would lead to a total breakout. The Dwarf army was locked in a stalemate.

Bahr whistled under his breath at the scope of devastation gripping the valley. Huge craters, presumably from the cannons, pockmarked the land. Burn marks, dark and terrible, littered the ground in angry scars. A handful of skeletons continued to rot in the middle of the no man's land. Smoke from a dozen funeral byres drifted up in lazy columns, contaminating the already dreary sky. Broken strands of wire and wooden posts lay in tangled heaps. Old shields and axes were scattered recklessly, forgotten where they'd fallen in one retreat or the next.

"So, you've convinced me to let you come to my forward command center and see the battlefield for yourself. What's next?" Thord demanded.

Bahr barely managed to shake his head in disbelief. "War is not supposed to be like this. I have seen battles before but this, this is slaughter without purpose."

"This is how Dwarves fight. Sooner or later one side will make a mistake and the gates will be opened," Thord replied. "We are a patient folk. Hasty decisions do not become us."

"Even at the expense of so many lives?"

"The gods claim us when they wish. Ours is a solitary purpose."

Bahr refused to accept the melancholic approach to war. "There has to be a better way, one that will end this siege and reduce the number of dead and wounded."

Thord crossed his massive arms across his chest. "What do you suggest?"

"Those cannons are your problem. Take them out and you can run the field."

The Dwarf king shook his head. "Don't you think we haven't tried? Their lines are too well developed. The cannons are dug in better than our own and out of range. We'd need a dragon to get to them."

"Or someone not attached. You say these Dark Dwarves were once your kin?" Bahr said.

Thord nodded.

"That means they think like you, act like you. They fight like you do, right down to the same weapons. We can give you the ability to think differently. We don't understand your ways and that makes us dangerous. Your enemies won't be expecting outsiders to come to your aid. We can slip behind their lines and take out those cannons. That will open the way for a full-frontal assault."

"You will not find the task as easy as you think," a new voice said from the doorway.

Bahr turned in time to see an Elf walk in and remove his plumed helmet. Long, dark hair fell past his shoulders, framing his smallish face. The very tips of his pointed ears stuck through the hair. His eyes were hard like diamonds. A small scar ran under his chin and down the right side of his neck, old and past scabbed over. The Elf was lean, wiry but full of strength. His armor was dark, befitting the grueling contest he had come to fight. Only his boots were clean. Bahr could see the reflection of his face in their shine.

"I am Faeldrin," the Elf announced and extended his hand in the Human custom.

Stunned speechless yet again, Bahr stumbled to recover. "Bahr. This is…"

Faeldrin bowed crisply. "Anienam Keiss, greetings, wizard. It has been a very long time."

"A long time for me perhaps but the days go slower for your kind," Anienam grinned back and embraced

Faeldrin with the warmth of rekindled friendship. "I had no idea you were in this part of the world."

"King Thord is a strong ally to our king in Elvanara. It is a great honor to fight alongside his Dwarves again." Faeldrin removed his leather riding gloves, cracked and faded from years of use. "The Aeldruin hold no true allegiance to the Elven kingdoms, nor do the whims of kings hold sway over us, but we honor our oaths of kinship and loyalty. Some wars need to be fought, my friend. But come, why are you here? This is no place for tourists or travelers."

Bahr's eyes widened and slowly reverted back to normal. The Aeldruin were legends. An Elven mercenary unit, they roamed Malweir in search of righteous causes. Bahr had read where they helped kill a dragon and defeat the Goblin hordes in the Dead Lands long ago. Fierce and relentless, they were counted among the very best soldiers in the world. His hopes sank. If the best were here and Thord still hadn't found a way to break the enemy lines, what could he and his small band of cobbled misfits do?

"We are on a mission of the highest order. I'm afraid more than just this war affects the northern kingdoms. Several kingdoms to the west have already broken out in war and violence. The dark gods are seeking to return and claim dominance. The Dae'shan are loose again."

Faeldrin's face darkened. "Their kind should have been wiped out long ago. It's only through blind chance they escaped us."

"Berating ourselves over the past is pointless, Faeldrin. We must look to the future if any of us are to survive," Anienam said.

"They killed my brother, Anienam. I have a debt to repay."

"Your loyalty is admirable, as always. Which is why I've counted on you like my father did during his time. The Aeldruin are one of the most valuable assets the power of light has. It is fortunate you are here."

Faeldrin barked a laugh, light yet crisp. "A healthy purse doesn't hurt either. No matter what else we may be, my Elves are mercenaries at heart. Why else would we fight someone else's war? Enough talk of me. We're stuck here. The enemy is just as powerful as our friends and we haven't found a way to move them from the field."

"What about the forest at the base of the mountains?" Bahr asked, wanting an explanation for his earlier dismissal.

Faeldrin led him to the map table. "The forest would be a good option if not for a few problems. The Dark Dwarves are cunning and malicious. They have spiked the lanes leading up to the forest edge with caltrops. Our horses cannot go there. Also, my scouts have reported recent earthwork done, but for what purpose I cannot say. My guess is for more traps in case any of Thord's troops have the same idea. Crossbows are ideal weapons for fighting under a canopy but with the way trapped we will be at the disadvantage. Our best bet is to cross the mountains and come up behind them from the south."

"There is too much at risk for such a maneuver. Those bastards would notice a sharp decline in my lines and charge the moment struck. They'd be at my doors before we could muster the strength to halt them," Thord snarled.

Bahr felt the conversation slipping away. He had to find a way to turn their minds in his favor. "Precisely why I am volunteering my services."

"A prince of the north is well and fine, but what else have you?" Faeldrin asked. "My Aeldruin are fierce warriors and even we are not strong enough to break this stalemate."

"I've got a Gaimosian Knight, a wizard, a woman from Trennaron, and my young Giant friend, among others," Bahr replied. "We can break through and destroy those cannons. All you have to do is be ready to attack once we do."

They stared at each other for a long while. Each processed what he'd heard in their own manner. The impossible slowly started to become reality. A new sense of optimism arose and it spread like an infection. Generals and captains immediately reexamined their plans for a mass charge, studying and debating where the enemy would be the weakest. Any distraction would draw combat power and attention from the front. Bahr's plan might work if only they could reach the cannons in one piece.

Thord's deep laugh broke the silence. "Damned foolish of us all to even be considering such folly, but by the gods I like it! This needs to happen quickly. Timing is everything."

"I agree," Bahr said, secretly thankful the others were coming around. "I can have my group ready to go within the hour."

"Don't leave until the middle of the night. That will give you enough time to sneak through the forest and come out by their cannons. I'll give you two hours before I have my commanders begin an artillery barrage. The distraction will take all attention from you."

"How can we be sure?" Anienam asked.

Faeldrin said, "Because they know their cannons can't reach ours. Neither side has bothered making an infantry assault for weeks. They won't have any reasons to expect one tonight."

"There's the possibility their front ranks will pull back, closer to their cannons," Bahr theorized.

"Possible but not too likely. Each side is dug in effectively. There's no need to pull back out of range. If you make it that far," Faeldrin paused, "You shouldn't face much resistance. I think I am beginning to find the merit in your plan, Bahr."

He rubbed his chin ruefully. "It hasn't worked yet."

"Nonsense. Every good plan begins somewhere," Thord encouraged. "Captain Ironfoot, select ten Dwarves to accompany you. I want them ready and inspected within the hour. We're going to break them tonight and put an end to this damned war. Come, let us feast before this great adventure."

They filed back into the trenches in silence. Each man contemplating what might happen once the sun went down and the vagaries of warfare took over.

EIGHTEEN

Drimmen Delf

An emissary from King Thord had arrived not long after Bahr and the others had been taken away. The former prisoners were now officially guests and allowed the liberty of exploring the mighty Dwarven kingdom. Maleela grabbed Skuld and took off exploring. The others chose to stay and rest. The unexpected freedom could only mean one thing: a deal had been made and the time for action was fast approaching.

Maleela strode through Drimmen Delf with caution and respect even though most Dwarves bowed politely to her. Word had already spread that she was a princess and all who encountered her did so with reverence. She'd blushed at first but had gotten to the point where she hardly noticed. Drimmen Delf was packed with Dwarves. She smiled back and returned the bows.

"This is a wondrous place," Maleela commented. She'd been in total awe from the moment they stepped into the smoothly planed corridors.

Skuld couldn't help but agree. "I expected a hole filled with worms and nasty dirt. I never knew anyone could make something like this underground."

"They are masters of their craft. Look at the designs in the columns and on the ceiling. We have nothing like this in Delranan. And do you see how polite they all are?" she breathed in wonder. "I would love to have such freely given adoration, but my father's rage and greed have stolen that from me. I am as unwanted as the cold winter storm."

"You have majesty about you," Skuld said suddenly. "I am glad you are my princess."

She halted and looked him in the eye for the first time since abandoning Delranan. It was hard to think of him as a man. He'd been a naïve boy when they first met aboard the

Dragon's Bane, but the combination of experience and necessity had turned him into a man. Ordinarily she never would have bothered with one like him. Born to the streets, Skuld represented everything wrong with the kingdom. Or so she had believed. *How wrong have I been, and about how much? This boy thinks unselfishly and I struggle to find a way to look past my prejudices. What does that say of me?*

"Why, Skuld, I believe you are growing up on us," she said lightly. "It feels good to have someone my age to talk to. The others are older and already jaded by their experiences. I think the world needs more people like us."

He gave her a queer look. Life was anything but kind, especially to people like him. He'd been pushed to the edge of starvation and had to steal everything he owned. What good could possibly come out of that? She, on the other hand, was born into a life of luxury and had been pampered for the majority of her life. Their worlds should never have mixed.

"I didn't think the world wanted anything to do with the dregs," he replied, careful to guard his true feelings.

He knew he shouldn't, but he resented her all the same. Born into wealth and power, it was only chance that left her abandoned by fate. True, Maleela suffered from the abject hatred of her father, but it wasn't technically her fault. She didn't choose to be born. Deep down Skuld recognized the shortcoming in his thoughts, but that didn't stop him from despising everything she stood for.

Maleela offered a sympathetic look. "Skuld, you are a very special young man. The others see it as well, else you wouldn't be here. Anienam chose wisely when he assembled this group. Even if they are misfits and conspiratorial outcasts," she added with a sly wink.

He couldn't keep from laughing. The idea of being lobbed into a group of like-minded misfits encouraged him. They walked on, exploring as much of Drimmen Delf as their legs could take. Dining halls and kitchens the size of Chadra Keep were strewn, seemingly at random, throughout the city. Fresh baked bread beckoned from giant ovens. A collage of smells clung to the walls and high ceilings. For such a diminutive race the Dwarves enjoyed towering ceilings and spacious rooms.

They'd been wandering for hours when Maleela finally guided them into a kitchen and, after a brief exchange with the cooks, sat down to a small meal of bread, cheese, and ale. "You know, I feel more at home here than I ever did in my own."

Chewing a chunk of bread, Skuld decided to ask, "What was it like? Growing up in a castle with a king for a father?"

If she took offense she didn't show it. "Torture. My father and I never saw eye to eye. He blames me for the death of my mother and still had the audacity to use it as a basis for his war against Rogscroft. Men are wicked creatures, Skuld."

"Bahr and the rest seem good enough," he countered.

Maleela saw the insult burning his cheeks and quickly corrected herself. "I didn't mean men as in males. I mean our entire race. Men. We could learn a lot from Dwarves and Giants."

He was about to reply when the most beautiful sound echoed into the kitchen. Even the cooks stopped what they were doing to listen. Skuld became instantly mesmerized. Even Maleela felt the dizzying effects. Soon she began to sway to the sound. Her eyes grew droopy and she felt like crying.

"What is that?" she asked dreamily.

One of the cooks ambled over and took up their empty mugs. "That is the sound of our mothers singing to the newborn. You will never hear a greater chorus in any land."

"It's beautiful," she agreed.

Skuld broke into a wide grin. His heart felt light for the first time he could remember. The simple song stole his tiredness and despair. His pains were forgotten. He felt like a new man; one capable of conquering the world in the name of freedom and justice. He was no longer Skuld the street urchin, but something else. Unnamable. Changed.

"Take a care though," the cook warned. "Dwarven women are stronger than men and twice as mean when it comes to the children."

He stomped off, leaving Skuld and Maleela free to wander on. Without even communicating the pair started to follow the sounds of the music. Both wanted, needed to see what could possibly produce such god-like sounds. Dwarves brushed past on their own business. Several sniggered and barked deep laughs at the humans. Skuld didn't care. He pushed on as if in a trance until he reached the entrance to a great hall larger than any he'd seen thus far.

What they found in the hall defied logic. Massive chandeliers filled with oil lanterns hung low, bathing the room in heat and light. Grand tapestries covered the walls. Most depicted epic moments in Drimmen Delf's history. Others portrayed the basest form of enjoyment for children of any race. Pillows and mattresses filled the room with opulence. Dwarf mothers ambled around the room, most holding young to their shoulders as they sang. There was an undeniable atmosphere of warmth, love. The luxury of the Dwarf nursery surpassed every expectation the pair might have held. Maleela felt her mouth drop. Skuld whistled low.

The nearest Dwarf nurse spotted them and smiled before walking towards them.

"I…we didn't mean to intrude," Maleela said once the initial shock began to wear off.

The Dwarf bowed. "Nonsense. You would know if you intruded upon us, Princess."

"You know me?" she gasped.

The Dwarf laughed. "Of course. This is a small hold. Word travels fast, especially when it concerns royalty. Be welcome here. You as well, young Skuld. We have learned of you too."

Skuld couldn't do much more than blush and look down at his oddly shuffling foot.

The Dwarf gave Maleela a wink. "The lad needs a good woman to strip away that shyness. I know a few girls who might be willing to help."

Shock ripped open Skuld's eyes. "No! Er, I.... I couldn't!"

"Relax, Skuld. I am merely trying to lighten the mood. Do not be so quick to take all matters so seriously. Life is very short, even for us with long lives. Time goes by so fast, too often we stand on death's door wondering where it all went and what we can do to buy another day or two."

"We have seen much death on our trip," Maleela echoed.

"Such is the way of things. There is but one thing you can do. Meet death with arms wide open and accept the fact that you have done all you wished to do. No true warrior is afraid of death. The brave are favored by the gods."

Dreams sparked in Skuld's mind. Buoyed by the intensity of his current feelings, he imagined storming across distant battlefields, armed with sword and righteousness. He knew he wasn't a great warrior, nor was he much of a fighter, but he also knew he was destined to make a difference. He just didn't know how.

"We should be going," he said to Maleela.

"So soon? Is it our singing?" the Dwarf chided.

He shook his head fiercely.

Maleela stepped in to prevent further embarrassment. "Your singing is divine. What do you sing about?"

The Dwarf watched Skuld for another moment. "We sing the songs of our mothers, back through time to the beginning. Our heritage is most important and we honor the past by continuing the simplest traditions. Each Dwarf maiden is taught the song from youth and trained to sing it for years. There is no higher honor than to be selected to attend the youth rooms and sing. I have been here for nearly five years."

Maleela watched the women cradling their children, not sure that any were paired correctly, and felt her heart swell. Several children ran about and played. There didn't seem to be a care in the world. She felt as if she could stay here for the rest of her life, but Skuld was right. They needed to get back to the others. No doubt Bahr had returned and plans were already being made.

"Thank you for granting us the opportunity to experience this," she said. "The honor is ours and I can speak for both of us when I say that we will be changed for the better because of it. Thank you."

The Dwarf smiled warmly and placed a gentle hand on Maleela's forearm. "You are quite welcome, Princess. Be safe on your travels and may the sun never set on you."

Maleela bowed, forcing Skuld to follow suit. The Dwarf returned to the nursery already singing. Satisfied for reasons neither truly understood, Skuld and Maleela all but skipped back to the hall.

They found the others right where they'd left them, with the addition of Bahr, Anienam, and Groge, who'd returned some time ago. A few heads picked up when Maleela and Skuld entered but went right back to what they were doing. Weapons were being sharpened. Packs lightened. Dark paints were being applied to exposed skin, faces and arms. Armor was piled neatly on the tabletops. Maleela noticed the handful of Dwarves busy conducting the same preparations on the opposite side of the hall.

"What have we missed?" she asked her uncle.

Bahr scarcely looked up from the small map Ironfoot had provided. "The king has granted us permission to end his war, or so that's what we hope will happen. We have to be ready shortly."

Rekka raised her freshly darkened blade up to the light and carefully inspected it for any spots she missed. Satisfied, she sheathed the weapon and went to her gear.

"We're fighting their war now?" Maleela asked, stunned.

"No, just helping turn the tide and break the stalemate. Maleela, we need to get to the river and this is the only way. The Dark Dwarves have us sewn in."

"But I thought he agreed to let us go?"

Bahr set down his pencil and looked at his niece. "Maleela, we must do this if we plan on getting to Trennaron on time. All other options are far too time consuming. If this works we'll be on our way by tomorrow night."

"If not?" she argued.

He shrugged. "It won't matter."

"Enough talk. We have much to do if we're to make it by the deadline," Boen grumbled from across the table.

Maleela felt instant rage at being casually dismissed by the Gaimosian. "I am speaking to my uncle."

"No, you are wasting his time. Much needs to be planned for if we are to come back with as many as possible alive, young princess."

Bahr stepped between them. "I'm sorry but he's right. Maleela, you'll be staying behind along with Skuld, Ionascu, and Anienam. Don't fight me on this either. My decision is final. We're going behind their lines and none of you have any battle experience. Captain Ironfoot is bringing a small troop with him to support us so we should be fine."

He grabbed her by the shoulder before she could protest and pulled her close. "I know you wish to fight. It makes you special but it also damages your perception. I need you here to watch over the wizard and our broken spy. We are still being hunted by more than just the Harpies. I believe Ionascu is still working for Harnin. Think what damage he might cause if he slips a blade in the old wizard's heart when no one is paying attention. You are the most capable one I have."

She didn't like it one bit but reluctantly admitted the logic of it. The few hours of casual sword training weren't remotely comparable to what the others had gone through. She watched Boen roll his shoulders, stretching out his muscles. He swung his sword in great loops. The whooshing sound filled the hall. Cold dread suddenly filled her as she realized they were preparing to go to war. She'd been wrong to want to go. Despite the strength of her desires, she knew she didn't have the inert ability to slaughter others. Maleela calmly walked over to Bahr and wrapped her arms around him.

"Be safe, Uncle. We need you back here," she whispered.

His heart filled with pride and worry. Bahr had always looked on Maleela like she was his own daughter. His only regret was never having children. Slowly at first, he hugged her back. "We'll be back before you know it. Have the others ready to leave. I don't want to stay here any longer than necessary."

"We'll be ready," she affirmed.

They disengaged and Bahr turned to the others. "All right, let's go. It's time."

One by one they finished sheathing weapons and filed out of the hall. Ironfoot and his Dwarves went first, leading them down through the winding tunnels to the edge of the mountain walls. They marched in silence. Everyone's thoughts were bent on doing what needed doing to survive. The Dwarves were the most solemn. They'd already spent far too long in the trenches, battling their one-time kin for reasons no one knew.

Bahr glanced over to Boen. He trusted the Gaimosian with his life but secretly wondered if that was enough? Boen was prone to bouts of extreme violence capable of ruining everything they'd worked so hard to accomplish. It was a partnership of convenience. Bahr needed the muscle to keep the others in line and the quest on track. That didn't keep him from worrying Boen might break away one day and go off on his own. They were friends, but how far did friendship really go when faced with the end of the world? He tried to push the thoughts out and focus on what came next.

It had been a long time since he'd last been in a battle. The tactics and movements were the same. War seldom changed. His strength wasn't what it had once been, nor his prowess. Bahr was much older now. His body ached in places he didn't know he had. He grew tired more easily. Thankfully he didn't have to stand in the shield wall. This type of mission suited him just fine. Get in, wreak as much havoc as possible, and get back out again. He only hoped they managed to take the enemy by surprise. Otherwise…

Ironfoot stopped abruptly and nodded to one of the others. The Dwarf reached into a shadowed alcove and unlocked the hidden door leading out of the mountains. Fresh air swelled into the small entry room. The skies were almost black.

"This path leads down into the forest. There will be no talking from here. Even the smallest noise will betray our position. We are entering the warzone. If you fall behind you will be on your own. The mission is too great to risk stopping for one man. Understood?"

"Time's wasting," Boen answered for them all.

Ironfoot nodded and drew his sword. "Let's go."

NINETEEN

The Rebellion Splinters

Delranan was consumed by a darkness no one understood. The evil taint clinging to the air permeated the most holy of things. Most felt like a curse had fallen and was slowly devouring the ancient kingdom with madness and despair. The days grew darker. Grey clouds choked the skies in an eternal blanket. Streets were largely empty. Parents of small children refused to go outside unnecessarily for fear of reprisal. Markets shut down. Trade ground to a halt.

Roving patrols filled the streets now. The five-thousand-man reserve of the Wolfsreik executed Harnin's bidding without question. Their numbers were bolstered by the hundreds of disgruntled citizens wanting to make something more for themselves. Day by day the kingdom fell apart.

The rebellion went deeper underground. They'd made their bid to take back the kingdom and failed. Now Argis was imprisoned and Joefke dead. Scores more lay in shallow graves. The war continued, however, and worsened the deeper winter became. Early successes were stymied by the gradual adaptation of their enemies. The hit-and-run tactics met with very small rewards, forcing the rebellion leadership to find new ways to continue the war.

"We can't sit idle any longer."

Fenning rubbed his bald head in frustration. "What do you propose we do, Inaella? We don't have the strength to storm the Keep. Joefke's loss hurt us more than even you imagined. Harnin is too powerful."

"All tyrants can be stopped. The One Eye is no different," she protested. Her dark green eyes flared hotly.

The others nodded in approval. Everyone was tired of the constant hiding, plotting, and looking over their shoulders. The toll was too much. Combined with the loss of so many good friends and patriots, many wanted to find a way out. Either out of the war or out of the kingdom. Fresh fears over traitors arose. It didn't take much before finger pointing and accusations raged back and forth through their ranks. The council was hard pressed to stop it before their order dissolved entirely.

"What would you have us do?" asked another from the far side of the room.

Inaella folded her arms. "Continue fighting! Delranan is our kingdom. We have a civic duty and moral obligation to stand up for what is right. The people need to know they have others looking out for them. Think about your own families. Would you abandon them to Harnin's depredation? How many children are you prepared to sacrifice on his altar of insanity? There is no other answer but none! We must continue to resist."

"But at what cost?" Fenning argued. "Seventy-five dead already. Homes have been burned. Families ruined. We can't continue at this pace."

"You suggest we just lay down our arms and let Harnin do as he pleases? Delranan is already at the bursting point. All it will take is a puff of wind and this kingdom will go up in flames, whether we wish it to or not. Soldiers now control the streets. We've lost the advantage. He no longer fears us."

"We need that fear if we're to survive."

Fenning scowled at the speaker, a newer member to their council whose name he couldn't recall. "The Wolfsreik is to fear us? You suffer from delusions if you think such a thing is possible."

"He speaks the truth!" Inaella barked. "We held all the advantages in the beginning. Now we flounder with indecision. A move needs to be made. One that will shake Harnin's confidence."

Frustrated, Fenning leaned back in his chair and drank deeply from his mug of water. "What do you suggest?"

"I don't know," Inaella replied sweetly. She was pleased with his sudden attitude reversal. Fenning was much easier to deal with when he couldn't find any viable option to get his way. She decided to step back and allow him to come up with the target. "Whatever we do needs to be big enough to inspire the people again and make Harnin realize he's not as secure as he thinks. And I am not suggesting we try to free Argis. I realize the impossibility of that, however sore his loss hurts us."

"We could always strike the new barracks complex," suggested Ingrid, a young woman with striking blonde hair. The scar running down the side of her face was still pink, fresh. She'd lost her husband to Harnin's soldiers and wanted revenge. Joining the rebellion was the only logical move.

"Ingrid has a point," Inaella reinforced. "They don't have many guards posted. We could burn it to the ground and be gone before they manage to bring in reinforcements."

Fenning considered the proposal. The new complex was designed to eventually become a fully operational fortress on the outskirts of Chadra city. Harnin's designs called for it to be a permanent structure to secure his powerbase as well as repel Badron's armies when they eventually returned. The ugly buildings mocked the majesty of Chadra Keep. Destroying them would incite Harnin's wrath but it would also cement the will of the people against the continued oppression. Fenning knew there was little choice in the matter. Doing nothing wasn't an option.

"We would need to burn it to the ground," he finally said. "That's the only way to draw enough attention is to completely ruin it."

"Kill everyone on site," Ingrid said. The anger in her voice was unmistakable. "The message needs to be clear."

Inaella frowned at her zeal. Fighting attitudes were needed but Ingrid might become a major distraction if she continued to allow her desire for vengeance to cloud her judgment. "Ingrid, we are at war but there is more to think on than the careless slaughter of life, even if it does belong to our enemy."

"What do you mean?" Ingrid demanded.

Inaella stood and went to the middle of the room so everyone could hear her clearly. "We are all citizens of Delranan. Right, wrong, or indifferent, this is our kingdom. The men we fight against have families that live among us. We are the same people with differing ideals. How many of those pressed into Harnin's service truly share his vision for the future? For certain the only ones that do are those miscreants who joined him after Badron left. If we casually slaughter our own people, how long will it be before we go after their families simply for being married to the enemy?

"We cannot turn against one another so easily. Not if we expect to rebuild this kingdom to what it should have been. This is not a war of attrition, Ingrid. We are fighting for the very soul of Delranan. It is their minds that need winning over. Not their bodies." Inaella clasped her hands and scanned the room. "We should not be so casual with whom we kill. It will only come back to haunt us before the end."

"What difference will it make if we don't make a stand now?" Ingrid countered. "I say we strike with ruthless aggression and make them tremble in their boots. Villains only appreciate one thing: strength. We must deliver a clear show of strength and force Harnin back into the Keep. It is the only way."

"Do you think he's just going to lock the doors and try to wait us out? No, Harnin will scour the kingdom and kill everyone and everything in retaliation. We can't kill our way out of this mess."

"As much as it pains me to agree with her, Inaella is correct," Fenning said. He longed for the days when he could be just a simple farmer again. This life didn't suit him. Failing health combined with his rapidly diminishing ability to control the rebellion conspired to render him ineffective. "These are our citizens we're talking about, not some random foreigners. Prudence is required. We must look to the future."

"Even if it means losing the war?"

"I don't have the answer you're looking for."

Ingrid fumed but said nothing more. Taking advantage of the momentary lapse in communication, Inaella addressed the council. "Assemble a task force. We will attack the new barracks as soon as we have the necessary intelligence to support our actions. Kill only those that get in the way. We can't afford to have the people turn against us, not now."

Several of the council bowed and excused themselves, leaving on Inaella, Ingrid, and Fenning. The three said nothing, content with searching the others' faces for signs of true feelings and intentions. So much effort went into secrecy they often lost focus. Fenning was a farmer. He wasn't sure of Inaella's background but she carried the air of aristocracy. *No doubt some officer's wife. Ingrid. Now Ingrid is a problem. She's a complete unknown and that makes her dangerous on too many levels. Perhaps we were wrong to include her into the council so rashly.*

Shouts mingled with the sudden roar of swords clashing. Inaella shot up, eyes focused on the door. Her heart leapt. They'd been discovered. The door burst open just as the others started collecting their belongings to leave. A young guard, no more than eighteen, stormed in. His face was shallow, paled from fear. His eyes wild. Blood trickled down his right arm from a small wound on the shoulder.

Breathing hard, he said, "You must get out now. The enemy has found us!"

"How did this happen?" Fenning demanded, even as he slid into his heavy jacket. "We've always taken great precautions not to…"

"Shut up, Fenning," Inaella snapped. She knew none of it mattered. All that mattered was escaping Harnin's men before she and the others wound up prisoners like Argis. "Which way, guard?"

"The enemy is assaulting the front of the inn. They've already set fire to it. Too many of my friends are already dead."

She laid a gentle hand on his shoulder. "What is your name?"

"Hrald, ma'am."

Smiling, Inaella said, "Hrald, you have done us a great service. Your brothers will not be forgotten. They've earned their places beside their fathers in the halls of the dead. Now come, lead us to safety."

Nodding slowly, Hrald's back stiffened and he led them out of the room and towards the back of the inn. The sounds of battle continued behind them. Curses roared above the din, followed by screams and the wet flesh-smacking sounds of steel piercing bodies. Hrald wanted to run, to flee as fast as his already weary legs might manage but knew he couldn't. He was all that stood between the council and certain death.

Inaella fled but knew in her heart she needed to stay. The rebellion would go on without her. Ideals were much harder to kill than people. She was just a small part in a greater machine. The idea of sacrificing herself for the rebellion's sake almost inspired her but the look in young Hrald's eyes forced her to go on.

Her thoughts turned to how the enemy had discovered their position. Harnin hadn't made a move against them for so long they had grown complacent. She frowned. The stalemate was clearly over and loyalist forces intended to cleanse the rebellion to the core. But how had Harnin known where to find them? The obvious choice was Ingrid. She'd been recently accepted to the council and little was known of her other than her intense drive to kill the Wolfsreik. Inaella briefly considered it a ruse but for the fear in Ingrid's eyes.

The others had been on the council from the beginning, all loyal members to the opposition of Harnin's tyranny. She'd fought alongside them, even bled with them.

Everything had been in their favor until Argis's capture and Joefke's death. They'd lost momentum and were sent scrambling to find a way to reverse their fortunes. Inaella couldn't imagine any of the others turning. They were her friends. The heart of the rebellion. Soldiers were expendable, but not the leadership.

"Are the horses ready?" she asked.

Hrald stopped running long enough to look back over their shoulders. "Yes ma'am. There is a squad standing by to ensure your escape. The horses are saddled and ready."

"How can we be sure Harnin hasn't found them?"

Hrald had no answer. Enough of his friends had already died, he didn't want to think about more. Besides, they both knew there was every possibility that the Wolfsreik had already secured the inn and stables. Harnin's men were ruthless but not the seasoned professionals King Badron had taken across the Murdes Mountains. The reserves were part time soldiers who lived as farmers and tradesmen. What they lacked in extensive training and discipline was made up for by sheer brutality and unmitigated violence. Humanity was a simple creature prone to extreme fits of violence and rage. Once that inner beast was loosed it became next to impossible to re-cage. Delranan languished under that beast.

They reached the end of the small tunnel. Hrald motioned them back and slowly pulled the aging wooden door open. He poked his head out into the cool night. Small snowflakes instantly peppered his hair and face. Satisfied the enemy hadn't yet discovered this place, Hrald led the council into the stable.

The stable was large enough for ten horses and built into the side of a small hill. Mostly underground, the rebellion knew that secrecy would keep them alive better than fighting. Dozens of similar facilities had been constructed throughout the kingdom for just this eventuality. Prudence became the teacher of great wisdom.

"Halt!" a quiet voice commanded.

A dozen guards suddenly emerged from behind trees and bushes. Crossbows were leveled, swords drawn. There was the briefest moment where Inaella thought the betrayal went deeper and that these were Harnin's men. That moment faded when Hrald broke into a great smile.

"It's Hrald. I have the council. They must flee, now."

The guard commander looked them over before ordering his men to lower their weapons. "Quickly. Get them inside. It won't be long before the One Eye finds us."

Hrald escorted the council in and helped Ingrid and Inaella into their saddles. "Ride safely, ma'am."

Confused, she asked, "Are you not coming with us?"

He shook his head. "I am needed here. You'll require a diversion to escape."

Her breath caught in her throat. Diversion meant death. Hrald and the others were going to sacrifice their lives so that the council had the chance to escape. She wanted to cry for his bravery but refused to dishonor the deed with tears. "You are a very brave young man, Hrald. Stay alive, for me. I have a feeling I will need you in the future."

He beamed with pride and watched the council ride off into the night. The forest was dark but their guide knew the route to the next safe house. Behind him the flames started to lick above the roof of the inn. Snow melted in great pools. Embers floated in the night sky. The sounds of battle were all but drowned out by the roar of flames. Hrald knew they needed to leave, to save their lives while there was still time. He also knew he was given specific purpose to ensure the council survived. What remained of the guard would stay and fight. Even if it meant death.

"Prepare yourselves," the guard captain said. "We get back into the tree line and set up an ambush if they decide to come. The council must escape."

The guards went about their task wordlessly. Death held no fear, not anymore. They'd all seen friends die and each Man expected the same to come to them before the end. No one really thought they'd live long enough to see the rebellion end. Hrald paused to give a final glance up the trail the council had taken and went to join his brothers.

Jarrik tipped his head back, enjoying the warmth of the flames on his face. The satisfaction of knowing his foes were trapped and being burned to death filled him with energy. He and the others had been forced to sit idle as Harnin dithered over his next move. Weeks of inactivity while the rebellion grew and organized. Weeks where men he knew and once trusted defected to their cause. Weeks of missing the opportunity to wipe out the rebellion while it was still pathetic, weak.

It was only through Jarrik's own subversion that they managed to get a spy inside the rebel council. He smirked at how easy it was to turn one of their own. And all it took was the promise of a longer life and a small pile of riches. Jarrik wanted to spit. Peasants were always so concerned with money they lost sight of the bigger picture. Their spy wouldn't live long enough to collect his rewards. All rebel leaders were going to be captured and executed publicly in the grand finale of the war. No one would dare rise against the throne again.

Harnin, no doubt, would be incensed when he learned of Jarrik's disobedience, but that didn't matter. He was doing what was best for Delranan, not himself. The rebellion had gone on for far too long already. Combined with the lack of information from the real war in Rogscroft, Jarrik was left with an uncomfortable feeling. Nothing made sense of late. Harnin's actions were becoming increasingly erratic. His designs for the future of the kingdom echoed madness.

Jarrik watched the flames and suddenly found doubt. *All this merely weakens our kingdom. Will we be able to repel the Wolfsreik when they return home?* He was certain something dark and cruel inhabited Harnin's mind, whispering to him when no one was looking. Insanity was the only logical reason for his recent decisions. Delranan was once the pride of the northern kingdoms. Now it wallowed in an unnecessary military state. The population was subjected to fear for no reason.

Delranan needed a king again, not a tyrant. Jarrik, regretting his decision to support Harnin's coup, frowned as thoughts of betrayal formed. He wasn't sure if the time was right to abandon the One Eye and go back to Badron, but the thought grew with every passing moment.

"My lord, there is no way of knowing if the rebels are inside or not."

Of course not you fool. "Secure the perimeter and keep guards posted. We won't be able to search the ruins until this fire dies out. Commander Flynn, I am riding back to the Keep. Find me, no one else, when you are ready to begin searching for bodies."

Flynn saluted. "Yes, my lord. What should we do with these prisoners?"

Jarrik didn't spare a glance at the six men kneeling with their hands behind their heads. "Execute them and post the bodies for the people to see. They are traitors to the kingdom."

That should keep Harnin's anger in check though I wonder who the real traitors here are. Jarrik returned the salute and headed back to his mount. He'd seen enough senseless slaughter for one night.

TWENTY

Night Raid

Ironfoot took point. Used to spending years at a time underground, secluded from sunlight, Dwarven eyesight went nearly unmatched by any other race in the dark. Bahr didn't particularly trust the Dwarves but knew enough to let the best asset lead the way. The Dwarves wordlessly spread out in a loose wedge and entered the forest with the grace and stealth of jungle predators. He hadn't seen such precision in a very long time. Bahr and Boen stalked the middle of the formation. Rekka and the sell swords brought up the rear. The woman from Teng would be more than a match for any dark Dwarf seeking to turn the ambush and having Dorl and Nothol with her only made the odds near impossible.

Fighting down a yawn, the Sea Wolf scanned the forest as they marched. The night was so dark it was a useless endeavor but it made him more comfortable. He'd never admit it but he couldn't see more than a few feet in front of him. The Dwarves had painted a single stripe down the backs of their armor. Faintly luminescent, the paint was visible only by Bahr and the others. He was thankful for the effort, otherwise they might get lost in the dark. The silver light was so soft he had to squint to find it most of the time. Bahr silently wondered if the others were having the same difficulties.

Ironfoot halted suddenly and dropped to a knee. The rest of the Dwarves did the same. Boen sidled behind the nearest tree. Still trying to see, Bahr failed to realize he was the only one exposed. A Dwarf on the right flank rose and crept forward. There was the sound of a brief scuffle. A twig breaking. Ironfoot doubled back to Bahr moments later.

"We're at the outer picket line. Grey Beard just took out the sentry but we must be cautious from here," he whispered in Bahr's ear.

Understanding, Bahr replied in kind. "How much further to the cannons?"

"Not far. Maybe five hundred meters. Once we get inside their lines we go to ground and wait for the diversion. We move now."

The Dwarf stalked off again, his intent doubled. Ironfoot had no problems with leaving them behind if they couldn't keep up. Bahr felt his age catching up to him as he watched the Dwarves move as one. The wedge collapsed into two files. A pair of Dwarves broke off, presumably to eliminate the nearest sentries. Knees aching and back tight from the cold, Bahr trudged forward, desperate to keep the stripes of paint in view.

Soon enough they found a small ravine, more of a ditch, and burrowed in. Crossbows were assembled and loaded as the strike team waited. Cold winds entered the ditch and howled through with ruthless fury. Boen eased his head over the lip and took his first look at the enemy camp. He'd expected to find a disorganized rabble but found anything but. Tents were arranged in orderly rows. Fires interspersed the plain, large enough for a score of Dwarves each. Smiths worked deep into the night fixing armor and weapons. Very few enemy soldiers could be seen walking about. Most had bedded down for the night, leaving a skeleton force of guards to watch the perimeter.

Sliding back down he smiled to Bahr. "This should be easy."

Bahr offered his most skeptical look. "How do you figure?" *We're outnumbered and don't understand how these Dwarves fight. This could be a slaughter.*

"The cannons are in the rear of the camp and emplaced in bunkers. I guess to keep the enemy from hitting them. The main army is fast asleep. They won't be expecting a run for their most important weapons. We'll be able to destroy them with ease."

But how about getting back out again? "They're unguarded?"

"No. The enemy keeps their cannons under heavy guard," Ironfoot provided. "It will be a fight to gain control of the weapons."

"Lovely. How many Dwarves does it take to operate one cannon?"

Ironfoot cocked his head in thought. "Seven. There is much to do to get the weapon in firing configuration. Why?"

"Would we be able to gain control of one and use it to destroy the others?" Bahr asked.

Even Boen's eyes widened. They hadn't considered commandeering one of the cannons. Each Dwarf brought a satchel charge of explosives, enough to destroy one of the great weapons. Thord called them gunpowder, though the idea remained foreign to Bahr and his men. They were promised an explosion bigger than any fire either had seen. Bahr remained dubious and tried to put the conversation out of his mind as the time slowly dwindled.

"We might but the cost would be much too high," Ironfoot replied. "Cannons take a well-trained crew several minutes to get ready to fire and my soldiers aren't trained properly. We are infantry, not artillery."

"Do we have enough to destroy all the cannons?"

"Yes."

Ironfoot's answer was definite enough to prevent any further questioning. Awkward silence settled over the mixed unit, each lost in their thoughts. The night grew colder, an ominous sign, Bahr thought. As much as he didn't like to admit it, he was forced to realize he wasn't a soldier. This sort of life wasn't for him. His lament abruptly ended when the first cannon ball struck the front line.

A hellish ball flame blasted high into the sky, spitting fire in every direction. The whistle of shrapnel slicing through the air inspired fear in Bahr. The second round exploded before he had the chance to say anything. Then another. The barrage continued with fury. Dwarves screamed. Others shouted and ran for water buckets. Still more burst from their tents and rushed to their defensive positions in the trenches. The entire sky seemed to burn. Reverberations trembled through the earth. Bahr had never felt so small.

"We move!" Ironfoot crawled out of the ditch and sprinted towards the nearest cannon.

Dwarves broke off in teams of two and three, each heading for a different weapon. Boen was the first to make contact. A half squad of Dark Dwarves stumbled from their tent, still half asleep and slightly drunk. The Gaimosian fell upon them like death's herald. His axe bit deep. A head was lopped off. An arm fell, hacked at the shoulder. He struck the third Dwarf in the chest, burying the axe head in a spray of blood and crunching bone.

Bahr fell upon the others as Boen tried to dislodge his axe from the dead Dwarf. Parrying a wild swing, Bahr deflected the blade, pushing it up and away, opening the Dwarf's midsection for a killing riposte. Hot blood splashed his torso but the next Dwarf attacked before Bahr could worry about it. He ducked just in time, narrowly missing the blow meant to cleave him from neck to groin. Off balance, the Dwarf was unable to recover before Bahr took his head from behind.

Breathing heavily, Bahr looked over to see Boen crushing a thick Dwarf skull between his hands. A second Dwarf crept up from behind, his small dagger cruel looking in the light of the flames. Bahr flung his sword. The great weapon whistled end over end and took the Dwarf in the neck. Blood fountained as the body collapsed. The smell of death clung to the air in a thick miasma, sickening Bahr. He dashed over and yanked his sword from the corpse, whirling to find another opponent. Boen's victim died with an agonizing scream as his head caved in. And then they were alone.

"You all right?" Bahr asked.

With so much blood covering them it was near impossible to tell whose it was. Boen looked himself over. "Not a scratch. You?"

"Good enough. Come on, Ironfoot is already attacking the first cannon."

The defenders were caught unaware and unprepared. Cannon crews raced to their guns the moment the first incoming round exploded. So focused on getting their weapons into firing order, they never thought that they were the actual targets. Each cannoneer was as valuable as the actual cannons. Ironfoot's Dwarves fell on them immediately. Dozens of Dwarves died in the initial moments. The first cannon was secure before Bahr reached it.

He stepped over a pair of bodies and drew even with Ironfoot. The Dwarf busied setting the satchel charge in the cannon barrel. A second Dwarf finished filling the barrel with large packets of gunpowder. Bahr didn't understand much of what he saw but recognized enough to know they had put far too much explosive charge in the barrel. He stepped back and took in the weapon. The barrel was roughly twice as long as a man is tall and bigger around than the thickest tree. A strange metal bracket gripped the rear of the cannon, much like a fulcrum. The entire piece was dug in and built on a huge wooden platform that was anchored to the ground. Presumably to keep it from rocking back out of position from the release of so much kinetic force.

He tried to imagine what it was like being next to the cannon when it was fired, gauging the size of the explosion on the other end. The weapon was a marvel, made of cast iron and painted flat black. It also inspired great fear for the future. *Surely it can't be long before the other races learn how to create such powerful weapons. Then where will we be?*

Ironfoot lit the long fuse hanging from the end of the satchel charge and grabbed Bahr by his collar. "Run!"

Another salvo of incoming rounds hit the dark Dwarf lines. Body parts flew through the air. Bahr ran for his life, unsure of what was next. He made it only twenty meters before Ironfoot tripped him and rolled over on top to keep him from getting up. The cannon exploded, peeled open like a banana. Flames washed overhead in a great sheet. Bahr held his breath as the oxygen fed the flames. Residue fell down around them. Grinning, Ironfoot rolled off of Bahr and looked back to admire his handiwork.

The cannon was completely destroyed. Most of the crew was dead. Two more exploded, reduced to useless bits of molten metal. By now the enemy became keenly aware of the subterfuge. Infantry units were turned from the front lines to protect what remained of the cannons. Time was running out and there were still seven more to sabotage.

"Hurry. We must get to the next gun before they can muster a defense," Ironfoot commanded and took off again.

Bahr rolled his eyes and struggled to his feet. *I'd rather face an infantry squad than continue like this.* He looked over and was surprised to see Boen trying to catch his breath. A lifetime of combat hadn't prepared him for the sheer destruction of this night. Bahr slapped him on the shoulder on the way past, shaking him from his daze. Decidedly out of place in this new style of warfare, the pair hobbled off after the Dwarves.

Another explosion rocked the ground. A piece of barrel struck the ground between the men, drawing a curse from Boen. He failed to see the honor in fighting this way. Men deserved to die facing their opponent, not cowering in the hopes of being missed by super-heated bits of metal. He'd killed more than a hundred men in his long life but none of them in any way comparable. This, this was a nightmare.

One of Ironfoot's Dwarves went down with a pair of crossbow bolts in his back. Dark Dwarves sprung up from behind a sandbag wall, falling upon the other Dwarf with Ironfoot. Bahr and Boen ran faster before Ironfoot got killed. They hacked and slashed at the Dark Dwarves. Unarmored and focused solely on their kin, the Dark Dwarves were practically defenseless. The battle ended mercifully quickly.

Ironfoot paused to look at his fallen comrades before grabbing powder charges for the barrel.

"Grab as many as you can and stuff them down the barrel," he shouted.

Bahr followed suit, motioning Boen to keep watch. The last thing they needed was to get caught exposed again. Each powder bag weighed close to fifty pounds. His muscles screamed from the excess strain. Bahr considered himself a strong man but tonight's activities left him with sudden doubts. He hurt in places he'd forgotten having and there was still much work left to be done. Another pair of explosions dominated the night.

Ironfoot waited for him to place the last charge before lighting his fuse and shoving the satchel charge down the barrel. He didn't need to order them to run this time. Nor did he need to worry about tackling them to the ground in time. All three were safe on the ground by the time the cannon exploded. He looked up from the cloud of acrid haze and, seeing the weapon in the same state as the first, nodded once.

"That's it. We need to leave. Exfil back to the ditch," he ordered.

"What about the others?" Bahr asked as he rose again.

Ironfoot didn't wait. "They all know their jobs. Once we rendezvous at the ditch we head back into the forests."

If any others survive. He thought of the two Dwarves that had died taking this cannon and prepared for several more casualties. Hopefully Rekka and the sell swords escaped with only minor wounds, if any. Bahr followed Ironfoot. Using the confusion for cover, the trio nearly made it to the relative security of the ditch when a patrol stumbled upon them and immediately opened fire.

Dark crossbow bolts whizzed through the night. Ironfoot grunted and shouted out. An arrow caught him high in the right shoulder. Boen roared as only a Gaimosian could and charged into the mass of Dark Dwarves. Bodies flew. His sword cleaved helms and plunged deep into bodies as he single handedly reduced the enemy squad to corpses and walking wounded. Small axes bounced off his armor, succeeding only in infuriating him. It was a testament to their honor that not a one tried to flee.

Bahr wanted to help but knew he'd only get in the way. Boen acted like a madman, hacking and killing with reckless abandon. It was one of the few times Bahr felt honest fear. The Gaimosian was out of control and worse, appeared to be enjoying it. Finally, when the bodies had all fallen and Boen stood alone in the center of the crude circle, Bahr edged closer.

"Come on," he hissed. "More will be coming."

Blood streaking his face, Boen casually looked down on his handiwork and gave a soft nod. Nothing needed to be said.

TWENTY-ONE

Warfare Undreamt

Acrid smoke dug deep into Dorl's lungs no matter how hard he tried to hold his breath. The fury of the cannonade shook him to the core. He'd never dreamed such hatred and power existed and now that he had, wished it didn't. The ground trembled and broke where the rounds struck. Black smoke announced plumes of white-hot flames. Super-heated bits of metal sliced across the field, shredding everything it came in contact with. Dorl was convinced the underworld had opened.

He glanced to his right and left, taking small satisfaction in seeing Nothol and Rekka flinching with each new sound. Not even her steel spine was strong enough to prevent her from reacting like him. Only the Dwarves seem undisturbed. They patiently waited for the chaos to grip the enemy camp with almost bored looks. These were soldiers who'd seen too much of war already. None of the usual horrors held much promise save release.

"We go," the closest Dwarf ordered and dashed towards the nearest cannon emplacement.

The others followed closely. Deadly crossbows were fired at enemy Dwarves that got too close and then they were in the bunker fighting hand to hand. Dorl and Nothol secured the perimeter, knowing they wouldn't do much good down in the cramped confines of the gun pit. Rekka slid away into the night. Dorl scowled, guessing what she meant to do. He almost felt sorry for the Dark Dwarves on the next cannon.

"Come on, set the charges!" the Dwarf in command hissed as soon as the cannon was secure.

This is ridiculous. I'm not made for this type of fighting. These damned Dwarves are going to be the death of me. Dorl bolted up with a grimace and jumped into the pit. Bodies littered the ground. All but one was enemy. The

Dwarves showed no sign of losing one of their own. Instead they went about their task of destroying the cannon with grim precision. Despite their naturally gruff demeanor, Dorl found himself deeply impressed with their attention to detail. The Dwarves moved as efficiently as any race he'd ever encountered. Charges were placed in the cannon tube and the Dwarves hastily ran clear.

The explosion threw Dorl meters across the field. He hit hard enough his breath went out in a great whoof. Rocks and dirt slashed his face and hands. Something heavy dropped on his chest. His ears rang, deafeningly. Blackness took him for a moment.

Rough hands pulled him to his feet. "Get up or you're going to get us both killed!"

Letting Nothol take most of his weight, Dorl stumbled towards the next objective. His ribs felt bruised, one or two possibly broken. "You're not my favorite person right now," he managed through the pain.

"Who gives a shit? I'm all you got," Nothol replied tartly.

Another explosion nearly threw them both down. Dorl groaned at the pounding in his head. Nothol pushed them harder. The need to contribute to the mission combined with the suddenly strong survival instinct urged them on. All around the sounds of combat raged. Ironfoot's Dwarves were giving better than they got back. Bodies continued to pile up. Dorl snuck a glance back towards the first rank of guns. Smoke belched from the wreckage of several. He thought he spotted Boen's massive form hacking and slashing his way through enemy soldiers before a cloud of smoke obscured the view.

A trio of Dark Dwarves emerged suddenly and attacked the sell swords. Nothol shoved Dorl away and hefted his sword. The Dwarves were taken off guard, expecting to find their kin. Instead they got a pair of men more than willing to kill all three. Nothol wasted no time in lunging in to take the first Dwarf in the chest. His blade made a sickly crunching sound as it plunged through the breastbone and into the lungs. The Dwarf died with an odd gurgling noise.

The survivors fanned out, deciding to ignore the prone Dorl. They circled Nothol, wary and hostile. Nothol shifted slowly, desperately searching for any tell as to which one was going to attack first. He didn't wait long. The Dwarf on his right ducked in, drawing Nothol's attention. The second Dwarf attacked quickly. His battle axe swung a great arc. Nothol shifted, barely blocking the axe before it bit into his kidney. He swung his sword in a low circle to fend off the first Dwarf. Beset from both sides, he started to retreat.

The Dwarves recognized his inadequacies and pressed the advantage. Nothol fought with every trick and partially forgotten tactic he'd ever learned and it still wasn't enough. The Dwarves pressed him all the way back to the first gun pit. Exhausted and covered in sweat, Nothol struggled just to breathe. He knew he'd been beaten. All that was left was how he was going to die. Then Dorl attacked from behind. His sword bit deeply across the back of the first Dwarf's neck. Blood fountained in a thick spray. Taken off guard, the last Dwarf made the fatal mistake of taking his eyes off Nothol. He died quickly, a last mercy from a fellow warrior.

"You all right?" Dorl asked.

Nothol said, "Enough. This is getting to be a dangerous place."

"Let's fall back and cover the rest of the Dwarves. The sooner they destroy these damned cannons the sooner we can get back to Drimmen Delf." *Or so I hope.*

Darkness was her strongest ally. Rekka's black, form-fitting clothes betrayed almost no sign of her passing. She was the kiss of night, a whisper after midnight. Alone, she immediately reverted to her training in her jungle homeland. She was death incarnate, stalking the land with blade and fury. Rekka Jel marched steadily towards the furthest cannon. She'd volunteered for the task, knowing it was the most dangerous and that she alone was capable of ending it quickly.

The Dwarves had been reluctant at first. Ironfoot argued that there was no possible way a lone woman could succeed against such odds. It took Bahr and Dorl to convince him otherwise and even then he wasn't convinced. Rekka didn't bother waiting for him to be. She stalked off the moment they broke from the ditch. While the Dwarves battled against the first few cannon crews, she whisked effortlessly between the tents.

She avoided confrontation when possible. She killed quickly before her victims had the opportunity to sound the alarm. Rekka made it to her target by the time the first cannon exploded. The sound and sight of it made her think of the awkward weight of the bomb she carried. Explosives were a relatively new concept to warfare on Malweir and she wasn't comfortable holding them. Enemies deserved to die with honor, by sword and arrow. Being blown to pieces by shards of metal and flames seemed almost indignant.

A Dwarf stepped across her path. She took his head in one swift move. He died without a sound. Rekka pushed forward. Her eyes scanned the area, never resting. She didn't relish the idea of being caught unaware. One of the dark Dwarf cannons managed to fire off its first round. She decided to make that her primary target. The initial surprise had passed and the enemy army was slowly coming to its senses. Dwarves ran everywhere to get into their battle positions.

Rekka adjusted the straps on her satchel charge and attacked. She made no sounds on her approach. She brought her sword up over her head and leapt down into the cannon pit. One Dwarf managed to get a cry of alarm off before the sword chopped diagonally into his neck and collar bone. Hot blood sprayed her face. A second Dwarf tackled her to the ground, hammering blows to her exposed ribs with his meaty fists. Grunting through the sudden jets of pain shooting up her side, Rekka managed to roll just enough to make him miss. Drawing the small dagger at her hip, she plunged it deep into the Dwarf's sternum and gave a sharp twist.

She brought her knee up into his groin and heaved with every last ounce of strength. The Dwarf toppled over, dying in great agony. Rekka pulled herself up and attacked the five remaining cannon crewmen. A thrown axe flashed past her head, catching strands of dark, brown hair. Her arms moved frantically as she cut and severed. One by one the Dwarves fell under her onslaught. The last Dwarf ran up behind her, hoping to take her head for a trophy but caught only a belly full of steel as she stabbed backwards. The combination of his momentum and her force buried the sword to the hilt in his gut. His face twisted in a rictus of pain. His axe dropped uselessly to the ground. Blood frothed from his lips. Rekka rose and turned, studying her foe before yanking her sword free. The Dwarf fell dead.

Breathing heavily, she did a full sweep of the gun position before dropping the satchel charge. She struggled to recall everything Ironfoot had instructed her to do. Exhaustion and the added pressure of adrenaline clouded her mind. Rekka started shoving the heavy bags of gunpowder into the barrel. A new set of explosions dominated the battlefield. Three enemy cannons smoked and burned. Forcing them from her mind so she could focus, Rekka lit the fuse to the satchel charge and ran.

She darted past Dwarves who were too busy trying to get to their positions to bother with her. Flames and shrapnel bloomed across the gun pit when she was already a hundred meters away. The thin line of a smile cracked her stoic face and she continued running. The rapid escalation of chaos consumed the camp, forcing the Dwarves to be cautious. A great number had been killed in the covert assault and that message was being passed up through the chain of command. The sudden delay in action was enough to give Rekka and the others time to escape.

A lone Dwarf stepped out of the shadows to confront her. He was the largest Dwarf she'd ever seen. Massive forearms strained from holding equally massive axes. His left eye was dead, blinded by the same scar that ran from his temple to his chin. Beardless, the Dwarf looked terrifying in the firelight. He was a warrior. Rekka recognized this before she slowed to a halt. *At last, a true challenge.*

She raised her sword in salute and planted her feet shoulder width apart. Sneering, the Dwarf gestured with his chin. Rekka obliged and attacked. Her first blow was meant to distract him, opening his guard to be ripped apart by the second. It failed. The Dwarf dodged the overhand strike to his head and parried low with both axes. He trapped Rekka's slender sword and lodged a mighty kick to her stomach. She flew back and dropped to the ground. He laughed.

"You'll need to do better," he said mockingly.

Rekka struggled to suppress her rising anger. Only a clear mind could dominate an opponent. Taking a deep breath, she rose and dropped back into a defensive stance.

Either being respectful or overly confident, the Dwarf allowed her enough time to reset before barreling towards her. His finely sharpened axe blades glimmered in the flames. Knowing she didn't have the size or fury of the Dwarf, Rekka crouched, bunching her strength for what she hoped was the killing blow. The axes scythed out. The Dwarf roared. Rekka saw the futility of her move and tucked into a roll as fast as she could.

Infuriated by his inability to kill her, the Dwarf began to circle. "Come to my blades, human. I promise to make it quick."

Trained by weapon masters from the age of five, Rekka ignored the bait. Distraction was a key principle in single combat. One she'd used often enough. To defeat this Dwarf she needed guile. She flashed a toothy grin and raised her sword with one hand. With the other she quickly pulled her dagger and flung it as hard as she could at his face. He easily blocked the dagger away but didn't see her second move until after the sword slashed across the top of his thigh. He grunted and staggered back.

Rekka pressed the advantage. She delivered a series of blows. High. Low. Right side. Left side. The Dwarf struggled to fend her off but had lost mobility and was losing blood rapidly. Rekka hacked and slashed. Every blow was aimed at ending the battle. Finally, she broke through the Dwarf's defenses and felt the reward of her steel slicing across his grizzled throat. Some life left in him, he dropped one axe and brought the second down with as much strength as he had left. Rekka narrowly sidestepped the attack and watched him pitch forward. Dead.

He'd been a worthy opponent and she honored that by wiping his blood in the snow rather than on his corpse. True warriors deserved better than what they mostly received. Finished, Rekka looked around for more Dwarves before heading back to the ditch. She was tired and abused, but still in the fight. The easy part was over. The enemy cannons were destroyed. Now they needed to find a way back to the forest and their own lines. All that stood between the tiny group and freedom was an army of angry Dwarves.

TWENTY-TWO

Escape

The last explosion threw mounds of dirt and debris into the ditch, prompting curses and menacing glares from the Dwarves. Ironfoot watched as his assault teams gained the ditch, counting each Dwarf. Several didn't return, confirmed by the dour looks of their friends and a curt headshake. The losses, while more than he wished, were still in acceptable margins. *Besides, what's done is done. We all knew what the cost might be. They died well. I will raise a horn to their honor when next we feast.* He took the remaining satchel charges and started digging them into the lip of the ditch. They would slow their pursuers down for a time. *Hopefully long enough to let us get a good lead.*

Rekka Jel brought up the rear. Her sword gleamed with blood. Dorl noticed her ragged state, worse than his own, and briefly considered going to her. Her stern look cautioned otherwise. She was a warrior. He had to remember that. There wasn't any room for weakness; it would only get them both killed.

"Is this it?" Ironfoot asked.

Rekka offered a quick nod. "I am the last. The enemy is disorganized but they know the primary purpose of the attack was to disable their cannons. They are searching for us, in great numbers. We must be quick."

There were shouts of panic mixed with oaths of vengeance as the Dark Dwarves organized into hunter-killer teams. The escape window closed by the second. Ironfoot looked to the nine survivors. *So few. The enemy shall pay for this.* "Grey Beard, take point. Bahr, you and your people follow. I will bring up the rear. Move, now."

Rekka laid her hand on Ironfoot's shoulder. "I shall walk with you."

One look at the determination etched into her face was enough for him.

"They've seen us," Boen grumbled.

Ironfoot looked to where Boen pointed and his heart fell. Hundreds of Dark Dwarves had assembled and were cautiously making their approach on the ditch. Time was up. He gestured to Grey Beard and the weary band hurried back to the perceived security of the forest. Ironfoot paused long enough to light the fuses before hurrying to catch up. They only made a few meters before the first shouts went up. Black crossbow bolts flashed past. Some struck trees in a shower of splinters while others went harmlessly into the forest.

Bahr ducked reflexively despite knowing it didn't matter. When the enemy was behind you there was no safe way to move. Still, he and the others started weaving through the trees in the vain hopes of avoiding getting shot. His knees ached with every step. Age and over exertion disagreed with him, giving him pause as to whether or not he was the right man to undertake a quest that could possibly save the entire world. He berated himself for such weak thoughts. *Now is not the time!*

"Burn the forest!" a voice bellowed.

Heart threatening to rip from his chest, Bahr doubled his speed. He'd seen forest fires before. The flames spread through the canopy much faster than anyone or anything could run. They'd be roasted alive in minutes. Fear drove him on. Thick plumes of breath froze on the chill air. Snow crunched under his boots. He knew it wasn't enough. Flames would engulf them and blacken their corpses without mercy.

Then the satchel charges exploded. Scores of Dark Dwarves died in the blasts. Screams of the wounded drowned out orders shouted by their leaders. The enemy advance halted abruptly. No Dwarf was a coward but seeing so many of their comrades ripped apart in the span of a few heartbeats gave them pause. They milled about, suddenly fearful of meeting the same fate.

Bahr didn't have time to savor the moment. The Dwarves were used to explosions and would regroup and redouble their efforts in short order. He stopped weaving and ran as straight as he could. Trees gradually thickened until Bahr was certain they were securely back in the forest. He used that base comfort to calm down and focus. Far few Dwarves returned with them, a sad fact that only made finding them harder. He desperately searched the night for signs of the iridescent paint marking their tunics. Darkness mocked him in reply. Panic struggled to win free.

His efforts were rewarded when he finally spied the soft glow of silver paint. Bahr hurried to catch up to the Dwarf before he was lost in the night. So focused on the paint, he nearly slammed into the Dwarf after he abruptly halted. The sounds of heavy panting filled the immediate area. Bahr felt like throwing up. His stomach clenched miserably. His eyes watered, red and raw. Smoke burned his lungs. The battle had been intense, much more so than any he'd been forced to endure in a very long time. His energy was nearly gone. It was all he could just to stay standing.

"Head count," Ironfoot's strong voice ordered from the night.

They'd gone a few hundred meters and the forest thickened. Without the benefit of torches or moonlight there was a very real chance many of them would get lost or worse. One by one the survivors said their names until the Dwarf captain was certain all were accounted for. He turned to look back at the flames raging through the Dark Dwarf camp. Any satisfaction of a job well done remained elusive. They still had nearly a league to go before they would be safe behind their own lines. He used his sleeve to wipe the sweat from his thick brow.

"We've got a little time. The satchel charges will have given them a reason to be cautious. We've stung them, but not enough."

"Enough for what?" Dorl asked between ragged breaths.

Ironfoot fixed him with a stern gaze. "For them to stop chasing us. We've cast great shame on their commanders. The leadership will view our success as an insult to their honor. They will not stop until we either escape or are killed for their own sport."

"Sorry I asked," Dorl replied. He snuck a quick look at Rekka. She seemed to be in better shape than he was. Not that he took much comfort in that. Dorl started to think they weren't going to make it back to the mountains. Right now he wanted nothing more than to take Rekka in his arms and whisper a last "I love you" before they made their charge back to Drimmen Delf. The threat of rejection kept him from doing so.

Boen cleared his throat and spit a large wad of phlegm. "Do you have any more of those bombs?"

Ironfoot shook his head. "I used the last of them at the ditch. Do not think of it. The enemy will send more than even you can stop."

Boen bristled at the challenge but relented. As much as he enjoyed a good fight, sometimes running was the best option. Besides, he'd already made up his mind to ask King Thord to be in the front lines of the main assault. The glory would be heaped upon his shoulders. A proud representation of vanquished Gaimos. One last challenge to prove his worth.

"We shouldn't stay here," Bahr cautioned. "I can hear them coming through the trees." *Which is odd, considering we didn't make a sound on our way there.* There was only one conclusion. The enemy wanted them to know they were coming, and in force.

"Let's move." Ironfoot drew his axe and turned to face the Dark Dwarves.

Rekka wordlessly hefted her sword and did the same. Grey Beard led the others away before anyone succumbed to heroic, and foolish, notions. They started to jog. Each was exhausted, pushed to their limits, but slowing down meant death. Bahr secretly wondered how the Dwarves knew which way to go. He was hopelessly lost.

"Come on, old man. I've got you," Nothol said as he kept Bahr from falling after tripping over an exposed tree root. "We're almost there."

Bahr shot him a menacing glare but didn't have the energy to reply. He didn't know how far they'd gone before Grey Beard slowed and then stopped. He turned and drew his axe in a fluid motion. The others ambled to a stop and followed suit.

"Why are we stopping?" Bahr asked.

Grey Beard sneered. "We can't make it. The enemy is too close. Prepare yourselves. We must fight."

"Shit," Nothol muttered under his breath and drew his sword.

They formed a tight semicircle and waited. Clashing steel rang out from the darkness, followed by a deep groan and then shouting. The same was repeated from another part of the forest. Bahr flexed his grip on his sword. His muscles trembled from over exertion. Heart pounding, he prepared for battle. The wait wasn't long. Short, squat shapes of more than one hundred Dwarves emerged from the dark. Rekka and Ironfoot raced ahead, narrowly avoiding being swarmed by the enemy.

Nothol dropped his sword and set an arrow to string. Finding no point in taking time to aim properly, he fired into the massed enemy soldiers and was rewarded by seeing one pitch backwards. Enraged, the others broke into an all-out charge.

"Get down!" a deep voice roared from behind Bahr, prompting him to obey unquestioningly.

Crossbow bolts sliced through the space where Bahr and the others had just stood. The front rank of advancing Dwarves was decimated by the unexpected assault. A second salvo followed quickly. Then a third. The surviving Dark Dwarves fell back, taking cover behind rocks, trees, and ravines. Any thought of pressing their attack died with half of their force. The remaining leaders ordered retreat.

Bahr finally looked behind him, surprised to see hundreds of Dwarves emerge from concealed positions. *Prepared positions, too. Thord had this planned all along. Sneaky bastard.* His first real sense of relief washed over him and it was all he could do not to break out in tears. Tired beyond belief, surprised and elated at having survived such an ordeal, Bahr gathered his dignity and wits and pulled himself up out of the snow. From the opposite side of the defense he watched Dorl and Nothol share a laugh and embrace. Even Boen had a smile. Victory tasted good. Only the Dwarves seemed un-phased by what had happened.

Ironfoot dusted himself off and met the Dwarf responsible for saving their lives. "Sergeant, you are a most welcome sight."

"Captain, the king sent us shortly after you were seen leaving Drimmen Delf. We feared we weren't in time. The explosions took us by surprise."

Ironfoot laughed. "They took many by surprise! How many Dwarves did you bring?"

"A battalion. I have two hundred Dwarves spread out through this part of the forest in case the enemy decides to counterattack."

"They will. We've bloodied their nose but failed to deliver the crippling blow," Ironfoot said and nodded. "We need to hurry and return to Bode Hill. Dawn is fast upon us."

The sergeant gave a shrill whistle and his forces began pulling back to the base of the mountains. Heavy pine boughs kept the sharp winds from slicing into the tired raiders. Walking single file so as to conceal their numbers and make movement easier, and having an established path, they quickly found themselves out of the combat the zone. The claustrophobia of the forest gradually gave way to open skies. Thick clouds obscured the moon and stars, deepening the shadows of the mountains in the process but Bahr had never felt freer. Almost.

He gave a final look back to the forest and the flames engulfing a large portion of the enemy camp beyond.

Satisfaction finally set in. They'd accomplished what he was never truly certain could be done and all his people had returned. The deaths of those brave Dwarves who dared to believe the cannons should be destroyed instead of revered were added to a lengthening list of the fallen and stored in a special place in his mind. He'd never gotten their names, nor had time to make friends with any of them, but they gave their lives all the same. Bahr was proud to have fought alongside the Dwarves. His thoughts turned towards finding Thord and securing their passage east to the Fern River and then south.

TWENTY-THREE

Preparations

"They did it!" Thord bellowed. His beard bounced across his chest armor as he broke into deep laughter. Months of waiting for the tide to shift had finally ended. Without their cannons, his enemies were vulnerable. Legions of Dwarves itched to be set free, to sweep the valley of their twisted cousins. But Ironfoot and the others hadn't escaped yet. Thord was forced to watch through the looking glass as the enemy encampment devolved into chaos. As much as he wanted to loose his armies he knew he couldn't, not while Ironfoot was still behind their lines.

Turning to his field general, a bitter-looking Dwarf with a long grey beard and a perpetual scowl, he said, "General Brek, form ranks. I want the legions ready to attack at first light. We're going to break these bastards here and now, by Krug!"

Brek slammed a fist to his chest armor. "Yes sire. The Feral Axe battalion will assume point. The field shall be ours by nightfall."

"Don't take unnecessary risks, Brek. The Dark Hammer Dwarves are just as fierce as we are. This will not be an easy battle."

Brek grinned, displaying a row of silver-capped teeth fixed after a Goblin hammer caught him in the mouth years ago. "No battle is easy. Besides, that would take the fun out of it."

Thord watched him depart with great pride and a pang of jealousy. He wanted to don his armor and take up an axe for the cause but his place was here, in the command center on Bode Hill. He wasn't a warrior anymore, not unless absolutely necessary. Any attempt to sneak into the lines would be met by a handful of guards forcibly dragging him back into the command center. He was a king and it was his place to rule, not fight.

The irony of it insulted him. His greatfathers had forged Drimmen Delf from rock and stone. They led charges and held the center of the line in countless battles. Time and laxity all but shoved him into lethargy. Thord wasted away, the sword at his hip all but useless as his armies fought in his name. *Curse this crown. I belong out there, with my army. A true king would stand at the break, leading by example. This is akin to cowardice.*

Already Dwarves were moving. Roused from unsteady slumber thanks to the cannonade, most were dressed and armored. Axes and swords were sharpened. Crossbow bolts and quivers were fletched and filled. The massive army of five thousand slowly spun into motion. At last, they were able to go to war properly, without fear of being pummeled by cannons the moment they left their trenches. Smiths stoked their forges. Surgeons prepped the hospital tents for the inevitable influx of wounded.

The general excitement of the camp flowed through the army, sweeping everyone away. The prospect of ending the war and reclaiming what belonged to them filled hearts with joy. Battle songs as old as the sun drifted up from around the camp. The Dwarves of Drimmen Delf were ready to go back to war and deliver the fury of their forefathers. The Dark Dwarves had broken a sacred covenant among the clans. They turned their backs on justice, intent on vengeance for some perceived slight no one could explain. They came burning and killing as they took their war to the very gates of the great Dwarven kingdom. It was only through sheer determination that the defense held. Now Thord and his army stood on the brink of reversing their fortunes. Each Dwarf knew his orders. Every last Black Hammer Dwarf was to be killed outright. No surrender. No prisoners. Such evil shouldn't be allowed to fester lest it return with even more strength.

Engineers and cannon crews pulled their weapons out of the protective bunkers and, using an elaborate system of pulleys and levers, moved the cannons close enough to drop rounds behind enemy lines. The additional range would throw the entire camp into chaos while covering the infantry advance. Without the threat of return fire, the battle was expected to devolve into a complete rout.

Another set of explosions broke across the night sky, much closer. Tacticians and strategists on the command staff instantly focused on the small part of the forest edge where great balls of black smoke billowed. Scouts used spy glasses to identify the source. Thord paced the bunker nervously. He couldn't attack while Ironfoot and the strike force were still unaccounted for. His hands were tied. Frustrated, the king exited the bunker to get some fresh air. His guards hurried to catch up.

"Not a word," he snarled without looking back.

Rebuked, the guards remained silent and shadowed their king.

Thord's frustrations suddenly got the better of him and he punched the cruel rock wall as hard as he could. "Damnation! I want to attack but can't out of fear of cutting off some of my most valuable assets. My damnable commanders are too stuffy to even think to allow me down onto the field like a true king and I am reduced to having nursemaids again! Which one of you four would like to wear the crown for a spell?"

They passed nervous looks, none daring to speak. Bad things happen when a king loses his temper. Fortunately each hid behind the partial facemasks of their helmets. Thord snorted and kept walking. The first jets of pain shot up through his wrist. He figured he'd broken at least two bones, if not more. By morning the hand would be swollen and a sickly combination of black and purple.

But it was worth it. Anything to vent some of this nonsense I'm feeling inside. Only it wasn't worth it, was it, you old fool? Punching that wall was the dumbest thing I've done since allowing my commanders to convince me of my value. I never should have listened. A king needs to be seen leading, not watching. Ironfoot needs to get back here so we can finally end this dithering and go back to our lives.

"You are a Dwarf with much on your mind," Faeldrin said, coming up from behind.

Thord stopped and turned. "You expected less? I am a Dwarf hidden behind bureaucracy instead of a shield."

"There are times when a king's life is more important than a battalion of soldiers. I have seen it a hundred times over the centuries, mostly in men. They do seem to enjoy touting the successes hard fought by subordinates," the Elf mercenary said.

"What made you break away from your traditions, Elf? I've never heard of Elven mercenaries before. Don't get me wrong. I'm damned glad to have you. Your Aeldruin have proven invaluable in terms of intelligence gathering and screening our left flank."

The Elf lord let loose a slow breath. It was a question he'd avoided answering for the first hundred years since leaving the city of Elvanara. None of his family and only a few friends understood his need to be more than just another Elf. Malweir was ripe with injustice. "There was a time when I was happy, content ignoring the troubles of the world. This was before the order of Mages rose. Before the dark times claimed us all. I laughed and sang like many of my kin. The world held no other promise than a very long, peaceful life. It was a better time, I think. Then the Goblin army came. So vast they blotted out entire valleys. They came killing and pillaging from their dark mountain holes."

He continued quickly before Thord could take offense. Secret histories had proven that the Goblins were once Dwarves, but that was a tale for another time. "No one race was prepared to withstand their might. Kingdom after kingdom fell before a coalition formed. We stopped the Goblins on the edge of the Jebel Desert. The slaughter was horrendous. So many lives were shattered that day. Several of the smaller races all but died out. What little remains of them are secluded in places long forgotten. It was in that moment, staring out across the ocean of bodies, hearing the weeping of hardened warriors, and seeing others wander aimlessly, broken in mind and spirit, that I knew our world was never going to be the same. So I gathered as many of my people to me that were willing to follow my command and formed the Aeldruin."

"A harsh tale," Thord grimaced. While far too young to have been there, the Dwarf king had read all the old histories and knew full well the amount of carnage in that first war. This war paled in comparison.

"It was a harsh time," Faeldrin replied softly. "What corruption claimed your fellow Dwarves, I wonder?"

"Greed. It's an old tale, my friend. I've never understood why some just can't be content with what they have."

Faeldrin shook his head regretfully. "They are the same who want hand-outs, mistakenly thinking life is easier if someone else does all the work for them. Only, life has other plans, so their wishes devolve into a series of successive failures. The world needs strong beings to rule it. And if there aren't enough of them there will always be orders like the Aeldruin to step forth and see justice done."

Thord looked up at the taller and decidedly leaner Elf with curiosity. They had more differences than similarities but he felt a connection with Faeldrin. They were brother warriors, soldiers who had seen and done too much to smile often. Because of that shared emotion Thord felt like he could tell the Elf lord almost anything in confidence. *I can't believe I've never told a soul this before.* "Faeldrin, I detest being king."

If the Elf was surprised, he kept it secret. "Very few actually enjoy it. The idea is more promising than the achievement. Great kings struggle through this dilemma from day one and seldom live to see the truth of their legacy revealed. One day your praises will be sung, Thord. Do not fret. The future is more forgiving than the present."

"Reputation be damned! I'm talking about grabbing an axe and making the charge with the front rank. I'm a Dwarf, Faeldrin, born and bred for war. Yet here I find myself mired in politics and caught between opposing factions."

He continued to stew as Faeldrin stayed silent. Briefly, he considered having his commanders strung up for blocking his desire to join the battle. *What legacy will I have? A doddering old fool who let history pass him by?* It was through great reluctance that he came to conclusion his advisors and commanders had his best interests in mind. They couldn't afford to let him risk being killed against the Dark Dwarves. Leaderless, Drimmen Delf would be exposed to attack from too many sides. Thord needed to be the king, not the warrior.

"Sometimes it's not what you say," he told Faeldrin.

The Elf merely nodded, memories of his own trials casually playing out before him. There was a time he might have been a king, before he decided to sacrifice the security and ease of a simple life for the greater good of not just the Elves, but for all the races of Malweir. He'd never looked back, never questioned that decision. Faeldrin convinced himself that he had done the right thing. Sometimes even heroes needed to be reluctant.

Another Elf strode towards them, stopping respectfully short and bowing. "My lords, our scouts report seeing a large force of Dwarves moving back through the forest. The men are with them as well."

"It's about bloody time," Thord growled.

Faeldrin said, "Thank you, Euorn. Summon the others. I have a feeling the final battle is about to begin much sooner than anticipated. Oh, and see that Captain Ironfoot and the Sea Wolf are escorted here immediately."

"Stop berating yourself, Ironfoot. You did good. You all did."

Ironfoot struggled to meet Thord's gaze. Deep in his heart he knew the words to be true, but that did little to assuage his guilt over losing half of his attack force. Enemy casualties notwithstanding, Ironfoot performed his duties admirably. Victory and honor were heaped upon his name. Scribes were already fastidiously composing his tale for the archives. Lore masters would tell of his valor in every hall east and west of the Kergland Spine. All Dwarves would bow their head in respect to Ironfoot and his raiders.

None of that mattered. He'd lost good friends destroying the enemy cannons. Good friends whose empty seats would fill his heart with sorrow come the morrow. He sighed and tried to accept Thord's words. Try as he might, he couldn't find solace. The war had already claimed too many and hundreds more were going to die when the sun rose. Ironfoot would be there, at the head of the advance. His axe would reap vengeance for lost friends.

"Sire, too many did not return. That is unforgivable," he replied dourly.

Boen looked at Bahr and rolled his eyes. A true warrior never apologized for surviving. Especially not after successfully completing a difficult mission. These Dwarves should be celebrating, not mourning as far as he was concerned. *War does strange things to us all*. Bahr took it in with his usual demeanor. He sympathized with Ironfoot, images of the *Dragon's Bane* burning to the water line and his crew killed on a whim fleeting past. He knew exactly what the Dwarf was feeling. The helplessness of not being able to do anything was strong, so strong it threatened to overwhelm those not strong enough.

Thord waved off Ironfoot's concerns. "Many more will not return from this next fight. It is a small matter, Captain. We are at war and I need you to act like one of my best commanders. Can you do that?"

Bahr watched Ironfoot's resolve stiffen his back. The Dwarf stood tall, head back and chest out. He had remembered his pride. "Yes sire. I'll head back to my battalion and get them ready."

"Good lad," Thord complimented. "You're already a hero, Ironfoot, don't let it go to your head and act foolish out there." *Not like your fool of a king*.

Ironfoot saluted and turned to Bahr. "I cannot thank you enough for your assistance. You have done our clans a great service. If ever you need my axe, you shall have it."

"The honor was mine, Captain Ironfoot. May fortune favor you in the coming battle," Bahr replied with a forced smile. Having seen the size of the enemy force, he didn't know how anyone was going to survive.

"He's one of my best," Thord said thoughtfully after Ironfoot was out of sight. "Would that I had more commanders as capable, this war wouldn't have happened. Hindsight is the great lament of kings. Sea Wolf, you have upheld your part of the bargain. The enemy won't be able to use their cannons to stop my infantry advance. What Ironfoot said goes for me as well. I name you all Dwarf-friend."

Bahr bowed at the great honor. What little he knew about Dwarves suggested the title was not given freely, or without cost. He and his friends had paid enough. It was time to leave and continue with his quest. "Thank you, King Thord."

"I can't let you leave just yet. There is the small matter of a rather large and very angry army between you and the river. Have no fear. We'll have them cleared out and sent crawling back to their caves in short order. I anticipate you being able to depart by dawn," Thord said.

Not what I needed to hear but without Anienam's correct deciphering of the book we don't know how much time is left. I need to get back and find out what the delay is. "I understand, though I would rather leave as soon as possible," replied Bahr.

"You may return freely to Drimmen Delf. Eat, bathe, and sleep. Your wagon will be supplied, weapons sharpened, and I'll see to it that you have enough supplies to last a month of travel. I'd weigh you down with gold if I thought you could use it," he added as an afterthought.

A lesser person would have demanded payment but Thord recognized the honor inherent in Bahr. *This is a Man who is good for his word. The world would be a better place if more strove to be like him.*

They paused to watch Anienam and Skuld amble up the soft slope of Bode Hill. The look in the wizard's eyes was wild, unpredictable. Bahr grimaced. The old fool clearly had something cooked up.

"Wizard," Thord said in greeting. "I hadn't expected to see you here."

"Wars are mundane, Dwarf-lord, but sometimes unavoidable. While I didn't come to help you fight there are certain advantages to having a wizard on your side."

Bahr felt his stomach tighten. *What are you up to?*

Thord eyed Anienam briefly, searching for signs of madness or genius. "What did you have in mind? It's about to get nasty out there."

"I have a few spells worked up that will aid your warriors during the advance. I don't promise victory, mind you, just a little unexpected help."

"Are you sure about this?" Bahr asked. Not what he wanted to say, but this wasn't the place for arguments.

Already the first battalions of Dwarves were assembling in formation. Time slowly ran off.

Anienam winked slyly. "Of course. There's no real danger to me and any army welcomes as much aid as they can get. Hopefully I can speed the battle along and get us moving south again. In a way, I need to do this."

Answerless, Bahr shrugged and took his leave. He'd seen and done enough. Standing idly by to watch hundreds of Dwarves die didn't do much for his stomach. Besides, sleep beckoned. He slung his pack over a shoulder and headed towards the trail leading back to Drimmen Delf. The others followed suit, all but Boen.

The Gaimosian stood and looked out over the battlefield. His eyes were clouded with debate. The warrior blood demanded he armor up and join the attack. It's what Gaimosians were born and bred for. Age and prudence demanded otherwise. Reluctantly, he gave in to common sense and followed Bahr. He'd seen enough war for the time being.

TWENTY-FOUR

Bode Hill

Dawn was especially cold. Evergreens taller than Groge swayed in the breeze. Ice crystals filled the air. Exposed flesh burned from the touch and soldiers shivered uncontrollably as their bodies struggled to find warmth. There would be plenty of heat coming soon enough. Thousands of Dwarves in full armor stood in ranks two hundred across and twenty deep. All waited for the deep horns bellowing across the snow-covered field. The call to charge.

For most it was long overdue. The Black Hammer clan insulted them just by being in the valley. The Dwarves of Drimmen Delf found themselves isolated for the first time since the Mage Wars, centuries ago. Removing the Dark Dwarves opened the path to liberty and a return to normalcy. It ended six months of stalemate and stagnation. Victory lay on the other side of the wide valley.

Anxiety spread through the ranks. Most had seen enough of war and were eager to go back to their normal lives. Drimmen Delf had no standing army. Each Dwarf assembled had another profession but answered the call, as all good Dwarves should, when the invasion began. Those too wounded to be returned to duty frowned and stewed as their comrades prepared for the assault while others managed to sneak from the hospital tents and join the rear ranks.

Banners and pennants waved over the army, each battalions' standard, crisp and saluting a long, distinguished heritage. The very air was electrified with excitement. Waves of frosty breath mingled with the ice. Hands clenched axe hafts. Hearts beat loud. Murmurs and general chitchat circulated the ranks, preventing boredom from setting in. After all, the soldier's life was to hurry up and wait.

Thord had snuck away from the command bunker with a handful of his closest advisors to be with the cannon crews in the moments before the battle began. He needed the time away from maps, troop dispositions, and strategies. The fresh air cleared his mind and prepared him for what came next. Ice and snow clung to his beard like old friends. His eyes, normally dark from being underground, were bright and shining. He glanced skyward and was surprised to find he wasn't disappointed with the sun being concealed behind an ocean of grey-black clouds.

"A good day for a fight," he commented.

"Not so good for those bastards on the other side of the field," Brek replied just as casually.

"No. I don't imagine it will be but make no mistakes about their ferocity. We've taken their long range weapons but not their will to fight. They'll dig in like badgers and make us earn every inch of ground."

Brek yawned. "We've got all the advantages, sire. Our cannons were moved closer to deliver maximum firepower down on their trench lines and we have close to one thousand muskets issued to the front ranks with enough ammunition to sustain ten salvos. The Black Hammer will break and fold."

Muskets. Thord snorted. There was a time when Dwarves fought with axe and iron. Engineers accidentally discovered gunpowder and it wasn't long before idle minds turned it into weapon-grade material. Warfare changed forever that day. Weapons now had range and were three times as lethal as any catapult or trebuchet. They had the ability to kill far more than anything the Dwarves had used before.

Dwarves trained daily to improve marksmanship. The sounds of gunfire transformed large halls into firing ranges and echoed a hellish roar throughout the hold. Cannon crews practiced gunnery for hours a day. Scorpions and ballistae were steadily phased out. Thord despised the gunpowder weapons but was forced to recognize their importance to the future. Thus far only the Dwarves had such weapons, but that wouldn't last. Soon enough all the kingdoms of Malweir would wage wars with musket and cannon. The death toll would be catastrophic.

None of that concerned the Dwarf king. His sole problem lay in the six-thousand-plus army threatening to steal his kingdom. Rumors said the Black Hammer clan had been bribed with untold riches and power by secretive dark powers. Thord thought the notion foolish, until Bahr and the others were brought to Drimmen Delf and explained their quest. Now the idea held greater portent. He became more convinced that the Black Hammer clan needed to be destroyed to the point where they'd never be able to rebuild. Total annihilation was the only way to ensure his victory and see peace return to the Kergland Spine.

"We still have to get through their trenches," Thord offered.

Brek snorted. "Easy enough. We've got ladders and breeching equipment. If worse comes to worse we can turn their own gear against them. I don't see this being an issue."

"You could show a bit of modesty. I appreciate your zeal and boasting as much as the next Dwarf, but we're fighting our kin. Not some Goblin rabble with their heads stuck up their asses. I am worried, Brek. We have never fought a war like this," Thord confided.

"War is war. It doesn't matter who the enemy is. We will crush them all the same. I have no doubts about our forces, sire." He lowered his voice so only the king could hear. "We will win the day and take the field."

"You're sure you can do this?"

Brek only smiled before storming off to take his place at the front of the advance. Dwarves cheered as he strode past. Axes were thumped against chest armor. Booted feet stamped the cold, frozen ground. Brek's zeal transferred to the rank and file. What he believed, they did. He was the fire in the forge, the shining example of what a true hero should be. Each and every Dwarf believed General Brek was about to lead them to victory.

Thord watched his most competent general march through the formation, slapping shoulders and sharing laughs. There was a Dwarf bound for greatness. *Much like myself, long ago. Where did those days go? Am I to spend the rest of my life watching others reap the glory while I sit back and receive the credit?* Jealousy was a base emotion that even a king wasn't above. He reluctantly admitted he wished he and Brek reversed roles. That he alone stood at the end of the battle and raised the banner of Drimmen Delf. Disappointed, he headed back to the command bunker. There wasn't anything left for the king to do here.

"A magnificent sight, don't you think?" Thord asked with pride.

His legions stretched out before him, a mighty metal phalanx strong enough to crush any opponent. A brief hint of sunlight snuck through the clouds long enough to shine on the Dwarven army. Rarely had Anienam seen such majesty. The wizard admired the Dwarves for a moment longer before turning back to Skuld.

"It is time," he said.

Skuld pulled a book out of the leather satchel and set it in front of the wizard. The tome was ancient. A relic from the glory days of Ipn Shal. Anienam's father gave him the secrets of the expansive libraries before he died. The book was but one example. Anienam whistled softly while flipping through the pages. Skuld watched him intently. He found it odd that he took more interest in what Anienam did over Bahr and the others. Skuld greeted them when they returned from the raid on the enemy camp. He saw their bloodstained armor. The cuts and bruises. The hollow looks in their eyes as they tried to put it all behind them. He realized that wasn't the life he wanted to live. Death and glory were polar-opposite ideals.

"Ah, here it is." Anienam cleared his throat and began reciting the incantation scribed upon the page. He'd performed this spell one time before and that was so long ago he couldn't recall the results.

Darkness swarmed across the battlefield in a great and terrible wave. Temperatures dropped another twenty degrees. Lighting plunged down from the heavens, melting snow drifts. Steam rose in waves. Fog and mist flowed down from the mountains, up from the river. Soon the entire valley drowned under a wave of fog so thick vision was reduced to practically nothing. Anienam slumped down into the crude stone chair and took the mug of cold water Skuld passed him. It had been a long time since he performed such a powerful spell.

The Dwarf army recoiled from shock. Only the commanders had been told what to expect but seeing it was a far cry from hearing about it. Many soldiers quivered and threatened to run. Nothing so immediate could be natural and all Dwarves were superstitious. Heavy winds drove the mist and fog across the battlefield towards the enemy line but went unnoticed by most. Rumors quickly spread that Freth, the goddess of the underworld, had risen to claim them all.

General Brek forced his commanders to go among the ranks to instill order. Hold the line at all costs. The unnatural darkness held no ill portent for them, or so Brek fervently hoped. The wizard may be renowned around Malweir but he had yet to prove himself to the Dwarf general. Horses brayed as Dwarves struggled to gain control of the situation. Brek needed the horn to sound before more psychological damage rendered his army ineffective.

"Steady lads. This is on our side," he told his soldiers. "We're going to use it to wipe those dark bastards from the field."

The storm deepened. Brek's stomach lurched. *No wonder we spend most of our lives underground. This isn't right. We should have used the tunnels and come up behind them. No storms, no wizards. Just Dwarves armed with axe and mace*. The sudden braying horn shook him back to the moment. His heart quickened. The time had come.

Thord listened to the horn bleat two short blasts followed by a long, bellowing one. *At last!* He turned to Anienam. "Wizard, I hope your storm works. My army is depending on it."

"I've done my part, your majesty. The rest is up to your Dwarves." Anienam winked at Skuld. Still too weak to rise, he sat and watched as the cannons began firing.

Twenty-four cannons erupted simultaneously. Hellfire and black smoke belched from the dark metal barrels. Two dozen balls of super-heated iron rolled across the sky, trailing fire and burning embers. Filled with twenty pounds of high explosives, each cannon ball had the destructive force of ten catapults. Unlike previous assaults, the enemy lacked the ability to return fire. Caught in the open, Thord's cannons had the potential to devastate the Black Hammer clans.

Skuld's jaw dropped. He'd been deep inside Drimmen Delf when the first cannonade covered Bahr's sabotage mission and didn't see or hear the horror unleashed. It was unlike anything he could ever imagine. The very ground threatened to break apart under him. He began to sweat under the intense pressure building in his head. The first cannon ball struck enemy lines and exploded with more fire and cold hatred than Skuld could stand. His knees buckled as the sky erupted in flames and screams.

Thord roared approval, shaking a fist at the inferno. A second and third salvo was fired. Then a fourth. The Dwarves bristled and started surging forward, rocking back and forth as they built momentum. Squat bodies bunched, muscles strained with power. Between the fourth and fifth salvo a lowly horn brayed over the field. The call to charge. Thousands of Dwarves roared as one and started forward. A slow walk quickly turned into a trot. The cannons continued firing.

TWENTY-FIVE

Badron's Fury

Badron stood atop Rogscroft's battlements watching another part of the city burn out of control. Flames licked high into the sky as buildings quickly died. Smoke clung to the air with a pall. Nearly half of the city had already been reduced to char and ash. Those few civilians who dared stay behind, believing one king no different from another, remained secure in their homes for fear of their lives. Badron had decreed that no civilian would die unless it was unavoidable. The Goblins broke that peace and slaughtered with ruthless abandon.

"Three nights," Badron murmured. "The bastards have been burning and killing everything they can find for three nights. When will it end? I feel like a hostage in my own hall. Can't you use your powers to stop this?"

Amar Kit'han hovered in the nearby shadows. "Why would I do that? The Goblins serve a higher purpose than just your call, king."

Badron fixed the Dae'shan with a wicked glare. "Why else would they be here if not to serve my will? This is my war. They will obey my commands or be sent back to their holes in cold, wooden boxes."

Simple fool, if only you had an inkling of what lay in store for you. Perhaps then you wouldn't be so hasty to claim your dominance. "They are angered. Grugnak believes you have betrayed him. Revenge is a natural course of events. The Goblins require blood to satisfy their sullied honor, but do not be so bold as to think you control their armies. Without me they would not be here and you would not be sitting on the Rogscroft throne."

"The Wolfsreik is the supreme military power in the north. You overestimate these ugly vermin. I didn't need them."

Amar drifted to the edge of shadows and stopped. "Yet they are here nonetheless. You cannot change the past, king. The real question is what will you do now? Grugnak is out of control and he knows you lack the power to stop him. All power is now in his hands and your wolf soldiers appear to have abandoned you in your hour of greatest need."

Badron punched the closest wall. Dust and concrete crumbled from the rock, staining his dark brown leather glove. "Don't make assumptions until I have all the necessary facts."

"What more do you need? General Rolnir disobeyed your commands. His soldiers turned on their Goblin allies, slaughtering them alongside the Pell Darga. Your greatest asset seems to have turned to your greatest fear."

"I am a king, I do not know fear," Badron replied weakly.

Amar sneered. "But you do. All kings understand fear better than the common folk. You sleep with it, eat with it, and even go to the privy in fear. Every shadow holds an assassin. Every dawn the prospect of failure. You cringe at the sound of the wind. Do not feign great strength or wisdom with me, king. I have seen your darkest fears and the very depths of your despair. Shall I show you?"

"No." Badron folded his arms across his chest and shivered. It had gotten cold and he was ill prepared for it. The winters in Rogscroft were much worse than his Delranan. "As you said, now is not the time to focus on the past. There is truth in your words, creature, but I won't condemn my entire army to die without hearing Rolnir's explanation first."

"Perhaps, but what will you do? Grugnak is not known for his patience. His army will continue to pillage and burn Rogscroft, ruining all you came so far to achieve. Are you willing to let him end your reign? Imagine, your name being unremembered in a hundred years."

Badron paused. His motives fell under question. The surety of his cause disintegrated around him. He'd gone to war under the pretense of avenging his murdered son. It was a ruse, a poorly played one at best. Stelskor and his success in Rogscroft had always been a point of contention and jealousy. Badron manipulated the situation in his favor and attacked his longtime rival. The campaign was brutal, especially with the involvement of the Pell Darga, but his banner flew over the Rogscroft parapet right above Stelskor's head. Victory was his.

Or was it? Victory belonged to the one with the most strength. All his was gone. He stood alone on the cold rock wall. A king without a kingdom. Worse, rumors of Harnin's betrayal in Delranan robbed him of much needed supplies and reinforcements. Badron stood alone in more ways than one. His closest advisor wasn't even human anymore and spoke in riddles. He had no doubts that Amar Kit'han was leading him to a predestined event and that left him truly frightened. Scared as he might be, Badron couldn't find a way to break the Dae'shan's grip. Nor did he want to. He enjoyed the lure of power. The lusty feeling of supremacy. The Dae'shan could be dealt with when the time was right, but for now they would continue helping him achieve his goals. *So long as my goals coincide with theirs, no doubt.*

"My legacy will be secured, spare your doubts from that," Badron said slowly. "I have done what many in the north said couldn't be done. My enemy is dead. His kingdom is in ruins. History will remember me as the king who unified the north into an empire."

"Only if you remain alive long enough," Amar countered.

Badron hated the hissing sound laced in his words. Hated the condescending attitude with which the Dae'shan spoke. He recognized he was being used and it burned his soul. Creatures like Amar went behind the scenes. They went unremembered, not kings. Amar Kit'han had spent several lifetimes without anyone knowing he was alive. Badron found the thought wasteful.

"Perhaps you'd like to see my head occupy the next pike?" he asked.

Amar was silent for a moment too long. "Live or die, it does not matter to me. I am an agent of a higher purpose. Perhaps your daughter would accept my position. She has been hated from birth. It is easier this way. No attachments. No motivations. Yes, perhaps I should find Maleela."

Badron spun. Anger crossed his features. He pointed his index finger accusingly. "Leave my daughter alone! She has no part in this."

Amar pressed harder. "But she does. You should never have blamed her for the death of Rialla. A child does not get to choose such things. The dark gods wanted your wife to die. Does that trouble you? She needed to die. As did your son. You needed to be broken. A haggard semblance of the man you might have become. Only then could I manipulate you into what you might achieve under the tutelage of the dark gods. You should be on your knees groveling, king. A great honor has been bestowed upon you."

Something in Badron's mind snapped in that moment. Decades of pent-up grief, aggression, and lethargy broke through their barriers and collided in the depths of his conscience. He wanted to cry. To scream to the heavens. To feel anything but hatred and contempt. Only, he didn't know how anymore. He'd been a shell of a man for so long he couldn't recall what it was to be human. It became his pride and damnation.

He tried looking deep into himself to find remorse, pity. There was none. He was as bitter and twisted as a failed attempt at making a sword. Darkness clung to him now. Badron slowly came to realize his life was one fated to despair. Winds shifted and blew the smell of rotting corpses into his face.

"You did all this." It was more statement than question. Badron wanted, needed, to hear Amar Kit'han's admission. It was the only way to soothe the demons growling in his soul.

For the first time, the Dae'shan was unsure about how to reply. He hadn't expected Badron to awaken from the delusions of power. Still, there was room to maneuver him back into the trap and ensnare him forever. "There are events that have not yet happened that I have foreseen you standing in a position of immense power and wealth. The very crown of the world will be placed upon your brow. All you need to do is reach out your hand."

"You murdered my wife and my son," Badron accused.

"Murdered? No, I merely watched and…"

Taking a step closer, Badron clenched his fist. "And?"

"Stood by. I could have saved them if it served my purpose, but their lives were already claimed by the dark gods. Even I have masters, king. Do not think me the independent renegade bent on souring kingdoms for some nefarious purpose. I do as my masters command. They demanded the sacrifice of your family."

"I should strike you down and cast your shadows to the ground below."

Amar laughed. "You cannot kill me. I am not from this world. Any blow you might deliver, any sword or spear would never touch me." He rushed forward quickly, taking Badron off guard. "But one touch from my finger and I will reduce you to a pile of smoldering ash. Mind your tongue wisely or I will have it removed and fed to the crows for sport."

Amar's hand glowed an eerie blue-green, giving Badron pause. As much as he wanted to rip the Dae'shan's heart out and feed it back to him, Badron recognized the error of his thoughts. Amar Kit'han was raw power. Wheels in his mind turned. He needed to find a way to sway Amar back to his cause, to regain control and continue with the execution of his plans for the northern kingdoms.

"Perhaps not, demon," Badron hissed. "So long as you assist my war."

Fool. This war was never yours. You are a puppet for the dark gods and a poor one at best. I shall let you have your little game for as long as it amuses me. He bowed crisply, a casual reminder of a life long forgotten. "It shall be as you say, king. What do you propose to do about your renegade general? And your Goblin problems? You will need one of their armies to continue."

Badron began to pace. "Yes, I know all that. I can't hold Rogscroft without an army and I need another to retake Delranan. Harnin will suffer greatly for his sins."

If you only knew. "Events developing in Delranan are unfortunate but there is nothing you can do about it until after you resolve the dilemma here."

"And until winter ends," Badron added. "Very well. I'm going to summon Rolnir and demand an accounting for his treason. Grugnak will be easier to placate once that is done. The Goblins will go back to their submissive ways and I can begin consolidating the throne."

By then it shall be far too late.

"Why settle for just two crowns? The whole of the north is ripe for conquest. You could march an army unopposed all the way to the Deadlands in the east."

"The Deadlands? There is nothing there worth conquering. Besides, the Goblins dominate that kingdom. Tens and tens of thousands of their filth. I would not march there with three armies at my back. No. I will look west and south, but only after Rolnir is brought to heel and the Goblin issue is finished."

Amar bowed again. "As you wish, king."

Shadows rose and swirled furiously, collapsing in on themselves as the Dae'shan disappeared. Badron stood alone again and turned back to what little remained of Rogscroft. A new fire sprang up from the distance. There wouldn't be anything left of the city if he didn't stop the Goblins from their insane looting soon.

"Your game grows too dangerous. You risk much in that fool," Kodan Bak snapped once Amar Kit'han finished materializing in the small, dark chamber.

"Ever you seek to supplant me, Kodan Bak. Kill me if you must and assume control but stop wasting my time with idle threats. We have work to do."

"There is always work to do," Kodan Bak retorted. "You turn it into a child's game."

"Have you forgotten so much of your past? All humanity centers on petty games. They scheme and play at divinity. Some dare think their will can contend with that of the gods. Humanity is a mockery of what life should be. They need to be culled and put back in their place."

"I remember what it meant to be human, and I have little use for those memories. This is what life should have always been."

Amar cocked his head. "Why then do you continually seek to challenge my authority?"

"All authority should be questioned. Rulers need to be deposed from time to time. Under your rule the Dae'shan have been reduced to playthings. Artiss Gran abandoned our true purpose. Pelthit Re seeks his own path to greater glory and I rot at your side. The future is not so bright as you would have us believe."

Kodan Bak drifted back. He'd seen Amar Kit'han angry enough times to avoid getting caught in his ire without being prepared. Kodan collected power, ready to unleash at a moment, and waited.

"The dark gods will be here soon. We have much work yet to do and you waste time reminding me of *our* failures. Was it not you that failed the Masters in that miserable kingdom of Aradain? There is plenty of blame to go around."

Aradain. The name was a stain on their honor. Long before the creation of the Mages and the crystal of Tol Shere, shortly after the prearranged fall Gaimos, the Dae'shan sought to open a nexus and return their gods to Malweir. It was only through a handful of Vengeance Knights that they failed.

"The Edaas paid for their failure, Amar," Kodan countered harshly. "The death cult should never have been given so much power."

"Power is relative to station. We cannot make the same mistake. The dark gods now have the Cracked Crystal. Once the appointed time arrives the portal will open and darkness will once again blanket the lands. They cannot do that as long as there is strength in the north. We must continue to use Badron to destroy what might remains. Only then will the path be open."

"What of the wizard? They found Venheim and all our efforts to stop them have failed. He is the only power capable of ruining our plans," Kodan asked.

"The Hags have failed me. I warned Freina not to make contact."

Kodan didn't care. Harpies were more inconsequential than humans. "Foolish, but not to the point of ruining our work here. They continue to harry the wizard but more is required."

"Send out the word. I will pay a large sum for their heads, especially the brother of King Badron and Anienam Keiss. There is a tribe of mountain men in the northern part of the Kergland Spine. The wizard must be stopped before he can reach Trennaron."

"They have already crossed over the mountains and are embroiled in the middle of the Dwarf civil war. It was wise turning one of the largest clans to our cause."

Amar agreed. The stroke proved masterful. Not only did it reduce the combat power of the Dwarves, it also took their focus off of events in the west. A Dwarf army might be too much for even the reborn dark gods.

"The war will not prevent the wizard from reaching the river, though it may delay him just long enough. There is still a chance to end his meddling. Go now. I will deal with the Hags and King Badron."

Kodan Bak disappeared in a puff of darkness, leaving the leader of the Dae'shan commiserating with his own monsters.

TWENTY-SIX

Traitors

Piper finished reading the parchment and crumbled it up. He gave Rolnir the briefest look before tossing it in the fire. "That's settled."

"Unfortunately," Rolnir agreed. "You do know what this means?"

Piper nodded slowly. "We can never go home unless Badron is dead."

"Or deposed."

"Six in one hand," Piper replied.

Rolnir looked at his senior commander and best friend. "How do you manage to find levity in this? We've been declared traitors."

"Look around. It's the coldest winter I can recall. We're running low on rations, trapped in a foreign kingdom, and have an army of Goblins ready to march against us. There's not much point in staying serious when you think about it."

Rolling his eyes, the general of the Wolfsreik circled the fire. "I never dreamed such a day would come. The very source of power for countless kings of Delranan has abandoned the throne and gone rogue. This is a war unlike any other, Piper."

"It could be worse. Your head would be on a pike next to King Stelskor's if you'd have answered Badron's summons," Piper speculated. "And the rest of us would be smashing into Goblin lines trying to avenge your death. I think this way works out better. We can fight on our terms."

"What are our terms?" Rolnir asked. "Everything I've trained for, believed in, has turned out to be a lie. Our tactics won't work against Badron."

"I can't see why they wouldn't. Badron's not the warrior-king he thinks he is. He may know our tactics but knowing doesn't give him the ability to counter. He's reduced to a Goblin army sorely lacking in proper military training and discipline."

"They don't need discipline when they have numbers. Goblins fight like wild animals, making them dangerous. They lack honor and refuse to adhere to the rules of war. The only way to beat them is to adopt their tactics." Rolnir finally resumed his seat on the large tree stump and reached for the coffee pot sitting on the rock wall lining the fire. "You know, I might have gone mad by now if it weren't for this."

"Coffee makes an army move, even in the dead of winter," Piper said. "What are your orders? We can't stay here for long."

"Agreed. The Goblins are more than likely already en route. We need to split up. Get in with King Aurec and his Pell Darga. It's the only way we can salvage some sort of victory and still retain enough fighting force to take Delranan back."

"It might be too early to think about home," Piper added. "The Goblin threat is too severe to make future plans."

"Our three armies combined should be more than enough to destroy the Goblins."

Piper shook his head. "Unless Badron calls up reinforcements from the Deadlands."

"You're full of good news, aren't you?" Rolnir scolded and emptied the dregs of his cup back on the fire. "Has there been word from Herger?"

"Not since he left with a battalion of Aurec's soldiers and General Vajna."

Since the battle in the mountains Herger and his infantry hadn't been back to the main army for more than a night to refit and resupply. Rolnir believed the Wolfsreik's only hope for survival lay in staying in the field and keeping Badron guessing. So far the enemy had been unable to adjust. Small Goblin units were being picked off at random. The death toll continued to rise. Rolnir considered himself fortunate to have sustained minimal casualties. But that wouldn't last. It never did. There'd be a reckoning soon enough.

"Vajna is a good man," Piper said. "He'll break the Goblins. Force them to withdraw where we can hit them with all our might."

"This war isn't going to end without a lot more death. The crows will eat well."

Piper grinned. "Are you trying to dampen my good mood? It usually takes rain to do that."

"I wouldn't be a general if I made everyone happy," Rolnir replied with a hint of humor. There were times he wished he'd never been promoted. *Better to remain in the rank and file and go about my life without knowing what was going on.* "I'm going to turn in for the night. You've put too much on my mind and my stomach is unsettled."

"That's what good commanders are for." Piper rose and saluted his friend and leader. "I'll check the lines to ensure you get a good night's sleep."

"Whatever would I do without you as my second?"

Piper held out his arms. "A question I've long pondered during cold guard shifts."

The truth was the Wolfsreik needed people like Piper if there was to be another dawn.

"We're under attack!"

Piper jumped up at the sound of the cry. He quickly slid into his boots and reached for his sword belt. He was halfway out the tent before strapping it to his waist. What he found disheartened him. Goblins had come in from the north and overran the pickets and first line of defense before the Wolfsreik regrouped and managed to counterattack. Bodies littered the camp. Most were his soldiers. Piper drew his sword and roared an ancient Delranan battle cry. Echoes sprang up from across the beleaguered camp as his soldiers rallied.

Men were running everywhere, desperate to get to their battle positions. Goblins that managed to break through the freshly formed line hacked and slashed at anything that moved. Piper watched arrows riddle the nearest Goblin. It was dead before it hit the snow. Enraged, the Wolfsreik commander headed towards the line.

He grabbed the nearest soldier by the collar and jerked him close. "Find General Rolnir and inform him that I am assuming command of the defense. Tell him the enemy is attacking in force and has broken through in several places."

The soldier ran off and Piper turned towards the fires. The first few rows of tents blazed out of control. *How many died in those tents? Even one is too many. Soldiers should die in battle, not their sleep.* A pair of Goblins crept from between two tents and charged. Their blunted tulwars were dripping blood. Each Goblin bore a crazed look. The killing had already gotten to them, making them wild, unpredictable. Piper snarled and attacked.

His sword swept low, a blow aimed at disemboweling a man but high enough to rip across a Goblin's throat. The Goblin blocked and jerked back, exposing his midsection. The second Goblin attacked as soon as Piper went off balance. Piper barely managed to slip aside. The tulwar sliced down where he'd just been standing. Piper continued to attack. Three quick blows, two high and one low, pushed the Goblin back. Unused to this aggressive style of fighting, the Goblin made the fatal mistake of lowering his weapon long enough for Piper to rip his sword across the Goblin's throat. Hot blood melted the snow it landed on.

Enraged, the second Goblin raised his tulwar over his head and bull rushed. Piper took a half step back and planted his feet to meet the charge. The Goblin never lowered his weapon, a fatal error. Piper's sword punched up under his jaw and out the back of his neck. Blood frothing from his lips, the Goblin's eyes crossed. He dropped the tulwar and reached for Piper's throat. It was a useless gesture. Piper stepped back and spun around, taking the Goblin's head. Out of breath and exhilarated, Piper raced to the line.

What he saw encouraged him. It wasn't as bad as his initial estimates. Scores of Goblins lay dead, compared to a handful of his men. The enemy hadn't penetrated more than a few meters before being repulsed. Piper grinned. Goblins were no match for his well-disciplined soldiers. Goblins died in great numbers as more of the Wolfsreik filled gaps in the line.

"Commander Joach! General Rolnir says to expect similar attacks around the perimeter. Scouts report movement to the east and west," the same soldier Piper had dispatched earlier reported.

Not standard Goblin tactics. Grugnak has never been this subtle. Piper's guard rose immediately. A quick glance back at the battle confirmed that most of the enemy was either dead or had pulled back into the night. He turned back to the soldier with new orders. "Find the ranking officer here and order him to dig in but not to expect another assault. I want every other soldier to displace and move to alternate positions to the east and west. He is to have a reserve prepared to move to any part of the camp in moments. Do you understand?"

"Yes sir!"

"Move! We don't have much time," Piper snapped and the soldier raced off.

The Wolfsreik camp was attacked three additional times that night. Goblins pushed in force but never managed to break the line at any point. Piper moved from engagement to engagement, offering encouragement and jumping in the line when the opportunity presented itself. He shouldn't have. Rolnir might demote him if he ever learned his senior commander risked his life so carelessly.

In the end the Wolfsreik held. Whatever remained of the Goblin force had fled back to whatever hole they'd skulked out of, but the damage was done. The Wolfsreik was no longer safe. Rolnir had no choice but to either break up or move en masse and he needed to have it done by nightfall. No one doubted the enemy wouldn't be back by the time the sun set. A sense of urgency spread through the army. Soldiers began packing what few possessions they had without orders in anticipation of the move. Sergeants conducted inspections and readied their squads and platoons for the next fight while low level commanders speculated what their next move was going to be.

"It seems our position is more urgent than we believed," Piper told Rolnir after offering a haggard salute. He was exhausted, physically and mentally.

Soot stains on his face and armor, Rolnir wasn't about to disagree. "Badron moved faster than I expected him to. We've lost the advantage."

"Not necessarily. There's no way he can cover us if we split the army."

Rolnir scratched the stubble on his cheek. "I'd rather not. We'll be too exposed, vulnerable to more of these Goblin-style assaults."

"I still think we need to draw them into the open and hammer them with a cavalry charge. There's no way they'd be able to withstand it."

"Piper, this is a war of attrition. We can't be too free with our lives. The enemy has the option of being careless, suggesting reinforcements are already coming in from the east. I need to meet with King Aurec. The only way to win is through a fully coordinated campaign. Aurec is adapt at guerilla warfare. A tactic we sorely lack."

Piper took the compliment with a measure of anger. His vanguard made first contact with Aurec's forces and suffered severe casualties. It was a stark lesson in warfare and he took it personally. Despite Rolnir's insistence otherwise, Piper felt shamed by failure.

"I'm sure there's a better way," Piper replied, but without heart.

Rolnir held up his hand. "I know how you feel but we're being pushed against the wall. We need Aurec's soldiers and his style of fighting if we're going to have enough soldiers left to retake Delranan."

"Perhaps I should sit this meeting out," Piper suggested.

"Don't make this more difficult than it needs to be," Rolnir reinforced with a much sterner voice. "I need you sharp. Badron's removed our debate by seizing initiative. Let's take the war back to him and end this now."

Piper gradually relented and nodded. "Fine, but don't expect me to be overjoyed by it. I'll extend my hand to Aurec because you command it. Now, General, what are your orders?"

TWENTY-SEVEN

Kings and Generals

The coronation celebration was weeks old and largely forgotten. Men and women quickly stopped their revelry and returned to the hard prospect of fighting a guerilla war. King Aurec paced Grunmarrow like a trapped mountain lion. He wanted to fight. To attack and end the Delrananian rule of Rogscroft. The idea of taking the war back across the mountains never entered his mind.

So many lives had been lost in the few short months of the campaign here he'd never be able to raise enough support to invade their neighbors across the Murdes Mountains. Not that he minded. The combination of his father's death and the destruction of his cities left him with a hollow feeling. He slowly came to realize just how tired he was. Wars were meant for others. Some greater, some lesser.

Grunmarrow was alive again. Scouts had returned with news of the recent Goblin attack on the Wolfsreik's main camp. Badron's kingdom was in turmoil. His alliance was shattered. Men and Goblins turned on each other. The people of Rogscroft rejoiced at the unexpected news. They saw it as the beginning of the end. Aurec didn't have the heart to dissuade their notions. He knew it for what it really was: a prelude to something far worse.

Aurec's council urged immediate movements while the enemy was in disarray. While there was some merit to that line of thinking, he couldn't commit the bulk of his forces without more concrete information. There was more at stake than simply taking advantage of a rare glimpse of sunlight.

Thus far Vajna's combined operations with the Wolfsreik and Pell Darga in the northern foothills of the Murdes Mountains proved mutually beneficial but wouldn't last forever. At the end of the day the Wolfsreik was still the enemy and needed to be removed from Rogscroft. The situation became more convoluted daily, enough that Aurec suffered from severe headaches at night. Worse, he missed Maleela more as the days sped by.

Reluctantly, he turned from the sanctity of his tent and headed towards the council tent. Meeting with his senior commanders was quite possibly the last thing he wanted or needed right now. Drawing a deep breath, Aurec returned the guard's salute and entered. Those assembled rose in respect to their king and leader. Aurec waved them down and took his seat at the head of the table.

Pitchers of water and wine sat between platters of cheese, day-old bread, and a meat he couldn't identify. One wall the tent had been transformed into map boards, with icons for every unit in the field. Fires burned at both ends of the tent, not enough to completely warm them but enough to kill the slight chill clinging to each man. Aurec idly wondered where his people managed to find a crimson tent but knew better than to ask. Sometimes the answer wasn't what you needed to hear.

"Who's going to begin?"

Venten cleared his throat and rose. "Sire, as I'm sure you are aware, we've received reports of the Goblin assault south of Rogscroft proper."

"I believe I've heard a passing word or two. What do we do about it?"

"General Rolnir has disbanded the bulk of his army and sent them into smaller task forces to confuse the Goblins. While I can't confirm it, I strongly suspect Badron has declared open war against the Wolfsreik."

"I disagree, sire," Paneolus countered. "The Wolfsreik has been the symbol of Delrananian power for centuries. It is ridiculous to believe he'd turn against them now in favor of the Goblins."

"These are trying times, Counselor," Aurec said respectfully. "We already have some of Badron's soldiers fighting alongside us in the north. It isn't implausible to think

Badron's gone to extreme measures to exact his revenge for disobedience."

"But against the entire army? He'd lose ten thousand soldiers."

Sergeant Thorsson added, "Highly trained and well disciplined. The Wolfsreik lives and breathes for war. They executed their campaign to conquer our lands ruthlessly but with honor. My opinion, sire, is that the Wolfsreik realized Badron was off his rocker and decided it went against their moral code. I agree with Venten."

Paneolus's cheeks reddened. Instead of barking a retort he merely reached for a chunk of bread. He was a lifelong politician and knew when the odds weren't in his favor. Best to let the discussion play out rather than risk evoking the new king's ire. There'd be a time soon enough when he could meet with Aurec one on one. Perhaps then Paneolus might be able to persuade the boy king to reconsider.

"This could just be a ruse. Men and Goblins don't mix. Badron could be using this diversion to cull his opponents," Aurec suggested. "We can't discount anything at this point."

Paneolus concealed his grin.

"But Vajna's operations…" Venten began.

"Are useful, but not necessarily in our best interests. Badron is more cunning than any of you seem willing to give him credit for. Tell me, what do you think, Mahn? You've been strangely silent this morning."

The older scout rubbed his chin while trying to figure out the proper way to say what he felt. He was a soldier, not a statesman. His life was an endless series of journeys deep into the wild and potentially hazardous situations. Only he never expected to find himself embroiled in the dangerous world of politics. When he spoke it was uncertain.

"Sire, I only know what I saw. We fought the Wolfsreik for months. There is no love lost between our two armies. Everything changed when the Goblins arrived. I believe that General Rolnir may have indeed gone against Badron's wishes. He is an honorable man. We should listen to what he has to say."

Aurec broke into a grin. "Good. He's on his way here with a small delegation."

"What?"

"Sire! You'll put us all in jeopardy," Paneolus spat, bits of bread and meat flying from his mouth.

"We're already in jeopardy, my friend. In case you haven't noticed, we're at war," Aurec said in a measured voice. "Our enemies continue to gain strength while we wither away here. We are weak, gentlemen."

"That will change once winter ends," Venten said. "We'll be able to go on the offensive and take advantage of the discourse between the Wolfsreik and Goblins. Badron can be beaten, sire. We must bide our time though."

"Time is a luxury we don't have, which is why I invited Rolnir here. It is my belief that everything has changed. Yes, we can win but only through joining forces with the Wolfsreik. The worst that can happen is we rid Rogscroft of the Goblin threat."

Aurec rose and went to the maps. "We have less than two thousand swords here at Grunmarrow. Another three thousand at Stormeir. Even with both forces combined we're undermanned by more than ten thousand. There are small units spread across Rogscroft, from the Murdes Mountains to the northern coast, but we have no effective way to coordinate efforts. The Pell Darga guard all the mountain passes but will be hard pressed to prevent convoys and wagon trains from going back and forth once the snows melt. Our efforts to defeat the enemy thus far have worked but only on a small scale."

He paused to look each in the eye. "We currently hold less than a quarter of our own territory and are being pushed further away despite our best efforts. We are losing this war. Show me another way to reverse our fortunes and

I'm all ears but until then we have no choice but to meet with Rolnir and try to salvage something of our kingdom."

"We simply cannot enter into an agreement with a foreign army without contingencies," Paneolus argued. "We'd be exposed, vulnerable to whatever they might set their minds to once the main problem is dealt with. You all know I am no soldier, but I know how rulers think and behave. This Rolnir is no different from any other politician."

"I don't see how," Venten said.

"He's looking after his own neck. A dead man can't do much," the former minister of state replied flatly.

"Regardless," Aurec interrupted. "I expect him within the hour. Have a tent prepared and food ready to be brought. I'm sure they will be hungry after riding through most of the night. Also detail some hands to clean out a stable for their mounts. I don't want them getting mixed in with ours." The very real threat of poison entered his mind. Above all else, Rolnir was a professional soldier who had been a fervent enemy until a few weeks ago. Every caution needed to be taken until Aurec was sure of the Wolfsreik's sincerity.

"Sire, thank you for accepting my request to meet," Rolnir said with a proper bow.

Aurec bid him rise. "General Rolnir, it is an honor to meet you at last. We have been enemies for far too long."

"Regretfully, but this was never our war of choice," Rolnir replied. The subtle edge of tartness laced his tone, enough to draw glares from several of Aurec's council.

"Perhaps that is a discussion best left untouched for now," Aurec replied. The muscles in his cheeks rippled. "I trust your trip here was unremarkable?"

"For the most part, though we were forced to take a few detours thanks to Goblin patrols. The vermin are everywhere these days."

"So I've come to understand. May I present to you my council? Paneolus, former minister of state. A harsh man out of necessity. He's the only professional politician among us. This is Venten. A one-time general turned tutor now my closest friend and mentor. Mahn used to be chief of scouts and now serves as liaison to the Pell Darga. Lastly, Sergeant Thorsson. He took a nasty wound defending the gates of Rogscroft and is my personal standard bearer. Regretfully Cuul Ol, the chief of the Pell Darga clans, could not be with us today."

Rolnir bowed and saluted each accordingly before turning to his abbreviated staff. "This is Commander Piper Joach. He is my right hand and executive officer. I trust him implicitly. Colonel Ulaf, master of engineers, and Colonel Mentyl, my chief surgeon. A man who has been unusually busy as of late. Colonel Herger, my infantry commander, is away to the north with your General Vajna. My understanding is our combined campaign is progressing nicely, though I would like it a little faster."

"We are all tired of war, General," Aurec replied and led the way into the command tent. He continued once everyone was seated.

TWENTY-EIGHT

Growing Darkness

Captain Ironfoot finally allowed himself to drop to his knees and bow his head. His muscles burned. Pain screamed from a dozen wounds. Blood stained his beard and armor, transforming him into a vision of death. It was all he could do to remain standing. So many conflicting thoughts disturbed him. He wasn't sure how he was still alive, much less on his feet and coherent enough to command his battalion. Or rather what remained of it.

He didn't need to look around to know that a good portion of the Feral Axe battalion lay dead in the snow. Honor demanded he felt shame for still living when so many of those he'd been responsible for weren't. Hanging his head, the Dwarf captain jerked his axe from the chest of his last victim. The blade tore free after some struggle, accompanied by a sickly crunching sound. Blood and ichor dripped from the nicked and dulled blade.

Ironfoot stood in the center of the field of death. Crows and vultures had come from the mountains to pick at the dead. Thousands of bodies littered the snow for as far as he could see, their dark shapes and the already frozen blood in sharp contrast to the once pristine snow. An iron taint clung heavily to the air. It was unlike anything Ironfoot had ever seen. He looked up at the sound of a Dwarf retching and wondered why he didn't feel the same.

The cannon barrage had proven horrifically effective. Believing themselves safe from the enemy artillery, the Dark Dwarves emerged from their trenches to erect a stern line of defense against the oncoming infantry. They never counted on Thord moving his cannons forward. Hundreds of arms and legs and the occasional head littered the ground around the trenches in testament to the brutality

Thord had unleashed. Those Dwarves that didn't die immediately soon bled out in their trenches.

But that was only the first line. Ironfoot and his battalion had much further to go before getting back to the center of the enemy camp. It was a fight worthy of legend. One he wished he never had to partake in. The sheer amount of slaughter turned his stomach and deadened his senses. *So many friends.* Ironfoot was a soldier, had been for decades. But he, none of them, had ever seen a battle this destructive. He prayed to all the gods that he never did again.

"Captain, I have the preliminary casualty figures," Sergeant Bridgestormer said with an uncharacteristically low voice.

Ironfoot couldn't find the strength to turn. He wasn't ready for numbers. Didn't know how the lives of his soldiers could so casually be reduced to facts and figures on a piece of parchment. Heart heavy, he waved Bridgestormer off. "Not now, Sergeant. Give them to me later, after I'm too drunk to think clearly."

"Yes sir. What are your orders?"

Orders? To whom? For what? The crows will have this place picked clean in no time. The sun will eventually melt the blood-covered snow and the world will go on much like it always has. Why would anyone need orders? "We cannot help the dead. Have the survivors regroup at the edge of the first trench and see to their wounds. Everyone needs to eat, if possible, and rehydrate. The enemy is broken but still has sufficient numbers to press a counterattack if they really wanted to."

"I don't see how anyone would want to make a second run at this," Bridgestormer remarked. "Was a damned slaughter from the beginning."

"Yes it was. I wonder if they had any idea what was coming."

Shrugging, Bridgestormer replied, "Does it matter? This is war. It's all any of us can do just to make it to tomorrow. Nothing else matters when the enemy closes with you."

"That's not very sympathetic, Sergeant. These were once our kin," Ironfoot said.

"They gave as good as they got. Well, a little less. We won the field, sir. That's what counts right now. We'll clear the field. Burn out dead and treat the wounded. Crops will be sown and Drimmen Delf will go on like it has since the First Dawn. We are Dwarves, Captain. Never forget that. I'll have those numbers for you when you are ready."

Ironfoot watched his second in command amble off. Bridgestormer offered words of encouragement to others and helped many off the ground. Every guide-on and banner he found he immediately raised to plant upright. The colors of Drimmen Delf soon covered the field, waving triumphantly in the crisp midday wind.

"My friends, brothers, comrades in arms! Raise your mugs! Tonight we toast our heroic dead. Each and every Dwarf who gave his life so that Drimmen Delf may continue is a hero. To the dead!"

Hundreds of Dwarves gathered in the main drinking hall raised their mugs, horns, and cups, echoing King Thord's words. The very ground trembled as Dwarves stamped their feet and pounded hammer-like fists on row upon row of wooden tables. Roaring fires lined the walls. Some cooked giant boars or deer. Others just for heat. Barrels of ale and beer, dark and rich, emptied almost as soon as porters managed to roll them in. Bands played harsh music in the style of ancient Dwarven custom that echoed around the hall.

The celebration feast was an old tradition. Dwarves gathered to give praise to the gods and their fallen. That didn't diminish the massive effort being undertaken on the battlefield as hordes of Dwarves recovered bodies, weapons, and any other paraphernalia from the battle. The feast came first, followed the next night by the funerals. With the amount of casualties it was going to take almost an entire forest to burn all the bodies. The Dwarves didn't think on it. Each funeral pyre was constructed with love and pride. It was considered a great honor to participate in a warrior's funeral.

Thord drained his mug and slammed it down, signaling for a refill. His beard was already sopping from spilled ale. His belch rivaled the beating drums, prompting laughs from those closest. Even Anienam barked a laugh or two, much to the surprise of his comrades. They were guests of honor, each having contributed to the Dwarf victory. Faeldrin and the Aeldruin occupied a table opposite of the Dwarf king. All fifty strong had come out of the battle unscathed. They secured the river crossings, burning bridges to prevent the Dark Dwarves from escaping.

"My ancestors must be laughing down on me!" Thord bellowed. "Elf, man, and Giant all celebrating in the middle of the Hraldfeist. Ha. These are strange days indeed."

Faeldrin grinned and tilted his head out of respect. "Very little surprises me after having spent centuries wandering Malweir. I must admit this is a first for my Aeldruin as well, King Thord. We are humbled to be part of such celebrations."

"The honor is mine. You have been immense aid in our war. For that I name you Dwarf-friend from now until the breaking of the world." They clasped forearms, one thickly corded and muscled, the other thin yet powerful. "Alas, I wish I could say having an Elf in Drimmen Delf was the strangest happening but so many forces have come at once."

"Wars seldom develop the way we envision before the first arrow is fired," Anienam said cheerfully.

"Or cannon," Bahr added. He still wasn't sure how or where he fit in. The desire to get back on the road proved almost overwhelming, making it difficult to concentrate on the sights and sounds of the hall.

Thord laughed again. "Damned right. I bet you've never dreamed of such weapons."

"No," Bahr admitted. "And now that I've seen them in action I pray the technology never makes it south into the kingdoms of men. Such a thing would change the face of Malweir."

"You can't halt progress, Sea Wolf," Thord countered. "Still, most men I know are petty and wicked. Cannons would ruin everything."

Boen listened intently, though with a different perspective. He imagined an army of Gaimosians with cannons. Gaimos would never have fallen. Western Malweir would be settled, instead of the lawlessness running rampant now. No, he reasoned. Too many kingdoms banded together because Gaimos had grown too powerful for its own good. Boen decided Gaimos would still have fallen and his people scattered, leaderless to all corners of the world.

Bahr found himself agreeing with the Dwarf. "Do you think the Dark Dwarves will return, or have we beaten them to the point where they know better?"

"It's been my experience evil always finds a way to return," Anienam said. "And good always finds a way to allow it. A very strange world, ours. Centuries later and I'm still trying to learn the rules."

"One of the sad state of affairs, I'm afraid," Faeldrin seconded. "Now that the battle is ended you will want to be on your way."

"As soon as possible, which will more than likely be the day after tomorrow if we keep drinking like this," Bahr said. "It's been a long time since I got drunk."

"Warriors deserve to feast and drink. We stand in the aftermath of great accomplishment. Your quest will hold a day or two I deem," Thord replied. "If the wizard agrees with that, of course."

"I think we can manage an extra day," Anienam said. "We've certainly earned the respite and sorely need the rest and refitting. Bahr would know better, but we need food, fresh water, feed for the horses. Much more I suppose but I am no logistician. I feel claustrophobic just thinking about it."

Thord leaned over to Bahr after the wizard wandered off and said, "What a strange, old man. Sometimes I think the world is a better place with only one of his kind."

"I know exactly what you mean," Bahr said. "He is right, however. We'll need supplies for the journey south. Also, I would like to take advantage of your armories. Our weapons are in a sore state after the raid and I suspect we'll have need of them soon enough after leaving Drimmen Delf."

"They are at your disposal. I'll have my quartermasters prepare everything once you give them a list of your needs," Thord replied.

Faeldrin said, "You make it sound as if you've been in one long running engagement."

"It feels like we have." Bahr finished his ale and recounted their misadventures since being hired by Harnin One Eye. He made sure to leave out his relationship with Badron as well as Maleela's affair with Prince Aurec. He finished with the wounding of the Harpy in Fedro. Both Elf and Dwarf stood with mouths agape.

"There is more going on than you know, Bahr," Faeldrin said. "My scouts have received reports from Rogscroft. The Wolfsreik succeeded in toppling the monarchy. King Stelskor was executed by Badron. His body swings from the battlements of the city proper."

From his table, isolated in the corner, Ionascu glanced up. Strips of cooked boar hung from the corners of his mouth as he listened intently to the Dwarf Lord.

"Rogscroft was the only force capable of keeping Delranan's aggression in check. I don't understand how Badron was able to defeat them so easily."

"He had a lot of aid," Thord answered. "We spotted an army of Goblins marching west. They must have been at least ten thousand strong. My army was in no position to give chase, however. The Black Hammer clans had already infiltrated our valley and were preparing to lay siege. I'm beginning to think the wizard is right. Dark times have befallen Malweir."

"All the more reason for us helping you crush the dark Dwarf rebellion," Faeldrin said. "The Aeldruin haven't seen this much action since we enlisted to attack the dragon in the Deadlands, with Anienam's father. I'm thinking it might be time to take my force west, to Rogscroft."

"Fifty Elves against twenty thousand Goblins and men?" Bahr asked. "Even you must find those odds too much."

The Elf lord grinned. "Odds are for gamblers, my friend. We Elves have been here since the dawn of the world. We know enough when not to interfere."

Bahr still thought the Elf was crazy. No one in their right mind would travel into the war-torn kingdom now, after it had fallen to a demented king intent on murdering his way to power across half the continent. His brother had always been consumed with gaining power and status but lacked the proper motivation to pursue his desires. Bahr quietly searched out Maleela, knowing she lay at the center of it all. *The poor lass. All she wanted was a quiet life married to the young prince of Rogscroft. I let love and false pretense ruin that. It's a wonder she doesn't hate me for my sins.*

He thankfully accepted the refill of ale and drank deeply. Guilt gnawed at him. He wasn't sure what his motivations had been when Harnin first came to him, but it wasn't out of pure love. Maleela was a dear girl. Of that he had no doubts, but they were never close. He'd always assumed it stemmed from her father's animosity. Bahr was all but an outcast. Badron had seen to that.

Now he and his niece were on the run and lost on an impossible journey. The dire warning of the Old Mother haunted him. Maleela was the only one of the family worth saving, at least in his eyes. If she should fall to darkness…He let the thought fade. There was no point in dwelling on the worst possible outcome.

"We drift too far away from the point," Thord said after finishing his second mug. "The Black Hammer clans have been defeated but we didn't kill as many as I would have liked. They retain a sizeable force, enough to cause havoc up and down the Spine. Even going by river won't be safe until you get south, down into the Jebel Desert and beyond."

"We don't have a choice," Bahr countered. "Time is escaping us. We must find Trennaron and get the Blood Hamr back to the north."

"Provided the city still exists," Faeldrin added. "Our records have no mention of Trennaron for more than a thousand years. Whatever splendor the city once held has either vanished into myth or been carefully removed. I profess to having great interest in your quest."

"More than I, no doubt," Bahr half joked. "We've sacrificed much already. Finding Venheim was a stroke of luck, or mad genius. I'm still not sure. Folk believe the Giants don't exist anymore either. That's the one fact that gives me hope in finding Trennaron."

That was enough for Faeldrin. "My Aeldruin will escort you to the Fern River and help secure passage south. Know this, the river is not safe. Bandits and highwaymen rove the water and shores. We suspect they come from the edges of the Graven Forest, just east of the river but haven't been able to confirm this."

"Bandits would almost be welcome after all we've been through. Thank you, Faeldrin. Your assistance will be greatly appreciated," Bahr bowed.

"That's settled," Thord proclaimed. "Enough serious talk. Now is the hour to drink and make merry. A great battle has been won and my Dwarves deserve every hangover they wake up with. Come, friends, drink!"

Maleela watched and listened to the festivities with great interest. She'd never seen anything so grand or entertaining. The depth of Dwarven culture left her stunned and somewhat hollow. Nothing in Delranan compared with any of what she'd seen since arriving in Drimmen Delf. The thought of staying amused her even though she knew the invitation would never come. Humans were strangers, unwelcome except in the direst circumstance. Maleela would find no warmth under the mountains once the aftermath of the war settled.

"You look troubled."

Bracing herself, she turned and offered her best smile to Anienam. "Restless perhaps. It doesn't feel right being underground for so long, even in a place as nice as Drimmen Delf."

"The mountain kingdoms have certain charm to them but we are people used to blue skies and fresh air," the wizard smiled. "I must confess, quietly of course, that I find the halls of this place confining as well. Just don't tell a Dwarf."

"My lips are sealed," Maleela replied.

"There is more on your mind. Tell me, child."

Maleela wasn't sure that was such a good idea. She enjoyed Anienam's company and conversation but didn't trust him the way she did Bahr or even Skuld. The wizard wasn't as straightforward as he tried to appear. Every action and comment had a hidden agenda with motives visible behind his eyes. The old man struggled with too much guilt even though he wasn't about to share with mere mortals. Mortals he had no problem using to achieve his goals.

"I miss Aurec," she said finally. While that was true, she hadn't thought about it for weeks. Aurec was her life but thinking about him hurt too much so she forced him out, pushing his image into the cold recesses of winter. She steeled her resolve and focused on getting the Blud Hamr and ending the threat of the dark gods. Once that was ended she and Aurec would be able to continue, picking up their lives where they'd been rudely interrupted by her father's campaign.

"Love is a fickle desire, though I confess to having never met him. One moment love is white hot, so much so that we cannot go near it and the next it can be colder than the deepest winter night. It's funny, but I don't think I've ever truly been in love."

Maleela cocked her head. "How can you have lived for hundreds of years without knowing what it is to love?"

"I didn't say I don't know love just that I've never been in love. Wizards and Mages are no different from everyone else. Much of the old orders were married and had families. Personally I have found a great love for the purity of nature. There is unmatched serenity to the breaking dawn or setting sun."

Anienam fell silent, lost in private reflection, regret. Too many times he'd awoken only to discover he'd missed more of life. Too many nights were spent hunting down wicked creatures or defending innocent lives; innocent being relative. There wasn't much left in the world that hadn't been corrupted in one way or another. He often caught himself daydreaming of what life must have been like before the bad times, or even if there was such a time. Mankind seemed destined to suffer.

"So you have never known a touch?" she asked timidly.

A sudden twinkle lit his eyes up. "Some things must remain secret."

She shared his laugh before her thoughts turned serious again. "Do you think he is all right? I try to think of something else but his face returns every time I close my eyes. It hurts too much to continue."

"Missing the ones we love is natural, Maleela. I would like to think he is well but wouldn't be so callous as to guess for the sake of cheering you up," Anienam replied solemnly. "Aurec is young and strong, an heir to a kingdom. He will come through the dark times and you shall sit to his right." He smiled. "A proper queen for better times."

I hope so. No god, light or dark, will save the people responsible for harming a hair on his head. I shall be a queen. A queen of vengeance and justice. Maleela savored the thought of putting her father to the spear while the celebration raged around her.

TWENTY-NINE

Departing Drimmen Delf

Winter somehow got colder while they were inside the warm halls of Drimmen Delf. Dwarven hospitality went above all their expectations, making it difficult to leave. But leave they must. The band of adventurers loaded their wagon, sheathed refurbished weapons, and drew their cloaks tight as they marched with heavy hearts down onto the main thoroughfare running down the middle of the Dwarf kingdom.

Dwarves lined the way, some coming just to see the Giant. Others showing appreciation for what Bahr and his group did for the Dwarves. Winter flowers were laid on the road. Children waved and ran in between the horses. An honor guard awaited them the closer they got to the exit. Resplendent in their silver armor, the Dwarves snapped to attention and presented salutes with long, freshly crafted pikes. Bahr couldn't help but feel pride in the amount of effort Thord had gone through for them.

Only it wasn't Thord. The Dwarf Lord and his delegation had already moved back to Bode Hill to oversee clean-up operations in the valley. It was Captain Ironfoot who stood at the head of the honor guard. The grizzled Dwarf was cleaned up and, not quite sober, patched up by the surgeons. His beard was plaited with bones and silver. Each one a mark of honor from different actions against enemies of Drimmen Delf. He stepped down from the raised walkways lining the road and bowed deeply as Bahr halted his group.

"Lord Bahr, I have been given the honor of escorting you to Bode Hill," Ironfoot announced. The pride in his voice echoed like thunder in the cavernous opening.

"Did he just call Bahr a lord?" Dorl asked Nothol quietly.

Nothol concealed a wry grin. "Sounded like it. Maybe he knows something the rest of us don't. Now I feel like being all proper."

"You've never been proper a day in your life," Dorl chided.

"The end of the world seems like a good time to begin."

Bahr heard every word of the exchange but chose to ignore them. Dorl and Nothol had their uses. He could add comic relief to that list. Instead he returned Ironfoot's bow, somewhat awkwardly. "Captain, the honor is ours. I welcome your company."

Enough said, Ironfoot nodded sharply and spun about. "Detail! Center, march!"

The Dwarves moved as one. Their booted feet marched in unison down the corridor towards the massive eastern doors of Drimmen Delf. Soldiers who managed to drag themselves up from where they'd passed out gathered in knots by the gates. They broke into raucous cheers as Groge came into view. The noise became so intense Bahr felt certain the ceiling was going to collapse on their heads.

A score of Dwarves rushed out of the crowds to man the doors. Each door stood twenty feet high and was three feet thick. Carved from ancient oak trees, the doors had stood for hundreds of years and had never been breached. They took ten Dwarves and a series of elaborate pulleys to open fully, an endeavor the Dwarves struggled with now. Scenes of battles and revered Dwarf heroes were intricately carved into the doors and buffed to a fine polish. Each door was testament to the ancient history of Drimmen Delf and went unrivaled by any of the northern kingdoms.

Snow blasted in, driven by harsh winds. What little sunlight that managed to pierce the endless veil of drab clouds gave the ground a haunted look. Perhaps it was merely the pristine snow drifts marred only by the dulled brown tree trunks. Bahr knew that further down the valley was an entire forest of pines. He tried to peer through the steadily opening doors to see what the valley looked like in the daylight.

The low whistle behind him caused him to turn. "Everything all right, Groge?"

The Giant grinned like a love-struck teen. "I've never seen anything so detailed. So impressive. It is a great honor to bear witness to such artistry."

Bahr didn't understand Groge's awe. Having been to Venheim, Bahr couldn't see anything in Drimmen Delf worthy of the Giant's adoration. The Forge of Giants was legendary and held many treasures and more in the warm stone buildings and forges. Not that the Dwarf kingdom didn't hold equal wonders. But he was a simple man and unused to seeing such attention to detail in buildings. Delranan certainly lacked anything resembling grandeur compared to these two great kingdoms.

"They certainly know how to make doors," Bahr replied. *Not that I know much about the subject or really care.*

His thoughts were already beyond the mountain kingdom and stretching towards what was coming. He'd been a seafaring man for most of his life. The lure of the ocean called him from an early age. Being so far inland made him uneasy. Combined with him never having been east of the Kergland Spine before and he was out of his element. Bahr knew he'd have to rely more heavily on Boen and Anienam to keep pace with the approaching storm. He spent most of the recovery day pouring over maps, trying to memorize major terrain features. Distances. Which kingdom came next. Who was considered hostile or friendly. He quickly found himself overwhelmed by it all.

Groge tapped him gently on the shoulder, but still hard enough to make Bahr cough. By the time the doors were completely open the pain was mostly gone. Bahr still shrugged his shoulder though. The horses pranced nervously. They wanted to be in the open almost as badly as Bahr did.

He slid his hand down the horse's neck. "I know, boy. I know. We'll be free again soon enough."

Snorting, the horse tossed its head back. Ironfoot led the procession through the gates. One hundred Dwarves stepped off on their left foot and marched in cadence down the snow-covered road leading into the valley. The cold breeze stung Bahr's face and it felt good. He closed his eyes briefly to enjoy the touch of daylight. The stern glares of half a dozen statues lining the road looked down on him. Dwarf kings all, each statue spoke of an important era in Drimmen Delf's history. Each bore a massive double-headed axe. Their faces were partially concealed behind helmets. Standing thirty feet high, the statues were carved from giant blocks of marble mined from the southern end of the Kergland Spine. They commemorated the passing of the great Dwarf kings. One day Thord hoped to have his own.

"It feels good to be back in the open," Skuld told Maleela from his seat on the wagon bench.

He and Anienam drove the heavily laden wagon with Rekka and Dorl riding in the back. Their wounds were still severe enough to keep them out of action for the time being. Everyone else walked. Halfway up the mountain they couldn't smell the rot from the battlefield. Bahr turned his head in that direction anyway. The sky was dark with thousands of carrion birds. Smoke still billowed into the sky. Huge piles of wreckage already gathered were being burned. Everything salvageable had already been taken back to the mountains. The Dwarves were fastidious and thorough. More than half of the field was already cleared.

"It's as if the battle never happened," Bahr whispered.

Boen grunted. "Proficient aren't they? Makes my people look lazy."

"Not the word I'd choose to describe them, Boen."

He chuckled. "I've been called much worse, though it didn't turn out well for the one that said it."

"How long do you think it will take to load the boats? As much as I appreciate Dwarven hospitality I have this pressing feeling in the back of my mind. Time is against us."

The Gaimosian didn't much care for the sudden change in conversation. More and more his thoughts turned against the tiny band, of returning to his roots and wandering the southern kingdoms alone. He wasn't cut out for working with large groups. Too many personalities and opinions for him. Boen enjoyed the quiet solitude of endless leagues of open plains, campsites by a small fire, and bathing in streams. Humanity tended to cluster so close they stifled each other. His natural distrust in society stemmed from generations of atoning for the sins of their fathers. Gaimosians were a hated breed, only thought highly of in martial matters.

He got along with Bahr and most of the others well enough but felt like he was missing a large part of himself. The raid on the Black Hammer Dwarves allowed him the opportunity to unleash his inner rage and sate the need for battle. Boen strode through the Dwarves like an avenging god and it still wasn't enough. He felt as if he was slowly fading the longer he stayed part of the group.

Bahr's concerns only made matters worse. The Sea Wolf was used to getting his way, but that was on a wooden deck with a boat and crew under his feet. Boen didn't enjoy being told what to do. Never had. He and Bahr worked well together but so much time solely in small company drove him past frustration. He needed to be free again. It was the only way to soothe his frayed nerves.

"We have enough hands to unload the wagon quickly enough. What do we do with the horses? We can't leave them. Dwarves have no use for horses," he said with a heavy heart.

"I've arranged for a barge to carry us. The Fern River is wide enough that we should only need the barge and one boat to get us moving," Bahr answered. *If what the Elf said turns out to be true, which I have no reason to doubt.*

"Can't say as that I'm excited to get back on the water," Boen grumbled. "I prefer my horse or my damned legs."

"Sacrifices need making," Bahr smiled. "We'll move far quicker on the river, leaving us with plenty of time to make the return voyage, on land."

"Assuming we'll still be alive to do so. I don't like our chances. Too much has gone wrong already," Boen confided. "Don't forget the battle with the Harpies in Fedro. We may have wounded one and lost the others when the Dwarves captured us but Harpies are relentless trackers. They'll soon be on our trail again."

"Harpies are the least of my concerns, Boen." He looked back to the wagon before lowering his voice and adding, "I only hope the wizard has his timeline straight. Otherwise this will all be for naught."

"There is more than time to concern yourself with," Boen said. "The river isn't as safe as you think. We'll be in a confined space for an extended period. Bandits and murderers prey upon travel barges. Once we get to the Jebel Desert we'll suffer under intense heat and beasts best left to the imagination. The Graven Forest is no better. Mind what the Elf said. His Aeldruin have fought in every kingdom. They know the dangers far better than you or I. It would be nice to have some of them come along."

"I tried. It's not their fight. What we have is what we've got," Bahr said.

"Are you convinced this quest is necessary? Look at our band. They're no heroes. Hells, half of them aren't fit to travel long distances, much less find an impossible weapon and defeat the dark gods."

Bahr exhaled slowly. Boen's concerns reflected his own fears but he didn't see any other option. He couldn't go home and wasn't entirely sure of Anienam's sincerity. The wizard had a habit of speaking in circles, a tactic Bahr felt certain was designed to confuse the others and conceal the wizard's true intent. Boat captains were a superstitious lot but

Bahr maintained doubts about the dark gods. So much negative had happened in his life he didn't need gods or servants of gods.

His lack of faith translated into deeds. Bahr lived in the now. Tomorrow meant little. He had no home. No family other than Maleela. Not even a boat to roam the sea. Everything he had been was gone. A lesser man would have succumbed to his hate and gone on a rampage. Bahr liked to think himself more civilized that. Instead he turned his aggressions inward and struggled to find some way to turn his fortunes about. Only, the longer he stayed on this quest the further he found his thoughts.

Confused and partially depressed, the Sea Wolf looked hard at Boen. "Every one of them has come through when they were needed. Each has a specific skill set that has aided us since leaving Delranan the first time. It almost makes me comfortable with who we have."

"Despite there not being a proper warrior in the bunch?"

"I've got you and Rekka," Bahr countered. "She's worth more than her weight in gold when it comes to a fight. Dorl and Nothol know their way around the business end of a sword. Groge is large enough to make a grown man shit his breeks. Skuld's a good lad as well."

"You left out the wizard."

Bahr debated what to say. Being unsure of Anienam's true intent left him confused. He wanted to trust the wizard but couldn't. "Yes, I did."

They went on in silence for a while longer as the road wound down out of the mountains and into the valley. Most of the road had been cleared of snow thanks in no small way to the army of Dwarves marching out to war and back. A thin layer of ice coated what snow remained, making the ground treacherous. Pine boughs drooped under the weight of the ice, giving the land a pristine look Bahr hadn't expected.

His memories of the raid distorted the views he took in now. He'd expected a land thoroughly devastated by cannon fire and worse. Trees splintered to shreds. Massive craters in the ground. Instead he found a world untouched by the horrors of war. *It seems the Black Hammer clans never made it this far after all. Thord embellished.* He chuckled softly. Kings were supposed to make matters sound worse than they were. How else did they expect to get anything positive accomplished?

Ironfoot marched them over a recently constructed bridge and down into the forest. Cool water flowed unhindered beneath them, reminding Bahr of simpler times. He suddenly longed for the days when he could build a small cabin in the middle of nowhere, prop his feet up on the front porch and enjoy a scene such as this. Too much of his life had been squandered on raiding and quests. He awoke one morning to find he was old. The better part of his life well past. Instead of wealth or happiness all he had were questions. *Where did it all go? Have I wasted what little time I have on this world?* Death beckoned. He felt it curling wicked fingers towards him from the distance, beckoning.

"Bahr seems troubled."

Dorl looked up. "He should be. We're in too deep."

Rekka stifled a short yawn. "He is a good man. I trust him to do the right thing."

"So do I, insomuch as I trust anyone. We wouldn't have gotten this far without his thinking. That doesn't change the fact that we're heading into trouble."

She smiled softly and cupped his cheek. "Dorl Theed, you are brave. You've no need to fear now."

"It's not fear, Rekka my love, it's common sense," Dorl replied, taking a moment to kiss her lightly. "Death is stalking us."

"Death stalks everyone from the moment of birth. My people do not share your superstitious beliefs in death's evil nature. We are born. We die. It is as simple as that. Death holds no nefarious purpose. What stalks us is the Dae'shan."

"There's been no sight of them since the woods around Praeg."

Memories of her confrontation in the middle of the night continued to plague her months after it happened. Why had the Dae'shan come to her? They must have known what role she was meant to play in the unfolding drama. Her people had been sworn defenders of Trennaron since Artiss Gran first arrived and had the fortress constructed. Killing her would prove a major setback in Anienam's plans but wouldn't halt them. *Perhaps they thought to turn me, to sway me to their dark cause. What glory would be heaped upon the one who managed to turn a guardian!*

"No, but that doesn't mean they aren't still after us," she said. "I fear the next part of our journey will be the worst."

Dorl studied her face quietly, searching for any sign of jest, but Rekka remained stoic. She knew what awaited and refused to tell more. He wasn't sure what worried him the most. The thought of turning back to Delranan began to sound much better.

THIRTY

Anienam's Tale

The Dwarf Lord watched his guests slowly wind down from the mountains and through the forest. Normally he wouldn't have seen anything but they had a Giant who managed to stand nearly as tall as half of the trees. *A Giant! Here in my kingdom. What would the other kings think should I deign to tell them our ancient cousins still exist?*

"Ironfoot seems to have taken his new task well," Brek said casually.

Thord grunted. "He's a stiff bastard. Reminds me of myself, long ago of course. I didn't think he'd change his mind so quickly though."

"He had his reasons," Brek replied. "Still, he was the one who captured them. It makes sense having him be the one now."

"It does. He's a good lad. I'm thinking about promoting him when he returns."

"His actions in the battle merit that. I can give him a regiment. Have you made up your mind about helping them?" Brek asked. The battle of Bode Hill aroused his martial instincts. His desire to return to war intensified.

Thord shook his head. "No. We still haven't taken account of our dead and wounded. Not to mention the remnants of the Black Hammer clans are still out there. We may have beaten them but they are still Dwarves and we all know how stubborn Dwarves can be."

They shared a laugh, though Brek's mind was already going over battle plans and tactics to hunt down the survivors. Wars were fought and won by ruthless persecution, not sitting back and waiting for your enemy to make their move. He'd lost too many Dwarves by doing just that. Thord's war of attrition ground the army down needlessly. Brek would have attacked and continued to attack until the enemy broke before they managed to get their cannons emplaced. When death finally claimed him he would stand before Gru and be forced to atone for his misdeeds. Brek needed to find a way to redeem himself before that happened, else he would be banished from the halls of his fathers for eternity.

"They are here," he said, looking up at the heavy sound of boots crunching ice.

"It's about time. I'm getting damned cold standing up on this hill," Thord complained.

"Company, halt!"

The Dwarves ground to an immediate stop and separated back into two files lining the road. Ironfoot motioned Bahr and the others through as his Dwarves saluted. Bahr tried to look at as many of the honor guard as he could, returning their hard stares with nods and an occasional grin. Several Dwarves offered curt thanks or cheers. They all knew what Bahr and his group had done and were grateful beyond words.

Ironfoot led Bahr up the last few meters and stopped. "Sire, our guests await your words before departing Drimmen Delf."

"Very good, Captain Ironfoot," Thord said, his tone jovial. "Bahr, it is with mixed emotions that I send you off. You and your people will always have a place among us for your deeds and service to the Dwarf kingdoms. Wars are never pleasant. We learned that the hard way. If it hadn't been for you we'd still be deadlocked in the trenches."

"We are more than happy to help. Darkness seems to be spreading. It is the hour for good people to stand together," Bahr replied.

"Indeed. You've received enough supplies to last your journey?"

Bahr nodded. "More than enough. I speak for all us when I thank you for your hospitality. We might have already failed if not for Captain Ironfoot's intervention on your western doorstep."

If Thord took offense he kept it to himself. Instead he clasped Bahr on the shoulder. "Fare well on your travels, Sea Wolf. Be mindful, the way south is not an easy one. Bandits and marauders will attempt to waylay you, in addition to whatever darkness stalks you."

"Thank you, King Thord. I am in your debt. Perhaps when all this is ended we can sit down and do proper justice to those kegs of ale you have stored for special occasions."

"Ha! No Dwarf needs a special occasion to drink! You are always welcome in my kingdom. Now go. Faeldrin and his Elves are waiting at the base of the hill. They will finish escorting you to the river and the boats. Captain Ironfoot, are you ready?"

"Yes, sire."

Bahr looked down in surprise to see the Dwarf strapping a heavy pack to his back. "Ready for what?"

"I've decided that your quest is so important that it cannot be allowed to fail. Drimmen Delf will have a representative to aid you in whatever way you necessary. Ironfoot has volunteered," Thord announced.

Only Anienam seemed unsurprised. "He is most welcome."

The group parted ways, offering a final chorus of cheers and well wishes to the honor guard. Their last sight of Bode Hill was of Thord standing with hands on his hips, cloak billowing in the wind. The merriment followed down to where Faeldrin awaited. The Elves were more than eager to be underway, as they weren't a people to be kept underground. Faeldrin introduced his chief lieutenants and they set out at a brisk clip. Time being of the essence, the two groups wasted little in formalities.

"I've never seen an Elf before," Maleela told Anienam. "They're so pale, almost like my people."

He smiled, old memories drifting lazily by. "Oh, they're not all like that. Some have pitch black hair and rather swarthy features. Others are almost bronzed from the sun. All in all, a very intriguing people."

The Aeldruin suddenly broke out in song though the words were in their own tongue. Maleela closed her eyes and let the tones take her to faraway lands. She quickly found herself lost in a more elegant time, one without the struggles miring her life. Longing for the days when she needn't worry about the crown or her place in Delranan's history, a thin smile crawled across her face.

Anienam watched her sadly. He'd seen too much of the future. Too many dark possibilities looming in her future, unavoidable and desperate. He knew of the warnings given to Bahr by the Old Mother. Maleela's destiny lay down foul paths best left untraveled. He wanted to take her away and keep her away from the coming storm, but he was only one man. There was only so much he could do. Worse, he knew he had to let her fall if the quest was to succeed.

"It's beautiful," she finally said.

Anienam cleared his throat. "Yes. It is an old song. One they used to sing before going into battle I believe. It's funny how only the Elves can make a song about going to war sound so nice. A very remarkable people."

"Your description somewhat spoils the mood, Anienam," she chided. "Were Elves ever in Delranan? I mean before man?"

"I'm afraid not, princess," Faeldrin said from alongside the wagon. "The weather is much too harsh for our kind to thrive. We don't enjoy the cold very much."

She laughed. "I don't either. The drab skies are the worst part. All you see is grey for months on end."

"Elves need warmth and life. We need to be in the forests, tending to the trees. Our culture lives to take care of nature."

"Yet you still carry arms and go to war. That seems contradictory," she said.

"Dire times call for strength. Malweir is a dangerous world. I can't recall the last time there was a lasting peace." He paused, lost in thought.

"What hope do we have for the future if peace is just a lie?"

Faeldrin smiled, impressed with her quickness. He turned to Anienam. "She is smart, my friend. Ward this one closely. Such wit is rare. Maleela, peace is not a lie, though it certainly seems like it. It is an unobtainable goal if anything. There are too many strong-willed people for us all to get along, or so that has been my experience. Every ruler seems to think theirs in the only way of doing things. Convoluted at best, considering each race has distinct character traits. Our inherent ability to strive towards what we think is right is both blessing and curse."

"But without that uniqueness we are all the same. There wouldn't be any great works of art or monuments to important figures," she protested. "There wouldn't be anything remarkable or memorable in the world."

"As I said, a cruel jest. There are times I wonder if the world would be better off if we all minded our own business and stayed in our own lands," Faeldrin's said as his voice turned sour.

Anienam, stifling a yawn, finally spoke up. "The first order of Mages began from a single race. More specifically, a single group of people. They learned they had magic within them, but they weren't alone. Magic flowed through every race. Soon, the founders roamed the face of Malweir in search of others with the gift. Mages from every race imaginable came to fill the halls of Ipn Shal. A grand time all but lost to the vagaries of time. The Mages brought us all together. They helped make the wonders of the world possible and took light, illumination to those lacking such basic gifts."

"I was there, Anienam, when Mage-kind disintegrated on itself. The world was not a nice place," Faeldrin replied tartly. "Sides were drawn. No race remained neutral. They couldn't, not if they wanted to survive. Even that wasn't enough. Tens of thousands died for reasons few knew. Even more struggled through the aftermath and attempted to rebuild what little remained of their cultures. Following generations were taught to despise magic and the Mages. I would not be so quick to sing the praises of your ancestors, Anienam Keiss. Not when the hurt is still too real for some of us."

"I am not accountable for the sins of my fathers," the wizard said, stiffening. "Regardless of their downfall, the first Mages *were* responsible for bringing Malweir together. Can you imagine how easy it would be for the dark gods and their agents to return if we were all keeping to ourselves? None of us would have a chance. Darkness would return and Malweir would devolve into chaos and hatred."

"And for their arrogance the Mages were run to extinction," Faeldrin said. "I am not arguing against you, my friend, but trying to make Maleela see a different point of view."

"I still don't completely understand," she said.

"Very few do," Anienam said before the Elf could open his mouth. "It was meant to be a grand time. An era of elegance that would ensure peace and tranquility between all races. Our greatest minds conspired to create the crystal of Tol Shere. Through the crystal kings, queens, and petty tyrants would all be on the same level. Knowledge is meant to be shared, not hoarded."

"A sound practice in theory. Reality is a far different creature," Faeldrin replied. "Could it not be conceivable that the enemy forced the creation of the crystal? Knowing how fallible mortals are, it is easy to think the Dae'shan might have influenced some of the creators. Sometimes even the best of us stumble and fall."

Anienam had no counter argument. The crystal was made flawed, whether by design or an accident. Half of the Mages turned to darkness under the leadership of Sidian, the order master of the Silver. Anienam prayed and did everything in his power to ensure such a thing never happened again. The death toll from the first war had been horrendous. Almost an entire generation wiped out; far worse than any plague. If the dark gods succeeded in returning, he let the thought die rather than discover the options.

"That is a sad fact of life. Strength does not always translate into wisdom or greatness," he finally said. "Let us hope we are strong enough to do what's right for the sake of all our peoples."

Faeldrin nodded in agreement. "Wise words. Let us hope."

They continued in silence for the time being. Each weighed the consequences of their actions. History often forgot the people but the deeds were recorded meticulously. Maleela knew her uncle wanted nothing to do with the crown, leaving her the sole survivor of the family once her father was removed. She didn't know if she had what it took to become a queen or even how. The doubts gnawed at her confidence, leaving her aching for answers.

Anienam saw the failures of his people and the inability of his father to accomplish what he'd spent a lifetime trying. The crystal was lost, presumably destroyed when Sidian was killed. Yet the dark gods continued to attempt their return. Why? How? The answers eluded him. Only Faeldrin rode with confidence. Everything happening now had happened before. He held little reservation that they would happen again. Life was circular, neither beginning nor ending.

"We are close," Bahr said.

Ironfoot shook his head. "No. The river is still a few hours away. We should gain the shores by dusk."

"You mean to depart at night?"

"I wouldn't. The rivers are too fast, too treacherous to navigate in the dark. It would be best to load the boats and post a guard, then leave at first light," the Dwarf replied.

Bahr shot Boen a quick look to see if he concurred. "You expect trouble this far north? I thought the bandits stayed south, by the desert."

"Goblins have been seen roving the avenues from the east. We believe they are funneling west to King Badron's war effort in Rogscroft."

Bahr refused to believe his brother had stooped so low as to enlist the aid of Goblins. Long considered the scourge of the world by most of the other races, Goblins existed only for fighting. They relished the opportunity to die in battle. *Why in the Hells would Badron want that sort of chaos? He has the Wolfsreik. He could conquer the entire north with their strength.*

"Thord wasn't very forthcoming with information concerning the war. Understandably of course given his own situation," Bahr replied. "What else do you know?"

The Dwarf cocked his head, stroking the bone fragments laced into his beard. "Not much really. We've confirmed the city fell and chaos has befallen the Delrananian armies. There are whispers of great evil at work."

"We've been hunted by this evil since leaving Chadra," Boen said through a yawn. "I'd like nothing better than to drop my axe into its skull and be done with this all."

"Unfortunately it is not the sort of evil than can be killed by conventional weapons," Bahr countered. "We've tried and failed." He paused to search the skies for signs of their pursuit. He wasn't foolish enough to believe the Harpies would have given up so easily. "I doubt it will be long before our enemies pick up our trail again. They'll know we went into Drimmen Delf."

"But not which way we left," Boen answered.

"East is the only logical direction. They seem to know where we are heading. How else would you explain them being ahead of us?"

"We should have engaged them better in Fedro," Boen said. "Rekka's a sure shot with her bow but there's no way to know whether we killed the creature or just wounded it. I say we make a stand and end this."

"End it how?" Bahr asked. "They won't come anywhere close if they're smart, which they've proven to be time and again. Besides, I believe we have worse to think about. Harpies aren't much danger and, if what Anienam says is correct, they're working for agents of the dark gods. Who knows what fell powers they have at their disposal? I think the enemy is going to try harder to stop us the closer we get to Trennaron."

"I'm not convinced the place exists," Boen said. "I've been across Malweir a dozen times and have never come upon so much as a rumor of it."

"You shouldn't discount something just because you lack proper knowledge," Ironfoot interrupted. "I learned that lesson well over the last few days."

Eventually the tree line thinned out to a soft, rolling field covered in untouched snow. The air grew colder. Fresh ice crystals shimmered in the low light. They could hear rushing water. An unending wave of water pouring in from the Northern Sea eventually emptying out into the Brodein Delta and the Southern Ocean. The Fern River was one of the largest freshwater bodies on Malweir. Whole communities sprang up around the waters further down. It took a special breed of man to live this far north, where winter claimed half of the year.

Bahr's first sight of the river left him impressed and worried. A storm was coming, but from which direction?

THIRTY-ONE

The River Men

Skuld held his breath. He'd never imagiend such an expansive body of flowing water could exist. The Fern River was massive, spanning more than three hundred meters across. He felt infinitesimal. Raging waters rushed by in an unending flow. The warmth was stolen from the air, leaving beast and man shivering. Ducks and sterling geese clustered on the far shore. An eagle circled overhead, screening for a quick meal.

Skuld sucked in his breath and whistled low. "This is amazing."

Anienam smiled. "It is a grand sight, but minimal considering all we've seen thus far. Not to mention what we've got coming to us."

"I had hoped the worst was behind us," the boy commented slowly.

Anienam laid a soft hand on Skuld's shoulder. "One can never tell where the road will lead. All we can do is forge ahead and plan for the best and worst."

Dorl crawled from the wagon bed and stretched. He listened carefully to Anienam, disappointed with what he heard. A boy like Skuld didn't need the doom and gloom speeches. He was too young to process it all. Shaking his head, the sell sword ambled over to Nothol.

"You hear that?" he asked.

Nothol nodded. "He's just being himself."

"Is that what it's called? He's filling the boy's head with end-of-the-world scenarios. It's not right, Nothol. We've come too far and been through too much to let him demoralize Skuld."

"Demoralize? That's a big word for you," Nothol joked. "I think Rekka is giving you a little culture."

Dorl barely missed with the rock he halfheartedly threw. "More than that. I never met a woman like her. Damn it! Stop trying to change the subject. What he's doing is wrong, Nothol. Mark my words, no good will come of it."

"He's acted the same way since we first left Chadra," the bigger man replied. "I don't see any cause for concern now. Besides, he's done just as much to keep us moving unhindered as the rest of us. Well, all but Ionascu. I still don't see why we keep him around."

Because Bahr won't let us get rid of him properly. "We still have plenty of time to see if he accidentally falls into the river, or worse."

"Murder isn't my style."

"Not mine either but I don't fancy waking up with a knife across my throat either," Dorl replied. "That man is twisted."

Ionascu suffered the worst out of all them in Harnin's dungeons. They'd beaten and broken him until his mind snapped, leaving a shell of a man. Now he laughed for no reason and gave them guarded looks. Everyone knew it was just a matter of time before he attempted to kill one of them yet Bahr and Anienam reasoned that he still had some small part to play in the coming days and weeks. What, neither could say.

"No point in worrying about that. I say we do what we've always done. You watch my back and I watch yours. The Sea Wolf will get us out of this. If anyone can I know it's him."

"I don't understand your blind faith," Dorl said. "Bahr's getting old and tired. He's making more bad decisions and the risks only get higher." His voice dropped to a bare whisper. "Do you think it might be time to pull out of this little endeavor?"

"Abandon him now?" Nothol asked even quieter.

Dorl shrugged. "We did what we signed on for. We rescued the princess and brought her back. Our contract is fulfilled."

"We can't abandon him now. The old man is going to need as many friends as he can get if he's to find the Blud Hamr and bring it back," Nothol protested. The idea of giving up on his friend and going against his word sickened his stomach. A man was nothing without his word.

"You really think we stand a chance? How come the wizard hasn't said where we're supposed to bring the Hamr? How we use it? When? There are way too many variables for me. None of this feels right."

"Right how? We are embroiled in a quest way above either of us, in the middle of lands we've never been to, walking with Giants, Elves, and Dwarves, and looking for a mystical city that may or may not exist. What could possibly make sense in any of that mess?"

Nothol didn't want to admit it, but his stomach remained in knots over their increasingly desperate situation too. There was an unnatural air cast about them. One he didn't know how to combat. Fighting Dwarves and Harpies was one thing, but agents of enemy gods went far above anything he'd ever encountered before. Truthfully, he wasn't sure if he had what it took to go the distance and see the quest to its conclusion. He couldn't find enough of a reason to go against his best friend, nor could he find it within himself to abandon the others. Nothol Coll stood on the edge of a predicament he didn't understand with no viable way out. He sighed. *When in doubt forge ahead and hope for the best.*

"Maybe we're not supposed to understand," he finally said. "Not much of it makes sense to me but my gut tells me Bahr is going to need each of us to stop the enemy."

"What enemy? We've been captured and tortured by Harnin's men. Attacked by brigands and Harpies since we escaped but what else? Rekka had her encounter with a dark creature in the woods around Praeg and you and I both know there are plenty of dark things in the world best left undiscovered. What else? I haven't seen any evidence of Anienam's dark gods or these shadow people that have him spooked." He shook his head. "I can't help but think we're trapped on a wild boar hunt."

The others started setting up camp for the night. A heavy barge was docked nearby, waiting to be loaded. There were a handful of swarthy-looking men lounging on the deck. Their skin was dark from overexposure to the elements, their hair long and unkempt. Each wore a hardened look that was more than just for show. They lived hard lives. Winter in the north was no place for weak men to try and earn a living, especially on the water. Only the very tough and very foolish braved working the river now.

"Hey, what are you two yapping about?" Boen growled from the opposite side of his horse. The look in his eyes told them he wasn't in a forgiving mood.

Nothol raised his empty hands. "Nothing, just talking about old times."

"If it's nothing you can do it later. There's work to be done, ladies."

Scowling, the Gaimosian ambled off towards the barge with Bahr and Ironfoot.

Dorl pointed an accusing finger at the big man's back. "That I'm tired of. We didn't sign on to be treated like children."

"You're reading too much into it. He's a Gaimosian and that means a pain in the ass. They aren't hired for their people skills, my friend. Come on. I don't want to get chewed out again," Nothol said and walked off.

Anienam sat on the driver's bench quietly listening to their conversation. He couldn't blame them for wanting to back out. He would if he could. Meddling in the affairs of the dark gods was no way to make a living. Wishing was a pointless endeavor. Rarely did dreams come true, even less did they work out anywhere close to what you wanted. No, disappointment was the currency of the realm. A universal statement that was unavoidable. He'd seen it hundreds of times over his life. Men and women struggled through their daily grind only to be caught up in moments much too large to handle. The crash and burn followed swiftly.

His life was a string of disappointments. There were times when he wished his father had never found him. Never initiated him into the order of Mages, or rather what little remained. Anienam often caught himself wondering what a normal life would have been like. One where he knew nothing of magic or the vagaries of the dark gods. One where he etched out his days on a farm or in a market, bartering and trading exotic goods from across Malweir. Sadly, such was not his destiny.

All the signs pointed towards the climax to many thousands of years of struggle between light and dark. He felt it burning in his blood. The time was fast approaching when opposite sides would collide and turn the world to ash. He knew balance would survive and past wrongs would be righted, but at what cost? How many tens of thousands needed to perish first before the tragedy finished playing out? One of the basic tenants of his teachings claimed all life was precious. He found it difficult to accept that the rule applied to the vilest of men, that any of the Dae'shan retained a shred of mortality or decency.

Anienam spent years debating with his morals but no answer ever presented itself. The Dae'shan were the worst sort of evil. They'd given up their souls to achieve a dark power locked to the rest of the world. His knowledge of the order was limited, for most of the records were destroyed during the Mage Wars or before. The Dae'shan hadn't always been evil. Once they served neutral purpose. They roamed the world executing the will of the gods. But as in all things, corruption took root. They fell. Darkness claimed them with an irreversible hold. What had been pure now festered.

He thought perhaps it had all played out the way it was supposed to, that the races of Malweir were intended to go through such trials. But to what ends? Nothing he imagined was worth the agony of the moment. Whole generations lived and died without ever knowing peace. The unending struggle just to survive was too much for many more. Whatever games the gods played he doubted it was worth so many lives. Anienam wondered if the world would be a better place without any of the gods. Certainly there'd be far fewer conflicts or threats of unimaginable disaster.

So he sat and listened to the sell sword's complaints, secretly sympathizing with him. Dorl Theed wasn't a good Man, but neither was he bad. He paid his dues and struggled through life in the best way he knew how. Tough men were forced to live tough lives. He and Nothol had gone into some of worst situations Anienam could imagine and come back out with barely a scratch. They were the kind of men he wanted at his side when things went terribly wrong. That such rough men were few and far between was both blessing and curse. Anienam liked to think that one or maybe both would still live when the quest ended. It was a pleasant fantasy.

Hopping down from the wagon, Anienam started whistling an old melody, the origins long forgotten. He was about to unpack his bedroll when Ionascu cackled.

"We're all going to die. You know this, wizard."

Anienam frowned. He'd nearly forgotten the crippled man was still with them. "Oh shut up. Or you'll find your way to the bottom of the river."

"Should I be afraid? I know one thing you don't."

"What is that?" Anienam winced, knowing he shouldn't have bothered.

Ionascu sat up and looked him directly in the eye with a moment of rare clarity. "I am already dead. My soul suffers as we speak."

Shaken, the wizard stumbled away. Alacrity was unexpected in one so broken and abused as the former spy. Ionascu was little more than a shadow of what he might have been. Harnin's torturers were professional if nothing else. *Why then do his words strike deep chords? A creature like this shouldn't do more than elicit a smile.* Anienam decided to clear his mind. He'd had enough double talk and nervous feelings.

Thinking the river might given him better clarity, he soon stood on the mighty shore, well downstream from Bahr and the others. This was no time to converse with them. Not in his current state. Still, that didn't stop him from eavesdropping on the Sea Wolf and the river men.

"Half now and half when we arrive at the final destination," Bahr argued.

The river man threw up his hands. "How can I feed my family if you not pay? We don't know you. You can rob us too easy."

"Nobody is going to rob you." *If anything it'll be the other way around.* "But we're not going to pay you for services you haven't performed. You get us there and you get the rest of the money. You don't and your kids will starve before spring."

Pretending to think, the river man held up a hand and went back to the rest of his crew. They spoke in a low, guttural tongue that seemed animated and aggressive. One of them barked a deep laugh before being hissed quiet by the others.

"We should just get take the barge and get rid of them now," Boen suggested.

Bahr might have thought the man was joking if he didn't know the Gaimosian so well.

Faeldrin shook his head. "No. Doubtless there will be tolls and unseen checkpoints along the way. The river folk may be hard workers but they are mistrusting and will slit your throats if you provide the opportunity. Bahr, do not waiver. They will respect you if you stand fast. I'm sure your offer is more than sufficient."

"We're risking a lot on a handful of scum," Boen added.

Ironfoot listened to the exchange and had to agree with Boen. River men were of the worst sort. They stole and killed when they had the numbers. Trusting any of them was a death sentence. Sent as King Thord's personal representative, he didn't feel it his place, yet, to get involved with their affairs. He'd never been in the company of men for long and learning the rules proved complicated at best.

Bahr nodded slowly, never taking his eyes off the river men. "They must know we're on to them."

Faeldrin cocked his head. "Doubtful. They're not counted among the wisest of any race. I think they truly believe we are hanging on every word, hoping for the best."

"More the fools them," Boen replied. "They don't look very crafty. Even if they get the jump on us I could probably take them by myself."

"Don't be so sure, my friend," Faeldrin cautioned. "Vengeance Knights are renowned the world over for being the very best, but our rather dim new friends aren't interested in reputations. You being who you are won't keep them from trying to kill you in your sleep."

"All the more reason to kill them now." Knowing he wasn't going to win this fight, Boen headed back towards the wagon. He'd spent too many months pent up with Bahr and the others. Too many easy nights sleeping in soft beds and eating better than a Gaimosian should. Bahr was a capable man who didn't need a Vengeance Knight hanging around to get him out of scrapes.

"We need more up front," the river man said upon returning. "Half not enough. Think of our families."

"I am thinking of your families. Without us you will all perish. Getting us down river as quickly as possible is in your best interests. Half now. That's final."

The river man pretended to think again. His narrow eyes constantly roved between Elf, Dwarf, and Man. He knew Bahr. Everyone on the water knew the Sea Wolf. That didn't change the fact he intended to rob him blind the moment Bahr wasn't looking. With a reluctant smile, the river man threw up his hands. "You hurt my heart, and I know my family will suffer but deal. Half. No funny stuff though. We have a reputation."

They shook on it, all the while Bahr tried to keep from bursting into laughter. The only reputation the river men had was one of murderers and thieves. "We'll load in the morning and set off right after first light."

"Fine. Fine. Night is no time to travel the river. Too many foul things lurk in the night," the river man agreed. "In the morning."

"Do you think they'll still be here in the morning?" Ironfoot asked once the river man was far enough away.

"We haven't paid them yet. They'll be here. Then the fun begins," Bahr said.

Indeed. There will be more fun than you can imagine. Anienam tried to clear the foul thoughts from poisoning his mind. He knew the river men's true intent. They'd been touched by darkness. It was only a matter of time before they turned and tried to kill Bahr and the rest. No point in lamenting what hadn't happened. The wizard sighed and cast a slender pebble into the river. The hungry waters lapped it up without so much as a ripple.

THIRTY-TWO

Schemes

Amar Kit'han studied the ball flame curled in the palm of his hand. The soft blue-heat tickled his shadowed fingers. It was a rare moment of humanity. So rare he'd nearly forgotten what he had once been. Life was so fragile, so easy to break. Becoming Dae'shan was the logical conclusion to what his life was. Branded a petty criminal and murderer, he was hunted down, driven from one village to the next. He had to abandon society and took to the wilds.

He couldn't recall his name nor where he originally came from. Those details didn't matter. He had no desire to remain human. To squander what little life was given to him. He wanted more. The gods heard his pleas. It was no accident the night the Dae'shan came to him with their dark temptations. Perhaps he should have said no. Should have turned them away but temptation proved too powerful. He gave in and sold his soul.

What happened next was the end of one life and the beginning of something else. Neither alive nor dead, he became a monster. The flames consumed him. Unimaginable pain wracked his body as the Dae'shan used their fell powers to un-create him. Flesh melted from his skeleton. His bones incinerated to dust, blown away in a soft breeze. It lasted months. They claimed the pain purified him. It removed the petty human jealousies. The weaknesses of flesh and mind. Through fire and pain he was reborn. Remade into a greater power. He mattered.

Stripped of his mortal frame, the fragility of his thoughts and limitations of body and spirit, Amar Kit'han immersed himself entirely in what he'd become. He'd found being unsubstantial disquieting at first. Having no body wasn't right. It was only when he began to explore his newly bestowed powers that he accepted what he was. Like so many who had come before, he fell under their spell and became a monster.

Amar killed because he could. With a thought he snapped necks or shattered minds. He reveled in the anticipation of ruining lives. All the people who had wronged him in his previous life became victims. Their bodies hung from the branches of large oak trees until they'd been picked clean to the bone. Even that wasn't enough. He kept their souls and tormented them every day for years. He thought he might find satisfaction but remained hollow inside. Their deaths were comparatively insignificant given his knowledge of the universe. Time and space were limitless, as was his ability to redefine everything he knew.

Torment became his favorite tool. He twisted and shaped minds into creatures so devolved from their Humanity. They became crawling deviants willing to do his foulest bidding. The power swelled his head. Amar Kit'han could do no wrong. He executed the will of the dark gods with ruthless enthusiasm. The only possible hindrance was the greed of his comrades.

"Badron has lost his army," Kodan Bak hissed as he entered the cold chamber.

Amar Kit'han didn't bother turning. His red eyes continued to stare off into the night, relishing the feeling of total oblivion soothing the cavity where his soul had been. "It was but a matter of time. He still has the Goblin army at his side."

"Goblins aren't much better than dirt dwellers. They will not be enough to accomplish what we need."

"What do we need, Kodan Bak?" Amar snapped. Power whipped from his shadows, cracking the walls and bringing part of the ceiling down around them. "New leadership perhaps? How you'd enjoy seeing me removed so that you might assume the role. The gods did not choose you though, did they? You were found lacking, weak. Unworthy of their greatest gifts. Remember your place, before it is you who finds the short path to nonexistence."

Energy rippled around the Dae'shan in waves, distorting the air with rancor and spite. "You know of what I speak, Amar Kit'han. We were charged with bringing ruin to the northern kingdoms. Badron cannot continue his campaign without his army. Goblins have their uses but they are few."

"Indeed, but there is more at work. Pelthit Re spreads corruption across Delranan. That kingdom is the key to all our plans. It must be in total chaos by the appointed hour. I did not expect him to turn the One Eye so easily to our will, nor the results. Pelthit Re should be commended."

"Delranan already slides towards irreversible doom," Kodan offered. "But it is not enough. With the Wolfsreik free of Badron's influence they will stand in our way. My spies confirm they have already linked up with the remnants of Rogscroft's army and the Pell Darga. Their leader refused to succumb to corruption."

"Do we know what his plans are?" Amar asked.

"There are whispers that he intends to take his army back to Delranan to put an end to the One Eye's tyranny."

Amar floated higher. The Wolfsreik had become a major problem, whether he chose to admit that to Kodan Bak or not. There was no way his forces could defeat the combined strength of three armies, no matter how many Goblins Grugnak managed to funnel in to Rogscroft. The war for the north threatened to sour.

"Perhaps it is time for a new direction," he finally said.

"What do you mean? We cannot stop now. The hour is almost upon us and we have yet to find and prepare the temple at Arlevon Gale. And what of the wizard? He has grown most worrisome. More is needed to halt his progress, if not stop him altogether."

Amar desperately wanted to forget about Anienam Keiss. The wizard was a poison. "How that old fool has managed to avoid being ensnared in our traps for so long confuses me. We have tried for so long to remove the Mages and their ilk yet he persists. He's been relatively harmless until now. I have no reason to believe he is capable of changing suddenly. Still, he has the potential to bring us all to ruin."

"He's assembled a powerful band of allies," Kodan suggested.

"Pah! Would-be heroes. We have seen their like before. One of them always cracks and brings darkness to the group. It is only a matter of time before we can achieve similar results."

"But the Giant…"

"Is of no consequence. He is a boy by their standards and ignorant of the true ways of the world. He will not live long enough to wield the Blud Hamr."

Kodan's robes swirled, billowing out briefly. "If they reach Trennaron and Artiss Gran we will not find it so easy to kill them."

"Artiss Gran has lived for far too long. His treason will be dealt with shortly. Even now he feels his powers wane. Trennaron was never meant to be a bastion of hope. He will fail and fall into disgrace. Perhaps I shall keep him around like these humans keep whipped dogs."

"He was once one of us," Kodan said. "His powers remain so long as the Dae'shan do."

"Not enough to save him from my wrath. Enough of him. Artiss Gran had his uses but was found wanting. The dark gods will abuse him in ways he could never dream. I will deal with him personally, but there is time. Our focus must stay on Delranan. The kingdom stands on the brink but is not yet ready to fall. Perhaps a change of strategy is required."

"What do you have in mind?"

Amar grinned, savage and ruthless. "We bring the kingdom to its knees, so low it will never recover. Only then will it be prepared to receive the dark gods. Bring me the prisoners."

THIRTY-THREE

Plague

Night had fallen on Delranan. The hard-working citizens of Chadra, those still able to work and go about their daily lives, shuffled back to their homes or, for those still single, to their favorite taverns or inns for a hearty meal and cold mead. Armed patrols marched through the streets enforcing Harnin's law. A strict curfew had been established for three hours after sunset. There were no exceptions. Jails were filled with law breakers. Others were beaten badly enough they didn't get caught again. Those few who managed to avoid the soldiers continued to tempt fate.

Word of the raid on the rebellion's headquarters spread much too quickly to be coincidence. Harnin's agents spread a talented mixture of truth and propaganda even before the raid took place. Many civilians believed the rebellion had been decapitated and left aimless in the gutters. Others didn't care. Some, some knew the truth and continued to fight. One thing was certain. The recent raid all but ended the rebellion's raids. Any effective form of fighting or communication was cut off. It was only a matter of time before the end.

Private Ragnar sheathed his sword and removed his heavy metal helmet. He'd spent the last eight hours patrolling Chadra and was looking forward to a good meal and perhaps a little attention from one of the women working the floor of Felt's tonight. His eyes gleamed with anticipation, though for woman or food he wasn't decided. The rest of his four-man team entered the Felt and assumed their usual table in the center of the common room. The atmosphere wasn't one he looked forward to. It stank of heavy smoke and old vomit and had seen better days. The walls were stained from decades of smoke and half of the floorboards were rotted. Still, the foot was decent and so were the Women.

"Damned cold out tonight," Ragnar said as he leaned back in his chair.

Sergeant Belk agreed. "Colder than a frostbitten she-bitch. Not the sort of night we need to be out in."

The others nodded. After all, he was the one giving orders. A long-haired blond who had seen better days and was a little heavier than the year before ambled up to them with her usual perfunctory smile. "Lads, what will it be?"

"Helga! Fair maiden of the Felt," Belk said loudly. "Just the sight of your bosom fills me with warmth."

She slapped his reaching hand away. "That'll not get you as warm as you think, scoundrel. Ales?"

"Ales and roast mutton and bread," he said glumly.

Ragnar piped in, "And yellow cheese. I'm hungry tonight."

Helga gave him a wink and walked off. The others immediately turned to the youngest soldier. They bombarded him with so many questions his head started to hurt. It took Belk to get them calm again. Then he took over.

"What's all that about, lad? She got something for you?"

Ragnar grinned sheepishly. He didn't know but wasn't averse to finding out. A woman like that would keep him warm all night.

The door burst open and a bedraggled-looking man limped to the bar. Those few patrons smart enough to look away did so at once. Those less fortunate found themselves helplessly attracted to the inevitable confrontation. Belk gestured Ragnar to follow and they took up seats on either side of the newcomer. The man coughed violently. His entire body spasmed. A tiny trickle of blood seeped from his nose.

"What happened to you, friend?" Belk tried to ask seriously. He already figured the man had run into another patrol. *Probably Tor's by the look of him.*

Coughing almost uncontrollably, the man gave Belk a deadpan stare. Belk shifted back with shock. He looked into eyes the darkest red, sunken and shallow. The man's face bore a haunted sheen. His skin was grey, like boiled meat. Small, dark spots speckled his exposed flesh. Belk had never seen the like. Then the man coughed in his face.

"What's the meaning of this?" Ragnar snapped. "You'll lose your head for that."

The stranger turned slowly, fixing Ragnar with a baleful glare. He smiled once, coughed, and fell dead at their feet.

Ragnar rolled off Helga, covered in sweat and grinning like a child. He hadn't had that much fun since before the Wolfsreik marched to war and it felt good. Helga yawned and stretched. The moment was lost on her. He was another customer and she was closer to getting off her shift.

"I could get used to having a woman like you around," he said, placing his hands behind his head.

Helga looked back over her shoulder as she slid from the bed. "You're a good boy, but a bit young for my tastes. It was fun giving you a ride though."

A damned sight more than fun. I've half a mind to ask for your hand. Ragnar chuckled at the thought. That's when he first noticed the slight burning sensation deep in his lungs. He idly reached up and rubbed his chest. The burn worsened over the course of the night. By morning both he and Helga would be dead. Unfortunately, Helga managed to slip from the room and go back to the rest of the girls first.

Belk shut the door to his meager home and went to the dying fire. Shuffling the embers to build more flame, he took a few blocks of wood and tossed them in. Satisfied he'd done enough, he went to check on his children. Belk had five boys and two girls and wanted more. He'd come from a big family, blessed with so few deaths. Having children made sense and eased his burden, allowing him to spend more time doing his job since the reserves got called up to active duty.

He loved his family but the Wolfsreik paid more. Lord Harnin even went so far as to offer bounties for rebellion soldiers. Alive was worth more than dead, but Belk wasn't that picky. He kept a fat purse and food on the table. Anyone with seven children knew how difficult it was keeping them all fed and clothed. He checked the girls first. Both were curled under heavy blankets and fast asleep. All the boys but one were also asleep. Belk spoke softly to the lad and closed the door behind him.

What more is there to say than I love you? A good lad. My strongest. He'll make a fine man. Belk removed his weapon belt and cloak and yawned. It wasn't until he collapsed in his favorite chair that he started thinking about what had happened in the tavern. Belk was no stranger to death, but never in such a personal manner. The look of the man's eyes left Belk haunted. He felt unclean. Contemptible. He didn't understand what could transform a healthy man into death walking.

Belk stared into the flames. "What happened tonight?"

He would never get the answer. By dawn Sergeant Belk would be dead, along with all but one of his children. His wife left before any of them awoke. Her body was found a short time later in the central marketplace.

By the end of that first day more than three hundred people were dead. Over a thousand by the end of the week. Panic gripped Chadra. People barricaded themselves inside their homes and refused to come out. Whole families would be found dead once the sickness passed and the final accounting took place. Priests offered prayers to any god they could. Shamans and self-proclaimed hedge sorcerers offered charms of protection. They couldn't keep enough. People bought them as fast as they could. Anything to protect them. It wasn't long before that singular word spread, almost as fast as the death toll. Plague. There was no denying a devastating plague now ravaged across Delranan.

Even animals fell victim to the plague. Horses and wild dogs lay dead in the streets. The city stank of rot and of sickness. Chadra devolved into a graveyard. Bodies were stacked along the side of the road. Others stayed where they fell. Those few who were unaffected by the plague reluctantly agreed to take care of the bodies, but they were quickly subsumed with work. Some quit and, packing their belongings, headed for other villages with the hopes that the plague was not there. Yet others drank themselves to sleep nightly.

Harnin One Eye stood atop the parapet of Chadra Keep, staring down on what remained of the capital city. The plague had come from nowhere and all but ruined Delranan in a matter of days. He paced the dark corners of his chambers, waiting, hoping for the Dae'shan to return, but Pelthit Re never did. The sudden absence left Harnin with the feeling something nefarious was at play behind his back.

Thus far the majority of his household was unaffected. Chadra Keep was higher on the hill and separated from the city proper. Naturally suspicious, Harnin ordered the gates shut the moment the first report came in. His move paid off but, despite hope, wouldn't last forever. He needed information from the outside world. Being trapped in his own castle left him impotent. Worse, Badron might already be returning.

"I have the latest reports," Jarrik said, coming up slowly.

Harnin turned sharply. "Has everyone forgotten their manners? Just because there is a plague ripping my kingdom apart doesn't give you leave to forget your place."

Jarrik halted. A momentary flicker of amusement and hatred flashed before he managed to calm down. "My apologies, Lord Harnin, but I have the latest casualty reports from the city."

"No doubt worse than the day before," Harnin said, turning his back.

"Naturally. Though it appears the disease is abating. Less people are turning up to be treated."

"Because we have far less people in the city that can," Harnin replied. "We must have lost more than half of the population."

"A fair assessment. We can only assume the outlying villages have suffered worse." Jarrik rolled the scroll back up and shoved it inside his cloak. "How much longer are we going to hide behind these walls? Like it or not we need to be out there. Reassuring the people and bringing the rebellion to a close."

"The rebellion is surely all but wiped out by now. Remember Jarrik, they are the people. The very same ones that now lie dead in the streets. They can't fight us if they're already dead."

"Damn it Harnin, we don't know that! Our soldiers are healthy and secluded in their outposts. All the advantages are ours. We must press now," Jarrik all but shouted.

"I'll remind you to keep your outbursts to yourself, Captain," Harnin said coolly. "The plague has put us all on edge. I will forgive you this time."

"I don't need forgiveness. I need actionable orders," Jarrik insisted. "Let me take a detachment into the city. At the worst you lose twenty men and myself."

"I'm glad you consider yourself so expendable. Losing you wouldn't be the worst that could happen. You're quickly outliving your usefulness, Jarrik." Harnin paused. "Very well, take your soldiers and scour the city. Kill any surviving rebels and report immediately."

Jarrik opened his mouth and closed it just as quick. He briefly considered throwing Harnin over the edge. Few, if any, would mourn the loss and possibly elevate Jarrik to the throne. He didn't want to be in charge. Nothing good came from bowing under the pressures of the crown. No, Jarrik simply wanted to be free of the lunacy gripping Delranan. He wanted a return to before the night Chadra Keep was attacked. Before they went to war with Rogscroft. Life made more sense back then. Months later and both kingdoms stood on the brink of ruin.

There was a time he thought differently. He'd longed for power only to see how corrupt it made men. Harnin's fall into madness was a brutal awakening. It wasn't long before Jarrik started to think Argis might have been the smartest of them. *And look where that landed him. The poor bastard is already dead and doesn't know it.*

Turning on Harnin and freeing Argis, while producing a potential ally as well as an unsuspecting informant to the rebellion, never crossed his mind. The hour had grown too late to think about switching sides now. His fate was cast. Changing sides would only infuriate another group of people. Best he wait until the storm blew over before making his bid.

He turned to leave and stopped. The chance to stab another barb in Harnin's side was too great to pass up. "What of *Lord* Argis?"

"His usefulness is at an end. He will be dealt with accordingly."

Jarrik cringed at the icy tone dripping venom. For a moment he almost pitied Argis.

THIRTY-FOUR

Insurrection

Chadra had become a ghost town. Not even crows hovered or perched on rooftops. Cold winds blew the overpowering stench of death through the streets, choking what little life remained. Several houses had already burned down, smoke and ash clinging to the rest of the city like a pall. Depression gripped Chadra and refused to let go.

Sneaking from house to house, unseen by all but the dead, shuffled the thief. She wasn't sure how the plague avoided her and the idea was almost irritating. Either she was too good for the plague or the other way around. Not that she had many complaints. Dying in agony didn't appeal to her. Most of her friends were dead, as well as most of her family. So much had changed since the beginning of the rebellion. So many friends lost, victories and defeats. She lost herself in the quest to reclaim Delranan. And now she had nothing to show for it.

She scavenged what she could and bartered for what she needed. Life only grew harder. The one decent fact was the plague kept Harnin's forces holed up, giving the survivors free reign to do what needed doing. Half-full pack already on her back, she crept around the corner of a blackened building. It had been a chandler before the plague. She frowned. Most of these sorts of places were picked clean. There was canned food aplenty throughout Chadra but her eyes were set on a much greater prize: medicine. It was the one thing she sorely lacked.

Hand on the front door, she froze suddenly. Echoes from heavy-booted feet marching through the ghost town sent chills through her lithe body. She knew that sound. Wolfsreik boots were specifically designed to echo the crunch and stomp of every footstep to instill fear in their enemies. She'd fought them before, though always on her terms. Only a fool took on any sized element of the Wolfsreik at their discretion. Worse, their sudden presence back in Chadra could mean only one thing: Harnin was no longer afraid of the plague. She had to flee. There were many to warn.

Panic threatened to force bad decisions. She slowed her breath and tried to think. Echoes ranged up and down the empty corridors. Without knowing the direction her enemy came from she risked running into their arms. She could hear voices now. The soldiers were close enough she managed to pick out individual voices. That familiar gnawing feeling in her stomach started again. She had to run while she still could, but where? Which direction?

She closed her eyes and listened. Moments later she was able to pick apart the band of sounds, ruling out directions and avenues of approach. The first glimmers of torchlight reflected from the main road to her right. She grinned savagely and took off in the opposite direction. When she figured she was far enough away she found a deserted building and snuck inside. She needed to get a good look at the enemy. The information would prove invaluable.

She didn't need to wait long. Two rows of soldiers marched into view mere moments after she tucked into the corner next to a second floor window. She began counting. While the numbers weren't insurmountable, the Wolfsreik moved with enough force to keep any survivors' heads down. Having seen enough, she readied to leave. That's when she noticed the man at the head of the column. Jarrik, one of the lords of Delranan. Not for the first time she wished for a crossbow and the skill to use it. Instead she was forced to wait for them to pass. Leaving while they were still roaming the streets was tantamount to suicide.

"This is dire news," Inaella coughed. Her body was covered with bruises and she lacked any strength. The plague hadn't claimed her but it came close enough. She'd been bedridden for days while trying to recover. "Thank you, Ingrid. I can't imagine how difficult it was to not get caught."

"They weren't focused on finding me," Ingrid replied through the wet cloth covering her mouth and nose. "The real problem is Harnin has begun sending soldiers back into Chadra."

Inaella attempted to smile but it hurt too much. "No. The real problem is we are too weak by far to combat the Wolfsreik. You say none of them seemed afflicted by the plague?"

"Not a one. They were as healthy as before the plague."

"We've lost over half our strength. Most of the council is dead and there is little chance of coordinating our efforts to start fighting again. I fear the rebellion is finished."

Ingrid clenched her fists. "Finished? This is the moment we need to strike! We have plenty of men and women who cling to death. Let us use them. Throw them at the enemy and infect their soldiers. Harnin is nothing without them and he knows it. We can break them here and now."

"And do what? Chadra is not the city it used to be."

"Let me call for reinforcements from the surrounding villages. We still have hope, Inaella, even if you can't see it," Ingrid protested.

Inaella admired the young woman. She had a fire too few of the rebellion's leaders possessed. Unafraid, she reminded Inaella of Joefke. Pride and fervor were a good start but without a filter to control her emotions she feared Ingrid would burn out much too fast and wind up a corpse before her time. Youth had advantages but it was wasted on the young.

"Ingrid, I appreciate your zeal. You have been a great asset to our cause since coming to us but I can't allow you to throw your life away needlessly. I have every reason to believe the plague was not contained in Chadra. Almost three days passed before anyone understood what was happening, and two more after that before they closed down the city.

Who knows how many infected managed to get out before then? All Delranan may be suffering for all we know."

"All the more reason to send riders out. We'd all be dead if the plague didn't burn itself out. Those still alive are immune. Anyone chosen wouldn't have any reason to fear getting sick," Ingrid said. "Either way we need to know. The rebellion isn't over, Inaella. Not yet. Not when there's still fight left in us."

A coughing fit drove her back down onto the cot and she waved Ingrid off. "I will think on it, Ingrid. For now get some rest and see to the others. I'm afraid I must rest."

Ingrid gave her a final glance before slipping through the curtain. Her mind raced through scenarios and possibilities. One inescapable fact stuck out from any angle she looked at it: the rebellion needed new leadership if it was to survive the next stage of the war. The plague took all the fight out of Inaella. Fenning was dead, killed in the attempt to escape the Wolfsreik raid on their headquarters. Several others died from the plague. Only a skeleton representation remained and practically all those didn't want to fight anymore.

She couldn't blame them. Her life was a bleak shell of what it had been, even before the plague struck. So many more had died during those first few days Ingrid found it difficult to wrap her mind around. She still caught herself turning to speak with an empty seat. The pain grieved her deeply. She used it for strength. Their deaths gave her purpose. It only took intent to force her point. The rebellion languished with inaction for too long. The time had come for a change.

Ingrid left the pitiful excuse for a command center and headed towards one of the safe houses set up throughout Chadra. Her mind blazed with ideas. The guards on duty were surprised to see her wandering about by herself but accepted her with smiles and open arms. She'd proven herself to them during the plague and they weren't the sort to forget debts. Ingrid collected a handful of eager volunteers and gave them their orders. By dawn rebellion riders would be ranging across Delranan to assess the total damage caused by the plague and make their attempt at rebuilding lost fighting strength.

Satisfied, she gathered the strongest and largest of the remainder and headed back to Inaella. If the former aristocrat wouldn't give up power peacefully Ingrid was determined to take it by force. None of them would survive the winter if she didn't. Harnin wouldn't waste any more time after the initial patrol returned with their report. That Jarrik himself had led the patrol spoke volumes, all terrible.

Inaella's eyes fluttered open when she saw the curtains part. Distracted, she waved Ingrid off. "Ingrid, I need to rest. Come back later. I will summon you when…"

"I'm afraid it's not that easy, Inaella. I've come to get a decision. Now."

"What is the meaning of this? I am the senior ranking member of the council and I will say when you get your answers." The weakened woman propped herself up on one elbow and fixed Ingrid with a scowl. "This is not the time to show division. Not with the Wolfsreik back in the city."

"This is the precise time, Inaella," Ingrid countered. "We have sat by and watched as our city slowly died. The council did nothing. We sat and watched dozens of our friends get rounded up and executed under Harnin's orders. The council did nothing. It is clear that this body is not capable of making the necessary decisions for our best interests."

Inaella's eyes narrowed. "What are you saying?"

"The time has come for new leadership. A new direction is required if we're to win," she said flatly.

"Traitor! I should have your head."

Ingrid didn't move. "If you wish, though you'll have trouble finding enough men willing to strike it from my shoulders. In fact I have a suspicion that many of those men you were counting on would be revolted with how quickly you adopted Harnin's tactics. Face it, Inaella, your time is ended."

"What will you do? Without weapons and the fighting force to use them your dreams will be washed away like rain through the gutter," Inaella sneered. "You lack leadership. Always hiding in the shadows of others. It was a mistake admitting you to the council."

"Some mistakes happen for reasons we don't understand. Chadra is no more. You merely delayed the inevitable. I feel sorry for you, Inaella, I really do."

"Save your pity, snake," the raven-haired woman said.

Ingrid moved closer and sat on the edge of the bed. "Poor, poor Inaella. Where have all your servants gone? Your attendants to dress you and ensure you meet your schedules? You claim to know me? I know you as well. A broken aristocrat without lands, title or peasants to boss around. You are everything wrong with this kingdom. It's time for a new order to rise out of your ashes. An order that will reshape Delranan into what it should be. Who knows, perhaps you'll even live long enough to bear witness."

Ingrid tossed her long, blond locks back over her shoulders and stormed off, leaving the stricken Inaella lost in the quagmire of her own contempt and self-loathing. Words wouldn't come. In the end, it was all she could do to collapse back into her dirty blankets and sweat and wonder what went so terribly wrong.

Fuming, Ingrid didn't understand why she felt hollow. Rebuking Inaella should have been satisfying. She'd been waiting patiently for this moment since Joefke died. He was only a second cousin and not very likable but he was family. She couldn't tell the council this. They never would have allowed her to take his place, fearing ulterior motives and a possible play for control. Truthfully, she never had designs towards sitting on the rebellion council. Rising through the ranks was hard but won through constant struggle with the enemy and careful planning.

She wouldn't be where she was if not for the dedication of those who mattered the most: the people. Ingrid figured it was time for the aristocratic class to fall. They'd had their chance to govern the kingdom and made a royal mess of it. Delranan more than likely would never recover. A sad fact but one she was prepared to live with so long as what rose from the dust was better. The plague's unexpected arrival was blessing and boon. So many good people had died that the kingdom was left with barely half of its population. She kept busy to keep from crying. None of her family that she knew of survived. The last of her name, Ingrid vowed to keep fighting until death or victory.

Inaella didn't know nor would she ever that Ingrid had discovered the identity of the one responsible for selling out their headquarters. She took a team of personally dedicated fighters and hunted the man down. He died lost in his own screams. She had watched it emotionlessly even as he begged and pleaded for his life. His claims that he only did it to protect his family fell on deaf ears. Once he lay dead and broken in the gutters Ingrid took her fighters and killed his family. There was no room for weakness in the new rebellion.

Armed with righteous fury, Ingrid presented her offer to the remaining rebels. Her impassioned plea struck the right chords. All but a handful of the older, more devoted rebels left with her. Inaella's rebellion was dead. She flirted with the idea of turning the secret hideaway in but thought the better of it at the last moment. She wasn't a savage after all. Ingrid ordered all the weapons lockers emptied, food stores and supplies removed. They left just enough to keep the leftovers in supply for a few days. After that they needed to look after themselves. They weren't Ingrid's problem any longer.

She had a rebellion to fight.

THIRTY-FIVE

Execution

Argis barely had the strength to lift his head. He'd lost muscle mass, strength, and will during his incarceration. He refused to eat or drink, hoping death would come quickly and save him the pain Harnin deserved. It had been days since guards came to shovel out the muck. His cell was rank. Fetid. Rats came every so often to nibble on his toes and shins. He didn't care. Argis was as close to broken as he'd ever been.

"You've looked better."

Argis started to laugh but it hurt too much. "Come to gloat, One Eye?"

"Yes, in fact I have. You've given me more trouble than you're worth," Harnin sneered. "I should have done this years ago."

"You always represented the worst of us, Harnin. Badron couldn't see it, even though we tried to make him."

Harnin stared back at the former lord. There was a time he considered Argis a friend. They'd shed blood together, broke bread, and drained endless flagons of mead. Harnin had few friends in life. They'd grown close during the Spring Campaign twenty-two years ago. Argis blocked a swing by one of the wild men that would have cleaved Harnin from neck to gut. Harnin frowned at the memory. There was no place for foolish sentiments in the new kingdom.

Instead of friendship he found only disdain. Argis was one of their best. A king in another kingdom. He lacked the fear required of most kingsmen, seldom lacking the patience to tell Badron those things he didn't want to hear. Every kingdom needed advisors like Argis. Harnin despised him for that. Every petty argument pushed Harnin that much further from Badron's favor.

Harnin spit. "Badron's a fool. He made his destiny and abandoned Delranan by doing so. This kingdom should have been mine. Even his father knew it. Bahr was the smart one. He left as soon as he could and made his own life. I should have killed both of them when they were still boys. Perhaps we wouldn't be in this situation?"

"You betrayed the king," Argis insisted.

Harnin laughed. "You dare accuse me of betrayal? It was you who left the forgotten door open so our enemies could sneak in and kill Badron's son. Your selfishness set us on a course to war, Argis. Not mine. I merely capitalized on your mistakes."

"My only mistake was not killing you that night. You are a snake."

Shaking his head, Harnin leaned closer. His nose crinkled at the overpowering stench. How anyone managed to stand such rot was beyond him. "I saved your life, you know?"

It was Argis's turn to laugh. "I'm better off dead."

"Yes, you are. What you don't know is that a plague has taken over the kingdom. Thousands are lying dead in the streets, rotting as we speak. Rumor has it your precious rebellion was most stricken. Does that distress you?"

Wet strands of hair clung to his face. His broken nose itched suddenly. He refused to believe Harnin's taunts. Enough harm had already been done thanks to the One Eye's lies. He refused to believe that everything he had worked for, everything he'd risked over the last two years was wasted because of a random illness. So many friends… He let the thought fade. Death awaited them all; it was merely a matter of how that separated each other.

He'd seen the results of a plague once before. The results were devastating. Worst was the smell. Years had passed and he remembered the smell vividly. Argis wanted to weep, knowing even Harnin couldn't conceive such hatred. No tears came. He'd used them all. Argis was a useless husk of what he wanted to be. For a moment only he thought his act of betrayal was the wrong decision. But no. Badron would have found another reason to go to war and many more would still be dead. The sad realization that he hardly mattered finally broke his spirit.

"A plague would have killed your people as well," he said through coughing fits. "You'd lose just as much."

"Sadly no. I was forewarned and able to protect the great majority of my forces. You should know better than that, Argis. Rulers always have private sources of information," Harnin gloated. "You know what I speak of. He's been in here. I can smell his taint even above your own piss and shit."

"The demon," Argis whispered.

Harnin shrugged. "Hardly what I'd call a demon, though he does display rather vulgar traits. Regardless, he serves his purpose and has given me a new outlook on life."

"How could you betray Delranan to work with a monster?"

"Would it surprise you to learn that Badron has been under the influence of another of these beings? They warped his mind. They must have convinced him to go into Rogscroft at the onset of winter. Only a fool would take his army across the mountains and get cut off once the snows piled up. But then, Badron always was impetuous."

"The pair of you are fit for each other. Can't you see? You're both working towards the same agenda. Rulers! Ha!"

Harnin slapped Argis, knocking a tooth loose. "Mind your tongue before I have it cut out! I am nothing like Badron. Nothing! His family has led this kingdom into the ground. It has fallen to me to raise it up again. Don't you understand you are on the cusp of witnessing true greatness?"

Argis spit a wad of blood. "Greatness and madness are close cousins, Harnin. You could have been so much more than the shadow you've become."

"Perhaps, but none of that matters now, does it?"

Argis shook his head. "No. I don't suppose it does. Have you come to kill me?"

"No. Well, not me personally. I have someone special for that. Your time is expired, Lord Argis. Tomorrow you will be taken to the main palisade and executed in front of as many survivors as we can round up. Your rebellion is finished. Your treason is finished. You are finished. I win, my friend."

The door creaked shut with enough violence it left Argis's ears ringing. Only when he was certain he was alone did he break down and sob.

Dawn was bleak, fitting of the day's task. Dark and troubled clouds clung like a pall to Chadra. Freezing winds blew in from the east and distant Murdes Mountains. Heavier clouds rode low, threatening snow or worse. It was the middle of winter and the northern kingdoms were buried under feet of snow and thick ice. Crows landed on the crenellations and leering gargoyles as if anticipating a feast.

The soldiers of the Wolfsreik reserves were in their finest uniforms. Every weapon was new and impeccably sharpened. Boots were polished to high sheen. Dents were banged out of armor and helmets. They marched up from the barracks in ranks of two, their dark uniforms in contrast to the mild wooden walls of Chadra Keep. Pennants fluttered in the wind. Some tore, leaving jagged stains on emblems.

Harnin followed the soldiers. Dressed in the finest crimson robes and black uniform, his one good eye was red, sore. Late night discussions with Pelthit Re left him fractured in mind and spirit. His flesh was gaunt and obscenely pale. Dark blue veins popped out of the backs of his hands and neck. Patches of hair had fallen out, easily concealed with his hood. Sallow bags clung to his eye sockets, lending him a malevolent appearance. Those nearest cringed away on impulse. If he noticed he didn't mind. Fear was a ruler's most powerful instrument.

A crow cawed. Harnin admired the carrion eaters. *You shall have your feast, bird. I want you to pick his bones clean while his precious people watch in horror. There shall be no new dawn for Argis.* Reluctantly he took his gaze from the crow and settled on the massive x-shaped rack dominating the center of the palisade. He'd carefully detailed Argis's torture and execution to the master torturers. A traitor's death was too simple, too nice for one of Delranan's former lords. Argis needed to suffer so much it carried over to the afterlife.

Hundreds of civilians had been rounded up and marched up the slope to Chadra Keep. Several coughed and sputtered with the lingering plague symptoms. Harnin cared less. They were all expendable at this point. He figured at least half were willing participants in the rebellion. The thought of turning his Wolfsreik loose on them the moment Argis's head sailed over the wall tempted him. He reluctantly decided against it, knowing the psychological damage of having one of their staunchest symbols carelessly tossed into the crowd would leave the pitiful remnants of the rebellion in utter shock.

The idea of crushing so many dissidents put a wry grin on his face. A bell chimed once and the crowd hushed. Harnin turned back to the entranceway. Four guards pulled and shoved Argis outside. The former lord immediately tried to shield his face from the blinding light. Weeks of captivity left him diseased, so weak he couldn't stand on his own. The guards laughed, shoving him to the floor and kicking him repeatedly when he wouldn't rise.

Harnin pursed his lips. Conflicting thoughts kept him silent. Much of his hatred fled as he looked on what Argis had become. Confronting the traitor in the quasi darkness of the dungeon was one thing. Seeing him exposed in broad daylight was vastly different. Killing him was a definite mercy. Still, he couldn't help but feel the pull of old emotions. They'd been friends once. Harnin ignored the niggling in the back of his mind. Keeping Argis alive was dangerous. The man needed to die for several reasons. Harnin straightened his back and clasped his hands in front of him. Steeling his gaze, he watched as the guards hauled Argis back to his feet and kept moving him forward.

A loud gasp rose from the crowds as Argis came into view. The strange combination of sickness and madness washed over them. Few could believe the degeneration Harnin had not only allowed but condoned for the former lord of Delranan. Many already knew how far the One Eye was willing to go to achieve total victory. The kingdom quickly swooned under this new dictatorship. More than one onlooker wept for Argis as he fell again. The crack of whips was crisp, bitter on the morning wind.

Harnin ignored the crowds. People were little better than cattle. Their time was fast approaching. His eye never left Argis. Every jolt of pain, nuance of suffering was noted. He wanted to savor it. But there was no joy to be found. Every emotion appeared hindered, as if the Dae'shan lurked just out of sight. A fleeting shadow in that special space between light and dark. So long as Pelthit Re and the others remained, Delranan would never be recreated in Harnin's image. But no matter how he tried to rationalize it, Harnin couldn't find a way to remove the Dae'shan threat and make the kingdom his again.

Argis was hefted onto the wooden x and strapped down. His hands hung limply. His body sagged under its own weight. The wood groaned and leaned forward slightly. *Good. That makes it easier for the people to witness what comes next.* Harnin nodded to the head executioner. The bigger Man gave gruff commands and attendants began hoisting the x by a series of pulleys and gears. The wooden x slowly inclined forward until Argis was suspended over the crowds. Receiving a curt nod from the executioner, Harnin took his place upon the podium erected for the occasion.

"People of Delranan, you are here to witness the execution of a traitor. Lord Argis has disgraced this kingdom through seditious acts and turned you against the crown. Pay heed to his fate, for the same will befall you."

Several shouted back and threw rocks but the walls were too high. Harnin searched the outskirts of the crowd for the men Jarrik prepositioned in the buildings to the rear of the field. One hundred soldiers hid in full battle armor, ready to strike on the lord of Delranan's command.

Reacting how he expected, Harnin frowned and turned his back on his people. "Lord Argis, you are charged with sedition against the crown and the willful intent to sow discourse among the people. For this crime there is only one sentence. Death. Have you anything to say for yourself before your head rolls from your shoulders?"

Straining to raise his head, Argis tried to look at Harnin. Instead of anger he felt only sorrow. Harnin had been a good man before his descent into madness. Perhaps the afterlife would be kind to him, more likely not. Argis then turned his gaze down onto the people he'd sworn to defend and serve. The anguish in their faces wounded him more than anything Harnin's men were capable of. He felt their pain and something else. A faint sense of betrayal clouded their faces. *How many have died for our hubris? We ruined this kingdom with our greed and arrogance. You deserved better, but alas such was not your fate. I pray you find the courage to continue and wrest Delranan back from the catastrophe we have left you.*

"Have you nothing to say? Nothing at all to calm your soul before the end?" Harnin persisted. He'd expected more. A rant at the very least. A desperate plea to continue the rebellion. Argis's silence offended him. "Commence the sentence!"

The executioner hefted a massive double-headed axe and took three ponderous steps towards the prisoner. Argis started laughing, much to the disdain of the crowds. Grunting from the strain, the executioner drew back and swung. Argis cried out and went silent. His head dropped down from the wall in a shower of blood. People screamed. Others fled. Most could only stand and stare at what remained of their last hope for victory.

Harnin stayed long after the crowds dispersed and the guards returned to their quarters. He stayed long after the sun set and darkness rose. The One Eye sat and stared at what had been his friend and peer. The corpse stopped bleeding long ago. Congealed blood formed a gruesome necklace. Nerves died. The body stopped twitching.

Harnin sighed. "What have we become, old friend? Delranan shouldn't be like what we've made it. I'm going to miss you."

Slowly he rose, stretched, and went back inside. He'd seen enough. Pelthit Re materialized from the darkness, watching Harnin leave. Hands folded within his robes, the Dae'shan struggled with sudden doubts. Perhaps he'd chosen wrong in the One Eye. Surely there were better men to lead Delranan into the thrall the dark gods. Scowling, he turned his gaze on Argis's remains and thought.

THIRTY-SIX

Battle of Grunmarrow

The Goblin army arrived at dawn and was immediately attacked from the flanks by the combined mounted force of Wolfsreik and Rogscroft defenders. Scores died in those initial moments. Panic threatened to break the massive Goblin column. Sergeants and their cruel whips forced them back into defensive positions and kept the army moving forward. In a move of unanticipated boldness, Badron and Grugnak decided to strike Grunmarrow. The bulk of the Goblin corps in Rogscroft marched on the hidden village.

Word of their approach reached Grunmarrow first. Nothing so large could move quickly or stealthily without being noticed. Riders flooded into Grunmarrow with reports of the coming doom. Aurec acted quickly, sending the civilians and non-combatants up into the mountains. Battalions of Wolfsreik and Pell Darga hastened into defensive positions before the Goblins could reach the mountains. When the battle began it was on Aurec's choosing.

The initial attack forced the Goblins towards the waiting spears of the Pell Darga. The stout Pell warriors attacked with zealousness as Rolnir's cavalry continued to force the flanks closer together. Once massed, Aurec began a devastating catapult barrage. Hundreds of Goblins were slaughtered. Gaps formed in the center of the formation but the Goblins refused to break. Ranks of warriors stopped moving forward and faced outward. Spears were leveled, forcing the cavalry to withdraw.

Thinking they'd stymied the attackers, the front Goblin battalions surged ahead. They died on the Pell's short spears but continued attacking. Soon the Pell were forced to withdraw, leaving a field of corpses being trampled under the weight of the Goblin army. Aurec ordered the barrage to continue in the hopes of deterring further offense but the Goblins had come to fight. They dug in and formed shield walls to block the Pell and deter Wolfsreik riders.

Mounted archers stormed across the killing field, loosing their darts into the exposed Goblin backs. They only managed to get off a few volleys before the enemy adjusted. Aurec slammed the looking glass shut and snapped off a string of curses that managed to get Sergeant Thorsson's attention. The latter had the good sense to remain quiet while the newly crowned king vented his frustrations.

"They've already brought up shields to block the archers!" he fumed.

Rolnir wiped his eyes with an old rag. "We knew they would. Goblins are professional thugs that know how to fight."

Aurec shot a furious look to the Wolfsreik general. "We need to break them or they're going to break us. Should the Goblins win through, all our women and children will be exposed. I don't want that slaughter on my hands, Rolnir."

"There will be no slaughter. We need to intensify the catapult fire, adjusting target areas at random to keep them guessing. Once the center of their formation is unstable I will order a full charge. No army on Malweir can withstand a heavy cavalry charge."

"They stopped your charge the first time," General Vajna chimed in. He'd been given command of the infantry for the duration of the combined operation while Rolnir had overall command.

"As we figured on," Rolnir replied calmly. Working with former enemies was new for him, and he expected certain levels of animosity and discourse, leaving him more than prepared to overcome their differences. "Have the infantry ready to attack as soon as the cavalry breaks into their formation. Attack from the flank while the catapults cover the head of the column. Order a ceasefire once the infantry advances and have the Pell attack again. We'll break these bastards and send them running back to their mountain holes in the east."

"I hope for your sake it works, General," Aurec said flatly. "There is a lot on the line."

"I'm not in the habit of losing."

Aurec turned to Thorsson. "Issue the orders. Wipe this filth off the field."

Thorsson saluted and hurried off. Time was of the essence if the Goblins were going to be pushed off the field before sundown. The battle had already raged for half the day. Casualties were rising at a rate neither side could sustain for much longer. Aurec found it increasingly difficult to sit and watch the battle unfold. His instincts demanded he take to horse and ride into battle with his soldiers. Being king was vastly different from a prince. That and not a one on his council was going to let him get anywhere near the front lines.

The bulk of the Goblin force in Rogscroft was in front of him. Should they be defeated, the road back to the city and Badron would be wide open. Aurec stood on the precipice of reclaiming his kingdom and beginning reparations. He had to be sure he defeated the Goblins here, now. Only then would Badron finally be at a severe enough of a disadvantage to drive him back to Delranan or, at the very best, capture him and ransom him back to his own kingdom.

Thoughts of sitting on his father's throne, his throne, were almost alien. Aurec hadn't dreamed of seeing his home city again. He almost got carried away with future plans. Rolnir kept him grounded. The Wolfsreik general was a consummate professional, focused solely on the task at hand. His vision of a battlefield was unparalleled, giving Aurec full confidence.

"General Vajna, take the field. I want the infantry formed and ready to attack within the hour," Rolnir ordered.

Vajna saluted. "Yes, sir."

"You move on my signal," Rolnir said. "Piper, you get the honor of leading the charge. Don't be a hero. Break their lines open wide enough for the infantry to do the real damage. Piper, don't get yourself killed. I'm going to need you."

Piper bit his upper lip, grave reservations nearly freezing him in place. His still hadn't gotten over the mauling his vanguard suffered in the initial engagement of the war. Worse, he was allies with the very same people responsible. Joining King Aurec was the logical and ethical decision but it didn't take away the sting of knowing they had spent so long trying to kill each other. Piper wasn't sure if he would ever lower his guard and allow emotion in. The hurt was still much too real.

He stared down at the battle with disinterest. Goblins were among the nastiest races in all Malweir. Eradicating them was vital, especially here, to win back the kingdom and get home again, yet Piper couldn't find the necessary hatred. They were being used much the same way the Wolfsreik had been used. Badron's deception went deeper than any of them understood. Piper failed to see how his king had access to an alliance with the Goblin tribes. What else was he holding in reserve?

"Piper?" Rolnir asked, suddenly concerned.

Piper shook the cobwebs from his head. "Yeah. I'm just trying to think this through. That's a lot of Goblins."

"Yes it is, but we can break them. I doubt we'll get a better chance," Aurec added.

Rolnir said, "You have the opportunity to be the hero. Break the Goblins and free Rogscroft."

Piper's eyebrow arched wickedly. "Heroes usually get killed."

"Try not to follow suit. Are you ready?" Rolnir asked. Time was up.

"I'll break them open, you do the rest," Piper confirmed to Vajna.

The elder general nodded. "Good luck to you, Commander."

Piper saluted and left for his troops. Aurec watched silently, admiring the man. Only two types of people would march into a desperate situation they didn't want to: a fool and a brave man. Piper Joach was no fool.

"You are fortunate to have a second like that in your confidence," Aurec told Rolnir.

The Wolfsreik commander agreed. "If I only had a few more this war would be over already. It's going to be tough winning the field."

"They'll break. All the engagements we've fought against the Goblins thus far follow the same pattern. They fight until there's no hope of victory and then break and run. Our biggest enemy now is darkness."

Night was fast approaching. If the alliance didn't win the field before dark the Goblins would regroup and fight twice as hard. They were infinitely more comfortable in darkness. All the advantages the alliance enjoyed now would be lost. Surviving would prove a struggle.

"General Vajna, can you cover the cavalry with archers? We can't afford to give them a moment." Rolnir watched the cavalry reform in the far tree line. Three thousand soldiers tightened straps and checked the weight of their lances. He could already imagine the thunder of hooves rolling across the field.

"I'll have them begin at once," Vajna said.

Rolnir and Aurec soon stood alone on the small hilltop. Two anxious commanders with little in common save the preservation of their respective kingdoms. Both flinched as the catapults began firing at a maddening pace.

Piper's cavalry crashed into the already unsteady Goblin flank like the vengeance of the gods. Shields and bodies flew through the air. Blood rose up in waves. Screams mingled with roars and curses. The catapult batteries began firing projectiles coated with burning pitch. Thousands of infantry advanced under the blanket of smoke and confusion gripping the Goblin army.

What began as a courageous defense devolved into an everyone-for-himself melee. Piper swung and hacked until his muscles threatened to give out. Dark Goblin blood coated his armor, running in sheens down his horse's neck. He stabbed down, running his sword into a Goblin's throat and down into the lungs. The immediate battle space clear, Piper was able to look around for the first time. His stomach revolted. An endless sea of bodies covered the ground. He watched one of his men pulled from his mount and hacked to pieces even as more Goblins were slaughtered around them.

Piper threw up as a Goblin head was ripped from the shoulders and flew across the air. Two horses were killed with horrible screams. The pitch and yaw of battle went back and forth until Vajna's infantry stormed into the fray in massive phalanxes of steel and hatred. Goblins fell in droves. So too did men. The cavalry floundered the deeper it pushed, trapping man and beast. A lone horn wailed over the field.

The Goblins broke. Hundreds threw down their weapons and fled back to the east. Rolnir deliberately left the rear open. He wanted word to get back to Badron. He wanted that doubt to spread through the remnants of his supporters. Doubt led to fear and fear was the path to total breakdown. If it went well, the war would be over by spring.

"Commander! We've taken the field. Permission to reform the lines and pursue," shouted a red-faced senior sergeant. His shield was split down the center. Bits of bone were wedged in the crack.

Piper knew the right thing to do was agree. The Goblins were too dangerous to be allowed to regroup. Every advantage was needed to continue the war. The order to attack stuck on the tip of his tongue. Piper made his decision. "No, Sergeant. There's been enough killing for one day. Order the men to form ranks and secure the field. I don't want any surprises. Not now."

Reluctant to follow orders, the sergeant saluted. "Yes sir."

"Sergeant," Piper said as an afterthought. "No prisoners, if you please."

Grinning savagely, the sergeant spun off and began barking orders. The Wolfsreik responded with zeal, killing every Goblin left on the field. Vultures were already circling by the time night fell. Piper finally allowed himself to relax. The battle was over.

THIRTY-SEVEN

Revenge

Badron smashed the aged glass vase against the nearest wall and bellowed his rage at the top of his lungs. Attendants cringed, some getting slashed by flying glass. One body already lay dead with Badron's dagger plunged through his right eye. Madness gripped the throne room. Those wise enough backed as far away as possible and even that wasn't enough. Goblins marched in on Grugnak's command to line the walls. Anarchy now ruled Rogscroft.

"I want them all dead!" Badron roared.

Grugnak glowered at him, arms folded across his burly chest.

Badron pointed an accusing finger at the Goblin king. "Your army failed me!"

"After yours betrayed you," Grugnak fired back. The Goblin was unused to being mistreated in front of his army by Humans. It took every ounce of restraint not to kill Badron and be done with it. Only Amar Kit'han's quiet insistence kept Badron alive.

Badron paused. The Wolfsreik's loss severely crippled the campaign. Without the weight of his army, his hold on Rogscroft became tenuous. The Goblins were already revolting. He'd seen it while half of the city burned. Grugnak either lacked the ability or desire to keep his forces in check. Lately Badron's suspicions seemed to turn for the worse. He felt the world slipping through his fingers. All the pain from having his family ripped apart and his kingdom stolen behind his back by a man he should have ground under his heel years ago was finally catching up to him. He fumed helplessly, knowing his actions attributed to little more than a child's temper tantrum.

"I am a king," he snarled. "Two kingdoms are under my rule and yet I have no power to control either."

Grugnak cleared his throat and spit a massive wad of phlegm. "Conquering is not about land. You must break the people to rule. Humans are too weak. They do not understand the hard truths."

"Yet we are the dominant race on Malweir while your kind wallows in caves and dreams of glory. A glory you will never achieve."

Grugnak roared. "My armies…"

"Have been all but destroyed by the Wolfsreik! It seems neither of us have power," he mused. "A king without an army."

"I have already sent for reinforcements," Grugnak snarled. "Fifty thousand Goblins are ready to march west."

Badron's stomach clenched. Fifty thousand was an unstoppable-sized force. Not even if all the northern kingdoms banded together would they be able to defeat the Goblins. Badron didn't see how so many existed without owning more lands. So much combat power would bury the north in a sea of bones. The death toll would be unparalleled. And Badron lacked the ability to prevent the Goblin force from invading.

He began to pace. Thoughts collided and broke apart as he desperately tried to find a way to salvage his rule. Rolnir's desertion proved problematic and left Delranan and Rogscroft without a proper military force. Compounding matters was Harnin's betrayal. Delranan was defended against the Wolfsreik's return, though Harnin was presumed to know nothing of Rolnir's actions.

Badron suspected Rolnir and his force would be trying to return to Delranan as fast as possible, which in turn would deprive Aurec of much of his combat power. Rogscroft would be ripe for conquering by the Goblins. A thought blossomed and Badron grinned.

"Grugnak, when your army arrives we need to sweep across this pathetic kingdom, killing everyone in the way."

The Goblin cocked his massive head. Drool spilled from the corner of his mouth, splashing down his chest armor. "We will destroy your dreams."

"Rogscroft is no prize. I've lost too much here already, as have you. This kingdom needs to be razed and rebuilt in a better image. Your image."

Goblins were naturally suspicious creatures. Their hatred and fears pooled in deep wells. It was an old fear. One stemming back from their earliest days when they devolved from the Dwarves. They'd been ostracized, hunted, and exterminated whenever possible for centuries, driving them to oblivion until only darkness remained. Grugnak wanted nothing more than to burn the world to the ground and raise a Goblin empire. Only it wasn't so easy.

The Dae'shan came to him with gilded promises too impossible to follow through. They offered riches and land, the freedom to move about in daylight without fear of persecution. Grugnak was no fool. He knew as long as other races lived his kind would be feared and hunted. In the end there was no real choice. Grugnak committed his forces to the Dae'shan without so much as a question. They marched from the Deadlands, unwilling servants to the dark gods' bid to return.

"No man can be trusted," Grugnak said. "Why should I believe you?"

Badron help up his hands. "What else is there? You've been defeated, handily. Your army wasn't enough to stop the combined forces of the Wolfsreik and Aurec's men. I no longer have an army. Your fifty thousand will turn the tide and together we can crush our enemies under our heels. I am through with Rogscroft. My revenge was against Stelskor. His head is now my trophy. His son is in exile. What little remains of his people will be crushed by your new strength. We can sweep the old rule of the northern kingdoms aside and rebuild the world, Grugnak. All it takes is a spark."

"What spark?" Grugnak demanded.

"Your army."

The Goblin barked a horrible laugh. "You mistake me. I do not need you. My army will take this kingdom. You cannot stop me."

"I don't want to stop you. I want your help," Badron said quickly before Grugnak was able to think matters through. He had gone from imposable figure to expendable in the span of a few short months. "Take Rogscroft and do what you will with it. I don't care. My purpose is complete. What I want, is your army in Delranan."

"Invade your own kingdom?"

Badron nodded. "Yes. Rolnir will no doubt try to remove Harnin upon his return. The kingdom will be in utter disarray, giving us a small window of opportunity to rush in and destroy both defenders and the Wolfsreik. Not even their vaunted strength will be enough to withstand the weight you bring."

A cold wind howled through the throne room. Grugnak and Badron glared at each other, trying to determine the conviction of their faiths. Strangely, the king of Delranan already came to view his army as a distinct entity, no longer his to control. The systematic removal of everything he once held dear made it easier to order their destruction. Badron had come to hate his kingdom and everything it stood for. His mind slipped, devolving into a darkened mess. What had once been important was no longer interesting. All he wanted, needed, was death.

"Think about it, Grugnak. I am the last great king in the north and I'm giving you the chance to slaughter entire kingdoms of Men," he crooned. "What would your ancestors have done if they were faced with the same situation?"

Grugnak's eyes narrowed, his thick brow furrowed in rugged rows of lined flesh. Thoughts of slitting Badron's throat entertained him. Their alliance was one forged through the manipulations of the Dae'shan. One in which he harbored no illusions of Badron's loyalty. The king of Delranan would turn on the Goblins the moment he thought it was to his advantage. Just as Grugnak planned when the time suited him. It was a delicate balance he wasn't ready to play.

"First Rogscroft. Then we shall see," he finally said.

Badron smiled inwardly. He couldn't help but think of turning what remained of the Wolfsreik back to his side once the Goblin army crossed the Murdes Mountains.

Amar Kit'han listened to the shrill screams pouring out of his latest victim as the flesh was burned from his bones. Blood, super-heated from the unseen energy, evaporated the moment it touched the air, leaving a thin, red mist in the room. He enjoyed flaying people. Their screams satisfied his carnal need for pain as well as soothed his worries.

"Why must you waste our time in this endeavor?" Kodan Bak scolded from his place against the far wall. He bore no love for any of the races on Malweir but saw little point in killing for no other reason.

Amar didn't bother looking up. "It amuses me. Our kind has been given ultimate power yet we remain part of this pathetic world, dwelling with these insignificant creatures. It's hard to believe we were once Human."

"That humanity should be a strength, not weakness," Kodan countered. "You turn your energies in the wrong direction."

"What else would you have me do? I am sick of this mortal guise. Aren't you ready to ascend, Kodan Bak? How much longer will the gods casually disregard us while we do their bidding here on Malweir? I am tired of being a pawn."

"What are you saying?"

Amar Kit'han had never been satisfied with his station. Not as a man, and certainly not as the head of the Dae'shan. He wanted more. The days when his order remained neutral, serving the best interests of the world rather than a single faction, were barely memories. He could hardly contain his blind ambitions. Amar Kit'han wanted what the gods offered. He wanted to become a god and forget the trappings of everything that had come before.

"We were meant for greater purpose," Amar said after slicing one of his victim's chest muscles apart.

Kodan couldn't believe his ears. Ever the reluctant agent of evil, he struggled with their previous lives and what the gods originally intended them to be. "We do as the gods instruct."

He was careful not to incite Amar further by accusing him of leading the Dae'shan away from the grey and into the deepest heart of the black. There was a time when white and black stood on opposite shoulders, the Dae'shan walking a narrow path. Amar changed that with ruthlessness and cunning. The Dae'shan fell from grace and had been servants of the dark gods ever since.

"As we always have, but aren't you curious?"

He wasn't. "Toward what? We have experienced everything Malweir has to offer. This has been our world since the creation. What more do we need?"

"To be free, Kodan. Do you recall the taste of freedom? I almost cannot." He removed the victim's heart and squeezed, relishing the feel of blood and gore spilling from his fingers. "For centuries we have obeyed without question, doing what the dark gods demand. But the gods are not here, nor have they been for a very long time. Perhaps our lives would be better off without them."

"Without them? You speak of sedition."

Amar finally turned and faced him. "Sedition? We are not vassals ruled by mere lords. I am speaking of deicide."

Kodan Bak recoiled at the waves of hatred pulsing off Amar. Cold and calculating, the Dae'shan were the ultimate powers on Malweir. Removing the dark gods was logical. They were a shadow presence; an abstract working against the natural progression of life. Who better to take the dark gods' place in the long, empty pantheon than their willful servants? While self-serving, the idea wasn't without merit.

Deviant intent flickering in his nightmarish eyes, Amar Kit'han folded his hands within his robes. "You begin to understand. I am tired of being a pawn. Join me and we will rule the world."

"How can we defeat gods?" Kodan protested.

"Any way we must. I have already set plans in motion that cannot be stopped. Whether you are with me or not doesn't matter. We shall conquer or be destroyed."

"You've damned us all."

Amar lifted higher off the floor. "We've been damned for a very long time."

THIRTY-EIGHT

Maleela's Descent

Maleela shivered. Cold winds drove down from the coast, following the track of the Fern River as it wound deeper into the heart of Malweir. She stared out at the seemingly endless snow-covered plains wondering how any land would be warm this time of year. Once, she almost couldn't remember when, she enjoyed the deep winter cold. The strange combination of the war and their unexpected quest convinced her otherwise. She despised the snow and what it represented. Instead of serenity she found hatred, emptiness. Boen and Rekka spun impossible tales of distant southern lands. Her heart tugged, conflicted between her unending love for Aurec and the impossible desire to flee to better kingdoms.

She hadn't slept well since leaving Venheim. The Giants made her comfortable with their mild manners and easygoing attitudes. Some of them at least. She enjoyed spending time with Groge. The youth was wide eyed, still capable of finding the good in things when so many others doomed themselves to ill will and twisted thoughts. Maleela often thought of leaving in the middle of the night and going off to find a new life. As much as she wanted to go back into Aurec's arms, the more she became convinced he was dead. There wasn't anything left in either kingdom for her. She needed a new beginning.

Her mistrust of the others grew daily. Bahr was the only true family she had left, but even he wasn't enough to keep her in the north. The street urchin, Skuld, was turning into a Man before her eyes. Maleela knew he'd make someone very happy if he managed to break away from the heavy macho nonsense surrounding him. The combination of Boen, Anienam, and those two sell swords was certain to ruin young Skuld. He deserved better. They all did.

"I don't know how people can stand this weather," Skuld said from behind her. "I can't feel my fingertips."

She smiled despite her earlier misgivings. "I used to stand on the walls of Chadra Keep and let the winds blow through my hair. There is purity in the wind."

"We used to stare up the hill towards the castle," Skuld replied. "We watched the guards patrolling the walls and thought only of taking what was within. Chadra Keep represented evil as far as we were concerned. I wish there was a way to go back and tell people how wrong they were."

"Perhaps they weren't wrong at all."

He looked offended. "I was being serious. You shouldn't mock me."

Maleela turned, sadness in her eyes. "I wasn't. I was being truthful. What fools we were, to think we were better than the people. I should have seen it sooner. Darkness festered in my father's soul. I've spent my entire life being ostracized. There is no love in the wooden halls of Chadra Keep, Skuld. It has grown lifeless and decrepit since my brother's death."

He went to stand beside her. "I remember his funeral. Even for a street rat it was very impressive. That's how I became involved in this mess."

"I don't understand."

Skuld grinned sheepishly. "I wound up following Dorl and Nothol, overhearing their conversation about adventure and treasure. I think I was the fool. Their tales captured me and I had to follow. Life in the streets is hard. You have to fight for every scrap of food, for clothes, for a dry place to sleep. Bigger, tougher kids are always trying to hurt you and rob you. What kind of king allows such conditions to thrive right under his nose?"

"You've grown since this journey began," she said appraisingly. "Badron never cared for the lower class. They were a means to his rule, nothing more. Life or death meant less to him as time went by. My uncle tells me it wasn't always like that. He said that he and Badron once viewed the world with open hearts. No one can say what changed. My father grew spiteful, choosing to covet what others had rather than cultivating his own holdings. He always wanted more. The world isn't made to live that way, Skuld. He let greed and avarice consume him until nothing remained but bitterness. My brother's murder finally consumed him."

"It's not too late. We can reclaim Delranan. You are the heir to the throne."

"There hasn't been a queen in Delranan for nearly a hundred years. I can't see the people accepting one now, especially the daughter of the worst tyrant in our history. They'll string me up and leave my body to the crows." She paused, lost in terrible thoughts. "I hate him."

He shuffled his feet, unsure how to respond. He'd always thought her lucky. She had a father, albeit one who hated her, and a roof over her head. He didn't know his parents. Hard life on the streets raised him into the man he was today. Not that it was much to brag about. Without a coin to his name, no family, home, or idea of what he wanted to become, Skuld stumbled through life hoping something good would fall into his lap. Only in the last few weeks had he learned that a man needed to make his own way in life, not wait for fortune's kiss.

"I trust Bahr. He says it will all work out once we get the Hamr and stop the dark gods," Skuld said.

She fixed him with a dubious stare. "Do you truly believe that nonsense about the gods returning? Why is it always the dark gods and never the light? Are we supposed to blindly accept the fact that any god willingly stepped away from his creation and allows evil to flourish? What separated dark from light if that is so?"

"I never believed in any god. There wasn't any point in putting faith in something no one could prove existed."

"Precisely! The wizard would have us believe that the gods of light are not interested in this world any longer and have disappeared, leaving the gods of darkness to reclaim what they've always been denied. His reasoning is suspicious at best. I have trouble placing faith in anything I can't see."

"Why are you here if you don't believe?"

She smiled. "I could ask you the same question, though I suspect our answers are similar. We are the same, Skuld. Homeless and without family. What choice do either of us have? Stay away from Anienam. I don't know why exactly but he leaves me with an ill impression."

Skuld left her, already lost deep in thought. So much had changed since he snuck aboard the *Dragon's Bane* he wasn't sure of much anymore. Once, he wanted to be like Boen: hunting down the wicked and reaping the rewards offered by kings and queens. His dreams of being a famous hero adored by the public and having to push the affections of women away ended quickly the day the first crewman was found headless on the decks.

They'd never figured out who was responsible, though Skuld had suspicions. He'd been seeing strange shapes in the sky since leaving Stouds, what seemed a lifetime ago. It wasn't until the battle in Fedro they learned a trio of Harpies were tracking them. Skuld's imagination was never great, making it more incredulous as time progressed. He'd seen Giants, been captured by Dwarves, hunted by Harpies, and hounded by a great evil for months. Nothing in his life on the streets could have prepared him for any of it. The longer the quest went the more convinced he became that he wasn't going to survive the end. Especially if what Anienam alluded to was even half correct.

Exhausted from thinking of the possibilities, he went to find a warm place to curl up and sleep. He'd had enough of frozen wastelands and the sloshing waters of the Fern River. Skuld took the time to slip his favorite horse, a large roan mare, a small apple from his pocket. The mare snickered and nuzzled against his arm. He smiled. Sometimes the animals were better company than the others.

Rekka's blade danced off Boen's much larger and heavier broad sword. The Gaimosian grunted and took a half step back. Sweat covered them both. The small woman from the southern jungles attacked Boen with cunning, precision, and unmatched skill. His size and indomitable power kept her at bay, for the moment. After an hour of sparring, Rekka lowered her sword and bowed gracefully.

"You are a worthy partner," Boen admitted. He rolled his massive shoulders, driving out the ache before inspecting the nicks on his sword.

"Your words are kind, Boen. I thank you for sparring."

He grunted, knowing she would have rather sparred against her newfound love, Dorl. But he was wounded and not in any condition to fight, at least not for a while. This quest was taking a heavy toll on them all. Boen wasn't half as young as he used to be. Every morning he awoke with fresh aches and pains. Old wounds haunted his movements. Though he'd never admit it, he was tired beyond anything he'd ever felt. The Gaimosian was beginning to think he'd finally met his match. The idea that this quest would be the end of him seemed almost pleasing after a lifetime spent fighting, questing, and watching friends fall.

"It is rare to find one capable of matching a Gaimosian," he went on to say. "Are all your kind so skilled?"

Rekka wiped her blade down with an oiled rag. Salt and spray from the river threatened to ruin the steel if not properly taken care of. She was used to humidity, not the unforgiving cold of the north. Each environment presented unique challenges. "Only those chosen by the dream masters."

"I have been to many lands, but I have never heard of yours until now," Boen admitted. "What is Teng like?"

She paused, the question taking her off guard. Rekka had been away from home for so long she forgot many things. The harsh discipline of the sword masters. The mysticism that often made little sense of the dream masters. Her entire people lived to serve the gods of light. Preventing the dark gods from returning and counteracting the Dae'shan were their ultimate purposes, though she wasn't sure how she was going to succeed in a task after so many already lie deep in the ground from failure.

Rekka sheathed her sword. "Teng is a difficult land. It is a hidden kingdom, deep in the jungles of Brodein. Those chosen are raised almost from birth in either martial arms or to interpret dreams. We are given no choice."

"A hard life," he agreed. "It is said my people were given no choice either. Becoming a warrior was expected if you wanted to eat. I understand where you come from, Rekka. It is an honor to serve alongside you."

She bowed, waiting for him to ask the inevitable question everyone wanted an answer for. A woman with little need to divulge her past, Rekka stayed in the shadows. Waiting, watching. Her life lost meaning, transforming into a metaphor. Lesser disciples cracked long before the training process was complete. Rekka was one of the few from each generation strong enough to abandon home and family and become something more than herself.

Boen, sensing her mild discomfort, asked, "What can we expect once we reach Trennaron?"

She blinked, taking a split second to decide how much to say. The secrets of Trennaron were known only to a handful. Secrets so great small minds burst, rendering those unfortunate ones insane or worse. "The citadel is deep within the jungle. Each year we learn of those foolish enough to go in search of it. We find their bodies partially devoured soon after. There is no record of anyone ever reaching Trennaron and returning alive."

"I am not afraid," Boen grunted. "Death is a Gaimosian's companion. We do not fear what awaits us."

"You should," she replied softly. "Darkness surrounds the citadel. Fell powers spring forth from the center of the world and are collected there. The dream masters say Trennaron is a reservoir of hostility. Only the guardian keeps it from spreading across Malweir."

The big Gaimosian scratched his jaw. "This guardian, whose side is he on?"

"He doesn't take sides. The guardian is neutral."

"Then how do we know he'll help us?" Boen asked.

She had no answer.

Day turned to night without incident. The barge continued downriver. Bahr and Anienam argued with the captain, wanting to press on while the crew thought it wiser to put to shore. Neither side wanted to work together and their argument nearly came to blows. A lifetime spent on the waters gave Bahr better understanding of their situation but he struggled to find a way to communicate effectively with the river men. Plenty of people called him a pirate, though in truth he was anything but. The river men, however, weren't ashamed of the name.

"What dangers await us should we continue?" Bahr pressed. Anger tinged his voice.

The captain grimaced and shook his head fiercely. "Rapids! Not safe to traverse in the darkness. Barge will capsize or worse. You want to kill us all!"

"Nobody's going to die, you daft bastard," Bahr snapped. "We're more than capable of getting through a set of rapids."

Barking a maniacal laugh, the captain asked, "How?"

Bahr passed a sidelong glance to Anienam but the wizard merely shrugged and shook his head. *Lovely. So the old buzzard isn't inclined to help.* "Let me take the helm. I've sailed on worse waters in worse conditions. There's not a cloud in the sky, damn it."

"I know you, Sea Wolf. But this is not the sea. River is very dangerous. You either do as I say or you can get off my barge."

The soiled captain folded his arms across his chest and gave Bahr his most defiant look, daring him to cross him. The urge to place a heavy fist in the river captain's face nearly won before Bahr managed to calm down. He wasn't accustomed to taking orders from others. Some were born to follow, others to lead.

Bahr prided himself on individuality and the ability to successfully manage his affairs with minimal difficulty. The river men's obstinacy tests the limits of restraint. Compounding his plans was the decided lack of support from Anienam. He briefly wondered what the wizard was hiding from, if anything at all. Ever since the morning of the battle of Bode Hill Anienam appeared reserved, uncharacteristically quiet.

Frustrated and without a clear plan of how to escape his quandary, Bahr relented. "How many days at this pace until we reach Brodein?"

Pretending to think, the smaller man rubbed the salt-and-pepper stubble on his chin. "Difficult to say. Four, maybe ten days. Weather is big factor."

"Ten days?" Bahr all but shouted.

Anienam quickly followed up, "Easy, Bahr, the journey would take weeks on land. We will still arrive in plenty of time."

"Provided your calculations are correct and there is no additional conflict along the route. There are too many variables to risk docking every night."

"Death is great risk," added the captain.

Anienam smiled, the sight of shark stalking prey. "Indeed it is. Sometimes it is most necessary. Captain, if you would allow me a moment to confer with my friend here I believe I can help see your point of view."

The captain dismissed them both with a curt wave.

"He's going to be the first one I kill when they betray us, wizard," Bahr threatened. "What game are you playing at?"

"No games, not this time," Anienam said with a sly grin.

"I don't like this. We have come too far to be waylaid by bandits. Boen has the right of it. We should kill them now and take the barge before they lead us into a trap."

"Killing them wouldn't solve any of our problems, Bahr. They will have scouts and spies staked out the entire length of the river looking for such. If we kill them now we'd make ourselves targets for every tribe of bandit or worse from here to Brodein. Prudence, Bahr. We must be cautious when dealing with these people."

He wasn't convinced. "Perhaps they need to learn respect from us."

"Killing them won't accomplish anything. Our quest is to save Malweir, not defeat a band of petty river pirates."

Bahr closed his eyes and exhaled a slow, deep breath. "I'm beginning not to like you, Anienam."

"It comes with my job."

"Which is what exactly? And what is this business about keeping your powers secret? You're known the world over. Do you truly expect the river men not to recognize you simply because you didn't perform a spell?" Bahr accused.

Anienam's heart clutched. He looked about to ensure no one overheard them. "This is not the time for me to reveal my true identity. If, as you say, they are going to betray us, any use of my abilities will only give them opportunity to develop their plans to counter me. I can't afford the risk."

"How can this rabble countermand a wizard?" Bahr asked.

"Magic is fickle at best. There are many old cultures with variants I have no defense against. Precisely the reason I need to use caution. Small tribes like these river men have had shamans and soothsayers long before the Mages rose. Their magic could be more powerful and from means I have no knowledge of."

"You're telling me the last descendant of the Mages can't fight off a handful of near primitive tribesmen? Why did you come along?" Bahr demanded, casually ignoring all the assistance Anienam had given since first arriving on his doorstep that night, on what seemed a lifetime ago.

If he took offense, Anienam was careful not to show it. He knew their quest went beyond the simple pandering to an old sea captain's ego. Friends weren't necessary for victory. He was the legacy of all who had come before. When Anienam died so too would magic, unless he managed to cultivate Skuld into an appropriate apprentice.

"Bahr, you must remember that we are but one small part of this world. These people have no idea what is coming nor would they be inclined to give us safe passage if they did. People are creatures of habit and culture. They will not change just because a strange old man in tattered robes suggests the end of the world is upon them. You aren't thinking rationally. Malweir has enough enemies in wait for us; it doesn't make sense to add more."

Bahr pointed a finger at the wizard. "I don't recall anyone asking my opinion about trying to save the world. I'm a washed-up seafarer with no boat, no home, or family. You came to me asking for help, not the other way around."

"I came to you because I had to!" Anienam snapped, finally allowing anger to take control. "Don't mistake my acquiescence for kindness. You are a vital part in all this, the hinge to success or failure. My task is to keep you alive for as long as possible."

Bahr stood in shock. He was many things: scoundrel, womanizer, disgruntled brother, but he'd never been important to anyone until now. The idea was anathema. He didn't need to be important. Didn't want it. All he wanted was a strong boat beneath his feet and the freedom of the open sky. Accepting his worth for all Malweir seemed wrong.

Anienam relaxed. His features softened back into the kind old wizard he preferred to assume. "Fighting won't solve anything. Let the river men think they are in control.

Should they turn on us you and the others will be ready to react. I don't trust them either, if that helps any."
"Only if they don't sell us out."
Bahr turned and called to the captain.

THIRTY-NINE

Ionascu's Venom

The frozen plains gradually gave way to scrub grass and sand. Temperatures rose in the same manner. It wasn't long before they abandoned their winter cloaks and furs. Rekka's mood changed almost at once. She'd never been exposed to the cold before and was immeasurably glad to be done with it. Soon enough she'd be back in the humid jungle, a more harsh and dangerous environment than the frozen north.

Normally she spent hours a day in deep meditation. The dream masters of Teng taught calming techniques to counter the intensity of the training. It took her years to learn, forget about mastering, the skills she'd need for the rest of her life. However long that should be. Her conversation with Boen left her shaken. The longer the quest lasted the more she felt impending doom bearing down on her. Death offered no promise for the likes of Rekka. Her life was a dedication to mortal suffering with the hopes of eternal enlightenment. Still, there'd been too many close encounters to keep her mind at ease.

"Your girlfriend doesn't seem like herself," Nothol commented quietly.

He and Dorl sat at the edge of the barge, watching the waters rush by, or maybe it was the barge moving. They'd already been on the water long enough to grow confused. Dorl had hoped to avoid being on water again, especially after their time on *Bane*. Although he had to admit the probability of finding a corpse on deck was heavily reduced.

Dorl looked at Rekka with the strange combination of longing and fear. Their relationship was a dream, more than likely incapable of surviving the trials to come, certainly not the aftereffects if any of them lived. She belonged to a mystic cult from a foreign land with little to nothing in common with the northern sell sword. His heart was confused. As much as he wanted to sit with her in his arms and watch the world race by he knew destiny demanded otherwise. Men like him weren't supposed to have easy, normal lives. They just weren't. Dorl sighed in frustration.

"Who is?" he replied. "Nothing has gone right from the moment we left Stouds at the end of autumn. The closer we get to this Hamr the more I can't help but feel like the pieces are being moved to block us. Do you think we can win?"

"I don't even know who we're fighting," he answered and shrugged. "Doesn't matter. You're sounding like a lovesick puppy lately. I think she's got your balls in her pocket."

"Don't worry about my balls," Dorl said and frowned.

Nothol broke out laughing and was rewarded with a halfhearted punch to his left shoulder. "Why don't you go to her?"

"And say what?"

Nothol thought for a moment. "Good point. What is to say? We're so far out of our element up feels like down. It's not too late to turn back."

"Yes it damned well is and you know it," Dorl said. "We're in this for the haul. Although a nice fire with good food and cold beer wouldn't hurt. Those Dwarves know how to eat."

Rubbing his stomach in thought, Nothol agreed. "Best cooking I've had in a long while. Maybe Ironfoot can cook?"

"Anything has to be better than the combinations Boen puts together. I had the shits for a full day the last time he cooked," Dorl said.

Their easy laughter spread through the others. Tensions were high, and with good reason. Hunted and alone, no one knew whether they'd live or die.

"Maybe you're right," Nothol finally gave in. "This is getting too dangerous. We're not heroes, Dorl. I know that, but I can't help feeling like a part of something special. Wouldn't it be nice to have people remember our deeds a hundred years from now?"

Dorl scowled. "That implies we're going to survive. What happens if we're dead and wasted away without anyone ever knowing? The stakes are too high."

"Anything worth fighting for usually is," Nothol replied. "This is war, Dorl. If half of what Anienam says is true there's no place for us to run that won't be affected."

"Don't tell me you've bought in to it?"

"Bought in to what? We're doing a good deed here," Nothol defended.

Dorl shook his head ruefully. "What makes you think we can take on gods and win?"

"What makes you think we can't?"

Dorl Theed had no answer. He'd never felt smaller, more insignificant. The sell sword didn't belong in this tale. He knew it. He was a simple man with few interests. Finding Rekka was a fluke, one he hoped to cultivate into something meaningful. He doubted she was ready or able to give up a lifetime of training and dedication to a singular purpose for the sake of love. Still, he wasn't willing to give up. His heart finally felt content, leaving him prone to rash decisions and worse.

He'd known his share of women, never bothering to constrict himself with only one. Dorl believed there was a time and place for love, but he hadn't discovered his own yet. At least, not until he met Rekka. Thoughts of her plagued him, stealing his focus from the task at hand. His prowess in battle lessened and made him more liability than asset. One day Dorl knew he'd put the others in jeopardy. Whether unintentional or through ignorance, his inability to concentrate was more than likely going to get one of them killed. He couldn't live with that.

Dorl recognized the best action would be to abandon his relationship and turn his back. Knowing and being able to do that were two opposite ideations. He'd never felt more strongly about anyone and had no intentions of giving up on what might be a promising future. Old doubts lingered. Questions that never should have been asked swirled in his mind. Stay or go? Should he leave his friends to their fate out of selfishness or struggle on to whatever end the Fates decreed? He hung his head, overwhelmed.

"It's not death I fear," he said after long moments of listening to the frigid waters lap against the barge. "You and I have both seen enough to be inoculated. What I fear is obscurity. Falling into an abyss from which there will be no escape. I don't want to die for reasons I don't fully believe in."

Nothol nodded understanding and placed his hand on his best friend's shoulder. "Our lives have never been easy, though they've certainly been more comfortable than this. We come from a hard land where making difficult decisions is the way of life. How many times have we been stuck in situations we had no reason being in?"

"I hear what you're saying and it makes sense, to an extent, but I don't feel it in my heart, Nothol. It's like, I don't know, being stuck on the edge of cliff without knowing whether to turn about or plunge downward."

"Sometimes the heart lacks clarity," Nothol replied.

"You sound like my mother."

"You're acting like mine. Snap out of it, Dorl. I need you to stay frosty. You've had my back through a hundred shitty situations and I need it one more time. Go cry to your girlfriend tonight and come back in the morning the man you used to be," Nothol admonished.

Dorl's jaw tightened as he contemplated punching his best friend. The barge gradually began to shove towards the near shore just as the sun was setting. Golden-pink light riddled the grey skies, offering rare glimpses of hope. The already weary band took heart. They'd been through so much hardship and toil it was all they could do to get up in the morning and carry on. Dorl's attitudes ran through them with varying degrees. Only through Bahr's steadfastness did they keep pushing, keep driving south towards Trennaron.

"We're putting in for the night," Bahr announced as he came back from the bow. "The river men say it's too dangerous to keep on." His voice lowered. "This doesn't feel right. I want guards posted throughout the night. Otherwise we might just awake to our throats being slit."

"Be a lot easier if you just let me get rid of them now," Boen said, continuing his earlier arguments. "I don't like having to watch my back for no reason."

"We're not having this discussion again," Bahr said firmly. "This is their barge and they know the river far better than any of us."

The Gaimosian snorted but stayed quiet. His mood quickly infected the others.

"You're too trusting," Dorl snorted. "Can't we use Anienam to help us out?"

The wizard suppressed his frown. "It doesn't work that way. Without a proper threat I don't have a target to channel my energies. Besides, any use of power will only alert our enemies to our whereabouts. Trennaron is still very far away. We need to maintain as low of a profile as possible if we're to find success."

"You would think having a Giant along would be enough of a deterrent," Nothol said. "I damned sure wouldn't try us."

"You've got a little more sense than most," Bahr added. "Establish the roster as soon as we dock and get some rest. I have a feeling these river rats are going to give us a few surprises before we arrive at our destination."

Ionascu listened to the banter with venom in his heart. Once, and only briefly, he considered joining them. Becoming a member of their group. It was in his best interests. Harnin's betrayal left him no better than Bahr.

Crippled and alone, Ionascu contemplated taking his own life but lacked the courage. His heart burned darkly. Revenge demanded to be fulfilled. The strange visitors continued to approach him in his dreams, giving him new purpose and the intensity he'd long forgotten. They whispered promises he couldn't ignore.

Ionascu thought back to his first moments aboard the *Dragon's Bane* and the almost immediate sense of animosity exuded by Bahr and the others, as if they knew his true identity. He laughed at their ignorance. Mild complacency kept him from striking out, that and the underlying fear of not knowing whom to trust. As great as his desire for revenge might be he still wasn't willing to completely trust the visitors in his mind. The crippled one pulled his patchwork blanket higher around his neck as cold winds tickled his flesh.

The hard tack of his dagger pressed tightly against his side. None of the others knew he was armed or they surely would have taken it by now. Ionascu studied his companions while trying to determine which to kill first. Hatred for Bahr was minimal. If anything, the brother of the king had been kind enough and even stood up for him when Harnin betrayed him. The One Eye needed to die, but he knew he'd never get the opportunity to exact such punishment. The wizard, on the other hand, posed the greatest threat. He watched Ionascu with suspicious eyes, suggesting he knew too much. But how to kill a wizard?

He frowned. Perhaps Badron's daughter should get the honor of having his blade rake across her throat first. She'd been a thorn in his side from before her abduction. The thought of killing her left him feeling warm inside. With Badron's son dead she was the last of his bloodline. Delranan would never be the same after his family was successfully removed from the throne. Ionascu contemplated the future, slowly falling under the sway of the voices in his head. They offered delicate temptations and the unforeseen paths to a better life. They promised to heal his broken mind and body, making him stronger, faster, wiser. They whispered his role for the future and the coming storm. He sighed contentment. The voices were his only constant. His true friends during the long winter night. A wry grin on his face, he drifted back to their alluring embrace.

During it all the river captain stood at the bow watching them with foul thoughts of his own.

FORTY

Expectations

Artiss Gran stood atop the crumbling battlements of Trennaron. His tired eyes endlessly searched for his approaching guests. His ancient body was on the brink of giving out. Long days turned into years and then centuries. All his hopes and dreams ended the day he became one of the Dae'shan. He became more than what his physical form restricted. He became a messenger of the gods, both light and dark, and all was well with the world.

Until Amar Kit'han decided the world was not enough. Amar subverted the Dae'shan, twisting them through vicious lies and wicked intent. The others willingly gave themselves to their new direction but Artiss couldn't. Too much of his Humanity remained to so callously abandon his own race. He stood his ground and broke away from the others. The Dae'shan were only ever four. No more, no less. Artiss's departure left them sorely lacking much of their combined strength. Amar never forgave him and never forgot his treachery. Centuries passed without conflict until recently. The veil between dimensions was weakening. The dark gods saw their way back into Malweir. Amar Kit'han and the fractured Dae'shan were sent back into the world to pave the way.

He sighed. Once, long ago, he relished the feel of fresh wind on his face. It was the only reason he could think that he still made the daily pilgrimage up to the top of Trennaron. Mortal needs and desires extinguished the moment he accepted his robes and was transformed. He looked down at the massive structure built deep in the jungle, wondering how he'd come to be the guardian of the Blud Hamr. Knowing it was the only weapon capable of killing the dark gods and how badly Amar Kit'han wanted it destroyed gave him purpose but no comfort. Part of him had always known he was meant to come here. Just as he suspected, without ever saying, that the rest of the Dae'shan would stumble and fall into shadow. Some things were just meant to be.

Massive stone gargoyles decorated the walls and towers. Their pointed ears listened to the winds, massive wings curled over their backs protecting them from sunlight and worse. A series of square towers ringed the interior complex. Artiss knew the actual chamber the Hamr was kept in was far underground. So deep that lava flowed around it. Ancient wards protected the building from evil, but those wards were weakening with time. Artiss took comfort with the knowledge that the last of the Mage bloodline was approaching. If only they could beat Amar Kit'han here Malweir might stand a chance.

The jungle had been cleared back a good hundred meters. A worn cobblestone road was overgrown and barely discernible even from his vantage. Brambles and snaking vines overran the road, a reminder that the jungle took what it wanted. Small tribal villages peppered the jungles. Many of which dedicated a large portion of their society to becoming guardians of Trennaron. Artiss had little to do with that but they provided a much needed outer layer of security. Human intervention had prevented many incursions, by the Dae'shan and worse.

Artiss looked down, catching the faintest glimmer of movement under the massive banyan trees off to his right. Squinting, he was able to discern the mighty outline of a Gnaal. A remnant of the dark Mages. Artiss frowned. He had enough power to defeat the genetic monsters, but little left to defend Trennaron. Gnaals were nearly extinct, and a good thing too. Nearly ten feet tall, the monster had skin the color of darkest midnight and was covered with boils and lesions weeping endless streams of puss and worse. Foul eyes watched the castle, searching for any exploitable weakness. Artiss knew it wouldn't wait long.

"So, my brothers have at last realized my hour has arrived," Artiss said. His grey-white robes floated in the stale wind. Having given up the black preferred by Amar Kit'han long ago, he quested to return the Dae'shan to the spirit of neutrality they were originally intended for.

Hot winds blew across Trennaron, carrying the stench of rot and decay. The war had finally come to this ancient and most holy place. Artiss Gran would be hard pressed to defend it long enough for Anienam Keiss and his selected heroes to arrive. Frowning, the former Dae'shan balled his fists and collected power. If it was a fight Amar Kit'han wanted, a fight he was going to get.

END

BOOK IV OF THE NORTHERN CRUSADE
EMPIRE
OF BONES
CHRISTIAN WARREN FREED

ONE

A Cold Winter Night

Winter was cold this year. Famine and misery had swept across Delranan with unabated fury. Hundreds lie dead, frozen in the snow and ice. Every corner of the northern kingdom was consumed with the strange combination of violence and misery. A rebellion against the twisted forces of Lord Harnin One Eye struggled to stay ahead of their enemy even after a devastating plague ravaged much of the major population centers. Hope faded. So many had paid the price to be free but the kingdom was no closer to losing its chains.

Delranan was once the strongest of the northern kingdoms of Malweir. King Badron's family established strong economic ties with neighboring kingdoms and had the best equipped, well-disciplined army: the Wolfsreik. What should have been a time of glory devolved into madness. Badron longed for the wealth of neighboring Rogscroft and only needed the proper motivation to attack. That came when Aurec, son of the king of Rogscroft, invaded Delranan and kidnapped his lover, Princess Maleela. Badron attacked with all his might, leaving his kingdom open to the depredations of Harnin and his Dae'shan manipulators.

Few realized the Dae'shan were the masterminds behind the war now engulfing multiple kingdoms. Immortal, their sole purpose was to prepare Malweir for the return of the dark gods. They started in Delranan, knowing the final entry point still intact lay in the forgotten ruins of Arlevon Gale. They twisted the minds of Harnin and Badron, turning them against each other. Worse, their leader, Amar Kit'han, had brought in an army of Goblins from the Deadlands. It was only a matter of time before the entire north lay in ruins.

Ingrid crouched in the knee-deep snow under the walls of Chadra Keep. Her breath came out in thin plumes. Her cheeks were bright red, nearly frozen from prolonged exposure. Soot smeared her face. Her blond hair was pent up under a heavy cloak. Her lithe body was hidden beneath thick, dark clothes. The short sword in her gloved hands felt cumbersome, almost alien. Blue eyes as sharp as ice glanced up towards the battlements where iron helmed guards patrolled the frozen winter night.

Sunrise was still hours away, giving her plenty of time to accomplish her purpose. Twenty of her best were lined up behind. They comprised the heart of the new insurrection. Ingrid stole the position, to be sure, through ferocity and her desire for revenge for her husband's death. Using the plague for cover, Ingrid used her influence to gather fighters loyal to her ideations and deposed the former ruling council.

All her desires and actions led her to this point. Only days ago Lord Harnin, in a fit of madness, had Lord Argis executed atop the very walls of Chadra Keep. He personally flung the severed head down into the massed crowds of spectators, laughing insanely to the winds. While Argis was certainly no paragon of virtue, it was he that allowed Aurec entrance into the Keep to rescue his love. He maintained the pretense of being faithful to the decaying monarchy while secretly joining the rebellion. Captured during a massive purge, Argis was dragged away in chains and held captive until his death.

Ingrid saw his death as the catalyst for igniting the flames of rebellion across the entire kingdom. She intended on making him a martyr for the cause. His death, hopefully, would spur the sluggish population into action and they'd be able to finally overthrow Harnin One Eye and King Badron. His murder inspired Ingrid. The one thing *her* rebellion lacked was passion. She aimed to change that this very night. All she needed was his body.

Dreams of a free Delranan were too distant for Ingrid to focus on. She still had a, thus far, mediocre rebellion to orchestrate. Many friends already lay deep in the dirt; something she blamed on improper leadership. Argis was strong, but he'd been too concerned with trying to keep from being discovered to be effective. Still, his death was precisely what the rebels needed.

"Quickly, take your team and get the body. The guards won't be back for seven minutes," she ordered quietly to Orlek, her second in command.

The dark haired Orlek nodded and gestured for his team to follow. Ingrid waited as the scene played out much too slowly. She was nervous beyond belief. A life of violence was almost alien to her. That didn't prevent her from stepping up and taking control of the defunct rebellion. The people of Delranan needed strong leadership if they were going to find their way out of the growing darkness and she was the only likely candidate. Heart pounding in her chest, Ingrid watched her fighters sneak to the base of the walls.

She knew this was the trickiest part. One of her middle men managed to bride Harnin's guards so they'd turn a blind eye to the recovery. Ingrid was no fool. She recognized that those guards could have easily taken the money and still intended on turning the rebels in. No one could be trusted in these troubled times. Of course, she fully intended on exploiting the recovery for her own aims, more than likely signing a death warrant for the greedy guards. She didn't think that was her problem. The only thing that mattered was recovering Argis's body and letting the kingdom know that Harnin wasn't invincible. He could be broken.

Orlek's team disappeared behind a series of small mounds comprised mostly of trash and offal. Chadra Keep had fallen far since the night Badron's son was assassinated. Ingrid paused in thought. If only she could find Princess Maleela, the entire kingdom would rally to her cause. Justice would return and life would improve. Only no one had seen the princess for months. Ingrid bore a worried suspicion that she was already dead, despite Badron's cause to go to war with neighboring Rogscroft.

Nervous minutes went by without any sign of Orlek. Any number of things could have gone wrong; death being the least. Ingrid wanted to follow, to take part in the task herself if only to relieve the rising tension of uncertainty building in her chest. She was suspicious, though not always. Once, before her husband was taken, she'd been overly trusting and of a good nature. The war changed her in ways she had yet to understand. Survival dictated many of her actions. Survival and the overwhelming need for revenge.

Finally, after what felt like hours, Orlek and his men came scrambling back. Ingrid flashed a wry grin upon seeing the body wrapped in old blankets being carried on their shoulders. The sudden stomp of boots striking cold stone broke the silence. She froze. Torchlight reflected off the top of the walls. The guards had returned too soon. Orlek was still twenty meters away and without the benefit of cover. He'd be spotted. She envisioned mounted guards pouring from the gates to surround them all. The rebellion would die and she'd be blamed.

Cursing her decision not to bring archers along, Ingrid tried to crouch deeper into the shadows. Orlek would be discovered at any moment and she was powerless to prevent it. She briefly considered fleeing while the window of opportunity was open but thought better of it. Any cowardice would travel faster than the recovery of Lord Argis. Doomed with either choice, Ingrid hoped for the best.

The guards were speaking loud, suggesting they weren't onto her scheme. Hope flickered. Ingrid was no fool. Her enemy was sly; cunning enough to burn the entire city of Chadra to the ground if necessary. Their select indiscretion atop the Keep's walls might only be a ruse. Desperately, she clutched the hilt of her tiny dagger. It was the only comfort she could think of until the moment passed.

Orlek's team halted abruptly and huddled to the ground. Ingrid cursed under her breath. A stiff wind sliced across the open field, slipping beneath her collar and down her back. Chills racked her body. Her teeth chattered noisily, so loud she was sure to be caught. She closed her eyes and waited for the worst. Gruff words were exchanged between the guards, followed closely by the torrential sound of water striking the ground.

Ingrid's eyes flew open in time to see buckets of waste splash against the rocks and snow-covered ground. The torchlight weakened and faded altogether. Then tension had passed. Ingrid could breathe easy again. It only took Orlek a moment to get his team up and moving again. They dashed the final few meters and kept running back to the cover of the houses. Ingrid and the remaining ten rebels picked up and followed.

"It was foolish to put yourself at risk like that, Ingrid," Orlek scolded. The slightly older man stood with his arms folded across his chest. His perpetual scowl seemed harsher in the low candlelight.

Anger flashed in Ingrid's eyes. "We must all risk much if there's to be any hope for the future, Orlek. What would you have me do?"

"Be a leader. Use your head, not your heart."

She balled her fists. "And be like those fools I replaced? Inaella and Fenning were fools. They sat hidden in the dark and expected everyone to die for them. Look where they led us. We were at the brink of ruin.”

“They did what they thought was right,” Orlek replied. “True leaders can’t be expected to get their hands dirty without proper cause. Inaella was a good woman. I knew her before all this. She led the rebellion in the best way she knew how.”

“She let us grow stagnant to the point we became ineffective,” Ingrid countered angrily. “How many of your friends were killed?”

Orlek stayed silent. The truth was too awful to admit aloud. He’d joined in the beginning, when everyone was bright and optimistic. They didn’t think about death back then. He smirked. Back then. It was only a handful of months ago when the rebellion started. He’d been there when Argis and Joefke led the raid on the arms locker at the docks. He’d lost friends at every turn and still kept fighting. His prowess on the battlefield led him to numerous promotions but it wasn’t until Ingrid usurped the rebellion from the former council that he attained his higher position. Now it was his job to keep her grounded and the war going in a logical direction. She didn’t make it easy.

He slowly licked his lips before answering, “Ingrid, we have all lost ones dear to us. It’s not about their deaths; it’s about how we measure their lives. Each man and woman in the rebellion died so that Delranan can be free again. Our enemy has over five thousand regular army troops and access to near unlimited weapons stockpiles. We fight and scrape for every used arrow or nicked sword. The process must be slow, orderly until the time comes when we can finally spread across the kingdom. That time is not yet.”

“You advocate sitting with our hands tied while the enemy gets stronger? Inaella tried that and look where it led us. We stood on the precipice of ruin.”

“The plague destroyed our ranks, not Inaella’s inactivity,” Orlek countered. “You don’t honestly expect me to believe we accomplished nothing during those first few months?"

"We didn't accomplish enough," her words were slow, measured.

He shook his head in disagreement. "This argument is pointless. We need to focus on the future, not the past."

She paused, lips pursed as if ready to continue her argument. Instead she relented," Agreed. Our mission tonight was highly successful. I congratulate you, Orlek."

"I don't need thanks, give it to the men. I did what was asked of me," he replied modestly.

Her opinion of him rose slightly. "Our next task is to spread the word that we have recovered Lord Argis's body from our enemies. He should be revered as a hero to the cause. Spread rumors. I want him martyred for his deeds. The rebellion needs to use his murder as a rallying point."

"We are still weak from the plague. Half of Chadra was quarantined and burned down. The Wolfsreik no longer comes down to patrol but the population is decimated. Nearly one in three died."

She closed her eyes briefly, knowing all too well the high cost the unexpected disease bore away. Ingrid was surprised there were still enough fighters left to carry on. "Turn that around. Two in three survived. What you said is true. Our enemy holds every advantage except one. He lacks the desire to be free. Harnin One Eye is a twisted monster, Orlek, but we can beat him by twisting our words. By only using hopeful messages and through the sheer determination of the people's fighting spirit."

"You ask much from a broken people," he said.

"No more than what I ask of myself."

"What are you really fighting for? You're no soldier. My guess is you've not done a hard day's work in your life," Orlek said, hoping to learn more about the woman he'd tied his fate to.

Ingrid fixed him with a withering glare. Until now she had kept all details of her previous life secret, fearing they'd undo her if anyone found out. Trust did not come easily. She'd been betrayed by those closest to her in the past and had surrounded herself with hardened killers. Anything to put the past behind her. Still, she needed as much support as possibly if her plans for the future were going to work. She decided it was time to include Orlek into her darkened vision of the world.

"You're right. I was considered a lady of society. I wore the finest clothes, went to the balls held up on the hill and had enough money I didn't need to work hard. I cooked, and kept track of our finances. We weren't wealthy but managed to live comfortably."

Orlek's suspicions confirmed, he asked, "There's no shame in that. Plenty of good women used to live like that. Of course I never had it that good. Sounds like you had a good life. What changed?"

"My husband was taken in the middle of the night on charges of treason and executed in the middle of the street by men he had known for years," she answered tightly.

It was a sad tale but one that had played out a hundred times over since Harnin assumed control of Delranan. He waited patiently, suspecting there was more to the tale.

Ingrid debated telling him everything. Some secrets hurt too much to expose. It was her need to have him totally on her side that won through, however, forcing her to tell him her darkest secrets. "My husband was an officer in the Wolfsreik."

For once, Orlek didn't know what to say.

BIO

Christian W. Freed was born in Buffalo, N.Y. more years ago than he would like to remember. After spending more than 20 years in the active-duty US Army he has turned his talents to writing. Since retiring, he has gone on to publish over 25 military fantasy and science fiction novels, as well as his memoirs from his time in Iraq and Afghanistan, a children's book, and a pair of how to books focused on indie authors and the decision making process for writing a book and what happens after it is published.

His first published book (Hammers in the Wind) has been the #1 free book on Kindle 4 times and he holds a fancy certificate from the L Ron Hubbard Writers of the Future Contest. Ok, so it was for 4th place in one quarter, but it's still recognition from the largest fiction writing contest in the world. And no, he's not a scientologist.

Passionate about history, he combines his knowledge of the past with modern military tactics to create an engaging, quasi-realistic world for the readers. He graduated from Campbell University with a degree in history and a Masters of Arts degree in Digital Communications from the University of North Carolina at Chapel Hill.

He currently lives outside of Raleigh, N.C. and devotes his time to writing, his family, and their two Bernese Mountain Dogs. If you drive by you might just find him on the porch with a cigar in one hand and a pen in the other.